Liza Alexandrova-Zorina, born 1984, grew up in a little town on the Kola Peninsula above the Arctic Circle (the setting of her novel). After graduation she moved to Moscow. She is a prolific journalist, popular blogger, and public activist. She is a columnist for several leading opposition periodicals and also heads the literature section of the "thankyou.ru" book portal.

Winner of the Northern Star Prize (2010) Liza was a finalist in two major literary competitions: Debut Prize and NOS (2012) with her novel *The Little Man*. Her other prize-winning book is the collection of short stories *The Rebel*.

Melanie Moore has been translating from the Russian, both fiction and non-fiction, for more than 25 years.
"My career as a Russian translator spans more than a quarter of a century. During that time I've seen the collapse of the Soviet Union and the emergence of today's Russia. And I've brought my sensitivity to the dislocations and continuities both in Russian life and in Russian literature to bear in translating *The Little Man*. Even though the novel is so dark, there's something that shines through as redeemable – perhaps it's just the ability to reveal the darkness for what it is without condoning it."

GLAS NEW RUSSIAN WRITING

contemporary Russian literature

in English translation

Volume 60

This is the tenth
volume in the Glas
sub-series devoted to
winners and finalists
of the Debut Prize.
Glas acknowledges
the support of
the Debut Prize in
publishing this book.

Liza Alexandrova-Zorina

The Little Man

A novel

Translated by Melanie Moore

GLAS PUBLISHERS
tel: +7(495)441-9157
perova@glas.msk.su
www.glas.msk.su

DISTRIBUTION

In North America
Consortium Book Sales and Distribution
tel: 800-283-3572; fax: 800-351-5073
orderentry@perseusbooks.com
www.cbsd.com

In the UK
CENTRAL BOOKS
orders@centralbooks.com
www.centralbooks.com
Direct orders: INPRESS
tel: 0191 229 9555
customerservices@inpressbooks.co.uk
www.inpressbooks.co.uk

Within Russia
Jupiter-Impex
www.jupiterbooks.ru

Editors: Natasha Perova & Joanne Turnbull
Cover design by Igor Satanovsky
Camera-ready copy: Tatiana Shaposhnikova

ISBN 978-5-7172-0124-7

"MUCH UNHAPPINESS HAS COME INTO THE WORLD BECAUSE OF BEWILDERMENT AND THINGS LEFT UNSAID."

FYODOR DOSTOEVSKY

Even Savely's surname was a joke: Savage, yeah right! He had a stammer, stumbled over his words and took refuge from conversations in solitude. When people around him laughed, he'd sulk and when they wept, he'd sneer. He always got out of bed on the wrong side and came upon people when he was least wanted, so that by forty, life had really started to grate. He was born in a little town and had grown up there too. From his window, he could see the school where the only thing he'd learnt was that while it's the hard-working students who solve problems, it's the failing students who set them and change the rules to suit themselves so that they always have the answer ready. Savage went unnoticed as a pebble on the road. But when the gangster Mogilev nicknamed Coffin was shot dead in broad daylight, Savely came to the notice of the whole town.

It was several hours' drive to the nearest village while the Finnish border was only a stone's throw away, so the town lived a life of its own, cut off from the rest of the country like a hunk of bread from a loaf. The gangsters ruled by terror, prowling the streets, collars turned up, a trail of ransacked wallets and destinies behind them. Several gangs shared the various districts, but it was a small town and there wasn't enough room. Coffin had the last word. He crossed himself with fingers clenched into a fig and could multiply any number by zero. The crumpled faces of his henchmen made you think of clenched fists. He had blood on his hands, right up his arms in fact. He had blown up his rivals when they were relaxing in a restaurant and thereby put an end to their protracted showdown. Only one survived. The blast ripped his legs off and the crock that was left they called Shorty. He walked on his stumps rather than crutches, supported by hands that were callused and scarred, and served as a reminder of what happened to anyone who crossed Coffin. He kept Shorty on as a mascot in the belief that he would bring him luck. And he did until the day Coffin was shot down right in front of everybody. Shorty, looking at the body, felt a gnawing pain in his stumps.

Savely's single life continued even after he got married. Life with his wife and daughter was like sharing a communal apartment. They took no more notice of him than they did of the pattern on the wallpaper. His wife's tongue was knife-edge sharp, she smeared Savely with taunts like buttering bread, and his teenage daughter aped her mother's manners so that Savely was caught between the devil and the deep blue sea, unable to understand how he had become so estranged from his own daughter. In her disinterested gaze, like a needle to his heart, he read, "So he's alive, fine, but it would be no great loss if he wasn't!" He tried to spend longer and longer at work and when he was at home hid away in a corner like a cockroach. The "life is fun" attitude of the TV made fun of him. "Someone's got to be the loser," he thought with a shrug.

The town was so small that a whisper at one end could be heard at the other. Savely's wife changed lovers like she changed clothes and she believed that marriage aged people while love made them younger. She wasn't ashamed to appear in public on the arm of her date and, envying them from afar, Savely would cross the street or look down if he bumped into them and his wife's lover, plastering a grin on his face, would pretend they didn't know each other. At night, twisting and turning in bed, Savely would often picture his wife in bed with another man but he felt neither jealousy nor insult, only envy. He was so lonely he could have howled at the moon like a wolf and talked to his own shadow.

At work, Savage huddled in a corner behind a cupboard. It separated him from his colleagues and sheltered him from the sidelong glances he so dreaded, although, in fact, no-one paid him much attention. Someone had stuck a broken chair in his corner and a fat clay pot with a dried-out palm and Savely would squeeze past the clutter he couldn't quite bring himself to throw out.

If not for his visible bald spot and the horseshoe curve of his shoulders, Savely Savage could have passed for a teenager. He was skinny and, like all dreamers, he dragged his feet like a child. The office grind had sucked all the goodness out of the years and now he was irritated when anything new disturbed his usual routine. He'd fume when the roads were resurfaced or the street names changed or when his slippers weren't where he'd left them. He met the same people every day and only noticed them when they disappeared. He lived his life as if he were watching a boring film.

The town clung to a mining factory like a baby to its mother. The smoking chimneys could be seen from every part of town. In conversation, people would say "there" and everyone knew they meant the factory. They could nod vaguely in any direction and everyone would still know they meant the factory even if they'd nodded in a totally different direction.

Karimov, the factory manager, looked like an Italian mafioso. He had black curly hair and a hawk nose and his appearance didn't fit into the local landscape where it resembled a glossy photo pasted over a pastel drawing. Karimov had been sent two years ago from Moscow, which from here seemed so distant it might as well have been abroad, and he lived out of his suitcases in a hotel, as if constantly awaiting a transfer. Karimov helped the local orphanage and that's why people forgave him his look of disgust and the cold half-smile that never left his face and could induce a shiver even on a hot day. He was a door-step baby himself with the sticky eyes of every abandoned child. His mother had wrapped her baby in a faded dress and left him on the steps of the orphanage. The baby lay there all night. He didn't cry, just fixed his angry eyes on the locked door. In the morning, he was picked up by a passer-by who took the bundle home and opened it up on the table, the baby splayed out like a frog. The man had no children and decided that the god he didn't believe in had sent him a son.

You could set your watch by Mayor Krotov. Rushing to work in the morning, Savely would see him outside the local municipal office and in the evening the burly mayor would tumble out of it like a potato falling from a torn sack. Keeping his eyes straight ahead, he would get into his car that would tip sideways. Rumour had it that the mayor had built a medieval castle with towers somewhere out in the forest, hidden away from the townsfolk. No-one had seen this castle, however, and encrusted with rumour, it grew to the size of a town. Krotov avoided meeting Coffin who did his best to avoid him too. They communicated through the chief of police, Trebenko, who travelled between the gangsters and the civil servants like a ferry between two shores. They had tacitly split the town in two. Each part had its own laws and regulations that didn't operate in the other.

Everything is in plain sight in a small town so no-one bothered to hide. The one place of entertainment, the Three Lemons bar, brought the town's big cheeses and its lowlifes together under one roof.

Trebenko would pop his head round the door on holidays but would hurry away after just one glass. Antonov, a chain store owner and an aspiring local Duma Deputy, left with a different girl every night. He looked like a kind uncle, capable only of taking you on his knee to tell you a story. Antonov didn't tell any stories but he did give generous presents. He had a furrowed brow and a well-padded torso that he covered up with wide jackets a size too big so that he always seemed to be wearing someone else's suit. Antonov drank life down in big gulps and his vodka in tiny sips and he believed that anything

10

that was for sale could be bought and anything that could be bought was for sale.

In the evening, lolling out on the veranda of the Three Lemons, Coffin would look everyone over with a glance as clammy as his moist palms and Shorty would set up a game of patience, slavering on his fingers and slobbering on the deck which bristled in his hand like a ruffled bird. He would draw the cards from a deck as if he were plucking feathers and set them out face down. The cards were marked so that he was able to guess them while the other bandits looked over his shoulder and tried to predict whether the game would work out or not. Coffin's guys would sit stiff as statues at the little tables, the passersby reflected in their shades.

Savely frequently came across his daughter at the bar. She had grown up on her own terms like nettles behind a fence. When she saw her father, she would turn away or give a laugh that was exaggeratedly loud. She wore too much make-up and blood-red lipstick and Savely wanted to rub it off his daughter's face with his sleeve. He tried to talk to his wife about it but she just brushed him aside. "Better a gangster than an insect," the gibe came. Savely felt like a beetle crushed under foot.

"A little man in a little town," he murmured to himself in front of the mirror, stroking his thin hair. "A little man…"

That evening, like thousands of other evenings before, he was on his way home from work and turning over his usual thoughts of life passing him by like the last bus home. "I've lived the wrong way, in the wrong place, with the wrong people," he told himself.

There were some girls sitting on a bench drinking beer, lazily checking out the passersby through the glass of the bottle. "They're even more bored than I am," thought Savage as he went past. He bought a loaf of bread from a stall and munched on it as he walked along. Family meals had gone by the board even earlier than the marital bed.

Coffin was snoozing on the veranda of the Three Lemons,

his legs stretched out, and a waitress nearly dropped her tray as she stepped over them cautiously. Shorty, curled up like a cat, narrowed his eyes in the sun. Rubbing his stumps, he clacked his teeth angrily, snapping at the air, and hated the entire world. The gangsters were drinking kvass in beer glasses, batting away flies and, with nothing better to do, were sizing up the passersby as if they were going through their pockets.

"You should look at every person as if they are condemned and going to die today," said Shorty, repeating the words of a sermon he'd read in a church newspaper. He'd been frequenting the church of late, leaning back to see the icons he couldn't reach to kiss. "Then people will all be kinder to one another and more tolerant…"

"You should look at every person as if he's been told to kill you and could pull a gun on you at any time," growled Coffin, without opening his eyes. "Then people will treat one another according to their deserts!"

The gangsters held unlimited sway over the little town. People were more afraid of them than of the police because the gangsters had been laying down the law for a long time. Sometimes, people would turn to them for help and ask them to intercede with an over-zealous civil servant. If it was a minor official, the gangsters would burst into his home, empty out the safes and get him to sign the necessary papers. Coffin's right-hand man, a gangster known as Saam, called this popular justice and there were people who were only too pleased to have someone in town who would stick up for ordinary residents. On one occasion the gangsters beat a local government official so badly that he died a few hours later. "Everyone does it and so did I," the man kept saying through blood-caked lips as the doctor examined him and directed the paramedics to the morgue. "Did I really ask for too much?"

One of Savely's colleagues had gone to the gangsters too, asking them to beat up an old school friend who owed him money that he had been unable to get back for many years. The old school friend had borrowed from his pals and tried to set up his own business but had gone bust and taken to the bottle to hide from his creditors.

"What's the interest rate?" Coffin yawned into his hand.

The man made a gesture.

"A hundred!"

The gangster raised his eyebrows.

"I'm not doing it for the money," Savely's colleague explained. "I don't really need it. You take it. It's the principle of the thing. If you borrow, you've got to give it back."

"It's a good principle," said Coffin, with a wry smile. "So, I'll be waiting for you to bring the money at the same time tomorrow. You'll pay me double: for you and your friend. You can pay in instalments…"

For several weeks, the man delivered the money to the gangsters, packing the tight little bundles into a plastic bag. He had to go into debt himself, sell his old car and his wife's rings and then, once he no longer owed the gangsters anything at all, he happened upon the old school friend and, pulling him into a hug, he dragged him into the nearest shop for a drink. "You can divide people up into those who don't pay their debts and those who pay off other people's," he mumbled after the second glass. His friend, rubbing his blueing nose, nodded in agreement.

Antonov came out of the Three Lemons gleaming like a polished boot. Looking at his red, fleshy face, Savely remembered the chubby little boy from the parallel class who was always eating between lessons, his sandwiches wrapped in greaseproof paper in his briefcase. His classmates used to laugh at him, clipping him round the ear, and he would wipe his hands on his trousers and chase them down the corridors. Savely was also picked on in class so he tried to make friends with the school fatty. When he went up to him, however, the boy looked him arrogantly up and down and turned away. Antonov hadn't changed much in thirty years. Savely looked at his own reflection in the bar's dark window and thought that he was still the same stooped and clumsy boy he had been thirty years ago, plodding home, his satchel clutched to his chest. Looking around, Antonov dived into a huge jeep and the driver, whose face looked like a hand giving the finger, switched on the engine.

After Antonov came Savely's daughter in a flashy dress of her mother's that hung on her like a lowered flag. Vasilisa was unsteady on her feet, treading cautiously in her high heels, her cheeks flushed crimson with alcohol. Savage had long been aware of a smell of tobacco and cheap wine when Vasilisa came home late but now he was absolutely stunned: one of Coffin's henchmen was putting the girl in the car next to Antonov. The whole town knew the boss never left the bar with the same girl twice and Savely, remembering all he had heard about his antics from the old ladies in the neighbourhood, was practically gagging with rage.

Gasping for air like a fish out of water, he hurled himself towards the car but the gangsters blocked his path.

"M–m-my d-daughter, d-daughter!" Savage stammered.

"Daughters flower after hours," chuckled Coffin, rubbing his swollen eyelids. "We'll bring her back in the morning."

He rocked back on the wicker chair again, a sign that the conversation was over. Savely was determined to drag Vasilisa out of the car come what may but, as he rushed forwards, he stumbled and fell onto the table. The glasses rolled onto the floor, sloshing kvass all over the gangsters. Furious, Coffin leapt to his feet, fists clenched, and seeing his Adam's apple bobbing in his throat and the vein standing out on his forehead, the gangsters prepared to fight.

Antonov opened the car window and hate pounded in Savely's temples at the sight of his shiny cheeks.

"Okay, mate?" smiled Antonov. "Nothing to worry about. We're just going for a drive."

"What are you talking to him for?" drawled Vasilisa. "He's no-one."

"You should be s-shot!" Savely exploded.

In a little town, either you kill boredom or boredom kills you.

14

"Get me a gun." Coffin told his aide, wiping his kvass-soaked trousers with a handkerchief. "And quickly!"

He devoured Savely with eyes that burned right through his pockets and Savely began to feel uncomfortable. Sensing fun and games ahead, Shorty jumped out of his seat and got under their feet. Smacking his lips and positively buzzing with curiosity, he was trying to work out what Coffin had come up with.

Saam brought over the double-barrelled shotgun Coffin always kept in the boot. He was breathing hard and his lips trembled with excitement. Coffin smirked when he saw this and raised an eyebrow in surprise but he failed to read his fate in the other's face.

"Take it. Shoot yourself," he said, offering the gun to Savely.

Two aides rushed over to Coffin, helpfully seized the gun and put the barrel to Savely's chin and his finger on the trigger.

"Or shoot me," Coffin said, looking straight ahead as if he were looking into a mirror. "If you don't, I'll shoot you."

Delighted at this unexpected entertainment, the gangsters crowded round Savely. Passersby slowed down and a plump woman hanging out washing on her balcony, paused, a sheet raised above her head. Savely was trembling. The palms of his hands were sweating and the barrel of the gun dug into his chin. His hands shook and he felt that with one jerk of his finger he would press the trigger. It seemed as though his body were no longer attached to his head and his head had been stuck on a spear. Scared to move, Savely looked askance at his daughter. One of the bandits grinned.

"Shush!" Coffin licked his lips.

A shot rang out.

Startled pigeons rose into the air. The gun fell to the ground. Savely, as if in a dream, couldn't tell whether he'd been shot or whether he'd shot Coffin but his nostrils filled with the smell of gunpowder that reminded him of bonfire smoke and made him want to sneeze.

Everyone stared at the spread-eagled body that only a second before had ruled the whole town with terror. Shorty whimpered, aware of a gnawing pain in his stumps as though they were sprouting new legs while Saam, looking at the spreading pool of blood, thought that it was possible to see into the future not just in coffee grounds but in swirls of blood as well. Coffin lay there, arms spread wide as if he wanted to embrace his own shadow. It seemed that at any moment he would get up as if nothing had happened, feeling the hole in his head in astonishment. Vasilisa, her hands over her face, shrank into the furthest corner of the car, while Antonov looked as if he were about to whimper the way he did as a little boy when he was clipped around the ear. He didn't take his eyes off the gun that was lying on the floor and his earlobes were white with fear.

No-one tried to stop Savely. The gangsters moved apart in silence, letting him through, and, moving backwards, he went further and further away from the veranda where his life had split in two like a vase falling from a shelf. Savely crossed the square on wobbly legs, his shirt soaked through, horror keeping a murderous grip on his throat until he threw up, stomach heaving.

A woman's scream cut through the silence. There were shouts behind him as though the sound had just been switched on. Savely could see the gangsters running towards him and, darting round a corner, he fled.

Teetering, he made his way through courtyards where people shrank away from him, assuming he was drunk. "Hello, Savely," nodded an elderly neighbour, putting down her shopping bags. He had always been polite enough to ask after her health and had been rewarded with lengthy accounts of her ailments, evil doctors and costly medicines. It was a shared ritual, unbroken for years, but now Savage recoiled, hiding his face behind his upturned collar and the old lady watched him go, her hand over her mouth.

The police were already waiting at home. Savely looked

up at the windows of his flat and had the impression that there, behind the tightly closed curtains, Savely Savage was taking his key from under his mat. Crossing his legs, he pulled off his boots, shuffled across the corridor into his room and switched on the TV. If he were to look out of the window, he would see someone, peeping out from behind a corner and looking up at his windows, imagining that Savely Savage was looking at him.

Patrol cars sped around town like mad dogs, spreading out through the streets one minute, forming a pack the next. Savely sat in the basement counting the drops of water falling from the damp ceiling. Cats yowled in the darkness. The roar of the patrol cars, excited conversations and yells reached him from outside. Savely tried to piece the evening into a single whole, like a mosaic, but its events fell to bits and got all mixed up. He began to imagine he'd shot Antonov from a gun his daughter had provided and that the gangsters had pressed the trigger just as they put the barrel to his chin. He couldn't believe what had happened to him and, huddled into a dark corner like a child, he simply trusted everything would sort itself out.

During the night, keeping close to the buildings, he made his way to the outskirts of town. Five long rows of brick garages formed a whole town, a rabbit-warren where Savely Savage took refuge. He stretched out on the bare earth and tried to go to sleep so that he could wake up from this bad dream.

Severina was so pretty she would look lovely even in a distorting mirror. Weeping drunken tears, the nanny at the orphanage could never admire her enough. The nanny had no children, her husband had left her and she spent all day and all night at work until eventually she moved in along with all her stuff. As she sang each child to sleep, she would imagine it as her own, that she had carried it and given birth in agony, until she completely lost her marbles, talking to her babies for days on end.

Severina struggled at school and when she stopped going

she could read only one syllable at a time and count only on her fingers and couldn't understand why the world was like an orphanage full of nasty abandoned children.

"My, but you're beautiful," said the gangster, taking her by the chin. He had got out of his car that had pulled up alongside her. "Let's go for a drive."

Severina had seen Saam several times at the orphanage where he would pick out boys for Coffin's gang. He got his nickname from his narrow, deep-set eyes and his short, stocky build. People said his stare could bend horseshoes but, unlike Coffin, Saam was cautious and went through life like a cat on a windowsill. No-one could remember when he'd arrived in the town or where he came from. He didn't talk about himself, joking that he was born when he first held a knife and that he first held a knife when he was born.

Saam took Severina to the town market which was squeezed into the old bus depot. Brightly coloured stalls huddled together. The clothes hung from string, dresses and suits dancing as they fluttered in the wind. Boys from the orphanage hung around but the women in the stalls, with their red swollen faces, never took their eyes off them. Sometimes the boys went back to the orphanage with their pockets full and then they would be surrounded by a noisy pack of girls cadging presents. More often, however, they would be brought back by a policeman and the hapless would-be thieves could long be recognized by their swollen ears.

"Pick something!" Saam urged. "Don't be shy!"

When Severina pointed to something that had caught her fancy, he pulled it down and threw it over his shoulder. The market women watched him go mentally calculating their losses while the ones who saw him coming from a distance hastily hid the expensive items away.

Coffin's gang met at an old wooden house left behind by the early settlers. Encircled by a high fence, it towered over the brick houses around it the way angry grown-ups stand over a naughty child.

"But she's underage!" exclaimed Shorty, stroking his stumps, when Saam brought Severina along.

"I've adopted her," snapped Saam.

Everyone looked at Coffin.

"Orphan girls are accommodating," he grinned, looking the girl up and down. "Let her stay."

Saam took her everywhere with him like a doll. Sitting in the car, Severina would count the gunshots on her fingers, trying to work out how many had hit their targets. The first time she saw a dead body, she wasn't afraid. They were trying to cram a lanky corpse into the boot but it wouldn't fit so the gangsters tossed it onto the back seat. The head, its hair caked in blood, was on Saam's lap while Severina held its feet and examined its polished boots.

She moved into Saam's two-room flat and when she was on her own she would run from one room to the other delighted that she wouldn't be seeing the institutional walls of the orpanage any more. Trying out the role of lady of the house, Severina spent whole days cleaning floors, washing clothes and decorating the rooms with flowers and knick-knacks.

"A woman's a woman," snorted Coffin, noticing the polka-dot tablecloth and violets on the window-sill. "She could be 13, she could be 50 but she's only got one thing on her mind. You watch, she'll be giving you little Saamkins…"

"Fine by me," said the gangster, shrugging his shoulders.

Severina only went to the orphanage for the nanny's funeral. The nanny had downed an entire bottle, then suffocated the babies, sobbing all the while.

"You poor, unfortunate things. What have you got to live for? You'd be better off dead," she wept, her hands around their tiny necks. Then, with a farewell kiss to each of the dead babies, she jumped out of the window, arms outstretched as if she expected to go straight up to heaven from the home.

The whole town buried the dead babies. As the procession went from the morgue to the cemetery, people stopped at the side of the road to see them off on their final journey. But the nanny's funeral was hushed up. The coffin was placed in the corridor of the orphanage and the children crowded round, sniffling, to gaze in silence at her tear-stained face, fixed in a grimace of pain. They remembered the nanny rocking each of them in her arms, her gruff voice singing a lullaby, and thought that no-one had loved them more than this awful woman. Severina went over to the body, kissed her on both cheeks and fell on her breast in floods of tears and the denizens of the orphanage wailed in chorus as they took up her lament. As evening drew nearer, the older children took the coffin to the cemetery and lowered it into the grave just as the nanny used to put them in their cots. Hastily, they covered it with earth and planted an iron marker without a name or photograph.

After what had happened, the room was boarded up and a priest was called to bless the home. "In the name of the Fa-a-ther and of the S-o-n," he intoned, swinging a smoking censer from side to side, while the children, picking the peeling paint off the walls, thought of their own fathers, who, like God, they had never seen.

Savely Savage woke up and turned to glance at the alarm clock. Instead of the bedside table, however, there was the rusted shell of a car, with crumpled cigarette packets lying around and bottles that reflected thousands of suns. In all his many years at work, Savage had never once been late and, driving away the vestiges of sleep, he thought about his unfinished drawings and a report he had to submit as if he could still put the finishing touches to his work.

In the north, winter doesn't end even in summer. It was a frosty morning. The ice crunched in the puddles and his breath was steaming. A hairless dog, tail between its legs, plodded along the road while up in the trees black crows resembled elderly gossips with dark shawls thrown around their shoulders. Shivering with cold, Savage walked past the closed garages, pulling at the heavy locks. Men used to congregate here once, drinking vodka and arguing noisily about nothing. He had often wandered in this area of single-storey buildings, picking up the echo of these squabbles and gone home drunk as if he'd downed a bottle himself. Strolling around, he secretly hoped he would be asked to join in, would be offered a drink and some homemade snacks, but on the one occasion he was invited to join two other drinkers, he chickened out and quickened his pace, without answering. These days, the garage get-togethers had been displaced by the TV and people spent their evenings with its programs as they had with their friends. Savage himself couldn't imagine his life without its yells, debates, laughter and tears, without the news, the slogans and the adverts, the dull reports, the songs, groans and gabbling that filled his room, giving its walls world-wide dimensions and reducing his ego to a mere pixel. Now though, his ears were full of silence like cotton wool that seemed as if it might burst his eardrums.

Savage had been on the move for several hours, not knowing what he was looking for, afraid of every sound, wondering whether to go home or to the police, and what to do next. Without reaching any decision, he went off into the taiga, afraid the garage owners might spot him. Savage tried to imagine his daughter weeping in self-pity, his colleagues whispering and the cleaner scouring the blood off the veranda. For a moment, he felt a pleasant warmth in his breast: the whole town was talking about him today. He remembered the drug dealer who sold pot to teenagers, the girls Coffin picked out for the Councillor, his own plastered daughter. "A little man in a little town. A little man in a little town," he muttered, sucking the words like lollypops as if finding new meaning in them.

When he was young every day ended before it began, an endless series of years stretched on and there seemed to be an eternity ahead. With age, however, the days had become dull and heavy and Savage had the impression that every page torn from the calendar counted off a year rather than a day, making life fly by like scenes from a train window that he could never make out properly. Now, he appeared to have got out at the station and could touch them with his own hands. There was

21

still dirty snow in the forest, patches of white in the gullies, and Savage rubbed it on his face by way of a wash. As he wandered he pondered his fate. Would he go to prison? Would the gangsters take their revenge? He had a feeling that he could go back to town as if nothing had happened. Coffin would be dozing on the veranda, the gangsters would be drinking kvass and his daughter would be getting into Antonov's car over and over again...

Afraid of getting lost, Savage kept his eye on the television tower which stuck out like a splinter. Every time he lost sight of it, he broke out in a sweat. By evening, he was dizzy with hunger. He chewed bitter unripe berries that burnt his mouth and drank water by wringing out the damp moss like a sponge. Towards nightfall he went back into town.

The windows glowed yellow in the thick twilight, breaking up the pavements with patches of light. The streetlights gleamed dully. Savage wanted to bang on all the windows one by one to ask for shelter. Standing on tiptoe, he peeped into ground-floor flats, picturing the inhabitants sitting at the table or watching television and couldn't understand why he had deprived himself of such normal, everyday delights.

Spooked by the infrequent passersby, he kept close to the trees, then sneaked across the road to look into a bin. He took out a stale bun that already had bites out of it and threw it away with a fastidious shudder.

It was quiet outside the police station. Even the patrol vans were dozing. A drunken girl in torn tights lay on the steps and there was thick darkness behind the barred windows. Bending over the sleeping girl, Savage straightened her skirt, crossed himself and stepped inside.

"Get out!" yelled the duty officer, pushing him out into the street. "Go on! Get lost! You can't come in here! Go away!"

"I'm Savely Savage who shot Coffin."

"They'll kill you. Go away, they'll kill you!"

"Go where?"

"Just go and don't come back!"

He slammed the door.

"Where am I supposed to go? Where?" Savage tugged at the door but it was locked.

Squatting next to the girl, Savely put his head in his hands. A phone box screeched under the arc of a streetlight, its door flapping in the wind, like an injured bird. Photos of criminals and missing persons hung on the walls. The photos were all jumbled up, making it impossible to tell straight away who were the criminals and who were the victims. An old man, trudged by, dragging his leg and leaning on a lacquered cane so that, from a distance, he seemed to have three legs. He looked curiously at the sleeping girl and at Savage and terror stuck Savely's tongue to the roof of his mouth. The old man continued on his way.

The duty officer flung open the window.

"Take this! It'll do for a start!" He handed some crumpled notes out through the bars. "Go away! You were never here!"

Taking the money, Savely looked at the officer. The bars kept them apart and Savage couldn't tell which of them was inside and which was free.

Savage was odd man out in any group. He propped up the wall at parties, he was alone in the crowd on municipal holidays and when his colleagues organized a party, he would sit bent over his plate all evening. At home he talked to himself. Now, he was creeping along the blocks of flats aware that the loneliness he carried within him like a child had finally let him go.

He checked his insides in astonishment and discovered that another Savage had taken up residence in the body of Savely Savage and realized in delight that he couldn't predict what the new resident would do next. "Maybe it's schizophrenia?" he chuckled, thinking that a madman among normal people was the same as a normal person among madmen and who knows, perhaps, it was only now that he had rid himself of the mental illness that had been his former life.

Previously Savage had felt that his future was over but

the past had never happened. Interminable grey days were breathing down one another's necks, and the tail end of an unbearably long dull line of them was already in sight. Now, though, the line had been interrupted by days that had turned his life inside out and Savage felt that the past hung on him like a clingy girlfriend while the future was at his back.

A rusty kiosk leant drunkenly against a block of flats. Only the plump breasts of the saleswoman could be seen through the tiny window and Savage suddenly wanted to pinch them. The kiosk sold beer snacks and he stuffed his pockets with dried fish, nuts and crackers. He spent the rest of his money on a phone card.

He didn't recognize his wife's voice.

"It's me," Savage croaked, surprised to find he wasn't stammering.

His wife let out a sob:

"Why on earth did I marry you? And now, now..."

A patrol call shot round the corner. Savage froze but the police went on by.

"I don't know what to do..."

"Die!" sobbed the receiver.

His wife promised to come out to the garages. Savage curled up on the ground behind a heap of scrap metal and watched the road through a hole in a rusty washtub. He had eaten the nuts and crackers which grated on his teeth like sand and now a leaden torpor came over him. He didn't think about anything, didn't try to remember or work anything out. At home, he slept under two blankets and wore pyjamas even during the summer yet now he didn't feel the cold of the metal he was lying on. His wet, dirty clothes were plastered to his skin and dry grass and chewing gum had stuck to his tangled hair.

A black spot on the horizon was getting closer and turned out to be a woman. Savage had told her to meet him a little way off so that he could check she hadn't been followed. His wife was wearing black as if she were trying out a set of widow's weeds. The pointed toes of her velvet boots wiggled predatorily

24

as she looked around her, nervously straightening her skirt. Savage wanted his wife to take him by the hand like a child and to stroke his head. He began to cry, feeling alone and unneeded like a spent cartridge. Frightened that his wife would go away, he tried to call out to her but he couldn't move his swollen tongue. He might as well have been gagged. Everything swam before his eyes and Savage fainted. When he came round he saw his wife with Saam. As Coffin's right-hand-man, he had taken over as head of the gang. Savage imagined he was holding a gun that was pointing at Saam and he was trying to work out whether he'd killed the gangster or not.

Sound carried on the empty street as it does on water and Savage could hear every word. A gesticulating Saam was swearing at his wife, trying to convince her of something. She was having none of it, lips pursed, and Savely reckoned with a chuckle that no way would a thug like Saam get the better of her. "A stubborn woman's scarier than your gun," Savage grinned, vengefully. Saam's sidekicks were searching the area, peering under cars, looking for him in every nook and cranny. As he tried to hide behind a piece of sheet metal, Savage knocked it over and the gang turned towards the sound.

"There he is!" Saam gestured, reaching for his holster.

Keeping close to the ground, Savage squeezed between the garages and fled into the forest. Tripping over rotting tree stumps slowed him down. Branches caught on his clothes and scratched his face. The only way to avoid being lynched was to go back into town but the way was blocked by his pursuers and the forest offered him no refuge. The gang were catching up and Savage weaved from side to side like a hare with hounds on its tail. He stumbled and rolled into a gully with a small lake at the bottom. He flopped, face first into the slime. Yells and the sounds of branches as they snapped under heavy boots came closer and closer. Savage sank into a stupor and resignedly awaited his fate. "It'll be all over soon. It'll be all over soon…" thudded in his head. Water got up his nose and in his ears and a grey shrew with a long tail like a rat clambered on to his shoulder and sank in its teeth. Savage brushed it off into the water. Then, he spotted a huge hole in the side of the gully where the roots of trees had been ripped out. It was a tight fit but he burrowed in and lay, face down, on the ground, covering his ears. To Savage, if he couldn't see the gang, they couldn't see him.

Saam was pulling Savage's wife by the hand.

"You said he trusts you!"

"You're the ones who frightened him off!"

She tripped and fell and, pulling off her boots in a fury, she ripped off a broken heel. His wife was so close Savage could have stretched out his hand and stroked her leg in its tight black nylon. It crossed his mind that he had spent twenty years with a woman he hardly knew. Married people are always unpredictable travelling companions but Savage and his wife hadn't even been on the same train.

"It's like the earth's swallowed him up!" spat Saam, sitting on a fallen tree.

"Maybe it wasn't him?" said one of the gang doubtfully, standing just a couple of steps away from Savage's hiding place.

Saam didn't answer. His eyes shone with malice.

"He won't last long in the forest," whined Savage's wife. "He'll be out there for a couple of days, and then he'll give himself up. Keep a look out for him at the police station. You're bound to get him. Where else is he going to go? He hasn't got any friends or relatives…"

They kept on looking for Savage until it grew dark, moving in circles and spreading out through the forest only to go back to where they had last seen him while Savely bit his fist till it bled to keep himself awake. He stifled a cough that felt like claws scratching his throat, struggling to breathe as he held it in with all his strength to avoid giving himself away.

"If a gun goes off in Act One, it must be hanging on the wall in Act Three," Saam shouted in the distance. "Keep looking and don't come back without him!"

26

Cold rose from the gully. Mist gathered over the water, sneaking under Savely's jumper like a cat and curling up in a ball on his chest so that he felt as though a cold gravestone had been lowered onto him.

The veranda at the Three Lemons had been sealed off. There were police officers all over the place, keeping curious onlookers at bay. All day long the townsfolk kept coming into the square to catch a glimpse of where Coffin had been killed still not believing it had really happened. The gang shot them evil looks and people tried to adopt sad expressions, hiding their smiles behind the handkerchiefs pressed to their mouths.

The gang, baring their teeth, patted their pockets, checking their knives.

"They grovel when you're alive, then they're chuffed to bits when you're dead."

"Slimy, worthless scum."

It was dark and quiet in the bar with the blinds down and napkins over the lamps to dim the light. The waitresses whispered. They couldn't bring themselves to talk out loud. Saam was hunched over a table, worrying a steak with his fork, feeling his back tingled and stung by people's stares. The gang were quiet, waiting to see what the new boss would do but Saam doused them with silence like boiling water. The first thing he had to do was to deal with Savely Savage for shooting Coffin but he'd vanished into thin air. Saam chewed these depressing thoughts along with his steak and his armpits prickled as he started to doubt whether he had really seen or only imagined Savage out by the garages.

Shorty tried to distract Saam, rustling up a couple of old jokes that he acted out but Saam kicked him aside and the cripple cringed in a corner, keeping a frightened eye on the new boss. Saam pulled a face and Shorty could read his fate in the lines on his forehead. Fatigue appeared on the cripple's face. It looked pinched as if he had aged several years in a couple of minutes.

Colonel Trebenko came in and sat down at Saam's table after checking the place out. They sat in silence for a long time, peering at the pattern on the napkins, unable to bring themselves to talk about Savely Savage.

"I used to have a friend who was a real daredevil," said Saam suddenly. "He went skydiving, drove around at 140 without a seatbelt, slept with other men's wives and ate off his knife. He didn't make it to 30…"

"Why? Didn't the parachute open?" snorted Trebenko.

"No, he went out to get cigarettes in the morning and was hit by a car on a pedestrian crossing."

The colonel raised his eyebrows.

"So?"

"So, we're rushing around in circles like hares all over the wood and fate's like a hunter watching us from a helicopter, keeping us in its sights. And however much we try to dodge it…" Saam narrowed his eyes into slits. "If it's someone's fate to be shot, what does it matter if a cop kills you or some bystander?"

Trebenko knew that Saam and Coffin had had their issues. The town had long anticipated a bloody ending and wondered who would come out on top. But now Coffin was lying in the morgue, stretched out as if he owned the place, and even as a corpse he was as terrifying as ever.

Many years ago, several ancient refrigerators arrived in the morgue for storing bodies but early next day they were put on a lorry and driven off to an undisclosed location. Rumour had it that Antonov had bought the refrigerators for a pittance and that they were now in his warehouse, full of frozen fish and ready meals. The morgue had just one room. Coffins and funeral wreaths were pushed back against the walls while the doctor slept behind a screen, feet up on the couch, and the attendant squeezed between the tables, swearing. The door was ajar and anyone outside could catch a glimpse of the sheet-draped bodies, the soles of their feet protruding and tags on their big toes like the ones usually put on newborn babies to prevent any mix-ups in hospital. Wielding his mop, the attendant drove away the little boys glued to the door to gape at the dead gangster, the mere mention of whom sent shivers up their spines.

"If you find Savage, let us have him," said Saam, leaning back and starting to rock on his chair. "We'll deal with him ourselves."

"Are you crazy?" asked Trebenko in astonishment. "Perhaps you'd like to hold a public execution in the square as well?"

"If you find him, just hand him over," Saam insisted.

He gave a short, dry laugh as if he'd cocked a pistol. When he did cock a pistol, it sounded like a laugh so that, hearing the familiar noise, Trebenko shuddered, not sure what it was. Saam just grinned balefully and played with his fork.

"It's a shame Coffin will never know who killed him. I'd love to see his face!"

Investigator Lapin, a callow youth and none too tall, who was just out of college, was hanging around near the police cordon. Lapin had his own issues with Coffin's gang. He would never forget the evening his Dad had come home later than usual. There was blood on his face and stains on his clothes and he reeked of alcohol. His mother was just about to tear a strip off him when he burst into tears, his face turned to the wall. He'd gone for a drink with his mates after work when a group had come round the corner already half cut. He wasn't scared when he made out Coffin's fleshy face. His Dad was a big guy. Tall and broad-shouldered, he stood a full head higher than the gangsters but legless Shorty held his knife as high as he could reach and his Dad's stomach turned to ice. The gang laid into him more out of boredom than anything else, nonchalantly and without enthusiasm, and then let him go as grudgingly as they had beaten him up. Lapin's Dad couldn't endure the humiliation no matter how much his wife consoled him. He took to drink, promising with every glass that he'd shoot the lot of them, the bullies, but before long he was dead.

His son, short and skinny and not a bit like his father, dreamt of vengeance, sticking to Coffin's gang like a burr. He dusted down the files, kept tabs on Severina and looked for witnesses but, fearing for their lives, no-one would speak out against the gang. His superiors, irritated by his zeal, were too cowardly to do anything obvious but behind his back paperwork got mixed up, test results vanished and records went walkabout. But the investigator didn't give up.

Lapin looked at the dried blood on the floor of the veranda and fought down a desire to touch it as if it weren't real. He looked over the shoulders of the scene-of-crime officers and questioned the witnesses hovering uneasily off to one side. He shoved a greasy note into the bouncer's pocket and from him he discovered what had happened the previous evening.

"Ah, Lapin, you're here too!" drawled Colonel Trebenko, screwing his eyes up after the darkness of the bar.

The investigator stretched, hands behind his back like a naughty schoolboy, and Trebenko hid the displeasure that made the vein on his forehead stand out behind a half-a-street-wide smile. He wasn't happy that Lapin had been allowed access to the murder scene and he was looking for someone to take his anger out on.

After college Lapin joined the police but he didn't last long. He would spend the night at work, digging into old files and in the mornings would wash off the archival dust in the sink, badger witnesses and search all the hide-outs and abandoned building sites. He slept in short bursts, ate standing up and when he was bowed down and oppressed by fatigue and despair, he would go to his father's grave to boost his morale. He didn't know himself what he was looking for but he hoped he would find the end of a thread and that when he pulled it he would be able to unravel the snarls that entangled the town.

"They'll kill you, lad," rasped the sallow old man who guarded Antonov's warehouse. "As sure as eggs is eggs, they'll kill you!"

Lapin knew the gang brought hostages to this remote

spot and held them in the cold cellar where there was an iron bedstead and a water bowl. Sensing there was a lot the old man knew, Lapin latched on to him like a tick. He pestered him with fictitious checks and turned up with threats or presents, but the old man, chuckling into his moustaches, stubbornly held his tongue, looking at Lapin with faded eyes.

"I was young once too, you know," he said, patting Lapin on the back and inviting him to share his meal. "Stubborn, like you, naive, kind... Now my life's like an old pair of pants... Why should that be, lad?"

The cramped room smelt of old age and sour milk. Damp seeped from the walls that were papered with magazine covers and Lapin, shivering, thrust his freezing hands into his pockets. Seeing this, the old man threw an old blanket round his shoulders and, topping up their tea, got out a jar of jam.

"I'm sure you're thinking: 'You're not long for this world, old man, so tell me everything you're scared of before you go'... Right?" he said, narrowing his eyes.

Lapin smiled, warming his hands on his steaming cup.

"And if I am?"

The old man didn't say any more, just licked the spoon and stuck it in the jar.

"Are you scared of them?" Lapin asked, trying to get back to the subject, but the old man, popped a spoonful of jam into his mouth, a sign that he had nothing to say.

Lapin looked at the faded pictures on the walls and remembered the events of years gone by that had flared up as news headlines and been instantly forgotten, leaving behind a void and an aftertaste of printer's ink. In the same way, the archives, yellow with age, smelt only of paper and dust while the crimes themselves seemed invented, like a detective story.

"Drop it. You won't dig anything up about them and, if you do, you won't send them to jail. They'll kill you first. And if they don't, you still won't change anything. New ones will come and take their place!" said the old man, frowning. The hopelessness of what he said was contagious and Lapin caught it like a cold.

31

"Is your Dad still alive?" asked the old man by way of goodbye.

"He's dead," Lapin replied. Then added, "He didn't kill himself."

"Not even cockroaches kill themselves," muttered the old man. "They get flattened with slippers but here in our town, well..."

From then on, the old man would ask Lapin to stop for tea and the investigator felt as though confessions were gathering on the tip of his tongue. He had lived alone for a long time and Lapin was his only visitor apart from the demons that cackled in the corners of the room. Lapin grew quite attached to him, talking to him about his job, about his Dad and taking revenge on the gang, about the fact that he couldn't find a single girlfriend in the entire town and about Chief of Police Trebenko who longed to be rid of his pushy junior.

"Come back again," the old man told him, wiping away a tear. "It's so lonely without you, son..."

Then once, as he left work early in the morning, Lapin saw the old man on the bench just outside the station. There was a wistful, plaintive expression in his colourless eyes and his head hung at an unnatural angle from his broken neck. Putting his arms round the old man, Lapin felt the same cold coming from him that had come from the walls of his room. He went back into his office, wrote out his resignation notice and swapped the police for the Prosecutor's Office.

Whenever Lapin met Trebenko he felt a chill pass through him as it had that morning he put his arms round the dead old man to ask for his forgiveness. Now, coming across the colonel by the veranda, he shivered out of habit and turned up his collar.

"This is the most extraordinary murder in many years," he told Trebenko keeping his eyes on the toes of his boots.

"Murder's murder. They're all the same," said Trebenko, pulling a face. "One guy kills another and hey, three's a crowd. There's nothing for the Prosecutor's Office to do here. We haven't got enough room ourselves. Get out of here, Lapin. Stick to your own business."

The investigator wanted to laugh in his face but, blushing furiously, he stepped back over the striped police tape and with one last look at Coffin's empty table, he ran across the square with the feeling that today, for the first time in several years, he wouldn't need to take anything to help him sleep.

Once Severina had moved in with Saam, Coffin started to spend more time with them. Catching his eye, Saam clenched his teeth and pretended not to see how Coffin was grinning at her budding breasts. Once when they were drinking at the Three Lemons, it was too much and he put his hand on Coffin's.

"There are plenty of girls. Take any one of them but leave this one alone!"

Coffin said nothing, knocking over his glass in silence.

One day he turned up when he knew Saam wasn't home.

"If God made you ugly, it was because he wanted to punish you. If He made you pretty, he wanted to punish those around you..." Coffin spent a long time practising how to say this, trying out various voices but they still came out wrong and, losing his temper, he reverted to his usual tone: "And you're hot!"

Severina's hands shook so much as she poured the tea that she spilt it on the tablecloth. Coffin, jaws working, stared at her for a long time then, knocking over the table, he dragged her into the bedroom.

At the orphanage, the kids had slept head-to-toe and even three to a bed when there wasn't enough room. Girls and boys shared the same rooms. They were in and out of each other's beds, used to being in an institution where everything around them belonged to no-one in particular and to everyone all at the same time. Bodies, included. Outside boys liked the girls from the orphanage because they would go to bed without a fuss, unaware of what they should or shouldn't do.

When Coffin left, however, Severina burst into tears. She

33

felt as if there were greasy stains on her body that would never wash off and spent the whole evening in the bath, trying to scrub away his kisses with a loofah.

Coffin began to call round with presents and flowers that he left on the bedside table and Severina threw out of the window. She said nothing to Saam, scared that he'd drive her away so that when she became pregnant she didn't know whose it was.

She rushed round to the orphanage and sobbed on her girlfriends' bosoms. They talked over one another as they offered prescriptions they'd overheard or come up with themselves. Severina tried them all. She sat for hours in a hot bath and hit herself in the stomach. When she went to the toilet in the Three Lemons, a dark red clot came away that she flushed down the toilet and in the bowl she suddenly saw the drunken nanny, keening, "You poor, unfortunate things."

Saam started to notice Severina blushing and biting her lips till they bled and Coffin grinning at her, and jealousy gnawed at his heart like a horde of mice. One evening, the gang had nothing to do and were knocking back beers, Severina was washing up loudly at the sink and Coffin put down his beer and went to find her in the kitchen. Saam waited a moment, then jumped up after him, arriving just as he put his arms round the girl's thin, bony shoulders and whispered into her ear. Severina gasped and dropped a plate. Coffin jumped back. His stare raked Saam's face.

They went outside and lit their cigarettes in silence. The moon clung to the old weathercock that creaked in the wind and the minutes dragged out like a funeral procession. Saam went for his knife. Coffin grabbed his. For a long time, they stood breathing heavily, neither able to make the first move.

"There are plenty of girls," said Coffin, lowering his knife in a conciliatory gesture. "You and me, we're like two hands. It'd be stupid for one to cut the other off."

Saam put his knife away and, after a long drag on his cigarette, he tossed the butt away.

"Was it her idea?" he asked.

"Course, it was," Coffin lied, knowing Saam wouldn't believe him. "I didn't make it easy. After all, she's your girlfriend…"

"There are plenty of girls," said Saam, repeating what Coffin had said.

They embraced and went inside. They were hardly through the entryway before they were falling about laughing.

Meanwhile, Shorty was hiding behind an old barrel. Coffin had beckoned to him as he headed for the street and the cripple, hiding a gun in his shirt, stole into the yard like a cat. Coffin knew that Saam wouldn't have time to use his knife before being shot in the back. Saam too noticed that the cripple who had been setting out his game of patience on the floor had vanished and he felt his gaze wandering over him from his hiding place behind the rotting barrel.

That evening Saam swore to get revenge, hiding away the hurt that pierced his chest like a knife.

He didn't drive Severina away immediately. She followed him round like a beaten puppy, afraid to open her mouth, and when she lay down beside him, Saam would shove her off the bed and that's where she slept, on the floor, next to his slippers. He stopped taking her with him and for days at a time the girl would sit by the window, her eyes tracing the rain drops that trickled down the glass.

One evening Saam came home drunk with a girl who was roaring with laughter. She wandered around the flat, still in her stilettos and the click of her heels pounded in your temples. Saam spent the night with this new girlfriend, putting Severina outside, where she sat by the door, legs crossed, ears attuned to the slightest sound. In the morning, the girl carefully stepped across her, wiping her smudged mascara with the edge of her sleeve, while Saam held out her bag. Severina didn't go away, though. She kept watch for him by the door. As he locked the door, Saam kicked her, swearing through gritted teeth. Then he disappeared for a few days so that Severina went back to the orphanage where the staff took her in without a word.

Even there, Coffin stalked her and Severina hid in her room whenever she saw his car parked by the fence. Then Coffin would send the boys to drag her out into the street and he would take her off into the forest to a bathhouse on the lake.

At the bathhouse, the elderly attendant provided clean, crisp sheets and, looking at Severina, would say in a singsong drawl, "Soft as the first snow". It wasn't clear whether he meant the girl or the sheet.

Severina curled up in the sheet, biting her nails in silence and looking askance at Coffin. Furious at her indifference, the gangster was eaten up by jealousy.

"But I'd like to marry you," he said huskily, sitting her on his lap.

Severina didn't believe him.

"One word from me and Saam's sweeping the streets!" he bragged. "I can kick him out of the gang if I want."

Severina lay back and looked at her reflection in the mirrored ceiling, at Coffin and the syringe on the table. She swayed like a sleepwalker. "Soft as the first snow, soft as the first snow, softasthefirstsnow," she repeated faster and faster until the words stopped making sense.

Furious, Coffin passed Severina on to a sidekick.

"Set her up somewhere. She can start dealing, whatever takes her fancy."

Severina was passed around and now it was her men that she counted on her fingers, men whose faces she couldn't remember and whose names she got mixed up. Coffin sent her into schools to swap heroin for crumpled banknotes. She liked standing outside a school, listening to the cheerful chaos of break times. Sometimes she looked through the windows, mouth open, repeating what the teachers said. They seemed completely different to the lacklustre teachers at the orphanage who were always gone too quickly for the children to get used to them.

"We've got to get that brat set up with one of our guys,"

Coffin spat out one day, scratching the stubble on his chin. "She knows a lot. We can't let her go."

"Who needs her?" said Saam dismissively, pursing his lips.

"I do!" hissed Shorty from his corner.

Boredom meant they set about the preparations as if they were giving away their only daughter. They decorated the house in white net, hanging it on the walls, wrapping it around the chairs and ceiling lights and draping it over the sofas. Falling about with laughter, they stuck paper angels cut out of newspaper onto the windows.

"We learnt that at the orphanage," boasted a boy who was skinny as a rake, had a squint and was diligently wielding a pair of scissors. "We cut snowflakes out every year."

They plied Severina with alcohol from early morning so that she was wearing a silly smile as she looked at them with drink-filmed eyes. The cripple was puffed up with importance. His suit had been ironed and he had a faded flower in his buttonhole. Coffin gave the bride away, bestowing his blessing on bride and groom alike. The whole night was spent carousing and dancing, every toast preceded with a rousing "Kiss! Kiss" that reached the entire neighbourhood.

The moon was frozen to the frost-covered window and the old tape recorder croaked like it had a cold. Barely able to stand, Coffin pulled Severina up to dance, leaping around and shouting to a slow, syrupy, sentimental song. Then, when the tape changed to something with a bit of rhythm, he spun in a slow dance and Saam, drinking from the bottle, pointed it at him as if he were taking aim.

"Life's like a bottle of vodka," Saam muttered drunkenly, his head on Shorty's shoulder. "You think just another shot or so and things will cheer up but the more you drink, the crappier you feel."

"No," laughed Shorty, shaking his head, "life's the bottle. And what you fill it with, vodka, water, or poison, is up to you. That's what free will is," he said, stressing every syllable.

As morning approached they jumped over the fence, all hot and bothered, and fell on the first person they came across who was going home after a night shift. They kicked him in the face till the dirty snow turned red and, abandoning him in the roadway, went off home, howling with laughter.

They woke up where they had fallen in a drunken sleep, some at the table, others on the floor or out in the yard, face down in the dirt.

"Get us some water!" rasped Coffin, rooting around in the ashtray. He pulled out the remains of a cigarette and lit it, coughing.

The cripple filled a pan and dragged it over to Coffin who clutched it greedily, spilling water down his front.

"We'll have a real wedding when she's eighteen!" he said with an evil grin, spotting Severina coming down stairs. Trembling, she was holding on to the wall and when Shorty reached out to her she shot out of the house to the accompaniment of Coffin's laughter.

An insult hurts like a splinter until it's taken out. The day after Coffin's funeral, Saam took a tied-up Shorty to the cemetery. He didn't know what he wanted revenge for – the evening the cripple had hidden behind the barrel or his wedding to Severina. The gang dug a fresh grave and threw Shorty in it. He wriggled like a worm and thumped on the lid of the coffin. When they had filled the hole in with earth, they drank to the memory of the dead.

Karimov, the factory manager, was looking listlessly at a cardboard model of the plant. Tiny pipes, production units, buildings, quarries and railway tracks: scale models of the real things. To Karimov this was like being God. He imagined someone up above, looking listlessly down at the real factory, while he, Karimov, scurried like an ant around the edge of that someone's table, which to him was the whole universe.

"Your father is God!" his foster father used to tell him, poking him in the chest. "And you shall have no other gods."

Karimov didn't believe there was no God. He sought Him passionately in sermons and travelled the world on pilgrimage until he was deadly tired and filled with hatred for people and God. "God exists and he is as evil and cruel as my father," he decided. He drew a line under his search for God.

He didn't read books. He preferred newspapers. Other people's inventions made Karimov yawn. His life was more convoluted than crime fiction and more complicated than drama. It didn't fit neatly into the literary canon and the women in it never stayed longer than one night so that their names and faces were gone from his memory before the scent of their perfume. He paid prostitutes in forged notes on the grounds that counterfeit love deserved counterfeit money. "Nobody needs anybody," Karimov loved to say and this epigram was always on the tip of his tongue.

The phone rang and Karimov reached out for it, his sleeve sweeping a cardboard building onto the floor.

"I've got a riddle for you."

The dry, grating voice made Karimov wince.

"Ten goods wagons leave Station A. Eight goods wagons reach Station B. The question is what happened to the two wagons…"

"What's this about," asked Karimov, snapping his cigarette case shut.

"Just a riddle. A child could solve it."

Outside, Karimov could see the production units, the rail tracks stretching away from them.

The line had gone dead. Karimov lit a cigarette, pondering who could have betrayed him and smiled: after all, so far everything was going to plan.

Karimov stole because he was bored. It amused him to put his hand in someone else's pocket so that they could see it but couldn't catch him. He was taunting the man who had made him factory manager, convicting him in that dry, grating voice. He wanted revenge for being exiled here, which was the worst possible punishment for Karimov. Hot-blooded and dynamic, he loathed the sleepy town and this factory where even the conveyor belts seemed unwilling to do any work and the trains loaded with ore had to force themselves to move.

The man with the grating voice was nicknamed Pipe after the fancy meerschaum pipe he kept packed with strong French tobacco. Even when he was forced to stop smoking, he carried on with the ritual, fiddling with his pipe all day and then throwing the unused tobacco away in the evening and cleaning the pipe carefully. The doctors had pronounced his sentence and now there was a pipe sticking out of his throat but he showed no signs of dying, looking so scathingly at the people around him that they felt naked and insignificant. When he spoke, he put a device under his chin that projected a mechanical, artificial voice, like the sound of metal on glass.

When he found out that Karimov was illegally taking loaded wagons out of circulation, Pipe suspected something. "He's not the kind of guy to be dealing in wagons," sniffed the old man, crumpling up the documents he'd been given. He realized Karimov was trying to distract him from something bigger but he couldn't work out what it was so he lost his temper, flying off the handle at his staff.

"You think you've got eyes in the back of your head and you know everything that's going on here, do you?" Karimov smirked, doing mental battle with Pipe. "And you can't see what's going on right under your nose!"

"You think you're giving me the run around but I'm the one who's leading you on – by the nose." Pipe insisted to himself, imagining he was talking to Karimov.

Karimov's only source of entertainment was the orphanage which he visited at the weekend. He made the staff nervous. They were scared of the hawk nose that sliced through the air like a ship's prow and of the sticky eyes like those of the babies dumped on the doorstep of the orphanage. Karimov brought toys and treats and, while his bodyguards dragged the boxes out of the car, he would stroke the heads of the children crowding round him and stare at a fixed point, wondering how life would have turned out if the stranger who adopted him hadn't picked him up from the steps of the orphanage one morning where he lay, wrapped in his mother's dress.

The cemetery nestled on the outskirts of town, entirely surrounded by new buildings. Savely Savage wandered among the graves looking for the food relatives brought the dead. Young faces looked out from the photographs on the gravestones. Savage could hear their cries and lamentations and their prayers. He felt as if he were the only dead person there.

Death had come to the cemetery. A hunched old woman with a crook, she was so bent over that the dead seemed to be drawing her to them. She had a huge hump like a tombstone and her eyes were empty black pits. Her crook struck the ground before her and the homeless people trailing in her wake collected the gifts left on the graves. Seeing Savage, the tramps grabbed hold of sticks, the old woman started to screech, thrusting her crook in the air, and Savely fled from the cemetery.

As he scrambled through the fragrant pine brakes, Savage looked back to that ill-fated evening when he had started to live back to front, knowing about tomorrow before yesterday and remembering when he was a little boy and it had seemed as though everything was still to come when in fact it was already behind him.

"You keep on studying, son," Savage's parents would say tenderly, looking at their boy bent over his books.

Savage's daughter would rip pages out of her textbooks and make them into paper aeroplanes which she threw out of the window.

"Why have I got to study stuff I'm not going to have any use for?" she yawned when Savage tried to talk to her. "You studied and where did that get you? Take a look at yourself. Studying makes people into failures!"

Savely blushed and bit his lip, while his daughter carried

on, swatting at him like a fly on the window: "Better no college than no money!"

If life were a book, then someone had torn out Savage's ending and stuck in pages from someone else's novel. Only yesterday, Savage had been drawing plans of mineral deposits. Now, here he was, striking sparks from a stone, which wouldn't turn into a fire. In the past, when he scanned an ethnography book, he had scarcely been able to hold back a smile at his sense of superiority over northern savages who worshipped stones. Now, here he was, crawling around a boulder, weeping and wailing, and waiting for a dry branch to burst into flame like Moses and the burning bush.

On Saturdays, the factory sirens sounded and the town fell still. Windows closed and the streets emptied. Explosions shook the ground. A dirty cloud rose from the quarry, covering the town like a shroud. Savage marked this latest Saturday by scratching his arm with a piece of glass so as not to lose track of time.

One lake flowed into another, stretching out in a chain across dense forest that was broken up by stony outcrops. There was a leaky wooden boat on the lake shore. A tiny creature lived underneath and jumped out when Savage kicked the boat. He walked along the water's edge, not knowing where he was going. There were no other towns around apart from abandoned workers' settlements. He didn't even know what he'd say to someone he met should he ever come across another living soul. His thoughts teemed like gnats, buzzing and biting, but they couldn't help.

Savage considered crossing the border or escaping to Moscow where he could disappear among the other down-and-outs. He imagined finding a job, buying a passport in a new name, starting a family, beginning again from scratch. Then he remembered an old school friend who had gone off to earn a living in the capital. He had spat with rage as he recounted rattling around in a train for several hours, without a seat, packed like a sardine into a stuffy, overcrowded carriage. Then

42

there had been backbreaking work until nightfall as a freight handler, too embarrassed to tell his fellow drudges he had a pocketful of qualifications. He swapped one job for another, choosing between jobs that paid where you were treated like dirt and jobs where you weren't paid for several months and then you were beaten up with baseball bats that damaged your kidneys. "What is life?" he had enjoyed philosophizing in the past, stabbing a bit of sardine with his fork as their glasses were refilled. "You know what life is?" he asked Savage when he ran into him on his return home. "It's this!" he said, pulling up his sweater and revealing the bruises. Remembering that black and blue stomach, Savage reckoned Moscow was scarier than the taiga.

A village of summer dachas could be seen beyond the trees. The houses were scattered like children's bricks, some of them set apart, others clustered closely together. There were picnics here at weekends. Children raced around shrieking during the day and bonfires were lit in the evenings. When one yard struck up a song, the neighbours would join in while stray dogs took up the melody, carrying it along the streets where it continued to be heard for a good long time. Only rarely could the white and purple flowers of potato plants be seen in the yards. The cold ground had no time to warm up in summer before it was autumn so only the most stubborn and reckless gardeners bothered with allotments.

A few years ago, Savage's wife had made him buy a plot of land for growing vegetables.

"There are potatoes in the shops," Savage had said, trying to get out of it but his wife had hung on with bulldog tenacity.

"You know how much they cost. We could all go on holiday on the money we'd save."

Savage succumbed to the temptation of a family holiday and bought a few buckets of potatoes and a sack of fertilizer. He spent all summer on the land, digging, weeding and watering. In the autumn he harvested exactly the same number as he'd planted and was happy.

"The season's nearly over. Shall we go for the tail end of summer?" he said, reminding his wife about the holiday and holding out the money he'd set aside from his wages.

His wife and daughter crammed their suitcases with clothes and went off on holiday. He saw them to the door, feeling like a beaten dog. Once on his own, Savage cooked jacket potatoes and ate them, skin and all. He dunked the potatoes in salt and reflected that life was better taken with too much salt than with too little.

Now, looking at those savourless days, he was astonished that in a matter of minutes he had swept his entire life off the table and begun again not from the beginning or even from the end but from a line in someone else's tune, which he had taken up like a drinking song at a wake.

The village was quiet. The dacha owners had gone home, smoke-blackened barbecues and bent shovels abandoned in the yards. The sleepy caretaker, who kept an eye on the dachas, protecting them from tramps and thieves, was strolling beside the fences. A ladder leant against one of the houses. Only part of the roof was covered in plywood. Savage waited for the caretaker to turn down another street then slipped through the hole in the half-repaired roof. It looked like a respectable sort of house and Savely decided it was bound to be stocked with food. Inside, it smelt of rotten wood. The old furniture had been covered in patterned tablecloths and old toys put away in a wooden box so that just for an instant Savage imagined he was back in his own childhood. He searched the cellar, pulling out a sack of gone-to-seed potatoes and dusty jars of mushrooms. There was a dry crust on a shelf and Savage ate it, slugging water from a pot-bellied carafe. When he had gathered up his supplies, he fell on the bed and, rocking into the springs, he counted the number of days he had slept on bare earth.

Previously the week had divided into two. Long drawn-out weekdays had given way to unbearable weekends. Now they were all mixed up and no day was like another. Savage

44

called the days it rained and he had to hide under branches getting soaked Mondays and if he'd managed to find something to eat, it was Sunday.

His cheeks grew wispy stubble, his face darkened and his skin was so stretched there didn't seem to be enough of it. Sometimes, Savage was overcome with despair. It made his hands shake and his tongue stick to the roof of his mouth. He would cry, sniffling to start with, like a child with hurt feelings, then getting louder and louder until he was sobbing out loud. Afterwards, exhausted, he would fall on the damp swamp-smelling moss and lie there, gazing up at the cold sky and trying to read his fate in the patterns of the clouds. Like a rabid wolf, circling a settlement, Savage could neither go back to town nor run away.

The residents of the town had stern, suspicious faces and cold smiles – looking into their eyes was like freezing in a snowdrift. They walked well-trodden paths, concealing their frost-bitten fates under fur coats and now that they had adjusted to the gangsters running the show they had long forgotten ever having lived differently.

The nine-storey block of flats stuck out among the five-storey blocks like a raised finger. Its residents tended to look down on everyone else, making them easy to recognize anywhere in town. A shop-owner's noisy family moved into one of the flats. He had three children, a shrill mother-in-law and a widowed sister who looked after the children. The businessman was pigheaded and grasping so that fresh bread was never put on the table until the children had finished the last stale bun and his bookkeeping was darker than the Polar night. But the gang weren't the tax service and they weren't taken in by forged records. Coffin demanded a round sum from the businessman that the latter couldn't bear to part with. Arson set light to his shops, the electricity failed because of sudden power cuts and auditors made frequent inspections. Coffin was stubborn but the businessman was a match for him. His losses ate away at his savings but he was prepared to sell off all he had rather than see anything go to the gang.

Realizing that the day of reckoning was nigh, he sent his family out of town and sold his shops to Antonov for a pittance. He hid the money in bank accounts and barricaded himself into the flat with a double-barrelled shotgun. No-one broke down the door, however. Nothing happened at all and the next day the businessman started to panic. He looked out of the window and saw Coffin's men surrounding the building. The way in had been boarded up. Hovering in the courtyard, residents who couldn't go home asked the gang to let them in or, as a last resort, to let their families out but Coffin shook his head. Anyone who tried to climb out of the ground floor windows was driven back inside with sticks. Soon, the businessman's doorbell started ringing. His neighbours asked him to come out and speak to the gang but, pressed to the spy hole, he remained stubbornly silent. They were running out of food. The residents organized a morning market, swapping their surplus for things in short supply. So, the hoarder on the first floor who kept sacks of potatoes on the balcony swapped them for tea and soap and a bakery worker exchanged flour for lard and washing powder. Fed up with waiting, the gang cut the electricity and water supply in the building, and the people shut up inside became utterly dejected. Since the plumbing wasn't working people had to use the entrance hall as a toilet and had to hold their noses when they went outside their flats. The businessman, ear pressed to the door, could hear angry footsteps but didn't answer any knocks. He no longer knew what he had hoped to achieve by locking himself in his flat and now he became totally confused and couldn't work out what to do. His rage only made him more stubborn, however, and, when he looked out of the window at the gang who were lying in wait for him, he laughed darkly and gave them the finger.

The businessman's neighbours were no cowards either. The whole block gathered outside his door, with hammers, axes, pliers and spades and, for several days, they battered at his iron door until it smashed. When they opened it, they found themselves looking down the double barrels of the shotgun.

"Now, now. Give that here!" cried the woman from the bakery fearlessly seizing the gun.

The neighbours grabbed the businessman by the hair, hands, feet and clothes and dragged him down the stairs. As his bones counted out the steps, he regretted ever moving into the top floor.

"Open up! We're bringing him out! Open up!" the residents yelled out of the windows and, spitting into their palms, the gang set about dismantling the barricades.

The hapless businessman was pushed into a car and driven away to an undisclosed location. His flat stood empty for many years, the crumpled door a reminder of the days of confinement, but then a new resident moved in and upholstered the door with leather, maintaining that he had purchased the flat from that same businessman whom he had allegedly seen safe and sound at the notary's office.

When Saam showed up at the orphanage, the little boys would crowd round him, making a racket and fighting in a bid for his attention.

"I've taken up wrestling. I can beat anyone. I'm just what you need!"

"I climbed into a flat through a tiny window while my dad was the lookout. I can still get through any window!"

"Saam, let me be in your gang!"

The children put part of their loot in a common pot to learn about the pecking order and the gang would help those who had been caught. The local children's officer, a tall butch woman, with police major's rank and a dark moustache above her thread-thin lip, released the little thieves, throwing the reports into a bin she would kick under the table with the toe of her boot. The woman had eyes like dried-up puddles. They seemed always on the verge of tears but she never actually wept.

47

"Little thugs," said the sergeant who brought the small robbers in from the market. He looked discontentedly askance at the major.

"What, you think they should be sent to a prison colony?" she said, dispatching yet another crumpled police report into the bin. "They've no future as it is and they'd make mincemeat out of them there. They'd come out brutal and full of hate..."

Listening to her, however, the sergeant smiled a crooked smile knowing that she was more afraid of the brats than they were of her and that her teary eyes looked the other way in return for gifts from Saam.

The gang put the smartest kids into a juvenile detachment. On an abandoned building site, avoided by tramps and dogs alike, they were trained to fight, use air-guns and hide from pursuers. Then, when they left the orphanage, they became full-fledged members of the gang. They called Saam "Dad" and were ready for anything for the sake of that word and how it felt to say it.

"This is a little town. It cramps your style," Saam would say, looking at the boys as he leaned on a slab of concrete. "With our lads, we could move mountains."

"Better to be a Big Man in a little town than a sucker in the capital," his comrade snickered.

Rain hammered the window panes, running down in streams that distorted the houses, streetlights and pedestrians, rushing along under umbrellas. It was noisy inside the Three Lemons, glasses tinkling as women laughed and conversations bubbling up and boiling over like milk on a hot plate.

"Take away the gang and there would be mayhem!" said Antonov, loosening the neck of his shirt and shrugging his shoulders. "You just try and hold them back," he said, nodding at the tables nearby.

"Why do I have to be involved with a killer and a bandit?" Krotov wondered tearfully.

Antonov sucked on a piece of lemon to go with his shot of vodka while Krotov screwed up his face as if he had a bitter taste in his mouth. They were so alike they could have been one another's mirror image and, for anyone looking at them, it was like seeing double.

"I'm no idiot either but I've been involved with them for twenty years now. You'd love to keep your hands nice and clean while Trebenko and I do all the dirty work."

Offended, Krotov stared at his plate.

"You're a businessman whereas I'm a civil servant. I'm not working for myself, after all." He spat the words out along with his olive stones. "While you were off having fun, I was doing the thinking for everyone."

Antonov threw back his head and roared with laughter as he remembered the accident at the power plant when cables had burst like old veins, houses were staring out of empty sockets, and satellite dishes protruded like ears that had been deafened by the silence. Clutching a bulging suitcase to his chest Krotov had fled in his official car from the electricity-deprived town which looked like a black foundation pit from the top of the hill.

That year, the winter was so cold the houses froze right through and people slept in sweaters and hats, the blankets pulled up over their heads. It was a long time since the decrepit electricity grid had been repaired and initially the cables, eaten away by the cold, stopped working in various parts of town, leaving first one set of buildings then another without light. Then there was an outage at the main power station and the whole town sank into an impenetrable gloom.

Sirens wailed like hungry dogs, alarms screeched, women shouted and then the town fell silent and everything was quiet. In the distance, the factory was all lit up, powered by a back-up substation. Residents scurried along the dark streets like moles, holding their arms out and bumping into one another. Cars raced around town for a few days, their headlights dazzling. Then the petrol station closed and the cars shuddered to a halt in the streets where they turned into giant snowdrifts. Some people hastily gathered their things together and managed to leave town. Krotov, the mayor, was one of them. He fled to Moscow. He had recorded dozens of different speeches and slogans for all eventualities so that every day his voice could be heard from the loudspeaker in the square, reassuring the citizens by the very fact that the mayor was sharing their common misfortune.

Only the factory's main production units carried on working. Schools and hospitals closed. Shops initially used generators and hastily sold the food in their defrosting refrigerators. Residents stocked up on food, not knowing how long they would have to manage without electricity. The cost of candles skyrocketed. They went for fabulous sums of money and whispers did the rounds that suggested the hardware shops and the church stall were making the biggest killings of all. Televisions didn't work. There were no newspapers and information about the failed power station travelled by word of mouth, acquiring more and more details and sowing panic among the residents.

Savage didn't know what to do with himself as he sat in his dark room. He looked out of the window as if he were watching television, trying to imagine what was going on in the black windows of neighbouring blocks of flats. What were other people doing? Dreaming, talking, pottering about at a loose end, making love? A useless lamp dangled from the ceiling like a hanged man but the telephone worked and Savage's wife spent days chatting to her friends, her legs swung over the back of a chair. Savage had no-one to ring, however. All he could do was listen to his wife's conversations as she bitched about her colleagues as if nothing had happened and discussed recipes to make with the food they had stocked up or talked about the bank robberies that had taken place in the town.

An inquisitive moon was glued to the window pane at night. Savage tried to read by its meagre light, taking forgotten books down from the top shelf, which had once seemed mysterious but were now as dull and simple as copybooks. Savage decided to read them back to front but instead of making nonsense of the plot it gave it new meaning. Turned inside out like gloves, heroes became antiheroes, executioners became victims and wives, husbands and children wicked angels biting their wings in rage and all the books that had previously differed so greatly in plot and ideas became impossible to tell apart. Read from back to front, each book told how man is born in darkness, lives in shadow and departs into the night.

Savage wanted to share his thoughts with his daughter. He knocked on her door but Vasilisa wouldn't open it.

His wife was banging pans in the kitchen and, poking his head in, Savely saw that she was trying to light a fire on the floor.

"Are you out of your mind?" he shrieked, afraid. "You'll set the place on fire!"

"Oh, you're such a wimp," snapped his wife. "You really are."

The residents found it impossible to stay inside their flats when they didn't know how to keep themselves busy and they wandered the streets like sleepwalkers, slipping on the icy, snow-covered pavements that weren't being cleared. There was a crowd outside the municipal hospital, faces bleeding and noses broken. Some people were picked up on the street and carried in or brought in on stretchers.

"Fellow citizens! The situation is under control. Keep calm!" In the square, the mayor's voice boomed from a loudspeaker that was plugged into a storage battery. "There is no need to panic!"

During the day when there were a couple of hours of sunlight, everyone came tumbling out of their homes. Midday in the polar region was like evening. In the lilac twilight, snowdrifts looked like cotton wool and stars shone dully through slate-grey clouds. When they looked at one another, neighbours found they had changed beyond all recognition: their faces were swollen and sleepy; their eyes teary. People walked with their arms outstretched automatically, testing the air to avoid bumping into a post that had suddenly sprung up out of the darkness.

51

Savage roamed around town, trying to find something useful to do. He wanted to help and hoped he would come across an old man stuck in the snow or a woman who couldn't find her way home but, as he wandered around, he blundered into fences and cut his knees when he fell on the icy road and didn't meet anyone he might have helped. From a snatch of conversation, tossed over the shoulder of a passerby, he found out that the hospital needed volunteers. Wearing his red armband, he longed to help the patients who had gathered at the hospital entrance where fires were burning, shedding light on the street and the lower floors. Instead, he was assigned to corpse duty, dragging away the bodies that were being dumped out of the back door and straight into the snow. He would put a corpse onto a sheet and slowly drag it through the snow to the morgue where the doors stood open in welcome.

In the first few days, Coffin's gang broke into several banks where the alarms and security guards weren't working. As a result, soldiers were dispatched from the military unit to protect the main facilities and posted outside the big shops and local government buildings. It didn't take the gang very long, however, to realize that the outage at the power station hadn't just turned the ordinary lives of the residents inside out. It had done the same to the residents themselves.

The mayor's voice resounded through the town: "The situation is under control. Repair work is under way at the power station!"

People lit bonfires inside their flats causing fires. The whole town was enveloped in thin smoke and a smell of burning hung in the air. The police couldn't cope with the number of calls to deal with robberies and murders involving ordinary citizens, who suddenly realized they could get away with it. Savage's neighbour strangled his wife then dragged her out into the street and left her there. This murder, like many others committed during those days, would have gone unsolved had the man not been so tormented by his conscience that he went and confessed.

Police Chief Trebenko could tell that the town was getting out of control and that he couldn't pacify the newly savage inhabitants. It had become dangerous to go outside and the police barricaded themselves into the station, frightened by rumours that the townspeople were planning to take it by storm. To play it safe, they released all their prisoners except those waiting to be sent to labour camps but when they found themselves in the dark streets they asked to be let back in.

Trebenko went to the gang for help.

"My boys can't cope," he said, with a helpless gesture, hovering ill at ease in the entry way.

The generator snarled like a dog on a chain and a dim light winked with an air of cunning, threatening to go out one minute only to flare up brightly again the next. Predatory shadows flickered across the walls. A rusty sink kept count of the seconds like a metronome and Coffin, an old checked blanket round his shoulders, warmed his feet on Shorty who was curled up on the floor.

"They're getting into it," he smirked, exchanging a look with his sidekicks. "By the time the lights come back on, this will be a prison camp not a town."

Armed for the task, Coffin's gang took to the streets, shoulder to shoulder with the police officers, dispersing bystanders and terrorizing anyone who tried to take advantage of the general misfortune to line their own pockets. Instead of the soft, soothing voice of the mayor, the gang leader's hoarse and baleful tones could be heard from the loudspeaker in the central square.

"Right, well, basically..." Coffin began, clearing his throat. "Break it up. Go home. Stay indoors, quiet as mice: not a sign, not a sound. We catch anyone outside..." there was a pregnant pause, "and, well, you all know what will happen... That's all I wanted to say."

And that was the end of the unrest. A couple of days later, when extra troops had already arrived in town, the power station had been repaired and the lights came back on inside and out, dazzling eyes that had become accustomed to the darkness. The town had been without light for two weeks but it spent a lot longer licking its wounds. Ransacked shops, burnt out houses and broken fences were repaired all over town, the dead were laid to rest and newly emerged criminals, who until recently had been law-abiding citizens, were hunted down.

Colonel Trebenko came from the Ukrainian town of Donetsk. They say a Ukrainian without cunning is like a bun without currents. Trebenko wouldn't lift a finger unless there was something in it for him. He would wink complacently at his reflection in the mirror but blushed to see his old photos. The young lieutenant dispatched to a small northern town a quarter of a century before had the steady gaze of a prosecutor and Trebenko couldn't look him in the eye.

"A person's not a needle. We'll find him," he said. Trebenko liked crime films and would repeat phrases from them so you could tell which serial he was watching. There was no let up from the gangsters though. The previous chief of police had tried to resist them but came to no good. Trebenko's stomach ached at the thought of what had happened to his predecessor.

"If you don't, we'll skin you alive!"

"Why do you need him?" Trebenko raised his voice.

"Not 'you', us," said Saam with a grin, thinking back to the accident at the power station. "If he's not punished, the next thing we know, they'll all be taking up pitchforks!"

That conversation with Saam stayed in Trebenko's head. He parked the car in the garage and took a bottle from the cupboard, which he kept hidden from his wife behind a petrol can. He poured himself a glass and drank it down, so unaffected it might have been water. There had been a call from headquarters that morning. "Can't you cope?" the general had asked, needling him. "Have you brought in the volunteers? There's always something happening in your blasted town!" Trebenko had stood to attention as if the general could see him but when he replaced the receiver he spat out: "And we all know where the stars on your shoulders came from."

A gun and hunting trophies hung on the garage wall. There was a deerskin too, shaped like a map of the Soviet Union, pinned with beer bottle corks to mark the village Trebenko was born in, Moscow where he'd set up his children and the godforsaken place he lived in himself. "This is a big case so I can't go but as soon as it's over, that's it. I'm taking my pension and going home!" he would say after the third glass while his wife just sighed, biting her bloodless lips. Trebenko dreamt of building a two-storey house with a turret and carved shutters. He would draw the layout of the rooms on the back of a police report for his wife, telling her which room was the bedroom and which one was the lounge. But when his wife brought a dusty suitcase down from the attic, Trebenko would sulk and claim that urgent cases were keeping him at the station until midnight and his wife would carefully fold up the report and the sketch, hide it in the table drawer and put her suitcase away. "I'm stuck," he would say helplessly, hiding his eyes. He dreamed that Ukraine, warm, passionate, sable-browed Ukraine, was calling him home but the North, like a shaman hag, wouldn't let him go now that she'd got her talons into him.

"Will my police force protect me?"

Savage stood on the doorstep, fiddling with his matted beard. Trebenko had a picture of him in his breast pocket and automatically clasped his chest as if he had heart pains. Then, backing towards the wall, he was about to reach for his gun when he snatched his hand back, thinking it wasn't loaded anyway.

Matter-of-factly, Trebenko took out a second glass and filled it with vodka. They both drank in silence, staring at one another. Trebenko looked perplexed and Savage's glance wandered over his face like a blind man's hands.

"I didn't mean... I didn't think, I thought... But look what's happened," Savage mumbled, grabbing Trebenko's arm. "What can I do, Colonel? Who am I? I've kept myself to myself, done my job and look what's happened," Savage said again, struggling for words.

"It's a good thing you've come in of your own accord, as they say, a crime confessed…"

"Nothing can help me now."

"The court will be on your side! You're a family man, law-abiding, god-fearing. Just keep on saying you didn't think it was loaded. You'll get a suspended sentence for involuntary manslaughter."

"And be left to the gang's mercy."

"Pah!" Trebenko laughed affectedly but he stopped himself. "We can provide protection," he said.

He could tell how insincere his promises sounded.

"Perhaps I should run away? After all, they'll kill me, won't they?"

"Run where?" Trebenko took out his mobile. "You don't need to run anywhere," he said, chewing over the words slowly and wondering what to do with Savage. "You don't need to run anywhere…"

Trebenko tried to text a message but his fat sweating fingers kept hitting the wrong keys so that he sent a text more like a telegram.

Saam's mobile squeaked like a mouse and he read the message: "Garage, now!" He didn't need telling twice and, grabbing their coats, the gang dashed out of the house, stuffing their knives into their top boots as they went. They crammed into two cars and were off to the garages.

Investigator Lapin, who had been keeping watch on the gang outside their wooden house, gestured to his driver and the patrol car followed them at a distance.

Trebenko looked Savage over and decided he was so emaciated he would be easy to handle. He just needed to seize his moment, grab him from behind, get him on the floor and tie him up. The colonel turned to look for a rope and Savage caught his eye.

He followed Trebenko's every movement. He recalled how the duty officer had tried to persuade him to run. He had a sudden feeling that Trebenko's kindly face was just a mask and underneath he could see the colonel wetting a finger and leafing through neatly bound bundles of banknotes, tearing up police reports, and saying: "Some are destined to be the cork, others the bottle."

Savage drank from the bottle and watched Trebenko squirm.

"I didn't recognize you right away, you know," the colonel said with fake cheeriness. "I didn't know if you were a tramp or a forest sprite."

Suddenly it dawned on Savage. "You're all in it together! They're sucking us dry and you're protecting them. You're in it together. You'll hand me over, too, you Judas. You will, won't you?"

"What are you talking about?" asked Trebenko with a forced laugh. Suddenly, he lunged forward.

Savage snatched the gun off the wall and hit Trebenko over the head. The colonel collapsed at his feet, prostrate on the dirty floor, like a guilty slave.

"Judas!" yelled Savage, clubbing the colonel with the butt of the gun. "You Judas!"

He was beating him about the head and couldn't stop as he worked off all the hatred that had built up over the years. Then, when Trebenko was no longer recognizable, he slid down the wall and sobbed. He writhed on the ground, sniffling like a child, and wiped the butt of the gun with a bit of oilcloth that began to take on shades of burgundy.

"Judas! Judas!"

Savage searched the cupboards, taking boxes of cartridges and the gun wrapped in the deerskin. He took the half-finished bottle of vodka and a penknife, put on a pair of rubber boots he found by the wall, pulled on a camouflage jacket, poured petrol over Trebenko and, trying to avoid looking at his head, threw in a lighted match.

By the time Saam arrived, the garage was in flames. Black smoke stole along the ground, creeping into holes and corners where it curled up like a cat.

Saam lit a cigarette from the blaze. The blackened frame of a car could be seen in the fire. Cartridges left in the garage exploded.

"We're out of here," he yelled, tossing the cigarette into the flames, and the gangsters raced for the cars.

A patrol car blocked their way.

"I hadn't fallen out with Trebenko," said Saam, swinging on his chair. "He was as good as in our pocket." He showed his fist for emphasis.

His henchmen were sitting along the wall, still wearing their shades. The office's narrow window let in hardly any light and the yellow lamp shed a dull beam on the paper-cluttered desk. Saam was questioned by a lanky police officer, who stood in front of him like a question mark while Lapin stayed in a corner, unmoving, arms crossed. Trebenko had refused to allow him to attend interrogations but the colonel was dead and the officer had relented and allowed the investigator to stay. He had caught Saam near the burning garage and was the only witness in the case.

Lapin couldn't get the previous day's meeting with the mayor out of his head, how he had pulled up at the side of the road and lowered the window to talk to him. The window barely framed the mayor's fat face and, bending, Lapin had stood in front of Krotov, wondering to what he owed this conversation.

"You're good at your job. You work hard. I've had my eye on you for quite some time," said the mayor, his lips stretched into a smile. "I know things aren't perfect just now but…" the mayor hesitated, glancing at the side mirror as if he was afraid they would be seen together.

"Well, that's the job," said Lapin, embarrassed.

Krotov lowered his voice.

"You are engaged in a brave fight against crime. We place a high value on that. I want you to know that your work has our complete support!"

Lapin was confused. He didn't know what to say. Krotov raised the window with a nod. Its exhaust coughing, the car drove off, leaving Lapin to stare down the road for a long time, trying to understand the meaning of this sudden support.

Lapin's colleagues treated him like a leper and he felt as though he were carrying a bell and they hid in their offices when they heard it.

"Good only triumphs over evil in thrillers," sneered the senior investigator, who was taking the career ladder two rungs at a time, twirling his finger in a you're-crazy gesture.

"What about real life? Does evil triumph over good?" asked Lapin, looking at him defiantly.

"In real life, they're on the same side," was the reply and he laughed in his face.

Lapin often thought his own life had become stuck in a vicious circle. It stubbornly declined to detach itself from other people's lives and to settle into a path of its own. It felt like a train travelling backwards along a dismantled track.

Saam and Coffin believed Lapin wanted to cosy up to them, to get in on the act. When they heard the story of his father they could hardly remember the passerby they had beaten up. Shorty drew the jack of diamonds out of the deck and suggested getting rid of the meddlesome investigator but Coffin screwed up the card and flicked the ball of paper into a bucket: "Getting killed's something you have to earn!"

"Perhaps you had old scores to settle?" the lanky officer asked Saam, lowering his head. Big rabbit-teeth protruded onto his bottom lip and the large gap between them meant that when he talked he whistled as if in surprise.

"What's to settle? He's got his job, we've got ours. That's why he was kept on, so that our paths didn't cross," said Saam, making a face.

The Chief, the crazy old man Trebenko replaced in office,

59

was shouting below the window. He used to call his deputy a gangster and threatened to catch him red-handed. He read Trebenko's cunning face like a court brief, seeing through all his tricks and hated him more than he hated Coffin. The Chief had no wife or children. It was as though he were handcuffed to his work day and night. "I am not for sale!" he warned the gangsters and, indeed, they didn't buy him. Instead, they loaded him into the boot of a car, drove out of town, and beat him so badly against a rock that it turned red with blood. They threw him out at the morgue, stark naked. "When the attendants turn up in the morning, there'll be a nice little body waiting for them," said Coffin, roaring with laughter as he settled the policeman on the steps of the morgue.

But he didn't die. A year later, people began to meet him in the streets, his shaved head bandaged. Puffing out his cheeks, the Chief would seize passersby by the elbow and demand, "Name?" They answered and he left them alone. Occasionally, though, he would stare with his mad eyes and ask all of a sudden, "What's my name?" Trebenko took the Chief to a psychiatric hospital and found him a place in a care home but he kept on turning up in town.

At Trebenko's funeral when the sealed coffin was displayed outside the police station, the Chief nearly knocked it over, throwing himself on the dead man and howling like the north wind as he hammered on the coffin lid. Later at the wake, remembering his cries, some people said he had been in tears, others that he was laughing, and an elderly cleaner in a headscarf as old and faded as the cloth she used to wash the police station floors maintained that she had been able to make out the words: "They got me in the head and they got you dead!" But no-one believed her and put what she said down to drunken imaginings.

Children teased the crazy old man, throwing stones at him, and then fled in all directions, shrieking. When Lapin remembered that he had thrown snow in the Chief's face himself when he was at school, he blushed.

"What were you doing out at the garage?" the officer asked the gangsters' Big Man timidly.

Saam clenched his teeth as he looked askance at Lapin.

"Visiting."

Lapin was cleaning his nails with a matchstick, turning the mayor's words over in his mind. He had already seen enough of life not to trust people but had not drunk sufficiently deeply of it to have lost all hope. As a result, Krotov's voice rang in his head like a bell and the investigator felt that he was getting closer and closer to the gang with whom he had vowed to settle scores when he heard his father crying in the kitchen.

The gangsters lit their cigarettes as they left the station where they felt as cramped as in a common grave while the bars on the windows had scratched their eyes like shards of glass. Once outside, they shook themselves down, stretched their joints and, peering up at the sun, yawned wearily not bothering to put their hands over their mouths. The police officers standing by the car shrank back uneasily and the Chief looked out of the corner of his eye, dribbling.

Saam had become as suspicious as Coffin, as if the latter's morose mistrust had been catching. He expected to find a murderer round every corner, read judgement in every regard and sought to cheat fate by being a nice guy on even dates and a bad guy on odd ones. To the gangsters, his face seemed to be taking on the features of their murdered chief.

Jaws working, Saam looked at his sidekicks, suspecting each one of betraying him. His gaze pierced their cheeks and foreheads, making the gangsters start scratching as if Saam's mean little eyes were biting them like fleas.

"Someone tried to set me up!" Saam said through clenched teeth. "Sound out your informers. Dig around. Find out anything we don't know but they might."

The gangsters rushed off in different directions like cockroaches startled by the light and the old cleaner, who was washing the ground-floor windows, crossed herself as she watched them go.

At night, they gathered at an abandoned quarry, the polar sun clinging to its edge. There was water at the bottom and the gang threw the people they had tied up down the slope. They rolled down and into the water, choking on the muddy slime.

"Silent as the grave," said the gangsters, shrugging their shoulders. "Seems they really don't know anything."

"Then let them go to the grave," said Saam, gesturing to them to bury the bodies.

His sidekicks weren't in any hurry to grab their spades. Exchanging glances they froze in expectation so that Saam had a sinking feeling in the pit of his stomach and reached for his gun to hide his fear.

"But they're our people," said one of the gang, digging at the earth with the toe of his boot. "They worked for us, trusted us…"

"One of them polished off Trebenko to set me up and there's no time to find out who it was. One of them," Saam said, looking into the quarry, "will get what he deserves. The rest will go to heaven."

The gangsters climbed down cautiously, sliding down slopes that glittered with mica, and set about burying the bodies lying in the water.

The town withdrew into itself when it found out about the gangsters' massacre. Petty thieves cowered in their holes and the police, sensing a war, were afraid of night duty since at night all cats are grey and the gang was armed. There were rumblings in the gang. They discussed the massacre at the quarry, which not even Coffin would have carried out, and Saam, aware that knives were being sharpened behind his back, panicked and grew more and more afraid.

He went to the cemetery at night when no-one could see him and sat down on a dirty chair left over from the wake. His eyes bored through the ground as he imagined Coffin and Shorty lying there. He already missed the good old days when Coffin ruled the town, and Shorty would set up his marked cards, face down, so that no-one could tell whether he'd win his game of patience or not. He remembered the look of surprise on the face of the dead Coffin who hadn't expected his second-in-command to have loaded the gun, and he knew that cards should be kept up your sleeve, fists behind your back and your gun never trusted to anyone, friend or foe.

Coffin and Mayor Krotov had avoided one another, had never met, as if they lived in parallel worlds, and the mayor hoped the new gang leader would do the same. When his office door swung open and there was Saam on the threshold, Krotov gasped in surprise. His frightened secretary peered out from behind the gangster.

"He just came in. There was nothing I..." she said thickly in an attempt to explain but Krotov waved her away.

Saam shut the door, walked through the office as if he owned it, pulled up a chair and sat down facing the mayor, legs crossed.

"Have you gone crazy turning up here?!"

"I'm here to get to know you better."

Since Trebenko's death and the gangsters' carnage, the streets had been as quiet as a cemetery and Krotov had begun to fear for his life. He couldn't sleep at night, alert to the slightest sound. When he looked in the mirror, he pinched his nose and cheeks with his fat, sausage-like fingers as if unable to recognize his own face.

Saam stared at the bridge of the mayor's nose and Krotov, sweat pouring off him and running down his neck, prayed moving his lips without making a sound.

"We live in the civilized world," he said, mopping his brow with a handkerchief, unable to keep silent. "Why do we need these brutal methods, these killings, spying, massacres, if everything can be decided round the table?"

"The autopsy table?" the gangster joked spitefully so that Krotov felt a pain like a scalpel slice into his chest.

"I'm an old man and I don't like change," the mayor said. "Let's just let things carry on as they were."

Grinning, the gangster slowly stood up and made for the exit.

"You leave us alone, we leave you alone," he said, jaws working. He turned at the door: "We stay friends and everything will be fine."

When the door closed, Krotov took his heart drops. He looked out at the central square and regretted that he wasn't an ordinary resident of the town, hurrying home at the end of his working day.

The bathhouse was on the stony shore of the lake. Slender pines bent towards the water as if looking at their own reflections.

Salmon was laying the table, taking cutlery wrapped in napkins out of the capacious pockets of her apron. She stuck a finger into the pudding and licked it, rolling her eyes in an attempt to detect the flavour. Salmon was painfully thin, her pointed features sharp as a skull. Her blackened skin hung like torn curtains from her cheeks. She was so ugly that she was kept hidden from customers in the kitchen and told not to show her face. Her cracked lips constantly mumbled some endless story no-one listened to and she was so used to her nickname that she had long since forgotten what she was really called. She cleaned and she washed the pots, humming some tune to the sound of the water and looked enviously at the beautiful, supple bodies of the girls as she helped them make themselves presentable.

"I was beautiful once," sighed Salmon but the girls just laughed and she laughed with them, revealing a toothless mouth.

The portly bathhouse attendant was cooking kebabs in the yard, bending over a smoky barbecue, while Krotov watched him lazily from the bathhouse window, wiping the steamy glass.

"I used to be afraid to go out. Now I'm scared even to go to sleep. I just can't relax."

"I'm the same," agreed Antonov. "Still, he's cleaned up the town. There are fewer robberies."

"And people," added the mayor.

"They made mincemeat out of Trebenko," Antonov nodded and Krotov felt sick. "Do you not think it was Saam?" he asked surprised at his own question.

"He loses more from Trebenko's death than anyone else. The cops and the gang are like Siamese twins. No way could you separate them. You'd have come off worse. Now he's lost his chief protector. This isn't the '90s. It's time to grow up but they just keep on running around with their guns, pretending to be real tough guys."

"Do you remember Lisping Pashka? He became a mayor..."

"Yeah but there are only a handful of people in his town," said Krotov, jealous and dismissive. "Normal guys swapped their knives for suits and ties ages ago. Take Vasya the card trickster, who worked the trains when he was a kid, he's a big man now. I get phone calls..." said Krotov, pointing upwards to show where the phone calls came from. "They say, 'Sort the gangsters out. Those days are gone'..."

"Those days are gone," Antonov agreed. "But you can't put them in jail."

To cool himself down, Krotov scooped a handful of cold water and splashed his face, slapping his cheeks.

"Unless we..." he said, stressing the word "we", "get rid of them, they'll get rid of us. You and I are in the same boat. I told Trebenko too but he was up to his neck in that shit. The cops have been getting above themselves recently. They don't want to do any work at all. They're as close to the gang as they are to their own relatives. The Prosecutor's Office is involved as well. There's no point contacting them."

Antonov pulled a face. He rubbed his nose. He was about to open his mouth but changed his mind and said nothing.

"In fact, I do have one investigator," Krotov said with a conspiratorial wink. "He's either got accounts to settle with the gang or is, you know," and he twirled his finger by his head. "Anyway, he's digging away at them like a bulldozer.

I'm relying on him. Once he digs up something substantial, we'll get Moscow involved, journalists…"

"Maybe it's better not to rock the boat? As it is, we're like a house of cards. Touch one, we all go down," said Antonov, raising his eyebrows.

Krotov rubbed his temples and sighed wearily.

"I want to retire. I'm tired. I can't stand this any more – talk about the devil and the deep blue sea."

The door opened a crack and a bleached blond head of curls appeared.

"Are you going to be much longer, boys?" the girl asked with a pout.

All she was wearing was cheap perfume so that the men's eyes began to water and their earlobes went red. Wrapped in their sheets, they had the appearance of Roman senators and, catching a glimpse of themselves in the wide mirror that scarcely had room for them both, they burst out laughing.

The attendant manoeuvred the bottles so that one opened the other. He poured them both a cold beer, looking askance at Salmon who had poked her head round the door. Krotov kept checking his pulse, worried about his heart which was increasingly making its presence known.

"We can survive everything but death," said Antonov with a grin, collapsing onto a leather sofa.

"Joking's not going to save you," retorted Krotov, recalling Trebenko's burnt-out garage.

He looked at the battered sofa and wondered how many times people had had fun on it, made love on it, soaked it in beer or tears, patched it up and dragged it from one corner of the room to another. Things live longer than we do and when we die they remember our hot hands, stupid jokes and the boredom that envelops everything like a spider's web, clings to the furniture, catches on nails sticking out of the walls and delves into dark corners. Krotov was dying of boredom, taking refuge from it in red tape and evening get-togethers at the bathhouse but even with his arms wrapped round a girl,

66

damp from the steam of the bathhouse, it was all he could do not to yawn. The mayor looked around at people laughing and was seized with envy, unable to tell whether they were really enjoying themselves or just pretending to in order to annoy him. He imagined himself already dead while his boredom would stay between the cracks in the planks, left behind at the bathhouse with its smell of birch twigs and cheap floral scent, and he had a sudden urge to get drunk.

Trebenko's murder stirred up the entire police station. A general arrived from the regional centre. He twiddled his thin moustache nervously and nodded his head, speechless, as he looked at the burnt-out garage.

"What's going on here?" he yelled at the senior police officers who trembled at his stentorian tones. "A pinprick of a town and the whole country knows about it!"

Looking at the hills surrounding the town, however, the general realized that living here was like being on an island, cut off from the rest of the country and even from the nearest settlements which were several hours' drive away or a whole day on foot via swamp and impenetrable depths of forests where the trees were as tangled as fates. Close to the border, the town was surrounded by dense forest and it couldn't care less what happened beyond its limits. Like a prison camp, the taiga has its own laws and this gloomy little town lived by the laws of the taiga that said the fittest survived and a man with no gun was a man with no rights. The general felt suddenly uneasy as if aware that he himself had no rights or protection here and he hastened to get away as quickly as he could, cursing himself for his groundless fear.

"Do you actually know who did it?" he asked from inside the car.

Trebenko's deputy shook his head.

"Gangsters?"

The same shaking of heads.

"Was it revenge? Someone who's been sent down? Just

a domestic?" prompted the general. "Do you know but aren't saying or do you just not know?"

The deputy said nothing and the general, swearing, slammed the door and set off the way he had come without so much as a goodbye.

Nothing is hidden in a small town. The walls have ears and the backstreets mouths so that it's only on paper that crimes go unsolved. And yet the case of Trebenko remained blacker than the soot that covered his burnt-out garage. The police officers, buried in paperwork, rummaged through the archives, questioned people who had happened to be passing and the junkies who had left dirty needles with traces of their blood behind the garages but the witnesses only confused matters further.

Saam, who had been caught at the scene of the crime, was the only suspect and the main witness, Investigator Lapin, rubbed his hands contentedly. Crimes that went unpunished in Coffin's times couldn't go unpunished any longer, and rumour had it that the gang was about to be arrested.

"Times have changed," said Antonov, drawing his head into his shoulders as if afraid Saam would go for his throat. "There's nothing I can do."

The prosecutor also made a helpless gesture. "You'll be behind bars until the trial and then you'll be let off…"

Trebenko's deputy was so like his late boss that from the back people took him for a ghost, quickly crossing themselves and spitting over their left shoulders. Krotov arranged a meeting. Saam came into the office and shuddered, taken aback by the deputy's likeness to Trebenko. The policeman was under pressure from people who were more frightening than Saam, however, and in his voice the gangster could hear the prison gates slam shut.

"If you're guilty, you'll go to jail. If not, they'll let you out," he snapped, leaning back in his chair.

Saam shot him a glance as piercing as broken glass but he remained impenetrable.

Loitering near the station, the mutilated Chief served as

a reminder of the day he was picked up outside the morgue, naked, his head split in two like a water melon. This only increased the investigators' rage.

"Name?" the Chief asked, grabbing Saam by the arm when the gangster arrived for yet another interview.

Saam wanted to push him away but the police officers smoking by the station door suddenly froze, staring at him. Gently, he withdrew his arm, patting the Chief on the shoulder.

"Will they really send him down?" asked the lanky officer doubtfully as he stubbed out a cigarette.

"Well if they do, they'll let him out again," spat the duty officer. He was immediately shushed.

It wasn't long before the driver of the patrol car that had taken Lapin to the garages went to his superiors and said that the gangsters only left the house after Trebenko was dead.

"Investigator Lapin and I had been watching the wooden house for several days," he mumbled, tipping his hat.

"Who gave the order?"

"It was unauthorized. Lapin slipped me a bit extra. And something for the petrol…"

"What about the gangsters?"

"They turned up when the garage was already on fire. Thirty seconds later, we showed up."

Lapin pleaded with the driver to say nothing so that Saam would be arrested but the officer had charged the gang a high price for his evidence and their Big Man was generous. Back to the wall, Lapin confirmed that the gang couldn't have killed Trebenko and the case collapsed.

Life is whatever we think it is, love whatever we call love. But hunger, sharp as a spear, was the strongest feeling Savage had ever known. He had become a wild beast, living to find food, and could now find his way around the forest as easily as the town, familiar with all the paths and tracks he walked every day, making up for the years he'd spent behind a desk, drawing his plans.

Fish splashed in the lake. Savage attempted to catch them with his bare hands, hanging from a narrow ledge of rock that stuck out over the water like a cap peak. He scooped up fistfuls of water, startling the fish, then lay for a long time, chilled to the bone on the cold stone, watching the pike swimming at the bottom, their smooth sides glistening. His stomach ached with hunger, as if he'd been kicked in the belly. Hunger pinched his throat, hammered at his temples and made his arms heavy, binding them like a straitjacket. Rolling onto his back, Savage wept as he remembered the fridge at home where his wife had allocated him the bottom shelf or the cold cabbage soup at his work's canteen where a rosy-cheeked waitress swept the crumbs off the tables and onto the floor. His wife cooked for herself and for their daughter and during the night Savely used to lift the lid and eat straight from the pan, quietly so that they didn't hear him. Now though he would have eaten the crumbs off the canteen floor and his wife's soup right in front of her. He so much wanted to eat that he would have eaten the cloud floating above him if only he could have reached it.

Seagulls circled over the town refuse tip and dogs scurried around, barking wildly when they spotted someone. Savage would make his way there, sniffing like a wild beast, rooting out leftovers by their smell, then move off again, covering many miles. He was scared of the tramps who lived there in a raucous family with their children and their shaggy dogs with ropes for leads. They would hail one another, their calls floating all day long above the tip like grey doves.

"Huh?"
"Well?"
"Ah!"
"Uh-oh!"

As he listened to their conversations, Savage was amazed that he had drowned in words when he tried to sort things out in endless rows with his wife. And words hadn't helped. Rather, they had hindered their attempts at mutual understanding.

He came to think that people needed words to hide the truth whereas feelings could be expressed by an eloquent silence.

He nearly died from eating rotten food, lying among the stinking heaps of rubbish, unable to bat away the birds that mistook him for carrion. He became delirious and heard voices arguing and a child's laughter and when the fever left him he saw that he was surrounded by piles of dirty rags that were digging in the rubbish, using sticks to keep the birds at bay. Men and women had the same black and swollen faces, with bunged up eyes and twisted mouths they treated like garbage chutes, tossing in anything edible they could find. Savage listened distractedly as they discussed his fate as if they were talking about someone else and everything that was going on was just a dream. Their conversations were brief. They spat out their words like the husks of sunflower seeds.

"Why kill him? He'll die anyway."

"He's better. He'll live."

"Is that a problem?"

"He'll bring his people here."

One of the women found a broken comb and, taking off her woolly hat, she combed out her red mane. The comb got stuck in her dirty hair and its last teeth broke. The woman hurled it away and put her hat back on.

"Are we taking him with us?"

"It's too much trouble. Let him be."

"We burying him then? He'll die. The cops'll come..."

The tramps set about covering Savage in rubbish: burst tyres, damp, soggy cardboard and packaging, slowly and solemnly to begin with, the way handfuls of earth are thrown onto a coffin, and then quickly, grabbing everything that came to hand so that first of all his arms and then his legs disappeared and before long a whole heap, indistinguishable from all the others, had formed over him. Too weak to move, Savage simply lay there, gulping in air through his mouth, aware of a broken radio pressing down on his chest. It had been thrown on top of him by a child with missing front teeth like gaps in a

71

fence. The tramps went away with a clank of the bottles they had collected and Savage listened to their friendly squabbling over the boots he'd taken from Trebenko.

Through a crack in the rubbish, Savage could see the gathering twilight, grey and limpid, that never quite became night. He imagined his wife drawing the heavy drapes to hide from the midnight sun and the room becoming as dark as it was under his mound of rubbish. At forty, Savage still had a child's fear of the dark so he loved these nights that were like days whereas his wife preferred the half-light that concealed her wrinkles and her colourless eyes, grown old before their time.

People had always thought of Savage as a "thing-in-itself" and now he grinned, suddenly thinking that, like all things, here he was, ending his days on the rubbish tip. Why bother with a grave for someone no-one would weep for? He'd probably never be found. He would be thought missing in the taiga and remembered as a joke; the furniture from his room would be thrown onto the rubbish tip, his TV, his clothes, photos of him when he was a child, his books and the drawings nobody wanted, rolled up in a tube and stored in the closet. And then his gravediggers with their swollen blackened faces would dig through the fresh garbage and find his clothes and swear as they shared out his sweaters and jackets, his down-at-heel boots and the scarves his wife had knitted him in the early days of their marriage.

Savage heard hurried steps and hoarse, feverish breathing. Someone began to dig him out, scraping the garbage away, and soon there was a swollen, smiling face staring at him. The woman stroked his face, like a child's and, smacking her lips, she kissed him on the forehead. Then, she took a mouldy bread crust out of her pocket and stuck it in his mouth like a dummy. Savage groaned. His stomach ached so much it was like being kicked. Pulling Savage out, the woman piled the rubbish up again as though there was still someone underneath it.

"Let's go. I'll hide you," she whispered, pulling him by the arm. "Come on. Be quick."

Keeping close to the ground, they crept through the dump. The woman looked around all the time, afraid the other tramps would see them. She began to hit out at old, congealed rubbish with a stick, making something like a burrow in the pile.

"Get in. Don't go wandering off."

She helped Savage climb inside and before she left she offered him the slimy greaseproof paper from a pack of butter.

"Don't eat it all at once," she said, stroking him on the cheek.

Savage curled up in his burrow, closed his eyes and, sinking into a deep sleep, prayed that he wouldn't wake up.

In the morning when he climbed out of his sanctuary, he strained his ears, afraid the tramps would catch sight of him but the tip was quiet. Only the seagulls cried as they wheeled above the sea of rubbish as if above water. Savage was in his stocking feet. Broken glass and metal stabbed his feet so he bound them in rags and put packaging on top. He tried to find the gun he had put down somewhere along with the cartridges wrapped in deerskin. He dug down into the stinking garbage but he couldn't remember exactly where it was that the tramps had nearly killed him. First, he rummaged through the garbage itself. Then he started to lunge around, thinking he could see the barrel of the gun sticking out of the rubbish all over the place. In the end, in despair, he took his head in his hands and fell face down on the ground.

A hunched figure appeared on the horizon and Savage tried to get back to his burrow but he was lost and couldn't find it. No matter which way he turned, everything looked the same and he didn't know which way to run. He froze and hoped the person would turn aside without seeing him. Then, suddenly, he recognized the woman.

"Why did you run away?" she called.

Savage said nothing.

"Let's go back," she begged. "Come on. I've got something to eat."

Her pocket, packed with leftover food of some kind, was

bulging and Savely obediently stumbled after her. The woman shared out the food then took out a quarter bottle of vodka from God only knew where. She offered it triumphantly and ceremoniously to Savage and, twisting it open, Savely took a swig. He choked and coughed. Everything swam before him and he fell, banging into the woman's knees. Laughing, she took the bottle from him, finished it in a single gulp and stretched out next to Savage, clinging to him. She quickly opened his trousers and Savage, drunk from that one mouthful, reckoned his new life was not so scary after all.

When he woke up in the middle of the night, however, when the woman had already gone back to the beggars' camp, he had a sudden vision of himself lying amid the rubbish, dirty and emaciated, being plastered with kisses by a drunken vagrant woman whose name he didn't even know and nausea rose in his throat. He bolted from the rubbish dump to where the forest was as dark, wet and safe as his mother's womb and lay for a long time on the ground, feeling the damp moss with his hands as if he couldn't believe that rubbish didn't grow in forests.

Savage wandered around the forest for a week. Then he went back to the tip, driven by hunger that was wringing him out like wet washing. He looked around and was picking at the rubbish when he heard a rustling behind him. Ready to run, he spun round to see the woman, skulking. He flinched, raising his arms in a helpless gesture and looked at her.

"What do you want?"

The woman came closer, her shopping bag clinking, a multi-coloured hedgehog of bottle necks sticking out of it. For the first time, Savage looked properly at her face. She wasn't even 40. Red hair speckled with grey poked out from beneath her hat and her wrinkled cheeks were dotted with freckles that jumped like fleas when she laughed.

"You coming?" she asked, lowering her eyes and adjusting her hat.

"I'm not going anywhere," said Savage. The stammer

he'd had in the past had suddenly returned. "I'm not going anywhere," he said again, shaking his head.

The woman put her head on one side and made her fingers into a gun.

"I've found the gun..."

Savely grabbed her by the shoulders.

"Have you? Have you really? Where is it?"

The woman didn't answer, her mouth stretched into a smile.

"Where's the gun?" Savage shook her. "Have you found the cartridges?"

"You coming?" she asked again.

Savely pictured her stretched out on the ground, lifting her messy skirts, while he bent to slash her face with a piece of glass.

"Bring me the gun. I don't believe you."

She shook her head.

"Bring me the gun or I'm not coming," Savage snapped.

Shrugging her shoulders, the woman shuffled away, startling the pigeons that were pottering about in the rubbish. Savage stared at her back, imagining how he would shoot her if he had the gun right now. The woman stopped and beckoned to him and he ran after her, swearing.

Savage sat down next to the woman. He ran his hand over the red locks sticking out from under her hat and was surprised at how wiry they were.

He remembered Lyuba with her snub nose, her memory preserved in the buttons sewn tightly onto his jacket and an opaque layer of sadness that had settled on his soul. For days at a time, the grey-haired secretary tapped away on the typewriter in his boss's office and, every time he passed Savage would try to decipher what she had written. The typewriter sounded curt and demanding and what he heard was: "Savage, Savage." On one occasion, however, he could make out, "sweetheart, sweetheart" and, unable to resist a look, he popped his head round the door. The typewriter had been replaced by a computer monitor rotund as the boss's stomach and a new young secretary was looking at Savage in surprise, her eyebrows raised in thin hyphens. Now whenever he passed the office, Savely would slow down to listen to the timid tapping of the keyboard, detecting words that made his throat dry. When he bumped into the secretary on the staircase, Savage dropped an armful of papers that scattered over the steps while she, with a cry, narrowly avoided falling by clutching at his jacket. She was left holding a button that had come off, so she pulled off Savely's jacket and rushed to sew it back on. "I've sewn the others on a bit tighter, too," she said, peeping round his cupboard and holding out the jacket. Savely blushed to the tips of his ears. In that blush, she discerned his cold bed and a wife who fell out of love with him before she got to know him. Savage, looking into her grey-green eyes, could see the cramped single room she shared with her mother and little boy and her tear-soaked pillow. They started trying to go to the canteen at the same time, eating at the same table, unperturbed by the silence.

"I was never a talker even when I was little," she muttered, embarrassed, playing with a tiny ball of bread. "It must be pretty dull for you..."

"There's a-a-always s-s-somebody to t-t-talk to. It's n-n-nice to have s-s-someone to be quiet with," Savage answered, stumbling over the words and keeping his eyes down.

Lyuba didn't ask about his wife and said nothing about the father of her child and Savage reflected that loneliness has many faces but the same taste of bitterness. Savage began to see Lyuba home after work and on one occasion he was invited in. Her mother fussed in the kitchen, clucking like a frightened hen, then hastily threw on her coat and shot out of the house, her arms not yet in the sleeves. The room smelt of nappies and the kind of floral scent used as perfume by middle-aged ladies to take away the smell of old age. The baby cried and Lyuba kept jumping up from the table, spilling tea and rocking her son, and Savage wished he hadn't come. He thought about his dishevelled wife

76

who came out in red blotches when they argued and his crying daughter, the nappies he'd had to wash because water makes your hands peel, and his mother-in-law who had been as sweet as Turkish delight until the wedding and afterwards was as sharp and biting as black pepper. Savage made his apologies by referring to the time and Lyuba, biting her lips until she drew blood, was barely able not to burst out crying.

From then on they avoided one another and, if they did meet in the corridor, they turned away as if that evening had never happened.

"Lumpy, dumpy, grumpy," Savage heard as he went past the office and this time when he looked in there was a new secretary, her mouth making a silly round "o". He never saw Lyuba again and was amazed that such a little town should be more than big enough for them both.

When he thought back to his failed romance, Savage realized that the sour smell of nappies and floral scent had been stronger than the murderous night-time attacks of loneliness. And now he lay, cuddled up to a down-and-out woman, on a rubbish tip among rotting food, yesterday's newspapers and broken furniture and no-one was closer to him than this woman whose name he didn't know.

"Have you lived here long?" he asked, stroking her wrinkled cheek with its smattering of freckles.

"A long time," she nodded, rolling her eyes.

"A year? Two? How long?"

She shrugged her shoulders and put her head on his shoulder.

"Where did you live before? What did you do? Do you have any family?"

"A long time," she said again with a wide yawn.

Savage hugged the red-headed homeless woman but she stood up, scratching herself, and with a nod of farewell, trudged off to join the rest of the tramps who were building a fire at the other end of the dump.

"Come back again!" Savage shouted after her.

One can get used to almost anything, even things that are impossible to get used to. Not so long ago, Savely had felt that it would be a disaster if he didn't have a job and an apocalypse he couldn't survive if he didn't have a roof over his head. Now, though, he recognized that the years had been spent in pointless toil doing a job he didn't like and in a marriage to a woman he didn't love. It had been a life without aim or meaning. He was scarcely any different from the down-and-outs who spent their entire day looking for food just as he had spent his trying to make a living. In the evenings, when Savage used to switch on the TV, the homeless people lit their fires and saw more in the tongues of fire warming their frozen hands than he ever saw on the screen. Savage dreamt of being back home, the day he killed Coffin erased from his life. He would give up work and spend entire days lying in bed, hands behind his head, looking at the patterns on the ceiling and picturing people or animals the way he did now in the clouds and then, strolling around town, he would acknowledge the people he met, known or unknown, and, shrugging his shoulders, would say instead of hello: "I've given up work, you know…"

"Having no purpose in life is worse than being on the road," Savage told himself repeatedly as he wandered round the tip. A stranger, with a dark face and piercing stare, looked out at him from a broken bit of mirror. He had matted hair and a pine twig poking out of a wispy beard. Savage dropped the mirror but it was a long time before the stranger disappeared.

Savely collected glass jars and stood them on a battered chest of drawers. Raising the gun, he aimed and the shot sent a flock of birds up into the air, clamouring and flapping their wings. He didn't hit a single jar and, in a fury, he knocked them down with the butt of the gun. There was an old sofa on the tip that had broken in half. Savage dragged over a broken TV and stretched out on the sofa, crossing his legs. He flicked through the pages of soggy newspapers and tried on a pair of worn-out trainers. Then, he stared at the television, pointlessly clicking the remote. The screen reflected the piles of rubbish, the sofa and Savage lying on it. Tossing the remote aside, Savely picked up a clump of barbed wire that scratched his hands. All he had to do was bite off the required length of wire and he could go into town. Savely had no idea how his plan would work out but the stranger in the mirror had it all sorted.

The street lamps that winked at passersby cast scarcely any light on the central street and the side streets were dark as a forest. Savage's fingers picked out the numbers to dial home in a telephone booth but he kept making mistakes and ringing the wrong numbers. Eventually, he heard his daughter's voice. For a long time, Vasilisa kept saying "hello" then stopping and listening warily. The dialling tone sounded like departing feet and Savage replaced the receiver.

He made his way along the deserted street, keeping close to the houses and was almost picked up by a patrol car when he was caught in its headlights.

"Hey, you!" called a police officer, lowering the window.

Savage dived into a garden and, crouching down, he hid behind a tree. If the officer got out of the car, he was ready to run into the yard to hide in an entrance or an open cellar.

"Hey, mate! Get over here!" they yelled through a megaphone and the echo rolled through the yards. Savage relaxed. He could tell the officer didn't want to leave the car. "Oh, to hell with you!" cursed the officer for the benefit of the entire town as he drove off.

There was no guard on the block of flats but a code was needed to access the entrance hall. A chill wind played in the aerials and the cables were as tightly strung as nerves. Savage pressed buttons at random hoping to break the code but the door stayed shut.

An old woman was dozing in a chair in the hall. She wore felt boots even in summer and she couldn't pronounce the word "concierge" calling herself a "conserve" instead. There was a chipped and dirty saucer on the table in front of her. Antonov's wife had come up with it in an attempt to teach the neighbours about leaving tips. The innovation didn't catch on. People threw sweets in the saucer or stubbed out their cigarettes and only rarely dug a few coins mixed up with crumbs and crumpled receipts from their pockets.

When some drunk went inside, Savage propped the door open with a stone. He waited a bit and went in, past the old lady whose head drooped on her chest as she slept. Gingerly, he took a sweet from the saucer. With the sweet stuffed in his cheek, Savage stole up the steps, his ears pricked for the slightest sound but the flats were sleeping, their leaky pipes snoring. There were shelves on the landings, full of spades from the dachas, body-warmers and smelly pots of paint which Savely examined carefully, picking out anything that might come in handy.

Antonov had bought up all the flats on the top floor and turned them into one, which had more rooms than the fingers on both hands. A ladder went up to the attic. Savage smashed the lock and hid under the roof. It was darker than the forest in there. There were stained mattresses on the floor, bits of stuffing showing, discarded by unknown residents. Snuggling into them, Savage thought happiness was an empty attic to hide in and a heap of dirty mattresses. He was prepared to stay there forever, just lying on the floor, looking through the cracks between the floor boards, not thinking about anything. Kitchen smells made his tongue stick to the roof of his mouth, laughter and the murmur of the TV reached him from downstairs. The lift rumbled and Savely imagined it as a giant mouth gulping down the residents then spitting them out on another floor.

Savely spent several days living in the attic as if he had forgotten what he was doing there. He slept whole days at a time, waking up only to eat. He was sparing with his matches as the box was nearly empty. He found an old newspaper and lit a small fire then took a rotting mushroom out of his breast pocket. He burnt his fingers as he held it over the fire. He drank the water he had saved in a bottle and once again sought the oblivion of sleep. If the residents had left food in the attic, he would have spent the rest of his life there like a house sprite, preserving the inhabitants' peace. When he ran out of water some days later, Savage got down to business.

Justice is blind. It wears a blindfold when it passes judgement. The innocent are always hardest hit. Savage was fed up with being the scapegoat of his own destiny. He set about putting right his mistakes as if his former life had been merely a sketch that he had now decided to rewrite, with the sin of doing nothing his main transgression. In the past, he would imagine slapping his boss across the face as he stood to attention in front of him. He would lower his gaze when he saw his daughter with the gangsters and stay silent when he longed to call out. He had thought mistakes were actions but now he had suddenly realized that the biggest mistakes of our lives are actions we don't carry out, the turnings we don't take, the words we don't say. No-one can enter the same river twice but life can be lived twice or several times over in a single life time, re-drawing its length and breadth. Or it's possible not to live even one life, leaving behind miles of roads untraveled and rivers of unshed tears and to die without being born. Savage had been born on that evening in the square when he shot Coffin and read his life's new commandment in the latter's evil gaze: "Thou shalt kill!"

Carefully lifting the trapdoor, he tried to make out the conversations coming from Antonov's flat. It seemed as if he could see the Councillor's wife through the wall in her flowing silk housecoat, pacing from room to room, lips pursed, tormented by boredom. When she left the house, the scent of her expensive perfume lingered in the entrance hall and Savage knew from the smell that she had gone out.

The Antonovs had a servant. She was a grey-haired woman who had come from a closed factory settlement, leaving behind the grave of her husband, twenty years of her life and her futile hopes. The Antonovs used her patronymic rather than her first name and the latter had been erased from her memory.

Mumbling away to herself, she called herself simply Petrovna. Savage recognized her by her shuffling gait and the sigh with which she put her heavy shopping bags down while she looked for the keys to the flat.

Antonov came home early. He sniffed at the stale odour that had appeared in the entrance hall. His bodyguards escorted him right to the door. Savage lay above the trapdoor but hung back, listening to Petrovna babbling as she opened the door to Antonov. In a flash of insight, he realized his plan was crazy, he would never pull it off, and he laughed at himself, wondering how he had ever dared to think he could. He had been mocked by the words "even a fly would hurt him" and now all of a sudden he had decided he was a cold-blooded killer. But then the hunger that blurred his thoughts dulled his feelings and only an animal fury remained. As Savage fell into a half sleep, his teeth chattered in anticipation of what he was about to do.

Savage heard the clatter of the lift arriving and looked through the crack. Saam stood on the landing and two of his henchmen had gone to the floor below. The gangster rang the bell, one long note and three short ones, and Savely realized it was a prearranged signal.

Antonov came out in his dressing gown, sleepy and bad-tempered. Saam leaned in to whisper in his ear.

"Savage? Bollocks!" exclaimed the Councillor pulling away.

"It can't be anyone else! I've checked out my guys. I've got rid of the others. Who else is there?"

Antonov shivered: "Even a stick may fire once in a blue moon, but twice and you've got a serial killer."

"So who's next?" Saam grinned, raising his eyebrows.

"Do you think he's not all there?" asked Antonov.

"Are you really bothered if the guy who kills you is crazy or not?"

Antonov thought back to his conversation with Krotov but hesitated to relay it to Saam.

"You're looking in the wrong place," he said choosing his words carefully. "Someone set you up. It's too complicated for an avenger of the people."

Saam could read wrinkles and find hidden meaning in what was left unsaid and the pauses between words. He believed there was a false bottom in everyone and didn't even trust himself. He could sense Antonov wasn't telling him the whole story but he didn't know how to make him talk. Stamping out his cigarette with his heel, he ran down the stairs without saying goodbye. With a frightened check round the corners, Antonov hurried back into the flat, making sure all the locks were securely fastened.

The hallucinations brought on by hunger made the world seem distorted, grotesque and alien. They had frightened Savage in the beginning but he soon got used to them, unable to tell his morbid fantasies and reality apart. After the taiga, living within four walls was like being in a coffin: the walls closed in, the ceiling appeared about to collapse and the floor seemed to be an oozing, squelching swamp so that Savage was constantly running his hand over it to persuade himself it was made of concrete and the squelching sounds were coming from the leaky pipes. Hunger made his stomach ache as if he'd swallowed a knife and his head hurt from the constant dizziness. He lay on a mattress, feeling like a rag doll unable to move without a puppet master.

That Saturday evening, however, he felt ten times stronger, as if someone had pulled invisible strings to set his wizened body in motion. Antonov tumbled out of the lift, laughing contentedly and giving off a harsh smell of brandy that reached even the attic. Dismissing his bodyguards, he disappeared through the iron door that clanked shut like a prison cell. Savage descended from his sanctuary and rang the bell – one long ring and three short ones – his hand over the spy hole. Antonov rattled the locks. "Who is it?" he asked in a drunken drawl as he threw open the door. Seeing a filthy, ragged down-and-out, he pulled a face and was about to slam the door, when Savage stuck out his foot. It was then that Antonov, instantly sober, recognized the foul-smelling tramp as Savage. He stamped on Savely's foot but the latter grabbed his shirt front and pulled him close, his stale breath making Antonov feel ill. He pushed Savage away and he tumbled down the stairs, almost breaking his neck. Everything went black and he struggled to get his breath, gulping in air like a fish out of water. Savage felt his face and realized he'd broken his nose. It was leaning drunkenly to one side. Antonov hurled himself at Savage and started kicking him as if he were beating a carpet. But Savely didn't feel the blows and only thought that even a film hero would have passed out by now whereas he still lay there, clutching his wire in his bloody hands. The drunken Antonov could hardly stand, collapsing onto Savage who threw the wire round his neck. He was no longer aware of any pain or terror or revulsion. He pulled the noose tighter, listening to Antonov splutter as the blood choked him. Savage remembered him as the fat little boy at school who had turned away when he offered him his hand. "If we could be told the story of our lives like the libretto for a ballet," Savage thought, "or meeting a person we could see in a flash everything that we'd go through, we would go mad. You can't cheat Fate. She will deceive you time and again and God forbid you should meet her when she's out of temper!"

Lying beside the now limp body, Savage was about to sink into the oblivion of sleep. "Daughters flower after hours": Coffin's voice rang in his head. "After hours indeed!" And Savely hit the body in the face. He looked at Antonov, disfigured in death, gathered his last strength and crawled down the stairs as if he'd lost the use of his legs. Blood streamed from his broken nose, leaving stains on the steps.

Once he had managed to leave the building, Savage hid in the children's playground in a tiny log cabin he could scarcely fit into, his legs in their bindings of rags sticking out of the window. He slept until morning, plunged into a heavy, viscous, drug-like sleep. When the yardkeepers arrived with their brooms, he fled the town where he imagined informers round every corner, their faces black with spite. He didn't know who these people were – police officers, gangsters or his colleagues – but whenever he saw them, he shrank like an empty stomach. Savage kept his face hidden and trotted through the sleepy streets, avoiding the rare passersby by crossing the road or diving into a yard so that he was soon in the forest that was now his home.

The funeral procession snaked blackly through the town. The coffin was carried on the broad shoulders of gravediggers, their faces sombre as the statues on tombs. Both sides of the street were crowded with people come to pay their last respects to the Councillor. "If you can't intimidate someone, you have to buy them. If you can't buy someone, you have to intimidate them," Antonov had loved to say. So people preferred to say nothing about him. And now they scattered curses as well as crimson carnations onto the black-draped coffin. He was remembered for the young girls he had seduced, for the murders of his rivals, and for flooding the town with out-of-date food. Pursing their lips, the old ladies spat in his wake while the menfolk clinked their glasses and drank to the killer's health. Only Petrovna, scurrying after the coffin her head hung low like a faded funeral carnation, wrung her hands and wept: "Oh, my master, my master!"

"Oh, yes, I know all about these 'masters'," Kolya the plumber used to spit when he came to mend the Antonovs' pipes. "Bloody aristocrats!"

But Petrovna, coming out in blotches at the insult, fingered the gilt cross she had been given by Antonov's wife.

"Of course, they're my masters, benefactors. They took me in, gave me work…"

Kolya tossed away his spanner, losing his temper:

"He's fresh from behind the shop-counter and his wife used to be the bookkeeper on a state farm. She used to steal frozen chickens," he muttered, lowering his voice as if afraid they'd hear him. "And you call them masters! I went to school with them. We learnt the ABC together. And now they're masters and I'm a servant?"

Shaking her head, the woman simply withdrew into the kitchen and with nothing better to do she washed the clean plates again, mumbling above the sound of the water.

"Masters!" the plumber repeated, rattling his tools crossly.

The crazy Chief ran behind the coffin, trying to see into the dead man's face. His pockets were stuffed with sweets and apples, given him by Antonov's relatives so that their kindness to the town fool who was once the chief of police might win God's favour and atone for Antonov's sins. His wife had taken refuge from his countless infidelities in a church on the outskirts of town built from the same grey brick that was used in the houses. She gave donations to the church and meekly attended services, singing along with the choir. And now she walked beside the local priest, severe and straight as a pole.

Saam watched the procession from a café window.

"That's not our style," he said, continuing an interrupted conversation. "Why should we want to kill him?"

Lapin squirmed in his chair. It felt like police questioning.

"Maybe it was someone from outside?"

Saam didn't reply. He fiddled morosely with the tablecloth.

"You run the whole town. All the dens, all the gangs... A cat can't eat a mouse without you knowing about it!"

Saam smirked but still said nothing.

"Why did you go to the garage? Who rang you? What did they say?"

"Oh, Captain, you'll never be a major!" sang Saam with an affected yawn to show the conversation was over.

As he watched the investigator go, Saam remembered him hanging around Severina, trying to make her tell him everything she knew. Lapin lay in wait for her at the gates of the orphanage, ambushed her at discos and tagged along behind her like a dog.

"You were with them all the time. They'll kill you," he said to frighten the girl. "If you tell me everything, we can make sure you're safe."

"Didn't see nothing. Don't know nothing," Severina doggedly maintained, twisting a lock of hair round her finger.

The investigator tried a different approach.

"You'll go down as an accomplice! They've got a real thing about pretty girls like you in the youth offender camps…"

Severina said nothing, batting her eyelids as if she didn't know what he was talking about.

"Come on, girl," said Lapin, close to giving up. "You're so young. What are you doing?"

"I'm not doing anything," said Severina, insistent as a woodpecker, and the captain mopped sweat off his brow.

Once he brought her a teddy bear, blushing at the absurdity of the gift. The girl hugged the teddy bear to her chest like a long-lost relative. From then on, it went everywhere with her. The investigator would often see her in town carrying it and wanted to take her in his arms like the toy.

When Severina was arrested near the school where she'd been selling heroin, however, the teddy was disembowelled and packets of white powder were found inside. Severina was taken to a cell and the teddy, turned inside out, was tossed into a rubbish bin where it looked like an abandoned baby.

In the cell, Severina curled up on the narrow bunk and immediately went to sleep to the sound of the dripping in the rusty sink, but a female police officer with hair like a wire brush woke her up and made her answer questions. In silken tones, she asked about Severina's friends, about drugs and life in the orphanage but she didn't sound sincere and the girl grimaced, saying nothing or giving the wrong answers.

"Do you like it at the orphanage?" the major asked. It was a stupid question and she was embarrassed.

Severina pointedly turned to face the wall.

"Who gave you the drugs?"

"I found them outside."

"You'll come to no good," the major said, a spiteful glint in her eyes as she left the cell.

The investigating officers gathered in a smoke-filled office. A dim light blinked wearily, barely illuminating the tired, sleepy faces.

"If she'd been outside my kids' school, I'd have used my bare hands and..." the lanky policeman demonstrated, putting his hands round his throat.

"What do you expect?" said another dismissively. "You know who she's working for."

"We pick them up but the Prosecutor's Office just releases them," a fat officer broke in, with an angry gesture.

"We should change places," the lanky officer laughed. "Let the Prosecutor's Office catch them and we can release them."

They all three fell silent. The fat cop finished his cigarette and went down to the cell.

"Drugs all over the place, gangsters." He scratched the back of his neck. "You're only fourteen. What'll it be next?"

Severina lay unmoving. The officer shook her with all his strength and she slid off the bunk.

"It's your choice, kid," he said. Realizing he'd underestimated his own strength, he helped her up. "It's either in and out of prison or you talk." He took a report out of a file and got ready to write.

"I'm not a kid," said Severina, pushing him away and rubbing her bruised knee.

"Who gave you the drugs?"

"I found them in the street."

"What were you doing near the school?"

"Waiting for a friend."

The officer spat and rubbed the spit in with his boot. He wrote the report, which he balanced on his lap with one hand and with the other he scratched the back of his neck wondering why he was bothering to dig out a statement like dirt under a fingernail if what appeared on paper was entirely the wrong way round.

"Who gave you the drugs?"

Severina was silent.

Once, when he was doing the rounds of the bandit dens, he'd come across Coffin. Sitting astride a chair, the gangster had said nothing, staring at the bridge of the fat man's nose and the policeman's shirt had been soaked through. With a nod to his bodyguards, Coffin stood up. He squeezed past the officer who shrank back against the wall when he felt a cold pistol hidden under a jacket against his stomach, and left the flat. From then on, whenever he heard Coffin's name mentioned, the officer felt a chill against his stomach as though he were up against the barrel of a gun and terror crept under his collar.

"Who gave you the drugs?" he repeated, yawning into a hairy fist.

"Coffin," Severina replied mischievously.

The officer gave a nervous shudder, scratched his nose with his pen but wrote it down. He had long dreamt of giving up police work, tired of his right hand writing something his left would then cross out.

"What were you doing at the school?"

"Dealing…"

Severina looked up at him defiantly and the officer wanted to hit her across the face with all his strength. It was said that Saam and Coffin had shared this girl between them and the fat man didn't want anything to do with either of them.

The police station provided plenty of shocking sights every day but since only the walls had ears all conversations about the gang stayed within its dirty, smoke-filled rooms. In the evenings when the station was empty, the old cleaner swept the conversations away with the dust so that she knew everything that was going on in the little town while the police forgot what they had heard more quickly than they filled in their reports.

The officer stretched his lips into a smile.

"Okay. Since this is your first offence, I'll be nice. I'll

89

let you go – for telling the truth." He sounded so insincere he actually winced. "Mind you don't come back!"

The officer threw open the cell door and, adjusting her skirt, Severina left.

"It isn't my first offence!" she called as she walked away.

Coffin and Saam sat in the car watching the entrance to the police station. Severina emerged from the dirty, scratched door, hopped onto the wall, stretched out her arms and, only just keeping her balance, walked along it, staring fixedly ahead. Slowly, the gangsters began to follow her.

"If we get rid of all our girls, there'll be nothing but old women left in this town," said Saam, drumming on the steering wheel.

"There are enough to see us out," replied Coffin with a vicious laugh. Then, suddenly serious, he looked right at Saam. "And it's not all of them, just one."

"How is she a threat?" Saam asked, shrugging his shoulders in feigned indifference.

"She'll bring people along and show them – they buried so and so here and so and so there. They got their guns over here, brought the drugs in over there…"

Saam snorted like a cat, never taking his eyes off the girl. He knew Coffin wanted to get even with Severina and what Coffin wanted was law.

"So?"

"Do you really think you can do whatever you want? Only until they know the details. After all, you knew I was sleeping with her. And you didn't walk in on us, you put up with it."

Saam went white and licked his dry lips.

"It's okay," said Coffin, patting him soothingly on the shoulder. "There are plenty of women. But she was ready as a loaded gun. If it hadn't been me it would have been someone else…"

"A loaded gun has to shoot," Saam had sneered the evening Savage shot Coffin who never even suspected there was a live cartridge in the gun chamber, inserted by Saam's trembling fingers.

"Sort it out. Trebenko warned us there was somebody digging away at us all: one minute there are phone calls from Moscow, then someone's freaking out the cops, then the inspectors are sent in. But we've got our own rules here!" said Coffin, blowing his nose and leaving with a slam of the door.

Severina turned round at the sound of the horn and walked over to the car when she saw Saam. He opened the door and the girl flopped down beside him just as she had on the day they met.

"I didn't tell them anything," she lied, biting her nails. "But they took the gear off me. What do I get for that?"

Saam said nothing, staring fixedly at the street and, turning away, the girl stared out of the window, flattening her nose against the glass. Looking at her from the side, the gangster took in her thin arms and dark, protruding veins.

"Was it Coffin got you hooked?"

Severina didn't answer, hiding her arms behind her back.

The car bounced along on the rutted road. There was a squeal then tinkling laughter from the girl and Saam suddenly slammed on the brakes. He lit up and took a long drag. Severina, leaning back in her seat, trapped the wreaths of smoke in her mouth as they spread thinly through the car. As if he had come to a decision, Saam got out of the car and thought as he slammed the door that there could be no going back.

It was quiet out of town. The bare forest was sombre as if it knew why they were there. Severina dawdled, dragging her feet. Saam followed, struggling to decide whether he should strangle her or use his knife.

The laughter of the waitresses took Saam back to the café. The memories made his throat dry just as it had the day he walked through the forest looking at the girl's delicate neck as easy to snap as a dry branch.

91

Rumours spread that the killings of Antonov and Trebenko were connected. The police were run off their feet and the townsfolk racked their brains, going over all the gossip and stories and someone began to whisper about an avenger of the people.

"It's got to be the Chief!" people said in the queues. "Maybe he's putting it on? Pretending to be crazy? Remember how brilliant he used to be!"

"Absolutely. What a guy! Honest and decent, not like that Trebenko, God rest his soul."

"Perhaps it really is him? After all he was the first to see through Trebenko..."

"Why doesn't he bump the gangsters off then?"

"We'll just have to wait and see..."

As he listened to the rumours, Lapin thought more and more frequently about Savely Savage, who was still missing without trace. His story was as big a puzzle as the murders of Antonov and Trebenko. The witness statements were contradictory. There were no motives for the murder. It was a mystery as to where the weapon had come from and there were people who couldn't believe that a seasoned gang member had been taken out by a quiet, inconspicuous engineer who had spent his entire life hunched over drawings of mineral deposits. Lapin was convinced the gang were on Savage's trail and that, God willing, his body would eventually turn up at the rubbish tip or in the forest, another one to add to the unidentified corpses buried on the edge of the cemetery.

Lapin went round to Savage's flat. He tried to read the answers to his questions in the cunning, slightly slanting eyes of his wife and the trembling lips of his daughter who looked sidelong at the investigator. He hovered awkwardly in the lobby uncertain whether to go in and Savage's wife pulled a face at the sight of his muddy boots.

The phone rang. Vasilisa answered but there was silence at the other end.

"Hello?" she said several times, looking apprehensively at the investigator. "Hello. Who is this?"

Lapin could see that she was upset and took the receiver away from her but the girl hastily rang off.

"They'd already hung up."

Savage's wife found a photo of her husband, which the investigator tucked away in his jacket. Whenever a case came to a standstill, Lapin would obtain a picture of the victim and use it to try and work out what kind of person the victim had been, what habits they'd had and what fears. He would try to put himself in the victim's place, talking to him and asking his advice and sometimes getting so far into character that he would shout at the criminal holding the front of his jacket: "I know you did it, you killed me!" He took Savage's photo in the hope of learning what happened the evening Coffin was shot, where Savely was hiding, who he was running away from and what he had planned.

"Were you in Antonov's car?" Lapin asked Vasilisa.

The girl nodded, mumbling something indistinct.

"And what was your relationship?"

"There wasn't any!" Mrs Savage replied on her daughter's behalf. "She'd been out for a drink with her friends and he was kind enough to offer her a lift."

"Did your father have an argument with Antonov that night?"

Vasilisa nodded.

"Where did the gun come from?"

"Coffin gave it to him."

"So why did your father kill Coffin and not Antonov?" Vasilisa shrugged and exchanged a look with her mother.

"Why would he kill Antonov? For wanting to give me a lift?"

"Why would he kill Coffin?" asked Lapin unsure whether Savage's wife was pretending or whether she really didn't know what her daughter had been doing in the Councillor's car.

"Perhaps when your father saw you in Antonov's car he didn't see it like that?" Lapin asked, choosing his words as carefully as he would pick his way through a minefield, annoyed for the umpteenth time that he couldn't go straight to the point and ask a direct question.

"Did you see your father shoot Coffin?" he asked without waiting for an answer.

"Yes," Vasilisa replied. "He shot him with the gun Coffin gave him."

"And why did Coffin give him the gun?"

"So that Dad would shoot him…"

Lapin raised his eyebrows.

"That's what he said? 'Shoot me…' And your father did."

Lapin was trying to imagine Coffin giving a passerby a gun and that passerby pressing the trigger like a coldblooded killer and he couldn't believe a word of it. There was something not right about this story.

"Can you imagine him strangling Antonov?" Lapin asked at which Mrs Savage got up, indicating that the conversation was over.

A woman's face is like a book. The face of a young girl reveals her foolish dreams. The face of a young woman is marked by thoughts that make her lips curl, tilt up the end of her nose or leave shadows under her eyes. The face of a mature woman contains her life story and she has to hide it under a thick layer of powder and lipstick as red as blood. As he struggled to put on his coat, Lapin studied Mrs Savage. He understood that marriage without love is like plain porridge and sleeping with someone else's husband adds a pinch of salt. But you can only eat one at a time.

As he went downstairs, Lapin cast a distracted eye over the smattering of confessions on the walls and went over the three killings in his mind, trying to imagine them all being carried out by Savage. It seemed so ludicrous that he gave a wry grin. "Truth is what you believe in," Lapin muttered to himself. "And you believe what you want to believe," he nodded, agreeing with himself.

When he went outside, he looked up and saw mother and daughter jump away from the window. The old lady on the bench looked like a crow, grey hair tumbling from a black headscarf, her nose long as a bird's beak.

"Who would have thought it...?" he began still at a distance, nodding up at Savage's window.

"Don't believe what people say. People are wicked. They gossip!" the old woman said, poking Lapin. "He wouldn't do any harm. He was like a mouse. He always asked after my health." She shook her head: "There's no-one to talk to now."

As he half listened to her chatter, Lapin was thinking about Shorty who, like Savage, seemed to have vanished off the face of the earth since Coffin died. In the old gang, Shorty, when he still had his legs and his own name, had a reputation for being reckless, a dare-devil, afraid of neither God nor man nor indeed the prosecutor, but after the explosion in the restaurant he had become the gang's jester. Hatred nestled in his heart like a cat. It could be seen in the lines around his mouth and Coffin would hear the cripple's teeth chatter in his sleep as he dreamt of getting even but the gangster enjoyed testing his own nerves so he kept him close like a time bomb. Gradually, however, Shorty got used to his fate and the gang leader got so used to him that he even seemed to believe the cripple would bring him luck. Now, though, Shorty had vanished as if Coffin had taken him with him, reluctant to give up his mascot. Had Lapin discovered how Saam buried Shorty he would have been astonished at his own insight.

Savage's sense of danger had dulled his hunger. When he was keeping watch on Antonov he had survived on mushrooms and two gone-to-seed potatoes. Back in the forest, however, he realized how deadly tired he really was. His hands and feet were as heavy as lead and Savage moved with difficulty as if there were an unseen wall in front of him. His head was spinning. Everything swam before his eyes and when he fell flat on his face, he lay there for what seemed like an eternity, too weak to move. Shivers wracked his aching body and he wept, praying for a speedy death. Savage felt as if someone were performing an autopsy, running a scalpel from his neck to the bottom of his stomach causing a sharp, intense pain and then with an almighty tear he was opened up and left to lie, eviscerated, like a tattered old mattress. In his delirium, he felt as if the wind were wandering through his intestines, chilling him through, while pine needles worked their way inside and pricked his stomach. The trees bent over Savage like doctors over an operating table and he was gripped by hunger-induced terror: it seemed as though the branches were reaching towards him to rip him to pieces and their dark hollows appeared as snarling mouths about to swallow him up. Suffering and tormented, Savage sank into a state of semi-sleep, semi-delirium, one minute feverish, the next shivering with cold. He lay unconscious for several days.

When he did come round, he couldn't remember where he was or why. Running his hands over his unfamiliar, wizened body that refused to do what it was told, he tried to stand up but to no avail. He had only enough strength to turn onto his side and stare at a pale patch of lichen that for some reason made him think of the fruit in meringue his mother used to make and he smacked his lips at the recollection. Other types of moss were coming up through the lichen like alien species. Predatory heads hung on slender stalks and their hollow tubes opened wide mouths. Savage thought that the jungle on some remote planet would look like this and he wanted to lose himself in the moss, escaping from the now repellent pines and birches that were all he ever encountered in the inhospitable Polar taiga. He could no longer tell whether he was roaming an alien planet in his imagination or whether he had shrunk to the size of a crowberry, darkening on its bush, and was lying amid mosses and lichens that towered above him. Reaching for the berries with a numb hand, he picked them, crushed them and licked them off his palm. They had no taste but they did quench his thirst and so Savage picked more, driving away the crazy thoughts and terrors that sent shivers down his spine.

By evening, Savage was feeling better and, guided by the television tower that could be seen above the trees, he trudged away from the town towards the dachas where he hoped to find something to eat. Plodding through the forest, he went in circles, losing the path. He was seeing double which made the television tower appear sometimes on the right, sometimes on the left. In the end he was completely lost and found himself on the outskirts of town.

Two teenagers were hiding behind the garages. One of them, a strap round his arm, was clumsily trying to find a vein. A couple of months earlier, Savage would have gone past with his head down but now, picking up a stone, he headed for the boys.

"Hey, you. Lose the syringe!" he yelled and the boys, seeing a tattered tramp threatening them with a stone fled. "If I see you again, I'll kill you-ou-ou!" His cry floated above the garages.

Savage remembered a teenager who used to spend the night in the entrance to his block of flats. At the time, Savage was on leave, spending it as he had for many years in front of the television, counting the days till he went back to work.

As usual, he woke up at the crack of dawn before the alarm went off but he had nowhere to go and was lolling in bed, listening to the sounds from outside. In the hubbub that reached him from the courtyard, he could pick out the shrill notes of his wife demanding that somebody call the police. When he looked out of the window, he could see his assembled neighbours.

Savage went out onto the landing. He could hear the disputes here too.

"He's blocking the way!"

"You have to step over him!"

"It's high time the door was locked. Otherwise, all the druggies come in. They've turned the entrance into a drug den!"

97

Someone shouted that the neighbourhood police officer would arrive any minute and people began to drift off. The entrance door slammed and, muttering imprecations, an old lady from the second floor began to climb the stairs, already out of breath.

"They'll pick him up now!" she said triumphantly to a neighbour who had poked her nose out of her door.

"There's no getting away from them," said the neighbour, nodding her head and adjusting a funereal headscarf. "It would be better if they all dropped dead."

Hanging over the banister, Savage could see a teenage boy curled up on the floor and he ran down, taking the stairs two at a time. The boy was lying with his eyes open, staring at a fixed point and his set face with its twitch recalled a theatre mask. Savage tapped his cheeks and tried to lift him up. Clutching his shoulder, the addict dutifully got to his feet.

Surprised at his own determination, Savage dragged the boy into the flat and shut and locked the door. His wife was at work, his daughter had gone to school and Savage had been left to his own devices until the evening.

He laid the boy on the bed, took off his dirty clothes and threw them in the washing machine. The boy's hair smelled of acetone. His complexion was sallow and his eyes still as glass. Savage wanted to call an ambulance but hadn't even picked up the phone when the boy went into the kitchen, dragging one of his feet.

"What's your n-n-name?" Savage asked, taking him by the chin,

"K-k-kostya," the boy replied, imitating him.

Savage didn't take offence and offered him a glass of water.

"Do your parents kn-n-ow you sniff glue?"

"They're dead."

Kostya lifted the lid of the frying pan. He rolled up the burnt omelette he found there and popped it into his mouth.

"Do you live in the or-or-orphanage?"

"No, on the street. They wouldn't take me. I'm nearly eighteen."

Savage was astonished. The boy looked about thirteen. He was short and painfully thin.

"You c-c–can't live on the street," said Savage, cutting slices of bread.

"Where else? I'll get a room in a hostel in a couple of months. I'll survive. I eat out of skips. There's always loads of stuff."

Savage watched the boy stuffing the bread into his mouth as if afraid it would be taken off him and he felt awkward. Pretending he had something in his eye, he wiped away the tears that had welled up.

The doorbell rang. Putting a finger to his lips, Savage indicated that the boy shouldn't make a noise and smoothing his fuzzy hair, he went to open the door.

"We had a call that a drug addict has been sleeping here," the officer barked, without any greeting.

"Wh-wh-who?" stuttered Savage.

"Sorry to have disturbed you," said the officer, ringing the bell next door.

When Savage went back into the kitchen, the boy was deftly going through the cupboards, looking at the jars of food. Lowering his head, the boy began to sniffle.

"I'm sorry, Uncle. I won't do it again… I only get to eat scraps and I'm really starving…"

Savage was embarrassed and, unable to find the right words, he put his arm round the boy who carried on sobbing, brushing the tears away with his fist.

"It's okay. I'll get a room and start a new life!"

While Savage ironed the freshly washed clothes with a sizzling iron so that they would dry more quickly, Kostya wandered around inspecting the flat. Savage was afraid some trinket would go missing and his wife would make a fuss so he put the iron aside and kept an eye on him. Even so, Kostya managed to sneak a couple of rings out of the jewellery box.

Savage saw him out, giving him a packet of groceries and a couple of jumpers, making Kostya promise to come back the following afternoon.

But Kostya didn't show up. Savage wandered around the entrances to various blocks of flats in the evenings, looking into basements that had been left open and gazing out of the windows. He was afraid that Kostya had got confused and would turn up at the weekend or in the evening when his wife and daughter were at home but the boy had disappeared.

Then, when Savage had forgotten all about Kostya, he suddenly came across him with his parents. His mother had the swollen red face of a drunk and his father looked like a living corpse.

Savage ran over to the boy.

"Y-y-you said you were an orphan! Why d-d-did you d-d-disappear?"

"What do you want? Beat it, yeah?"

Kostya had changed in six months. He looked like he had Down's syndrome. His nose had swollen up and his mad eyes gawped crazily. He went through Savage's pockets and took out a couple of crumpled banknotes. Then he rushed to catch up with his parents who had gone on ahead.

As Savage watched him go, he was overflowing with an unspent love that nobody needed.

He had thought he would never see Kostya again but a few days later, he suddenly felt someone tugging at his sleeve as he queued for bread.

"Uncle, spare some change... For a bit to eat..."

He dug into his pockets.

"Where are your parents?" he asked.

"I'm an orphan," said Kostya, taking up the old refrain. "I live on the rubbish tip. I eat whatever comes my way. My parents died a long time ago..."

Rubbing his swollen nose, Kostya turned to the woman who was next in line.

"Aunty, aunty, can you spare a little..."

Savage had a catch in his throat. He remembered the colourless hair that smelt of acetone and the whiny voice, and he thought that Kostya was probably already dead and there was only Savage to make amends for the absurdity of the boy's life, tossed away like an empty bottle of acetone.

Karimov often imagined being a serial killer. He entertained a fantasy in which he would steal out into the night and walk the empty streets, sticking close to the houses and hiding from the dull gleam of the streetlights that turned faces into wax masks and shadows into lead. Somewhere in the distance, a solitary individual who had stayed late with friends would appear and Karimov would hide behind a tree and wait for him to draw nearer. Then, he would jump out in front of him, stab him in the side and, leaving him there on the road, he would go home and, after smoking a single fragrant cigar, he would go to bed. Walking past the police cordon the next morning, he would look at the body, draped in a sheet, and be unable to remember the face of whoever lay beneath it.

Shaking a boxful of matches onto the table, he laid them out one by one, calculating that if he killed one person every week, it would come to 50 in one year, 500 in 10 years and 1,000 in 20 years. No motive, no evidence – chance passersby chancing to be killed by a chance murderer. Who would ever suspect him?

Karimov justified his crazy scheme by thinking: "How am I any worse than God? Doesn't he hide away from us like a criminal? Doesn't he kill us on the sly when we least expect to encounter him?"

Karimov didn't watch television and, when television programs were being discussed, he would leave the table, noisily pushing his chair away. Loneliness rose like bile in his mouth. He was bored in the evenings and lay on his bed, listening to Bach in an attempt to drown out the mutterings of radios and televisions in the neighbouring hotel rooms.

"All the world's a hotel and we are merely random

guests," Karimov would say with a helpless gesture in reply to bewildered questions as to why he didn't move into a flat of his own.

Winter lasts for six months in the Arctic Circle, night gives way to night and in the impenetrable darkness all sense of time is lost so that it seems as though the winter and the night will last forever. Looking at the frosted window, Karimov thought life was like the patterns frost makes on glass: from a distance it seems beautiful and ornate but up close it means nothing. Karimov drove these thoughts away and once again imagined himself as a killer. He got dressed quickly and left the room. He waved away the security man and ran down the steps, whistling a Bach fugue, and the soles of his feet tingled with anticipation. Turning up his collar, he concealed the predatory nose that could easily give him away and plunged into the darkness.

The infrequent streetlights only illuminated parts of the streets and people walked as though blind through the scrunching, glistening snow. In Moscow the snow would melt straight away into a dirty sludge but here it was like flaky pastry, layers of snow alternating with layers of mineral dust that settled in a grey film on snow drifts and faces. A fat woman, laden with shopping bags, waddled along, cautiously descending an icy hill, her arms held out so widely she seemed to be carrying buckets on a yoke. Following her, Karimov turned down a side street. He was mulling over how he would take out his pistol and silencer, hold it to her ear like a finger, shoot twice and, supporting the now limp body, lower it carefully onto the blood-reddened snow. Hiding the gun in his jacket, he would cross the courtyard, leave via the archway and, lighting a cigarette, hurry back to the hotel. Crossing the courtyard, Karimov discovered that it really did have an archway and if he did shoot the fat woman he would be able to hide there. He turned and went back the way he had come, without even looking at the woman who had put her bags down in the snow to catch her breath.

"They're killing each other!" The Chief's cry rang through the town. "They're all killing each other!" Rolling his mad eyes, he tried to grasp passersby by the hand.

"And that's the truth," agreed an old man as he hurried by, not even slowing his pace. "There's death everywhere! People got on better in the old days. Even dying was a cheerier business."

Karimov sneered and hurried across the road.

As he went back to the hotel, he measured himself against the people he encountered: some he strangled in dark alleys, others he waylaid in entrances. Even so, Karimov decided as he banged the snow off his boots against the steps, it was too risky to be killing people in the evening, in full view of everyone. He was so exhausted by his murder rehearsals that he hardly had time to take his clothes off before he fell on the bed and into a deep and dreamless sleep.

The idea was becoming an obsession. There was no let-up day or night. Karimov was scared he'd kill someone, get a taste for it and be unable to stop, but if he didn't at least have a go, he'd go mad. He ruminated on murder, relishing the details and roamed the streets in the evenings mentally picking potential victims out of the dusk. The bodyguards he left behind when he went walking were worried about him and gave him a gun. Weighing the cold and heavy barrel in his hands, Karimov finally made up his mind. He asked them to attach a silencer and, trembling with excitement, could hardly wait for nightfall.

The town was preparing for the end-of-year holidays. Multicoloured fairy lights twinkled and decorated Christmas trees looked out of the shop windows like nosy neighbours. Someone could die right now and the lights would continue to sparkle, painting the snowdrifts with all the colours of the rainbow, and when Karimov pulled the trigger and put an end to someone's life the residents of the little town would be asleep, unaware of the victim's groan or the killer's footsteps.

Karimov shivered as he remembered freezing on the steps of the orphanage as a baby. It had been so very cold that it had stayed with him all his life. It had penetrated his soul and everyone he spoke to could feel the chill. Loneliness is our original sin. We carry its mark when we are born and we die without knowing why we went through such torment. Only death as it closes our eyes momentarily shares the burden of our loneliness. Death, however, which had already been creeping up on the baby swaddled in its mother's dress, was frightened away by a stranger who clutched the child to his breast. Karimov walked the sleeping town and wondered why he felt neither gratitude nor love for his foster father but only a cold, detached hatred. Was it because he'd driven away Karimov's death, leaving his soul the permanent dwelling place of all-consuming loneliness?

His thoughts were interrupted by a reddish fur coat lying in a snowdrift. When he went nearer, Karimov could see a drunken woman trying to stand up by clutching at a tree. Her tights were in shreds, her neck was crimson under the scarf and the lipstick smeared across her face was like a bleeding wound.

It couldn't have been better engineered: the street was deserted, the woman was defenceless and Karimov decided that he could easily strangle her and not waste a cartridge. He reached for her neck, then drew his hands back as if they'd been scalded. Cursing his own cowardice, he again went to take her by the neck where he could see the blue of a swollen artery. He squeezed and the woman, opening her puffy eyes, moaned something softly. Karimov relaxed his grip. Hovering uncertainly, he lit a cigarette and looked around. The woman was looking at him, smiling, as she muttered drunkenly. "Coward!" Karimov cursed himself. "Loser!" Grabbing his gun, he trained the barrel on the woman and turned his head away, ready to shoot. There was the sound of a car. Headlights flashed in the distance and Karimov, hiding the gun, made off, slipping on the icy road.

Back at the hotel, he opened a bottle of the reserve brandy he kept for special occasions, ran a hot bath and sat in it until morning, sipping at the golden elixir until the water was completely cold. He went over and over his night-time adventure in his head, trying to work out whether the woman he had had in his sights would be able to remember him and then, calming down, decided that even if she could, no-one would believe her.

From then on, Karimov put his crazy scheme out of his head. His murders were only on paper as he sacked employees and shut down factories. Staff lists that were just a meaningless set of names to other people took on particular significance for Karimov. There was a face behind every name and a destiny as grey as the town outside and crossing the name out was like slitting someone's throat and hearing their death rattle. When Savely Savage shot Coffin, however, Karimov was suddenly wracked with an envy that stuck in his flesh like a sharp thorn and he didn't know how to take it out.

Time passes more slowly in the provinces and news from the capital arrives with chunks bitten off, like a half-eaten apple, and with a new meaning. In the metropolis, just like in a lift, people pretend not to see one another whereas in small towns everyone is exposed and other people's lives become more interesting than your own. Savage's life, though, was inconspicuous and uninteresting even to him. He was the sort of person who is only remembered when his obituary appears in the local paper. His wife had long considered herself unmarried and his daughter couldn't care less about him while Savage himself didn't know if he existed or not. And yet, in his dreams he lived nine lives every day like a cat and tried on thousands of destinies without finding a single one to fit.

He saw people as the living dead. Cold emanated from them and their souls were dark as the grave. They resembled photographs of themselves as children as much as the dead resemble photographs of themselves on tombstones. When was it that someone died and went on living? What was it that killed them – work, marriage, children?

"We're like bedbugs living in a sofa!" he heard once and, spinning around to find who had uttered something so like his own thoughts, he suddenly realized he'd said it himself.

At that time, he was too embarrassed to talk to himself aloud because people might think he'd gone crazy but now, as he made his way through the dank swamp of the forest, he gesticulated freely, debating with himself as he would with an old friend. As he remembered his old life, he cursed himself and tried to explain himself to himself.

On public holidays, a stage was rigged up in the central square in front of the statue of Lenin. Mayor Krotov was first to speak, the wooden boards bending under his weight until it seemed the stage would snap. He was followed by local government officials who all looked alike and Savage, shifting from one foot to the other, imagined hurling a stone or a rotten egg at one of them.

"Why did I even go?" he wondered, shrugging his shoulders as he scrambled through the fragrant fir trees.

"It's as lonely as the grave within your own four walls!" he told himself by way of justification.

"And being in the square's like being in a common grave, is it?" he asked, scoffing.

"If only…" Savage sighed. "Everything used to be held in common – life and death. Now, everyone even breathes their own air…"

On the town's holiday, its residents gathered as usual in the square, swapping gossip that did the rounds before coming full circle, turned completely inside out. The mayor, puffing out his cheeks, shouted into a microphone that whistled when he put it too close to his mouth. Savage held his bag to his chest. There were four eggs inside, neatly placed in a box, and he listened to the official speeches that droned in his head like mosquitoes. He had tangled his sheets up all night long as he imagined hurling an egg into Krotov's face. People said of the mayor that he ate for five and stole for ten. Savage imagined his wife's eyebrows rising and his colleagues clapping him on the shoulder approvingly, saying: "What a guy! Well done, what a man!" Savage nearly dropped one of the eggs as he carefully placed it in his pocket. He began awkwardly pushing through the cluster of people around the stage and in the end he crushed the fragile shell and his pocket was covered in runny egg. He couldn't quite bring himself to take the other eggs out of his bag so he just stood in front of the stage for the whole event, listening to the mayor and his aides and some visiting bureaucrats from the regional centre. Then at home, he spent ages washing his coat which bore the memory of that day forever after in the dirty marks on the pocket.

"I did know a chap who was always bothered about what other people were thinking. Even in his coffin, he was embarrassed by his cheap suit."

"Have you just made that up?"

"Your whole life's like a broken egg that's left dirty marks…"

"Stop it, will you? People will remember me for ages, now!" he said, spitting out the bitter recollections.

At that time, Savely Savage had been one of the living dead. Now, though, he had been reborn. He could feel the world around him through his skin and single out millions of smells, colours and sensations. He wasn't living out thousands of other people's lives in a day. He was living his own.

The North is headstrong and stubborn. In winter-time, it plunges the land into Stygian darkness while in the summer, it won't allow the sun to set, turning night into day. As if governed by the Arctic Circle his life had been grim and dark and yet now it was bowling along like the Polar sun, drawing circles on the horizon and keeping the townsfolk from their sleep.

The nondescript grey house surrounded by a fence didn't stand out from the other buildings. Looking up, there were identical white tee-shirts and darned and faded uniforms drying on the stretched-out washing lines. The military unit was billeted near the town market and on Sunday afternoons the soldiers lined up along the fence, begging food from the women going home with their shopping.

The unit commander was tall and broad-shouldered, with a spring in his step and big hands that easily encompassed government property. Initially, he sold decommissioned weapons to Coffin and then just anything assigned to the unit. In the end, the gang even took the training rifles. The sight of them was enough to make the police recoil. The gang flaunted the AKs slung over their shoulders and gave the training rifles to the kids at the orphanage making the town look like a fortress under siege until Trebenko begged them to hide the weapons away.

"Who's this penguin we've got here?" said the commanding officer looking at the pale, gaunt boys lined up in the yard. The soldiers snickered and the tubby little runt he'd spotted shrank back, afraid. "I order you to reduce weight and grow half a metre taller by the time you're demobbed," barked the commander and the soldier saluted, pulling in his chest.

"Yes, sir!"

The soldiers were always pleased when they were sent to work in town, painting fences or clearing snow. Crafty Krotov even came up with the idea of equipping the soldiers to lay asphalt but the next day the road they built buckled and dimpled so that little plan had to be abandoned. Then all the town yardkeepers were sacked and, in the mornings, the conscripts donned their orange jackets and flourished their brooms, begging change and cigarettes off passersby hurrying to work.

The commander personally picked out five soldiers to build a dacha for his daughter, feeling their muscles and patting their cheeks as if it were a slave market.

"Take the penguin too. That'll be fun!" he urged the lads he'd chosen, nodding at the runt.

Winter in the North lasts half a year and spring comes at the end of April. Like a party girl running late, applying her lipstick and pulling on her shoes when she's already running down the stairs, the Polar spring hurries to melt the snow and put out leaves. There were already dandelions flowering in town but the lakes in the forest were still covered with ice so that the soldiers left the town in spring time only to arrive in a winter forest. They were put out of the lorry and, huddling up close, looked around at the snowdrifts.

"I'll be back with food in a week," yelled the sergeant, lowering a box of canned meat onto the snow. "And the fence had better be up!"

Crestfallen, the soldiers set about nailing boards of wood together as they gazed around at the taiga they were going to have to live in. There was a rusty metal trailer on a piece of waste ground. It was colder inside than outside. There were grubby sleeping bags on the floor and the boys climbed inside and curled up, cursing the unit commander.

"At least, we'll get a good sleep," drawled the Penguin and was immediately pushed outside.

The thought that the fatso was freezing in the forest made the others warmer and they fell asleep. In the morning, they rolled up their sleeves and got down to work. When the sergeant arrived a week later, the fence had been thrown up, their supplies eaten and one soldier was in the sleeping bag in a fever of delirium. The sergeant unloaded the food and equipment, gathered up the soldier with the cold and promised to send back-up.

"The Penguin's lost weight," he winked as he left.

A month later the foundations were in place, the walls had gone up and, straddling the walls, the soldiers had cobbled together a roof, counting the days to their discharge. Once a week, the sergeant arrived, inspected the house, brought them food, gave them a swig from his water-bottle and jollied them along by talking about how soon their military service would be at an end.

"I'm due to go home next week," shouted a boy who was sitting on the roof.

"You finish building, then you go home," the sergeant said, dismissively.

"What do you mean?" he asked in surprise.

"You finish building, then you go home," the sergeant said with emphasis.

The unit commander descended to take delivery of the work. He inspected the house from all sides, banged the walls and examined it inside.

"Well done, lads. What a team!"

The soldiers straightened their shoulders.

"Now you can go to another town and do the same there for a friend of mine. He'll pay you."

"It's time to go home," said one of the soldiers, scratching his neck. "We're already overdue."

The commander went over to him and laid a heavy hand on his shoulder.

"And where might you be from?" he asked.

"Near Pskov, a village…"

"So what have you left behind? What are you going to do when you get there?"

The soldier didn't know how to respond. He looked round at his comrades.

"What? You don't need money? I said he'll pay!" yelled the sergeant.

Taking a deep breath, the Penguin stepped forward.

"I'm due to go too… I'll be building at home… My Dad'll help."

The commander pressed his lips together, jaws working, and the boy shrank still further under his gaze.

"You were told to grow another half metre. Have you? You're staying on!" said the commander, turning away and striding back to his vehicle. "That'll be all. Load them up."

They drove for several hours, trying to guess the direction they were taking away from the town. The soldiers said nothing. They stared at one another and when the lorry bounced over potholes, they bounced up and down in the lorry too.

"Attempting to escape is desertion," barked the sergeant. "Then it's goodbye, Mum!"

"But we've done our time," the soldiers complained. "Our parents will be looking for us."

"We've already phoned them to say their sons are in the disciplinary battalion," said the sergeant with a grin of farewell.

The unit commander's friend was a local civil servant. They were building a dacha for his son next to the plot on which his own sturdy house stood. The soldiers were put up in the barn on camp beds that collapsed when the legs buckled in the night and then the lads woke up on the floor in the small hours.

"Built by soldiers," said one expert, patting the walls.

"So what, by the time we've finished building for their children, their grandchildren will be grown up," spat the soldier from Pskov, kicking off his boots. "There's no shortage of work."

The owner's wife, old before her time, her grey hair pulled back in a bun, brought them hot pies that she'd wrapped in a towel to keep warm.

"Ooh, you're so skinny," she said, shaking her head and trotting off across the courtyard for more, tucking up her hair that had come loose.

She loved to sit on a folding chair, listening to their discussions. It reminded her of her own childhood, spent in the military town to which her father was attached. When she saw their ragged uniforms in the light, she brought along some castoffs of her son's, which hung on the soldiers like clothes on a scarecrow.

"Meat pies," she smiled, looking at the boys who were hovering impatiently. "And one has a peppercorn in it."

"Peppercorn?"

"Yes. For luck. Whoever gets it has to eat it and then he'll have good luck. That's what they say."

"That's about my luck, a mouth full of pepper," grumbled

111

the boy from Pskov although he looked enviously around to see whether anyone else had got the "lucky" pie.

The Penguin started to howl, his eyes on stalks, and the woman clapped her hands.

"He's the lucky one! Eat it up. You mustn't spit out good luck!"

Gathering up the plates, the woman set off for home and the boy from Pskov caught her up at the fence.

"Aunty, could I ring home from your place?"

Her kind eyes became small and sharp as pepper: "It's not allowed," she snapped in the voice of the unit commander.

When the house was finished, the sergeant came for the soldiers again in the ancient lorry with its angry cough. The women crossed the boys' path and thrust a packet of pies at them. Then leaning on the gate, she watched after the departing lorry for a long time.

"Just one more little house and back to your Mums," the sergeant shouted from the cab. "What were you before you joined the army? Soft as shit. A waste of space! Now you've got qualifications. When you go home, you can go and work on building sites, earn yourselves a bit of money. There's just one last house…"

When the lorry braked at a turning, the Penguin jumped over the side and made a dash for the forest, not really looking where he was going.

"Stop!" yelled the sergeant but there was no trace of the soldier.

The sergeant didn't dare look for him in the forest. He was afraid the others would make a run for it as well. Instead, back at the unit, he sent soldiers with dogs out to find the deserter. They spent several days looking for the Penguin until a shaggy sheepdog, its throat hoarse from barking, hurled itself at the tree he dangled from, hanged by his belt.

His father, also short and fat, came to collect the coffin but he never saw how his son had stretched out and slimmed down. The plain wooden coffin had been nailed down and he ran his hairy hands over the lid as if trying to make out the shape of his son. Clearing his throat, the unit commander offered his condolences and the sergeant handed over his effects, which smelt of the forest and of death.

His father hung around the unit, picking up hints and allusions, from which he built up a picture of his son's life in the army. When he realized what had happened, he lay in wait for the unit commander, fists clenched, but the latter, looking down at the shorter man from his full height, pointed to the morgue and his son's coffin:

"Take it and get lost! Come back and you'll end up there too!"

The soldiers were glued to the barrack windows, noses pressed to the glass, but when the commander looked up they sprang away as if he might remember their faces.

Medics loaded the coffin onto the roof of an elderly car that looked like a slave bent under an impossible weight and the father took his son home, chatting to him all the way as if he could hear him.

Everything in Savage's room had been turned upside down. Clothes, crumpled papers and drawings had been tossed around everywhere, books had been thrown from the shelves like birds from a nest and the mattress lay, disembowelled, on the floor. A sturdy lad was busy leafing through the phone book and Saam, slouched on a stool, was flicking cigarette ash onto the floor.

"Maybe it wasn't him?" suggested Savage's wife, leaning wearily on the door. She was dishevelled and her sleepless nights showed in the blue under her eyes.

Saam stubbed the cigarette butt out on the sole of his shoe and threw it into the corner.

"Well, the others certainly weren't him!" she said, shaking her head.

"So who was it?" the gangster asked phlegmatically as he inspected his nails.

Savage's wife moved closer, nervously fiddling with the belt of her housecoat.

"Come on, he's a complete pushover. Anyone could wipe the floor with him. He's scared of his own shadow. He sleeps with a night-light on!"

"Did your daughter see him fire?"

"She doesn't know whether she did or not. Sometimes, she thinks..."

Exchanging a look, Saam and his sidekick burst out laughing.

"Well, I believe my own eyes," Saam smirked, giving her the once over. "And if I saw that hubby of yours fire the gun, no-one's going to persuade me that Coffin shot himself!"

Savage's daughter was hiding in the bathroom where she was plastered against the door. Hearing the gangsters' heavy tread, she cautiously locked the door. There, sitting in the darkness, Vasilisa listened to the sound of water from the neighbours' and once again went over the events of that evening in her head. In the beginning, she had known her father killed Coffin. After all, it had happened right in front of her. But then doubts crept in and eroded her memories the way water wears away a stone and she began to think her father hadn't fired or that he fired but missed, that there was a second shot and a third.

"The minute he turns up, ring me!" barked Saam in the end. "Don't forget, he's dangerous!"

"And what'll you do to him?" Savage's wife asked and Vasilisa held her breath, her hand clapped over her mouth.

Saam didn't answer and from his expressive silence Vasilisa realized that her father would not be coming home.

Closing the door behind the gangsters, Savage's wife went into the kitchen, splashed some vodka generously into a glass and drank it down in one gulp. She recalled how once her husband came to her room at night when he'd had a drink. She was already asleep and her husband spent ages feeling along the wall to find the light switch.

"For goodness sake?! For goodness sake?!" said Savage, lurching from one side to the other. He wanted to shout: "I'm a person too. I'm suffering from a loneliness that I drown by watching TV and you, the only people close to me, bait me like a wild animal!" Instead, he became tongue-tied and simply kept saying, like a wind-up doll: "Me... person... you... wild animals! Me! Person! You wild animals!"

"Will you shut up?" his daughter yelled, banging on the wall. "You're keeping me awake!"

And Savage, his arms flailing like a windmill, plodded back to his own room, still mumbling the truth that had suddenly been revealed to him: "Me – person, you – animals..."

"Savage can't be living in the forest!" said Saam confidently. "Someone's hiding him! Have you checked out all his friends?"

"He didn't have any friends. We've been round to all the people from his class and the people he worked with. They were so scared they'd have been only too happy to hand him over but they don't know where he is."

The gang were sitting in their small house, hunched over a map and pointing to where Savage might be hiding.

"The dachas?"

"The yardkeeper says someone's been into a couple of properties and stolen food but that's normal."

Saam made a mark on the map.

"Have you been to the old workers' settlements?"

"Yes. There's no-one there."

Saam sniffed angrily as he rocked on his chair. He was amused when Savage shot Coffin. He bore no grudge against him. He looked on him as the weapon by which he took revenge on Coffin for Severina and for his position as second fiddle for so many years. Saam was disoriented by Trebenko's death and his blood ran cold when he was shown Antonov's disfigured corpse. He was sure he was dealing with someone as ruthless as himself, someone who'd stop at nothing, who would take revenge for being humiliated and wouldn't stop until he'd taken out everyone he hated.

"I know it's him," he spat through the gaps in his teeth. "The little man has taken on the role of justice but that's what we do and people are happy with it!"

He jumped up and paced the room, and the gang, quiet now, awaited his orders.

"Get the hunters involved. Ask the tramps at the tip. If he really is in the forest he'll turn up for food there sooner or later."

Saam felt he had been driven into a corner. The police had gone quiet after Trebenko died. They avoided Saam. They didn't attend meetings or take his calls and he didn't know what was happening inside the station. When Saam lost control of something, the ground went from under his feet.

A nondescript official appeared at the door with some papers and announced that the little wooden house was to be demolished. Saam felt giddy. He couldn't make his tongue work. He couldn't say a word and just stared, disconcerted, at the visitor.

"A swimming pool's going to be built here," the terrified official explained, swallowing hard. "It's an old house. It's falling down," he gestured at the room. "Its time was up a long time ago."

"And yours!" A gangster with a wide scar that split his fierce face in two took a knife out of his boot.

"Oh!" the official gasped, clasping his hands to his chest.

"Stop it!" yelled Saam and the gangster, grinding his teeth, put the knife away.

Leaning over the table, the gangsters scratched their heads unable to understand who would be so bold as to raise a hand against them. The official, meanwhile, putting his paperwork in his briefcase with trembling fingers, kept talking:

"I'm a little person. My job is to provide information. I don't decide which buildings need to come down or go up..."

"No, but I do!" said Saam, interrupting.

He could tell how unconvincing he sounded and silence hung in the room like an axe.

When the official had gone, the workers arrived. They wound building netting round the house like a shroud and the gang cut a hole in it so that they could go in and out of the house. The workers walked around timidly, measuring up the house, but couldn't bring themselves to go inside. When they started to cut down the fence with a whir of their electric saws, people came rushing out of the surrounding houses to watch. The gang sat at their table and poured out their drinks in silence, listening to the sounds from outside. Saam cracked his fingers, gnawing on his gloomy thoughts, while the others attempted to read them in his small, mean eyes.

The gang often remembered Coffin: in his day, not even stray dogs had come up to their house. Behind Saam's back they began to talk about treachery, something for which there was no forgiveness, not just from people but from God, who had turned his back on the gang.

"Coffin never kept his gun loaded," ground out the gangster with the scar. "Saam was the one who loaded it."

"They were a fine pair, fighting over a chick!" said another through gritted teeth. "What about us?"

"If we get rid of Saam, we're finished for sure! Let's just hang on a bit!"

Saam could sense the murmuring that was starting up in the gang and could turn to mutiny. As he lay chain smoking at night he could hear Coffin laughing as though he were watching him from Hell and making fun of his failures.

Swathed in netting, the house without its fence looked naked and defenceless and the gangsters, cowering and drawing in their heads, shrank in size. They sharpened their knives and didn't put a foot out of doors if they could help it but the workers still hesitated to start the demolition. After hanging around for a few days, they brought along a metal trailer. In it, they set up an old, stained sofa, a couple of camp-beds and a crooked table. The workers came out to answer

117

calls of nature among the willow trees and they rattled their bottles on the way back from the shop, shaking their fists at the gangsters.

On one occasion, the foreman, who was well and truly hammered, banged on the door, shoving away the workmen who were trying in vain to hold him back. Barely able to stand, he insisted that the gangsters should be gone there and then. Even when the gang dragged him inside he continued to threaten to demolish the house, residents and all.

The gangsters flung the foreman into the corner and then took up their seats, their massive malice-filled shadows surrounding him. Sitting astride his chair, Saam took a strong-smelling cigarette from the packet and licking his dry lips, lit up and puffed out smoke rings. The foreman, who had instantly sobered up, shrank back against the wall and could tell from the gangsters' faces that things were not looking good. A clock struck the hours in the next room, counting off the time that went endlessly on and on. Every time it struck, the foreman's hope that the workers would call for help diminished still further. Laboriously and with seeming reluctance, night tipped over the half way point and still the gangsters said nothing, still as statues. With a girlish sob, the foreman dropped his head onto his chest but the gangsters were unmoved. Only towards morning did they begin to yawn, opening their gap-toothed mouths while tiredness and boredom appeared in eyes that were red with lack of sleep.

The workmen, glued to the net-covered windows, tried to work out what was going on in the house but all they could hear was the sound of the clock drowned in the viscous silence. They couldn't bring themselves to ring the police and, tired of waiting, they went back to the trailer and collapsed onto the old, sagging sofa. They awoke in the morning to the foreman's heavy footsteps. He bundled up his things without a word and left without so much as a goodbye.

From then on, the workmen avoided the house and kept to the trailer. The local officials, grey as mice, wandered around, mopping their sweating brows and wondering what to do. The piled-up boards of the fence rotted in the rain. The gang gradually unwound the building netting, making holes for windows. Investigator Lapin was undaunted, he was certain that clouds were gathering over the gang and, mindful of his conversation with the mayor, he decided to go and see him.

There was a quiet, solemn air about the local government building and as Lapin ascended the red-carpeted marble stairs he felt as if he were in an important department in the capital or the museum he had visited with his class. He had fallen behind and gone down to the café where he sat till the end of the lecture, contemplating the stucco ceiling. But an old woman in reindeer-skin slippers barred his way, bringing him back to his back-water town.

"Where do you think you're going?" she demanded with a menacing lift of an eyebrow.

Lapin sighed and produced his ID. Peering at it short-sightedly, the woman brought it up close to her nose and moved aside with a gasp.

"So very young and an investigator already. I'm sorry I didn't recognize you, duck," she said, running after him, clasping her hands.

Krotov barely fitted into his chair, like dough spilling out of a pan. He took two tiny glasses out of the desk and a bottle of amber liquid that gleamed in the light.

"How's it going?" asked Krotov and Lapin was so embarrassed he forgot the speech he had prepared.

"We're doing our best," he muttered.

Lapin was intimidated by the mayor even though he despised this portly individual who had taken root in his chair like one of last year's onions sprouting in the cellar.

"You did mention support," Lapin began, the drink giving him courage. "I really need support."

The mayor always took fright when asked for something so he drew himself up, pursing his lips. "Supplicants are worse than terrorists," he would complain to his secretary seeing out visitors who whined that you couldn't get fresh air let alone snow out of the mayor.

"It's not right for a gang to be running the town!"

"True," Krotov agreed. "The place for crooks is behind bars!"

He filled their glasses and proposed a toast to justice. They drank in meaningful silence as if trying to come up with a solution.

"What is this stuff?"

"Reindeer velvet moonshine," said Krotov, smacking his lips and filling the glasses again. "Powerful stuff, eh?"

"Certainly is," nodded Lapin. He drank and leaned forward, "So about that support?"

Krotov fidgeted nervously in his chair.

"Support?" he said, wide-eyed. "What kind of support?"

"You know, to put the crooks behind bars... Oh, no, thanks. That's enough," he said, putting his hand over his glass.

"You insult me, Captain," said Krotov shaking his head. He poured out more of the moonshine and drank, tipping his head back. "We'll help! Carry on with your work, Captain, searching, digging around and we'll help!"

Lapin brought his chair nearer and looked Krotov in the eye.

"They keep letting them out!"

"Who does?" said the mayor in feigned surprise. He loosened his tie.

"Trebenko, the prosecutor, all of them..."

"Not Trebenko any more, may he rest in peace," said Krotov, crossing himself. "Dig around, lad. They'll go down. We won't let them out. You have my word!"

"If I drink any more, I'll be on the floor," Lapin admitted when Krotov poured out the last few drops. "Honestly, I will. Will you have a word with the prosecutor so that he doesn't get in the way? Otherwise, he'll send me away on business. It's happened before." Lapin drank, wincing. "I knew where they'd buried that businessman, on the building site when they were laying the foundations... But they got rid of me for a month... When I got back, the house had been built."

"Don't worry, Captain. I'll make a call. There won't be any more business trips," Krotov promised. Propping the unsteady investigator up at the door, he shook his hand firmly. "Don't let me down, Captain. You're my only hope!"

And Lapin took the marble stairs like an ice run, planting a kiss on the old woman in the reindeer-skin slippers.

As he drove past the jerry-built grey-brick church, Karimov asked the driver to stop. It was a long time since he'd been to church, disillusioned with the platitudes the priest mumbled into his beard. The priest, who believed the world was created in seven days, was a thin man, curved by life into the shape of a pretzel. He depicted paradise as rather like a church, gilded and glittering, and hell as smoke-filled taverns where music was replaced by the gnashing of teeth and the seductive girls drinking cocktails through straws were fiendish and foxy demons. Once, sitting through yet another sermon, Karimov, without a word of farewell, walked out of the church, causing the priest to make the sign of the cross over his departing back and to whisper a prayer for the sinner's salvation.

Today, however, Karimov suddenly felt like popping into the little church with its ridiculous, blue-painted domes, looking at the cunning faces of the saints and breathing in the coarse, cloying scent of incense that made fears and anxieties melt away and eyelids droop as if closed with copper coins.

Antonov's wife, eyes cast down, was cleaning the soot off the candles. She gave Karimov a barely perceptible nod when she saw him as though the Lord might not approve of them knowing one another.

His gaze wandered over the icons and a wrinkled, hunched old woman, noticing his haughty bearing, crept over to him, dragging her leg, and gave him a pinch in the side. It hurt.

"People come to ask God for things!"

"I don't need anything," he replied, laughing and rubbing his side. "I've got everything!"

"They ask forgiveness for their sins!" she whispered, pointing heavenwards.

"You old witch!" thought Karimov, livid. Aloud he said only:

"My sins are His mistakes. He should be asking my forgiveness."

Karimov headed for the exit but stopped in the doorway, made the sign of the cross, and called out to the hunchbacked woman, "Oh, I don't hold it against Him by the way!"

Karimov, who had previously hated the fanciful polar landscape, took to driving into the countryside, bowling along the bumpy roads, the fire breaks and the stony tundra wastes that lay in bald patches beyond the forest. The chauffeur was used to not asking questions and, unruffled, he kept his eyes on the road. Karimov, however, made fun of himself for still hoping to come across Savely Savage, seeking refuge in the forest from prison and the reprisals of the gang.

He didn't know what he would do if he did find Savage, what he would say to him or why but he couldn't get away from an obsession that had driven out his crazy preoccupation with random killings. Karimov couldn't forget the night he failed to shoot the drunken woman. He was humiliatingly aware of his own weakness and wanted to look into the eyes of the little man who had stood firm and pulled the trigger. He couldn't see any difference between himself and Savage. He didn't regard the murder of an innocent person as a crime and the murder of a gangster as a just punishment. He regarded all murders as murder and all deaths as death.

Karimov despised the residents of the town who for so many years had put up with the omnipotence of the gangsters, a venal police force, thieving civil servants and dishonest deputies and not spoken out against them. Flicking through reports, he remembered the years when no wages were paid at the factory and everyone in town had slaved away for food that was allocated by coupon. Not knowing where to put the money, the previous director had spent it abroad and rarely appeared in the town. Karimov, with a fastidious shudder, recalled the workers bowing when they encountered his motorcade in town.

But Savely Savage was made of different stuff and Karimov felt they would have something to talk about if he could only find him before the gangsters did. Karimov was a fatalist through and through and believed that if something was foreordained it would come to pass even if it defied common sense and he continued to cruise the forest roads, certain that he would come across Savely Savage sooner or later. If, of course, it was meant to happen.

The phone card cracked. Savage pushed the broken piece into the voracious payphone but couldn't make his call. He thumped the phone with all his strength and it rattled like a money-box full of coins.

Savely had been ringing his daughter to stop himself losing his mind. Her thin voice was the one remaining thread connecting him to the past. Vasilisa seemed to realize who it was saying nothing at the other end. Her voice would get softer and more playful the way it did when she was little and was asking for a new doll and Savage thought affectionately about his daughter and forgave her everything. Listening to the silence at the other end of the phone, Vasilisa longed to shout at her father, to say horrible things to him and then tell him how awful she felt and how frightened that each new day seemed like the night to her. And so they said nothing, neither wanting to put the phone down first. Afterwards, Vasilisa would lock herself in the bathroom and spend a long time crying, unable to answer her own question as to whether she wanted her father to come home or never to come home at all.

Now the card had broken and the last thread had been snapped. Savage was no longer able to listen to his daughter's voice and he felt as though he were turning into a wild beast, that his skin was covered in bristles and his curved, yellow nails were turning into talons. Like a rabid dog, he might leap at anyone's throat.

He hung around the town rubbish tip looking for the red-haired woman but she didn't turn up. Savage looked for the rest of the tramps. He wandered between the piles of rubbish and, clambering onto the highest mound, he yelled: "Hell-o-o-o! Hell-o-o-o!" Then he fell back on to the stinking heap and laughed. There was no answer. Only the stray dogs growled, giving him a wide birth.

One evening he finally spotted the smoke of a fire in the distance. When he went closer, Savage could see the tramps warming themselves around it. They were baking potatoes on sticks dangled over the fire like fishing rods. Savage was looking for a fight to let off steam and waited for the tramps to attack him and tear him to pieces. Looking at his fierce, crooked face, they moved aside, making room for him by the fire. Someone stuck a potato in his hand and his hairy neighbour, enveloped in a woman's shawl that was full of holes, offered him a plastic bottle of neat alcohol as if welcoming him into a brotherhood. Taking a gulp, Savage looked over the people seated around the fire. Like the grey rats that scuttled around the tip, they all looked the same. Sniffing, they turned their heads from side to side and there was nothing reflected in their small, red eyes but rage against the whole world. A couple of steps away, a man and woman lay together in a pile of rags. They were unembarrassed by the others present and their coupling was as desperate and as primitive as their lives.

Savage imagined he could become king of the tramps, kingpin of the rubbish tip, imposing his laws on the homeless and ordering them about like slaves. They would bring him the best scraps and surrender the best women to him and the female tramps would give birth to his children so that before long all the little vagrants would look like Savely Savage. After a second swallow, the idea no longer seemed crazy and after a third he started to like it.

The red-haired woman came over to the fire. She sat next to Savely, flopping against his shoulder like a rag doll and he was as pleased to see her as a sweetheart.

"Life's hard," said Savage, staring into the fire.

She laughed, scratching.

"Dying isn't," chimed in an old chap sitting nearby and Savage nodded in agreement.

The tramps kept a close watch on their bonfire, stamping out tongues of flame that threatened to leap onto the sprawling rubbish, but on this occasion they didn't watch closely enough and smoke suddenly filled the air. In an attempt to put out the fire, they began to pile rubbish onto it but the fire only raged more strongly and they scattered. Savage leapt up, throwing his potato away and the woman grabbed his hand to help herself up. Savely pushed her away instinctively and fled, his hands covering his face.

Later he came to his senses and went back to where the fire had been raging to collect the red-haired woman. Pungent smoke stung his eyes and filled his throat like cotton wool. Savage couldn't find the woman in the haze of smoke. He crawled along the ground, feeling with his hands like a blind man, but the woman wasn't there. He stumbled across two prostrate bodies in the smoke but could tell they were men from their whiskery faces. Savage felt he was about to faint and fled into the forest, hoping the woman had managed to escape the flames on her own. The wail of sirens could already be heard in the distance. Fire engines were speeding towards the tip and the vagrants were hurrying to get away before they arrived.

Lapin was emboldened by the feeling that the mayor had his back. When he was summoned to his superior's office he strode down the corridor, his boots stamping so loudly it seemed as though he wanted the prosecutor to hear him from a distance.

"Captain Lapin," said his superior, donning his official smile. "Any progress? Is it a case of no case without Savage?"

"I'm going through all the options…"

"Ah, yes, the options." The prosecutor nodded sympathetically. "You're not getting carried away, are you? After all, the killing took place in front of so many witnesses. Bystanders, the late Antonov, Savage's daughter. You can hardly suspect them of aiding and abetting."

"Even so, I'm going through all the options," said Lapin, shifting from one leg to the other.

"Do you want to pin the murder on Saam?" the prosecutor asked, rubbing his temples. "That's stupid. And if you are so keen on him, tackle his other crimes. The gang keep us busy."

When Lapin demurred, the prosecutor cleared his throat and said, "I've been talking to our boss. Local government thinks highly of you…" He screwed up his face as if it hurt him to say the words. "I see a dazzling career ahead of you if you want it!"

Lapin, mopping his damp brow, made a dash for his own office. On the way, he couldn't resist dropping in on the senior investigator who had been his mentor.

"How's things?" Lapin asked, putting his head round the door.

"Okay," the surprised response came. "Why?"

But Lapin had already rushed off, muttering under his breath.

The abandoned workers' settlement clung to the town like a baby to its mother but the forest advanced ingesting the deserted streets and houses. Slender young trees were pushing through the cracked and buckled asphalt. Moss had grown all over the walls and roads and birch trees peeped out of the windows like curtain twitchers. Over the years, the furniture left behind in the houses had grown damp and it was enough just to touch, say, a chest of drawers for it to fall apart on the spot. All around lay old photographs, books and the open maws of empty suitcases. "Buy greens. Ring S." Savage read on a damp-eroded note, left on a table. Where was the person who wrote it? Did he ever buy any greens? Did he ever ring someone called S.?

The settlement had its own tourist attraction. Local drunks took the rare tourists who showed up, their enormous rucksacks sticking up over their heads and looking, from a distance, like children sitting on their shoulders, to a flooded mine. It was haunted. The settlement, built thirty years before, had been home to many miners and their families but one stroke of the pen had shut it down, boosting the list of dead settlements that were starting to outnumber living ones in the area. The mine's director had aged ten years when he found out that the mine was about to be flooded. His eyes, widened in horror, were as black and empty as two mine shafts. When the water was turned on, the director disappeared. He didn't come back the next day or a week later and, scratching her face, his wife rushed to the pit, sobbing and calling her husband's name.

For a bottle of vodka, the drunks would tell the tourists how at night the director would emerge from the mine, take people by the hand and drag them towards him. The tourists wrote in their notebooks that he once drowned a young boy by grabbing his leg. True, the wizened old crones ticked them off, yelling out that the boy had been dead drunk and had fallen down the mine himself but the tourists didn't believe them and looked superstitiously askance at the fearsome spot.

The village started to empty once the mine had closed but not everyone left. Some wanted to die where they had lived. Others had nowhere to go. All they could do was drink themselves to death, competing to see who would live longest.

"I'm not coming to your funeral!" one old man shouted out of the window, shaking his fist at a neighbour.

"And I'm not coming to yours!" came the retort.

They died on the same day, poisoned by industrial spirit procured from some passing soldiers so they were both true to their word.

The shops closed and once a week Antonov would send in a bus-load of out-of-date food that people bought initially but then began to swap for other things. When the things ran out, the bus stopped coming, leaving the residents on their own against the taiga.

The settlement's last resident was the director's wife. Every day she went to the mine and sat on a cold moss-covered stone running cherry-stone beads through her fingers. She would talk to her dead husband, reproaching him for leaving her alone so soon. Then she would sob and, on going closer, you could pick out swear words amidst the muttering. Weeping, the woman prayed for the suicide with whom she had hoped to spend her afterlife but on one occasion her husband appeared to her in a dream in the form of a devil and after saying three Our Fathers she set out on foot for the town, dragging a battered suitcase along the ground and looking over her shoulder as if she were afraid that her husband was in hot pursuit, pointing the end of his tail like a finger. In the church, she was gathered up by Antonov's wife who gave her a job as a servant and the settlement sank into a deathly hush that was now broken by Savage, shattering the silence with a shout:

"Is there anybody there?"

"Anybody there…" replied the echo, drowning in the flooded pit.

Savage went round the houses and, despite all he'd seen in his wanderings, he felt suddenly ill at ease. It seemed as though the settlement only looked empty, that its residents, whether dead or departed for the town, were sitting inside, watching Savage roam the streets from their windows and grinning wickedly as he went through their things. He imagined that no-one went anywhere after death. They stayed put, living where they used to live and, sooner or later, every flat became a communal one, packed like a piggy bank full of change, with its residents, the living and the dead.

Hunger, clenching his stomach into a fist, painted crazy pictures in Savage's head. He felt dizzy and imagined there were people around every corner. Trying to escape from his persistent delirium, he hastened to leave the settlement, looking over his shoulder as if afraid that some unseen residents were wagging their fingers behind his back, sniggering around the corners, like devils.

"Nobody needs anybody," muttered Karimov, flicking through the telephone book and wondering why he needed an expensive, designer phone if there was no-one to ring. He had long ceased to see faces behind the names entered in a neat, even hand but only their bank accounts, crossing off the ones who had no money left.

His scheme was a simple one: to take the factory away from Pipe by buying up shares, turning his place of exile into his property and ridding himself of Pipe forever by severing the ties between them. He found an investor who smacked his lips in delight when he looked through the papers and the deal was done. Karimov himself rang round the shareholders, starting the conversation with meaningless small talk. The person he was speaking to felt as though Karimov's wheedling tones were sliding down his throat like a probe to examine him from the inside. Once he knew the listener would accept his terms and not reveal the scheme to anyone else too soon, Karimov named his price.

"Nobody needs anybody," he thought, rubbing his hands as he drew up yet another contract.

One of his foster father's friends had been known as a good family man. He spent his weekends with his wife and children and once a week dropped in on a young mistress who had wound herself around him like ivy. He was fond of a drink and of riotous parties with friends bringing other friends and ear-splitting laughter. Once, as he passed the cemetery where the crosses leaned companionably towards one another, he pictured his friends and relatives gathered at his funeral. His wife would sob as she hugged their children while his mistress, face hidden under a wide-brimmed black hat, crept stealthily up to the coffin and kissed his cold lips. He felt his eyes fill and looked away in embarrassment so that his driver didn't notice. At that point, he came up with the idea of staging his own death to fulfil a childhood dream of seeing how his loved ones would mourn him. He didn't go home that day. Instead, he hid in a hotel out of town and his minions presented his wife with the burnt-out wreckage of his car along with their condolences.

He hired a car and, sporting shades that hid half his face, he went from his office to his house and from the restaurant preparing the funeral feast to the morgue, observing his family. His wife spent a whole day going round the shops to pick out her widow's weeds and decided that black was definitely her colour. The children did what they always did and met up with friends. In the evening, the father watched them through the café window mixing martinis and whiskey and discussing a soccer match. The funeral was as dull as the tenth repeat of a show in which every line was familiar. His friends and sidekicks delivered short speeches with one eye on the time, gazing mournfully at the closed coffin. His wife didn't cry and his children, shifting from foot to foot, fidgeted with their lavish bouquets while his mistress didn't show up at all. The mourners heaved a sigh of relief when the coffin was lowered into the grave, which cut the man hiding behind the trees to the quick. When his wife got home from the funeral feast, flushed from the wine, she found the husband she thought she had buried earlier in the day, hanged in the bathroom.

"Nobody needs anybody," Karimov reiterated, recalling the would-be prankster's second funeral which was even duller than the first.

The phone rang.

"I've been hearing the bodies haven't even got time to grow cold up there in your Chicago of the Arctic Circle..."

Karimov cringed and thought that even the grinding of teeth sounded pleasanter than that voice. He imagined Pipe putting the electronic device to the hole in his throat and soundlessly moving his lips, his unlit pipe between his teeth, his useless tongue, flapping in his mouth like a fish.

"Have you got anything to do with it?" asked Pipe after a pause. "Have you got your hands dirty?"

"Local business. I keep out of it. First, some crazy guy shot the local gang leader, then the infighting started. So, things are pretty hot around here."

They both uttered senseless phrases, a completely different meaning showing through.

"God fashioned man out of clay but I made you out of shit and I gave you a name, money and power!" was what Karimov heard during the pause. "And you bit the hand that fed you!"

"You can win everything by force except love," Karimov told himself by way of justification, wiping his bristly, dimpled chin.

"I love a good settling of scores. There's less work for the cops," said Pipe, breaking the silence. "But that's not why I'm ringing. People want to play us off against one another…"

"As if they could," said Karimov, interrupting.

Pipe pretended he hadn't heard.

"People are telling me you're planning a mutiny. That you want to take over the factory…"

"Rubbish! How? A factory isn't a wallet. You can't just grab it and stuff it in a pocket…"

The dialling tone was the only response.

The old man never said hello or goodbye. He would break off a conversation mid-word by replacing the receiver, get up from the table without taking leave of his guests and never stayed the night with a woman, his trousers already half-on as she fell back onto the pillows. Karimov had often tried to beat Pipe by ringing off first or pushing back his chair and leaving a meal before dessert but the old man was always a fraction of a second ahead. Just as he was getting ready to leave, Karimov would see his hunched and already departing back. He once thought of leaving as soon as Pipe arrived. He waited in their usual restaurant, drumming the funeral march on the arm of his chair. He picked a table by the window and had drunk a cup of coffee when he heard a knock on the glass. Wagging his

131

finger at Karimov as if he were a naughty child, Pipe walked past, laughing.

Karimov looked at the telephone and decided it was time to be rid of his bothersome guardian.

Out where the ground was frozen and cold even in the summer, the taiga merged into tundra. The slender trees with their fantastically twisted trunks were smaller than the gigantic boulders. The tundra stretched for miles, blending into the swollen clouds on the horizon, and the sky seemed low enough to reach out and touch. Savage wandered among the dwarf trees like Gulliver in Lilliput and, looking around in fright, he began to stoop even more as if he wanted to be more on their level. In the taiga, severe and louring as a strict mother, he hadn't felt lonely among the laughing rivers, whispering trees and cackling wading birds. Here, though, it was so quiet that Savage suddenly wanted to shout out loud so that he could be heard on the other side of the tundra and, crossing himself superstitiously, he went back the way he had come.

Savage had been the master of his fate only in his dreams where he reworked his life over and over like a rough draft. It was like role play: he created stage sets and costumes, one minute trying out the role of a mover and shaker, the next going back to his own childhood. "What's hotter: the flame of a candle in our imagination or the cold drops of wax on the candle holder?" he thought by way of consolation. He tried to persuade himself that all those around him were circumscribed by their own fates, had come to terms with it and were living their lives as though asleep, to see the dull and dismal dream through to the end. Now he realized that you were only aware of blood if it was in your mouth and that blood shed by someone else [another] was like red paint in a film.

Soil samples left behind by geologists looked like shallow graves. Water had collected in the abandoned quarry. Its walls glittered with mica in the sun, driving the crows crazy. The ground had been trampled all around. The soft grey earth bore the wounds of vehicle tracks and the mounds at the bottom of the quarry brought to mind a cemetery without crosses. It was here that Saam had organized the bloodbath liquidating those he suspected of betraying him.

Savage was sitting on the edge of the quarry, legs dangling. He was dizzy with hunger but wasn't afraid of falling in.

"I'm not a person any more, I'm a wild animal. My life's like an animal's, my feelings are like an animal's. Have you got that?"

"Got that, got that…"

"A wild animal should be in a cage. Once it gets out, you won't get it back in, ever…"

"Ever, ever…"

Savage buried his face in his hands and the echo took up his sobs.

When no-one was using the bathhouse, the only people there were the attendant and Salmon, disfigured and hiding away from prying eyes in the back rooms. Saam had brought her here with an order to watch her day and night. The girl knew so much that she should have been got rid of long since but Saam didn't lift a finger. Coffin hated Salmon and when the Big Man put in an appearance at the bathhouse, the girl hid in the forest. Some people said that Coffin had doused her in petrol and tried to burn her alive, others that she had put her head in the stove and stupidly switched it on. One half of her face had been so badly burnt that when he saw Salmon the tubby attendant lost his appetite. There was a wan smile on her lips and her eyes were so sad that looking into them made you want to cry for nothing. But people tried not to look at Salmon, shrinking away from her face that looked like a scorched pie crust.

Once, when he went quietly into the steam room, the attendant happened to overhear a conversation.

"Just let her die in peace!" Saam yelled. "She hasn't got long!"

"Do you want her to take us with her?" asked Coffin. "If they get a whiff of her being here, they'll put the frighteners on her and she'll be delighted to rat on all of us! Can't you tell times have changed? If they can find something they can get their teeth into, they'll get rid of the lot of us."

When Coffin was shot, Salmon laughed all day long as if she'd gone mad and then wept all night long so that the girls spending the night at the bathhouse drove her off into the forest and she howled outside like the north wind. Since then, though, her disfigured face had never lost its smile as if Coffin had taken her sorrow with him when he died.

Steam rose from the kebabs that were cooking outside, the tubby attendant fussing over them. The girls, wrapped up in towels in the arbour, whiled away the time discussing TV serials, celebrity gossip and clothes. Previously, girls were brought in from the fishing villages where a net-load of fish and a night with a girl cost the same, and it was possible, by arrangement, just to buy the fish and have the girl thrown in on top. The girls had rosy cheeks, plump calves, and heels as hard as pumice stone but they laughed so loudly and infectiously that Trebenko loved going to the bathhouse just to hear them laugh.

"You're decent, hard-working girls," he would say, gathering them in his arms. "You should be getting married!"

The village girls, like fish, went off quickly. Their teeth fell out, their cheeks withered and their eyes became as colourless and woebegone as a pike's. The gangsters loaded them into a car and took them home and brought back fresh new giggly girls who struggled in an embrace like a herring on a hook.

When Karimov saw the solid, country cut of these girls, he pushed the fleshy creature snuggling up to him away in disgust and demanded that prostitutes from town should be brought in when he was due to visit. The village girls were replaced with girls from town, who were tempted by offers of clothes and money and brought in straight from the Three Lemons.

134

Karimov and the mayor were sitting in the steam room. Krotov, with a frown, was stripping leaves from the birch twigs like telling fortunes with daisy petals.

"Will they? Won't they kill someone?" grinned Karimov, splashing water onto the stove. "Once upon a time, there were three fat men. Then there was only one…"

"God only knows," said the mayor, shaking his head. "It used to be a quiet little place, people just got on with their lives."

"You can't hide anything in a hole like this!"

The mayor sighed heavily, pouring with sweat. The latest edition of the local paper had carried a photo of the town festival. Trebenko, Antonov and Krotov, the Three Fat Men as they were called behind their backs, could just about be squeezed into the frame. It occurred to Krotov that in old photographs he was more and more often surrounded by the dead and cold air wafted from the snap. The mayor carefully cut himself out of the picture, superstitiously touched wood, spat over his shoulder, and crossed himself. Deciding that even that wasn't enough, he went off to church and lit a fat candle at the altar.

"Have you talked to Saam?" asked Karimov, splashing on more water to increase the steam.

"He swears he doesn't know. So who does? A gangster's a gangster. Trebenko was the only one who knew how to put pressure on him. I've got no influence over those guys. They've got their own bosses."

"I have heard you decided to get rid of him…"

Karimov scooped up more water.

"For goodness sake, stop making steam. It'll kill me," Krotov burst out. "It doesn't bother me. It's a small town but there's room for everyone. Recently though I've been getting calls: 'Deal with the gang. The town's turned into a den of thieves. Normal people are too scared to come here…' As if normal people would come all the way out here. Why on earth would they want to come here? Now I have to choose between the frying pan and the fire…"

"What do you mean?"

"Between being fired by the bandits and being fired by the bosses."

"Not much of a choice," Karimov laughed.

He was only half-listening to the mayor. He was thinking about Savely Savage who had vanished in the taiga. It seemed to Karimov that Savage hadn't only killed Coffin. Lying awake at night, he imagined Savage dispatching Trebenko and Antonov and felt fear creep under the covers. When he looked at Savage's photo, taken from his personal file, however, Karimov understood that the timid individual with eyes like cups of clear broth lacked the stature of a calculating criminal, capable of premeditated murder. And yet Savage had managed to do what Karimov couldn't do: he had pulled the trigger.

"He pulled the trigger," Karimov said, out loud this time.

"Who did?" asked Krotov, puzzled.

"Savage."

"Oh, him… What do you think? Have they got rid of him?"

Karimov's shrug was non-committal.

"They must have done." The mayor provided his own answer. "Our guys don't like to mess around. God, I'm so sick of them! Bloody mobsters – can't sort their issues out in a civilized fashion."

"What do you mean civilized?"

"What? Through the courts!" said the mayor helplessly.

Karimov guffawed.

"There's a clash of opinion between you and them. They prefer crime without punishment. You prefer punishment without crime."

"Enough of the slogans, if you don't mind," said Krotov, pulling a face.

The men left the steam room. Savage watched them from the forest. He saw Karimov shed his towel, take a flying leap and flop into the water. The cold drops made the girls shriek. Savage had been training at the tip and had gone through a whole box of cartridges but he wasn't a particularly good shot.

He squinted and took aim at Krotov who was lowering himself cautiously into the lake and testing the bottom with his foot before going any further. Savage's hands shook with tension and he lowered the gun. Crossing himself, he came out onto the shore.

Salmon, a tray in her hands, was first to spot him. She froze. The girl turned to the bodyguards but they were downing cans of beer, sprawled in the plastic chairs. They hadn't seen Savage.

He fired. He shoved in two cartridges with shaking hands. He shot once, twice. The girls shrieked and dashed for the shore. Loading the gun, Savage fired and missed again.

The bodyguards leapt onto the shore but Savage was too far away and they took off along the edge of the lake. Savage kept on shooting and the shots landed at random near Krotov without hitting him. Karimov dived, taking refuge under the water and Krotov, gasping for breath, beat his arms on the water like a goose with clipped wings.

The gun coughed as if clearing its throat. Savage patted his pockets but there were no more cartridges. He threw the shotgun away and disappeared among the trees. Shots whistled after him. The bullets injured tree trunks and branches but Savage was already long gone.

He ran towards a turbulent narrow river with a stony bank and boulders poking out of the water. The tops of the trees leaning over the river merged to form a tent. Savage decided to cross the river to avoid the dogs they would no doubt send after him. The lake separated him from the gangsters. They would have to go round it which gave him some time.

But someone was catching up. Breathless with running, Salmon was hot on his heels. When she saw the man with the gun, she ran towards him, recognizing Savely Savage who had shot Coffin. Now she was close behind, afraid of losing him. Savage couldn't understand who was following him. Was it a child? A little old woman? A small creature in a faded dress clung to him like a tick.

"Who are you?" Savage cried. "What do you want?"

"I'm on your side!"

The river of salvation glinted through the trees and Savage had a glimmer of hope that he could escape his pursuers.

"Get lost!"

He pushed Salmon away, the girl fell and cut her elbow.

"I'm on your side. Wait!" she cried, jumping up and racing after Savage.

The river was only knee-deep but the current threatened to knock them down. Salmon clung to Savage's shoulder and they both went over in the water, tumbled like pebbles in the river. Eventually, he grasped an overhanging birch tree. He grabbed Salmon by the hair and pulled her from the water like a kitten.

"Now, get lost!" he said, pushing the girl away again.

Salmon was having none of it. She hung onto his hand and wouldn't let him go and Savage didn't know how to get rid of her.

"I know you! You're Savely Savage!" she shouted, stumbling on the boggy hummocks. "Everyone knows you!"

Savage realized he wouldn't get far. He was worn out by his wanderings and hunger. He could barely stand and the girl was hanging on to him like a stone round the neck of a drowned body. Voices could be heard in the distance as he spotted a refuge under the roots of an old fir tree. They hid in this lair that was laced with black, resin-scented moss and froze, hoping the gangsters would miss them.

"One squeak and I kill you," croaked Savage, a hand over the girl's mouth.

Salmon nodded, sniffling. They were both chilled from the cold river and their trembling passed into the fir's dry branches. A shower of yellow needles fell. Savage clasped Salmon tightly. One minute he thought she was his daughter, the next the red-haired vagrant woman, or a rotten log, sticking painfully into his side, and he felt like sobbing out loud.

He could hear his pursuers: shouts, branches crunching under foot and the hoarse breathing of the bodyguards who were more afraid of him than he was of them.

The men went past, ears pricked and trembling at the slightest rustle.

"He's gone," said one with a shrug.

"Saam'll have our skins," said another, wiping his forehead, but he too was uncertain and also decided to go back to the bathhouse.

Savage and Salmon waited for the gangsters to disappear then emerged from their sanctuary.

The police were first to arrive in response to the shots.

"Did he manage to hit many people?" asked an officer without any preliminaries as he jumped out of the police car. His shirt buttons were fastened the wrong way and an empty holster flapped at his side.

"No, not really," said the attendant dismissively. "One girl got a bit of a scratch. She'll survive to get a husband."

Karimov, wrapped in a white robe, was smoking on a rock. His hooked hawk nose made him seem like a giant bird on its nest. The girls were fussing over the one who had been wounded, washing off the blood and bandaging her arm with the shreds of a nightie. As he walked past the table laid in the courtyard the officer took an apple, wiped it on his sleeve and bit into it eagerly. Suddenly, he stood stock-still. There on the shore, arms flung wide, lay Krotov, naked.

The officer threw the apple core away.

"What about him?" he asked, pointing at the mayor.

"Looks like his heart. He was going under. We dragged him out but he was a goner. I nearly dropped dead with fright myself when I heard the shots."

Smoke was rising from the neglected kebabs and a smell of burning hung in the air. The attendant kicked the barbecue over, scattering the burnt meat, and poured water on the charcoal from a crumpled plastic bottle.

"A good thing it was his heart," said the officer, opening his notebook. "That way, we're not involved."

The attendant lifted an eyebrow.

"There's always trouble with these high-ranking corpses. There are phone calls from Moscow every day as it is."

A car slammed on its brakes. Saam leapt out. The corner of his mouth twitched edgily as if he was laughing. His face and his thick neck were covered in red blotches and his Adam's apple jerked nervously. He bounced as he walked along, surrounded by his bodyguards. He shot mean looks in all directions, his damp hands hidden in his pockets so that no-one would suspect his terror. He had hurled the telephone away from him like a scorpion that had stung him when he heard that Savage had turned up at the bathhouse. Saam could sense that Savage was getting closer and closer to him, picking off everyone to whom he, Saam, was close.

The bathhouse attendant took refuge in the steam room pretending to be cleaning to keep out of Saam's way. He had seen Salmon run off into the forest. She still hadn't come back and the gangster had told him to keep her close, like the apple of his eye. Embarrassed by her ruined face, Salmon never went further than the lake and now she had disappeared and the attendant's knees were shaking so much that he was wondering whether to flee into the taiga himself.

"Look at that!" said Saam, walking around Krotov.

Obscenely fat, the mayor looked like a slab of dough slapped onto a chopping board. He evoked no pity even as a corpse. Saam took off his windcheater and threw it over the lower half of the body.

"You worried about his prostate?" drawled Karimov puffing out smoke rings.

"Worry about yourself," grinned Saam. "Death's catching."

Karimov laughed, nodding. He had already felt fate threatening him with a knife and wondered whether it would hit him in the back or in the chest. He looked with distaste at

Krotov's obese white body and a wave of dumb indifference swept over him. In a detached fashion, as though he were standing on the sidelines, he was afraid his own death would be just as dull and stupid, dealt him by a madman at the back of beyond, in a town where malice was blacker than the polar night and the people, like the stone idols worshipped by the Saami, stayed put, overgrown with moss. Karimov felt fatigue leaning on him like a drunken woman, and he had a strong wish to get out of this town where death was more frequent than conception.

"Offer a million as a reward!" Saam told his henchmen, dispelling his thoughts.

Karimov grinned and lit the next cigarette in his chain.

"Do you believe anyone's going to try and catch him? He's more likely to become a local hero."

Saam shook his head:

"Only the dead become heroes. The living hate the living. They hate him more than they hate you and me because we are the powers that be and he's just a little man, the same as them, and suddenly he's smashed through the barriers and become different. They'll never forgive him for that!"

The polar sun hung above the horizon at night as though nailed in place. Four hunters walked through the forest, gloomily clutching their guns. The dogs had picked up the trail and were barking hoarsely as they pulled on their leads. Their wet fur bristled as if every hair were on the alert, ready for the chase. The bog squelched under foot. The hunters' heavy tread left dents in the soft moss. The depressions immediately filled up with water and before the men vanished into the trees their traces had disappeared as if no-one had ever been there.

The hunters lived in old wooden houses that even the dogs avoided. The dilapidated, two-storey blocks, clustered on the edge of the forest were known as "stumpies". Each contained eight flats, the residents living as one big family, their doors never locked. Neighbours could tell the creaks of the cracked and pitted staircase apart, knowing that when the old one-eyed hunter was coming home the stairs moaned like a woman but when his drunken wife stole in they squealed like the whispers of tattle-tales.

There was a smell of rotten wood, dirty washing and a burnt stove. The flats had no bathrooms and people washed in huge tubs, pouring the water out into the street. In the winter time, dirty mounds appeared at the entrances, the children sailing down them with a shriek. The residents of the "stumpies" could be recognized by their shaggy faces and bent, stooping figures that were the legacy of their crooked houses. Many of them had dogs which they let in for the night and out again during the day so that animals formed a pack and went careering around the streets.

When there was a knock at the old hunter's door, his neighbours glued their ears to their doors, listening to what Saam would have to say.

"Take people and dogs and comb the forest. He doesn't appear to be armed."

"And when I find him?"

"You know what to do with him better than I do. I don't want to see him."

"How much do I get for his hide?"

The neighbours held their breath but no matter how they strained to hear, they couldn't make out Saam's answer.

Ropes were stretched across the entrance hall with children's tights, colourful blouses and sheets drying. His heavy boots stamping as if putting nails in a coffin, Saam went downstairs and the stairs sobbed under him like a young widow.

When the one-eyed hunter left in his camouflage gear, there were three people waiting for him in the yard.

"It's dangerous in the forest," said a thickset youth who lived on the same floor, adjusting the rifle slung over his shoulder.

142

"You're getting old for hunting. You won't manage on your own," agreed a neighbour from downstairs.

The third neighbour said nothing, working his jaws. He merely indicated the double-barrelled shotgun sticking out of his bag.

The old man looked them over with his one eye, grinned without giving them an answer and they all four set off for the forest.

The dog runs were out of town, set back from the road. They were home to the hunters' huskies, pining with boredom behind their netting. When Savage's daughter was a little girl, she would run there to feed the dogs. Vasilisa would wait until her father set off for work and her mother, after quickly making dinner, went to a friend's until late. Then, she would stuff her pockets full of bread and go off into the forest. She didn't wear a watch so she hid the alarm clock inside her top so as not to be late for her parents getting back. When they saw her, the dogs would hurl themselves barking at the netting and, uncertain about going closer, Vasilisa would toss them the bread which the dogs swallowed instantly with greedy yelps. As she went home, she picked blueberries and stamped on any inedible mushrooms because it seemed a shame just to leave them. At home, the little girl would put the alarm clock back on the shelf and dash into the bathroom to wash the blueberry stains off her lips. Once, however, when Vasilisa got home from her walk in the woods, her father was already warming up yesterday's soup on the stove and realized from his daughter's blue lips that she'd been off in the forest. Savage began to think his daughter was growing up to be like him, a solitary dreamer, getting on better with the forest and with dogs than with people. He hoped that when she grew up, they would have things to talk about. From then on, however, his wife never left the little girl by herself. She took her with her to the shops and to her friends'. Savage, seeing how quickly Vasilisa acquired her mother's mannerisms, began to regret he'd come home early that day.

Scenting the hunters, the dogs started rushing about and jumping on their hind legs as though they could see them through the trees. When the runs were open, they ran round in circles, making up for the time they'd been locked up.

The dogs picked up the scent near the baths and tore into the forest, duplicating the route taken by the fugitives. They sped into an impenetrable thicket, forcing their way through a thorn-bush, and sank into a bog hidden beneath a shaggy blanket of flowering moss. Wild rosemary made them snort as if they were uttering expletives. They appeared to have lost the trail. They turned circles on the spot in confusion but caught Savage's scent again and shot off, noses to the ground.

"What're you doing here?" the returning policemen called after them.

But the hunters didn't reply, keeping tight hold of their shotguns.

The scent, a mixture of sweat and fear, vanished at the river and the huntsmen resorted to guesswork. The one-eyed hunter examined broken branches and looked for tracks on the mossy ground, crushed berries or a torn-off flower. Hillocks rose above the forest like women's breasts and the hunters turned back more and more often, wanting to go home. They no longer believed they were going to find Savage. The dogs trotted along, tails down, forever dashing off after a squirrel or a polecat. The forest grew gloomier and the old man pressed his lips more tightly together, tensing like a racing dog at a fence. His own dog plodded along beside him as old and mean as his owner.

The town was so small the gang could hold it in their fist and for those who couldn't get along with them, there was always the forest. Then the one-eyed hunter would track down the runaways, setting his dog on people the way others set dogs on wild animals. He preferred dirty banknotes to fox skins and would store them in a secret hiding place under the floor.

"Why does Saam want to find him? Why doesn't he let

the cops deal with him?" asked the lanky hunter, bored and making conversation.

"Probably because the gang are scared he'll find them first!" said the other with a shrug.

"I'm not against him getting his comeuppance. Our lives were calm and quiet till he turned everything upside down! Coffin looked after the town. If you kept your head down, he didn't bother you. What was so wrong with that?"

"Better the gangsters' laws than no laws at all!" said the thickset youth in agreement, ending the conversation.

The tree tops entwined as they leaned towards one another like conspirators. The hunters began to feel the forest was creepy. As they watched the old man's back they were frightened he would turn round and run them through with his one eye. The thickset kid kept adjusting his gun and slowly started to fall behind as though he couldn't keep up with their leader. The gap between him and the others got wider and wider and once the old man was no longer visible through the thick fir trees bedecked with black moss, he ran back towards the town. The lanky youth dawdled alongside a spirit stone that rose up from the ground to the height of a man. The Saami believed it was a dead wizard who had turned to stone. When the last hunter saw he was the only one still with the old man, he made a break for it as well, running into the dagger points of protruding dry branches. As for the old man, he grinned and went on, never slowing his pace, and embracing his shotgun like his girlfriend. The one-eyed hunter could sense Savage nearby. It was as though he could feel Savage's hands shaking and the sweat of fear breaking out on his back.

In the morning, there were suddenly so many people in the forest that the whole town seemed to have turned out to pick berries. The townspeople were combing the forest in a never-ending chain. In their waterproof jackets and knee-high boots and armed with guns, rusty rakes and kitchen knives, some of them were angry, their faces furious, while others were having a good time, staring curiously around as if at a picnic.

"The mayor never did me any harm. I always voted for him," they told one another.

"And Trebenko was a decent chap too. His dacha's next to ours."

Karimov had declared a day off at the factory. He had bet Saam a sizeable amount that Savage wouldn't be found and now he was driving through the deserted town, keeping his eyes skinned. He thought he had plumbed the full depth of human foulness. Now, he realized with astonishment that it was unfathomable. "Truth is like glass," his foster father had taught him. "You can only see it when lies make it dirty." Even so, Karimov did not abandon his plan to meet Savage in order to look into his colourless eyes and ask whether he had seen his own death in the other deaths or whether every death, like every life, was different.

A helicopter hovered, a giant dragonfly, above the trees. The women had stayed by the cars which poked their noses through the edge of the forest. They were discussing Savage with so much cold curiosity he might well have been the hero of an evening soap opera. The women turned their heads in unison as though they shared a single neck and spoke in chorus, interrupting one another. Two men, their legs stretched out, sat leaning against a broad tree stump dark with moisture. One was unwrapping sandwiches, the other pouring tea from a flask and both were thinking about going home as they watched people walk past, mired up to their ankles in the swampy ground.

"Such is life! It makes even normal people go off their heads!"

"You think he's normal? They say he chopped Trebenko up and set the garage on fire so that no-one would see he'd carried off whole chunks of him ..." The man spread his arms wide to demonstrate the size of the chunks.

"So what? You think he's a cannibal?"

"Well, how do you think he's survived so long in the forest? He's been eating Trebenko!"

The deeper they went into the taiga, the more strained their expressions and the scarier the thoughts they kept to themselves like a gun under their coats while their conversions lodged in the mossy bog. Coming across one another in the depths of the forest, people tried to get away again as quickly as possible.

"Remember: Savage is highly dangerous. If you see anything suspicious, call for back-up. Do not try to catch the killer yourselves. It could make you the next victim!" they were instructed via a loudspeaker by a man in a red armband.

Several military vehicles were parked by an old wooden bridge that had collapsed into the river. The unit commander used them to transport fish, carrying it in the cabs so that the inside stank of rotten fish. A fat-faced officer with a crimson neck was lining his shaven-headed boys up along the road so that those at the head of the line couldn't see those at the other end. Every now and then, townspeople would appear on the road, holding a rake or spade out in front of them like a bayonet, but spotting the soldiers they retreated into the trees. The officer barked out his final instructions and the soldiers dashed into the forest, sinking in the swamp that clutched at their legs, preventing them from running.

Most people were too scared to go into the dark, bristling forest and kept to the roads that divided the taiga brakes, hoping Savely Savage would jump out under their wheels like a hare pursued by hounds, scurrying along paths picked at random.

Those who stayed behind in town were struck by the silence that set solid in the streets, so dense it seemed possible to reach out and touch it. Little boys ran between the houses, sticking mug shots of Savage on the walls and entry ways. Above his picture, just like in a western, an award had been daubed in heavy ink. Saam raised it to three million.

"In memory of Coffin…"

"How are you going to pay?" Karimov asked him.

"Do you think they want the money? A hundred thousand's more than their wildest imaginings but they want blood. There's a wild beast in everyone. It's just that it can't get out. Give it its head and the whole pack will turn on its own!"

Karimov turned away in disgust. Outside, steam was coming out of the factory chimneys. The hills stood like sentries around the town. "There's a gangster in everyone and a prison guard too," he thought. "And which you end up as depends on how the cards fall. Maybe you have to be both more than once in the course of a lifetime."

In a small town, destinies are sewn together like patchwork. It only needs one to be ripped off for the stitching of the others to come out. Investigator Lapin roamed the quiet, deserted streets, looking at the pictures of Savage on every corner. He had been taught that to get an answer it helped to ask the right question. Now, though, Lapin had the answer in his pocket but there wasn't a question and he was trying to find one in the dust of the road and the faces of the downcast passersby but it kept escaping from him like a criminal, vanishing around a corner. And yet the answer was written on every lamp-post and Lapin kept repeating it until it no longer made any sense.

"Savage, Savage," mumbled the investigator, shaking his head. "Savage, Savage, SavageSavageSavage..."

A bar was open in a corner of an old house with dirty, peeling plaster. The grey bricks showed beneath like underwear. The cramped bar, packed to the ceiling, hummed like a hive and men, red-faced from the fug, stood around tall tables, blowing froth from their fat-bellied glasses and shuffling their feet. The bar took Lapin back to his childhood. His father would come here on Sundays, leaving him at the door. He would hastily down half a litre in one go, shake hands with friends, then taking his son by the hand, he would leave, ducking out of the low doorway. He would then buy him a small bar of chocolate and his son promised not to say a word about the bar to his mother: to keep mum. He wouldn't have squealed anyway but the chocolate, like the glass of beer and the waiting by the door, were part of a ritual they observed for years until his father came home, beaten up, and cursing Coffin's gang.

Lapin moved towards a table where two workman with rough, dark faces exchanged placid invectives, seasoning their dispute with words as pungent as black pepper. One had lost his left eye and the other hid a crippled hand beneath the table. Lapin wondered whether they had been disfigured at the factory or in a drunken brawl.

"No, you ask him!" the one-eyed man said, issuing a challenge as he stared at Lapin with his single eye. "What's he say?"

"Exactly. What can he say?! It's a rotten generation," came the dismissive reply.

"Maybe he has an opinion about that, about it being rotten?"

"A rotten opinion," said his friend with another dismissive gesture.

Unable to resist, the one-eyed man himself leaned towards Lapin.

"So, tell us, what can an ordinary person do when the cops are for sale and the courts are corrupt?"

Embarrassed, Lapin blushed, took a tissue out of his pocket and set about wiping down the sticky table.

"Go on then," the one-eyed man insisted. "Does he have the right to take the law into his own hands?"

"Only if he's not doing something illegal," Lapin blurted out, unsure how to answer.

The men exchanged a look.

"I told you, it's a rotten generation!"

"What if they did away with your mother, dragged off your wife and burnt your house down and everyone was in the pocket of the guy who did it?" the one-eyed man went on. "And then you took him out?"

149

"That's what prison's for," replied Lapin, flushing more deeply still. "Otherwise what makes us better than gangsters?"

"When in Rome..." said the one-eyed man reaching for the nearest cliché.

"You can't fight killers by turning into one yourself or wipe out theft by stealing," Lapin stubbornly maintained. "The court's for sale because we buy it and gangsters rule the roost because we've agreed to live by their rules."

The men didn't answer, noses in their glasses. Their grim silence made Lapin uneasy and he left, without taking even a sip. He bought a chocolate bar from the stall. It fitted into the palm of his hand and, popping it in his mouth as he had as a child, he was sorry his father wasn't there with him to lift him up on his shoulders and tell him right from wrong and explain why his son's life was like an overcrowded tavern, where there were plenty of people but no-one to have a drink with.

The smoke of bonfires rose above the trees, and shouts and the barking of dogs were carried on the river, its waves the measure of its width. From his hill, Savage could see his pursuers in full view in the clearings among the trees. He could see the men stoking the flames and heating tins of food over fires, eating hastily and throwing the tins for the dogs to lick clean. Salmon smacked her lips, imagining the aroma of the stew.

The more ground they covered, the gloomier people became, hearing in the murmur of the leaves the rustle of the banknotes promised as a reward for Savage's capture. When they came across one another, they pulled their hats down and hastened to hide in the trees.

Squelching through the swamp, a stumpy runt of a man, blue with tattoos, was on Savage's trail. His eyelids were without lashes and his heart without pity, his face hidden in scars. The first time he went to prison it was for killing two people in a fight and the second was for throwing a drinking companion out of a window because he declined to go to the shop. The runt didn't even have a knife with him, relying on

150

fists as big as pumpkins. He had a torn-off mug shot of Savage in his pocket and would take it out in order to wind himself up still further. By nightfall he was already looking on Savage as the source of all evils, hating him more than the prison guard who had burnt his face with a cigarette butt.

The one-eyed old man was more vicious, however. He took pleasure in killing, delighting in his bloodstained victims the way other hunters delighted in animal hides. His dog pulled on its lead as if it could sense that the fugitive was close at hand and the old man's one eye roamed over the forest as if his stare might be the net to catch Savage.

The soldiers wandered off in the forest like a herd of goats and the fat-faced officer dashed this way and that, gathering up his boys like mushrooms. Their lips were stained blue by berries and their smiles broader than a forest track. The soldiers massaged their shaved necks, itchy with gnat bites, and roared with laughter, pointing at one another. Picked up on the wind their laughter swept through the forest rolling down into the dank ravines. The soldiers covered miles of taiga and emerged on the rocky shore of a lake, so calm and smooth it seemed as easy to walk on as solid ground. They cast off their clothes and plunged into cold water that took their breath away. Their officer, stretched out on the shore, drank liquor from a flask and hesitated over whether to push on or turn back. He thought back to how Antonov used to supply food that was past its sell-by date and spurned even by the dogs while Coffin had bought up their weapons. He even got it into his head to acquire a grenade-launcher and was barely talked out of it. The entire unit had only a few submachine guns and many soldiers went right through their military service without firing a single shot. They were sent to work on municipal projects or construction sites and treated as guest workers. The officer imagined himself in Savage's boots, shooting Coffin and strangling Antonov who choked on his own blood. Then he fled from his pursuers, the soldiers who had been put on his tail and the hunters with their dogs, who had oiled their guns as if they were chasing

151

a wild animal. He could see his picture, pasted on the walls of the houses and imagined being surrounded and making a break for the border. He swallowed and thought he ought to go back, assume the role of a military court and shoot the unit commander. Tossing his flask aside, he jumped to his feet, yelling at the soldiers to get their kit on while his imagination painted the shooting scene.

"Back to town! And be quick about it!" he shouted, striding along the shore and rounding up the soldiers. His heart was pounding like a time-bomb, primed to go off at any moment.

Meanwhile, Savage and Salmon ran through the forest, not looking back. They were both too weak to evade pursuit and made frequent halts, collapsing onto the wet grass to gather their strength.

The girl stroked Savely's matted hair telling him the gang was frightened of him. "They're more scared of you than of anyone else!"

The forest was getting darker and denser, damp rose from the swamps and their feet sank into the squelchy moss. Birds called balefully and the firs linked their wide branches as if joining hands. The branches scratched the fugitives' faces and hands and gripped their clothes, refusing to let go.

Salmon had caught cold and thrashed around in a fever, coughing. Savage tried to carry her but found even Salmon's tiny, jaded body as immoveable as a boulder. On several occasions, he attempted to abandon her. "They'll pick her up," he said, deceiving himself as the girl slept, curled up in a shelter hastily thrown together from fir branches. Hardly had he gone a couple of steps, however, than Salmon woke up and came rushing after him with a cry.

"Who are you? Where did you come from?" Savage asked but Salmon just shrugged as if she didn't know herself.

"I haven't always been like this," she said once, gazing into the mirror of the lake. "I was very beautiful once."

Savage climbed a tall pine, sticky with resin. He made his way up its thick, strong branches as if it were a ladder propped against the side of a house. From up in the tree, he tried to make out their pursuers but no bonfire smoke rose above the treetops and he decided the hunters had fallen behind or gone home.

"We seem to have escaped," he said as he climbed down.

"There's no escape from the gangsters," said Salmon, shaking her head. "No-one's got away from them yet."

Bilberries hung like droplets on the bushes. Crawling on all fours, the girl picked the berries with her lips and wiped her mouth with her sleeve. Savage remembered the red-haired tramp he had abandoned at the burning tip. He had no idea whether she had survived or died, suffocated by the acrid smoke.

"I'm a murderer," Savage whispered recalling how the woman clutched at his arm and he pushed her away to escape from the blaze.

Salmon understood what he said in her own way.

"Tell me how you killed Coffin," she asked for the umpteenth time. She curled up in a ball as she listened, like a small child being lulled to sleep by a children's story.

"I was coming home from work and Coffin and his mates were out on the veranda," he began, stroking Salmon's head. "When I was going past, Coffin shouted something at me but I couldn't make it out. The others laughed and pointed at me. I went over and slapped him across the face." Savage clenched his fist and showed how he had struck the gangster and the girl laughed and clapped.

"Then his second-in-command came out with a gun and I thought my time was up. But he came too close and I grabbed it by the barrel and pulled it out of his hands and shot Coffin!"

"You should've shot Saam too," Salmon said every time, pressing her lips together. "You should've shot him!"

To Savage, it seemed as if they were circling the town as

153

they wandered through the forest, the town drawing them to it like a giant magnet. He recognized stones and roots, imagined houses behind the trees, and they would take a different turn, getting more and more lost. Then, suddenly, emerging from the trees into a clearing, they came upon a reindeer herders' camp.

Several small houses, made of dark planks, nestled in the clearing, together with a couple of nomads' tents and a barn, towering above the ground on two long piles. Perfectly normal clothes, the kind sold in any shop in town, were hung out on lines to dry. Brightly coloured sweaters, jeans and tracksuit tops, spattered with English writing, made an odd contrast to the wooden houses and reindeer skins.

The men had left with the herd. An old Saami woman, wizened as a baked apple, had stayed at the camp, preparing food over a fire, and two Saami teenagers, humming as they crafted something from a reindeer pelt. Savage dashed towards the fire, snatching the food out of the old woman's hands. He greedily devoured the flatbread and dried fish and then, coming to his senses, thrust a chewed-up morsel into Salmon's toothless mouth. The old woman, pointing a gnarled finger, called out in her own language and a reindeer herder, his eyes narrow and his face as round as a plate, took an ornate reindeer-skin cloak from his shoulders and wrapped it round Salmon. The Saami showed no surprise at having guests, as if they had been expecting them for a long time.

Warily, Karimov gazed at his reflection until the dark window was slowly lowered. Looking at him was a yellowed old man with a broad, fleshy nose and colourless eyes. He was holding an electronic device to his throat and talking through it. His grating voice raised goose-bumps like the scrape of metal on glass.

"I decided to take a look at this place for myself..."

They talked through the car windows, the vehicles standing still in the middle of the road. A traffic jam developed

154

but no-one honked their horns and the drivers lit up cigarettes and patiently waited for them to finish their conversation.

"It's just a town like any other, nothing special," said Karimov with a shrug and a defiant look at the old man.

"You know me well," said Pipe slowly, emphasizing each word meaningfully. "But I know you better."

Karimov pursed his lips.

"Do you think I want to know whether you've managed to get the factory off me or not?" The old man kept licking his dried lips as his gaze bored into Karimov. "I know that anyway. I want to check whether I'm so old some snot-nosed kid can get the better of me."

With a gesture to the chauffeur, Pipe raised the window.

Karimov nervously drummed his nails on his teeth, trying to predict what the old man had come up with but lost himself in his conjectures. Pipe didn't make idle threats and was known for having a great many enemies, none of whom were still alive. Tugging the hair at his temples that was as silver as a winter forest, Karimov pondered the fact that the pitiless old man was not about to show him any mercy.

"What's it all about?" Karimov had once asked, watching Pipe concentrate on filling his pouch with tobacco. "Don't you ever wonder?"

"There are only two questions in life that ought to bother you," the old man laughed, "what to do and who's to blame."

"And what should we do?"

"Make money!" Pipe guffawed, shedding tobacco. "As for who's to blame? Anyone who hasn't got any!"

Remembering the self-satisfied laughter, Karimov winced as if he'd eaten a lemon and decided he needed to get Saam involved. He would find a quick and simple solution. Karimov imagined looking Pipe in his colourless eyes at the very last moment and saying with his hands round his throat, "So, what was it all about?" Karimov inhaled deeply and, releasing the smoke through his nostrils, asked the driver:

"What about you? What's your life about?"

155

The driver shrugged and turned the key in the ignition.

"That's something nobody knows and thank God for that," he said.

Seeing a raised eyebrow in the mirror, the driver turned round to explain: "Maybe I was born to drive you around and you were born for me to drive. Just think, somebody was born just to die of a cold at two days' old after passing the cold on to all the other newborns in the hospital. If you knew why you were here, you wouldn't want to go on living."

Karimov screwed up his face at this homespun philosophy, thinking, "However you live the end's the same."

Military vehicles drove by, tarpaulins thrown back and soldiers poking out of the trucks like mushrooms in a basket. The jowly officer was dozing in the cab, his forehead leaning on the window, and Karimov grinned at the fact that once again Savely Savage appeared to have escaped his pursuers.

Back at the unit, the officer sent the soldiers to their barracks, dived into his own tiny room, opened a full bottle with trembling hands, cleaned his boots, and went off to get a gun. It was dark in the metal-lined stock-room with the spy-hole in the door. Since the unit commander had sold off all the weapons, there'd been no guards on the stores and the officer was able to remove the one remaining submachine-gun from the open safe entirely unseen. But he couldn't find the cartridges. He threw the gun angrily at the wall and stormed out of the stock-room, slamming the door. In the kitchen, he grabbed the enormous knife the cook used to saw stale bread and, holding it out in front of him with both hands, he crept along the corridors, jumping at every sound. The unit commander wasn't in. The officer checked the storerooms, went round the barracks, the enormous knife frightening the soldiers as its blade flashed, bouncing sunbeams off the walls. He even looked into the shed where broken motorbikes and various clutter were kept but, failing to find the commander, he lost his temper and thrust the knife into the wooden wall of the barn, where it stayed and grew rusty.

That evening the officer looked in on the neighbour with

whom he decanted his wistfulness into glasses. The miner's face was so grey it was as if his skin were covered in ore dust from the quarry where he had worked all his life. They both drank more than usual and, creeping out onto the top of the stairs in the morning, the officer couldn't remember why he had been looking for the unit commander the previous day or why his soul was as dead and dusty as a quarry.

The visitor from Moscow created an uproar in the little town. He walked everywhere, peered inquisitively around corners, his bodyguard trotting after him and his car moving slowly along the street, the driver never taking his eyes off his boss.

"The doctors recommend walks in the fresh air," he said, greeting Karimov at the hotel.

"The environment's not good here," said Karimov, pointing at the smoking chimneys. "This town's bad for your health, some people even die here."

"Don't make promises you can't keep," said the old man, pulling a face. "And don't drop hints about something you can't say out loud!"

The hotel doorman, smoking on the steps and holding the door open for Pipe, listened in surprise to their conversation. It was as if they were speaking in code.

"It's a long time since I was a child," Karimov began.

"Some are born children and some are born old," said Pipe, interrupting. "The children never grow up and an old man will never be a child. And they'll never understand one another…"

The old man stuck his speaking device in his pocket to show that the conversation was over and, with a facetious bow, Karimov ran down the steps. Pipe watched him go waiting for him to turn round, but Karimov slammed the car door without looking back and the doorman felt his soul shrivel. Pursing his lips, the old man went into the hotel, leaving a tip, and the doorman, grinding out his cigarette butt with his heel, flicked through the banknotes without taking his hand out of his pocket.

157

Pipe was seen in several places at once. He popped up in various parts of town, elusive as a ghost. He stayed under an assumed name, producing a well-worn passport and the hotel administrator noted in astonishment that several passports flickered through the old man's hand. The gangsters tried to keep an eye on the suspicious guest but he slipped away from them like water through fingers.

"He's one of us," said one of the gangsters, chewing his lip. "He can sense when he's being tailed without even looking. I turned away for a split second and he vanished into thin air, along with his bodyguard and the car."

"He's a high-flier that one," said another, shaking his head and pointing upwards. "You don't want to cross him too often. He's got radar for eyes. He saw me on the street and looked at me as if he could see right through to my bones."

"What are you, some girl people are making eyes at?"

"He can see you miles away. He's a scary guy!"

Listening to them chatter, Saam rubbed his temples, trying to fit together the murders, Savage running away, Severina disappearing and the arrival in town of the strange old man.

"How can there be any link?" asked his sidekick doubtfully. "The old man's one thing, the girl's another."

But a bad feeling tormented Saam, making his feet itch and his eyes water.

"Troubles never come singly," the gangster ground out. "If one comes along, you can expect more to follow. And when there's stuff like this going on," he said, using his hands to show what he meant, "not even the rain comes down just like that and the sun's got an ulterior motive."

Shrugging their shoulders, the gang stared at the toes of their boots, examining the dirt they'd picked up, but Saam went on:

"That old man hasn't just turned up. Don't take your eyes off him!"

Pipe hung around the police station, frowning at the officers darting about. He started up conversations with the locals and spent time in the library, leafing through a binder of local newspapers.

"Did you know this Savely Savage?" he asked the librarian, pointing to a picture of Savage on a two-page spread.

"Who doesn't?" she said with a gesture. "His photo's pasted up all over town."

"Not like that," the old man said, impatient and dismissive. "Did you know him before all this?"

"Of course," said a skinny young woman coming out from behind a stack of books. "He was in here a lot. A quiet type, shy, not someone you'd notice."

"What did he use to read?" inquired the Pipe.

"A bit of everything – literary magazines, popular science. Sometimes he asked for reference books. He took crime fiction out a couple of times but soon brought it back. He said it was boring."

Pipe went to the Three Lemons, spending the day out on the veranda where Coffin was killed. He sat in Coffin's chair, which had been empty since that evening. No-one, not even Saam, could bring himself to take Coffin's seat. As a result, the bouncer at the bar squinted suspiciously at the visitor and passersby looked round in fright as if they'd seen a ghost downing freshly squeezed juice.

Pipe inspected the area, taking particular interest in the windows that looked out on the square. He copied the witness statements that had appeared in the local press down in a notebook and checked his notes by questioning passersby.

"Lovely weather," said Pipe to a woman crossing the square, tipping his hat.

"Isn't it?" she said, shuddering at the mechanical voice and embarrassed as she looked at the overcast, grey sky.

"Such a pleasant, homely little town and such terrible things going on," the old man said, beginning at one remove. "I mean the gangster who was shot..." he explained in response to a puzzled stare.

"Oh, him... Yes, we're all in shock!"

"Do you think Savely Savage shot him?"

"Who else could it be?" the woman said in surprise. "Everyone knows he... Have you heard something different?" she wondered but the old man observed a meaningful silence and didn't answer.

With a smirk, Pipe looked at the gangsters who were keeping their distance, occasionally glancing his way. They were as alike as twins with their shaved necks, the leather jackets they wore in all weather and their eyes sharp as shivs, kept hidden behind shades. But Pipe's glance also cut like a knife so that the gangsters turned up their collars and shrank from sudden fear that made their armpits prickle.

"What is public opinion?" Pipe asked one gangster, grabbing him by the arm as if he'd caught him red-handed.

The gangster had been keeping watch on him outside the Three Lemons and was so taken aback he merely shrugged.

"It's what they say on TV! But what about the opinion of the individual?"

"Erm..."

"That's what they say on TV too!" Pipe said again pointedly and raised a finger. "Or at least write on the front page of the local rag!"

"He said people have more faith in the TV than in their own eyes!" the gangster said when he relayed his conversation with Pipe to Saam. "That, he said, is the miracle of technology!"

"What did you say?" asked Saam, picking at his teeth with a matchstick.

"Me? I said, sure it's a miracle..."

"What did he say?"

"Nothing. He hid his speaking device in his jacket and went off."

"What did you do?"

"I went after him. Saw him as far as the hotel."

Saam flicked the matchstick into the bin, turning the conversation with the old man over in his mind. He couldn't get his head round what the strange utterances might conceal.

It seemed as if the old man were offering a coded message. Saam played with the words and moved them around. He clicked the remote to try and find an answer on the TV and leafed through the latest newspapers, full of dull news and bureaucratic reports, but he couldn't solve the puzzle. In the end he became convinced the old man was making fun of him and there was no sense at all in what he was saying.

Karimov could feel the Arctic Circle tightening like a noose around his neck. He could see Pipe inquiring about Savely Savage, hanging around on the veranda and striking up acquaintances with everyone who was connected, one way or another, to the recent killings but he couldn't understand exactly how the old man hoped to make use of Savage. It even occurred to him Pipe would try and use Savage as a weapon, directing his hatred at Karimov. But to start with, he'd have to find Savage and that had proved impossible for the police, the gangsters, and the hunters.

"There was an old man in here," he said, leaning towards the young librarian, bored with her glossy magazine. "What did he want to know? Did he read anything?"

Karimov knew women liked him and he bestowed one of the smiles he kept for special occasions on the librarian. Casting an eye at the mirror, however, he saw the smile hanging from the corners of his mouth like a torn curtain. Turning a page, the woman scanned the headlines.

"He read the papers and asked about the murders. He's probably a journalist," she said with a yawn, covering her mouth with the magazine.

"Luck is like love: once it's gone, it won't come back," his foster father taught him, carving his simple truths on his heart like a knife shaping a wooden balustrade. "One door closes, another opens," joked Karimov. "Luck is like love," his father repeated, more loudly. "It happens for the first time, it just happens, and it happens for the last time!"

Karimov tried to talk to Saam who had set spies on

Pipe but the gangster had too keen a nose: he could smell putrefaction on someone who would die soon and money on someone about to have a lucky break. He shied away from Karimov like a vampire from garlic and, sensing that Karimov was going out of the game, he began to keep away from him.

Documents arrived from Moscow stating that Karimov now had a controlling interest but the news made him as black as thunder, aware that victory over Pipe would cost him dear. He regretted his haste and felt the ground shift beneath him like ice on a river in spring. At one point, he decided to run away and at night, tossing in bed, he tried to pick a country the vengeful old man would never be able to reach. In the morning, however, exhausted from lack of sleep, he refused to run.

His foster father's words rang in his head: "Some people play with fate and play to lose, others enjoy the game. Still others meekly watch as fate lays their lives out like a game of patience. But fate's an inveterate cardsharp and cheats every time!" He remembered the steps outside the orphanage where his foster father found him, wrapped in his mother's frock, and thought that the trials he had escaped and the misfortunes avoided had not stayed in the past but were running after him like unborn children so that the orphan who had been adopted would always be an orphan and the killer who hadn't been able to kill would still be a killer.

Pipe only started a game if he had all the aces up his sleeve so he never lost. Karimov came across him more and more often with a rolled up picture of Savage sticking out of his pocket as if the old man were teasing him deliberately. They were alike in this. They both liked to wind their enemies around their little fingers and to lead fortune a merry dance. As a result, they understood one another without speaking, reading each other's thoughts from a look in the eye or a pair of pursed lips. Pacing his office, Karimov fumed as he went over Savely Savage's story in his head but he couldn't grasp what revenge the old man had devised.

He summoned the head of the security service who was so suspicious people said he switched bugs on in his wife's bedroom when he left home.

"No news about Savage?"

"Not a trace. It's as if the swamp had sucked him in," he answered, shaking his head and Karimov winced at his harsh glance.

"Any calls from Moscow? Shareholders, the board of directors?" he asked casually, thinking about the packet of shares he'd bought.

The man curled his lip and made a helpless gesture:

"It's as if they've forgotten all about us."

Foreboding made Karimov's chest hurt.

He ran into the visitor from Moscow at breakfast. The hotel was empty and they sat in different parts of the dining room, separated from one another by empty tables. When he saw the dark shadows under Karimov's eyes, the two-day stubble and the nervous movements of his Adam's apple, Pipe shivered for a moment, feeling sorry for his ungrateful protégé. He had forgiven him so many times, smoothing his unruly curls with a rough hand, that he could forgive him as many times again.

The old man smiled, leaning back on his chair, and had Karimov looked up at him then, he would have known himself forgiven. Aware of Pipe looking at him, however, he kept his own eyes stubbornly on his plate, poking at his fish with a fork. The silence in the restaurant was so intense that the waitress threw open the windows to let in the fresh air. Fed up with waiting, the old man lost his temper and his grievances flooded back with renewed strength. His face flushed, he tore off the napkin, loosening his shirt collar, his mouth twisted. He'd been more malicious in the past and once he'd made up his mind was implacable, but he had aged now and loneliness tormented him like gout, twisting his joints. The old man shuddered and gave Karimov one last chance, looking at him the way people look at a foundling, hugging it to their breast. But Karimov hunched even more over his plate. Pipe got up and headed for the exit.

He met Saam on the veranda of the Three Lemons. The old man sat in Coffin's seat, which infuriated the gangster, but Pipe pretended he couldn't see his angrily narrowed lips and kept his eyes fixed on Saam.

"A killer shouldn't be small and pathetic. So other people don't get the idea that they can be killers too. And we really don't need avengers of the people. That's dangerous. Anarchy's not out on the streets, it's in people's heads!"

They were sitting by themselves like conspirators, surrounded by empty tables. Faded flowers drooped in plastic cups and sparrows hopped around their feet, pecking up crumbs of bread from the floor.

"People in small towns don't like change," the visitor said, nodding towards a huge election poster. The late Antonov beamed from under the slogan: This is our deputy! "Before long they'll believe it."

"What about the cops? The witnesses?"

Pipe held a small leather suitcase out to Saam. Bound packets protruded like ribs. The gangster wanted to open it and count the money but had second thoughts.

"That's for current costs. You get the rest when he's sent down."

"That's not our style. We're very straightforward here, nothing fancy."

The old man laughed and stuck his unlit pipe in his mouth.

"Putting a bullet in your rival's forehead is tacky. You don't get to see him suffer. Later you'll start to envy him. You'll be bent over with lumbago and immediately think: 'His sufferings are already over.' You look in the mirror and see a relic! Women look the other away, children are frightened. And you'll be remembered as an ugly old man as if that's all you'd ever been. Whereas he died young and will be young forever. You're still a novice but at my age you stop being scared of dying. Because you understand that nothing's more terrifying than life."

Saam's nose itched from this chatter. He couldn't get used to the old man silently moving his lips while what he said came from the device held to his throat. Saam wriggled on his chair, unable to make up his mind to agree yet scared not to.

The old man impatiently fingered the tie that snaked around his throat. Then he tapped the gangster on the hand:

"I'll tell you an amazing story that happened in the town of X a couple of months ago," he squeaked. "It was evening and people were going home from work. The streets were crowded. A gangster, Coffin, was sitting on the veranda of the Three Lemons with his pals." Pipe left a long pause after every sentence. "A car braked by the bar. Karimov got out. It's hard to remember what started the argument but Karimov and Coffin began making threats against one another..."

"So what did they argue about?" Lapin asked, reading through the statement.

"Seems to be about the protection money Coffin extorted from some of the workshops," said Saam with an enormous yawn. He didn't bother to put a hand over his mouth.

The office was dirty. Cigarette butts stank in the ashtray and the sun glinted off the walls. The investigator was sitting on the table with a thick telephone directory underneath Saam's statement, while the gangster slouched in front of him in the only chair, rocking back and forth as if it were a swing.

"Catching him lying is like trying to nail a sunbeam to the wall," Lapin thought.

"You can't have truth without lies. Like good and evil," said Saam as if reading his mind.

He'd come to see Lapin without ringing first, announcing on the doorstep that he wanted to make a clean breast of things. The investigator was so stunned he couldn't speak. When the gangster said it wasn't Savely Savage but Karimov who shot Coffin, intimidating Saam into saying it was Savage, Lapin felt

165

completely out of his depth. He couldn't tell what Saam was up to but he had a suspicion the gangster was playing it blind, wanting to make use of him by taking him for a ride as always.

"Why would Karimov pick a fight? He's not involved. He'll be removed the same way he was appointed – here one day, the other end of the country the next. Why would he quarrel with Coffin about the workforce?"

"Karimov's not like the managers before him. He's stubborn and arrogant. He's canny."

"You need more than that to kill someone."

"You don't need much to kill someone," said Saam pulling a face. "For Karimov the town's the town and the factory's the factory and our authority doesn't extend to its territory. People even say his problems started back in Moscow. Word got out about some scheme or other... He obviously decided he couldn't be doing with any complications. There was an inspection coming up."

It was as if the old man had materialized behind the investigator, with his electronic voice and spiteful chuckle, crumbling bread for the sparrows darting about under the table. Saam felt he was just moving his lips while Pipe provided the sound like a ventriloquist and his doll. Saam could tell that not once in his long life had Pipe ever lost. Not for nothing was Saam aware that, beneath the scent of expensive cologne, Karimov smelled of a damp, airless room, cold barley porridge and unwashed bodies. Saam trod cautiously through life like a cat on a windowsill. He never played against people who were always lucky so when he took the packed suitcase from the old man, he agreed to play by his rules.

Lapin reminded Saam of the penalty for perjury but the gangster shrugged and practically laughed in his face.

"But I'm here of my own accord."

The investigator didn't know what to think.

"So how did Karimov kill him?"

"Coffin said, 'Shoot me!'" said the bouncer from the bar.

166

"Why?" asked Lapin, shuffling his feet.

"How should I know what goes on in their heads?" The bouncer threw up his arms. "Maybe he was trying to be funny. Maybe he just thought he wouldn't shoot. Saam brought the gun out and everyone was laughing because they didn't think it was loaded. But Karimov checked and when he knew it wasn't empty, he went and fired."

The bouncer was one of the main witnesses. He'd been standing so close to Coffin that his trousers were spattered with blood. When Saam left, Lapin, confused by his version of the murder, immediately went to the Three Lemons. The investigator had a bad feeling and it didn't let him down. As soon as he started asking questions about the murder of Coffin, there was the bouncer, wringing his hands, and confessing to having lied when he gave his statement about Savely Savage. Lapin, however, didn't believe this hasty confession, blurted out by the bouncer as if he'd been carefully rehearsing his role.

"But you said something completely different before," Lapin said, showing the bouncer the record of his interview.

The man's shoulders drooped in poorly acted contrition:

"Yes, but you know how intimidating they can be. How many people have just vanished? And why? Because they said the wrong thing, or did the wrong thing, or looked in the wrong direction... We live in terror: the gang on one side and the big guys from Moscow on the other. And I have a family to feed. If you lose your job, you won't get another one."

Lapin believed the gang had got to Savage and settled their scores over the murder. Why had they decided to hang it on Karimov though? He suspected Saam wanted to blackmail the manager of the factory but he couldn't put the pieces of the mosaic together. There were fragments missing and now they had suddenly started to make a completely different picture. Lapin was losing sleep as he racked his brains over the puzzle.

"Then what happened, after Karimov fired?"

"He got in his car and drove off. They're not scared of

anything. They come here and think they can get away with anything! And we're like outsiders in our own homes!"

"So why did you give evidence against Savely Savage?"

The woman snivelled, wiping her face with a handkerchief. Lapin remembered this witness very well: she'd been hanging washing out on the balcony. She gave evidence as if she were recounting her favourite soap opera and her hands, unused to being idle, had either fiddled with her crumpled, stained skirt or adjusted her uncombed hair. Watching her fidget, Lapin lost the thread of the conversation. The woman liked thick soups and would throw in whatever came to hand and when she told a story she would season it with lead-ins and sayings tossed into the narrative like spices into a boiling pot.

"And could I really see who fired the shot when I was on the second floor? My eyes are bad as it is. I can't see anything beyond my nose."

"But you said you saw…"

There was a sour smell in the flat that made his gorge rise. From the corner a one-armed man, his spindly legs with their varicose veins dangling off the bed, fixed him with empty sockets.

"What else could I do? They made threats! 'Say it was Savage or we'll make short work of you!' I've got a daughter who's divorced, grandchildren, a husband who's worked all his life in the quarry and it's crippled him. He's worse than a child… Yes, I've sinned. I accused the wrong man!" she said and crossed herself in front of the paper icon hanging on the wall. "It surely can't be any worse in Hell than it is here."

Lapin shrank back, looking automatically over his shoulder.

"So who were those people?"

"Who knows? Scary ones. I even thought they were devils come to get me."

"Coffin's men?"

"Of course, not," the woman said, waving her arms.

168

"Definitely not. I know all the gangsters. They're from round here, they're our lads. No, those were from somewhere else but I can't remember their faces."

"Was Savage even there?"

"I clearly remember him getting into the fight. He was a round-shouldered little chap, not someone you'd notice, not much hair. I used to see him in the office at the factory sometimes. I think he worked there."

Biting his pencil Lapin looked at this new witness who had suddenly cropped up in the case. His head was spinning. The old witnesses had changed their statements, saying they had testified against Savage under duress and new witnesses were practically raining down.

"Why didn't you come to us straightaway?"

"I thought about it first. There were plenty of people without me. The square was crowded. 'What are things coming to?' I thought. 'Now the director will be going to prison!' But when I read in the paper that Savely Savage not Karimov had killed Coffin, I started to wonder if I was going crazy. I even told my wife I'd seen the director kill the gangster. She really lost the plot, screaming that I'd had too much to drink and just imagined it but I hadn't had a drop that night."

"So what, you can't believe your own eyes?"

"Who can?" said the witness. He smiled a cunning smile that showed off a gold tooth. "If everyone says I'm the Pope and it's in the papers and on TV as well, are you not going to believe it, Captain?" he asked with a wink.

"I'm used to believing my own eyes," replied Lapin, irritated, as he made notes in his pad.

Re-reading the new statements, however, he felt as if he were seeing double, like a man who was drunk. Lapin considered Savage as the murderer, then Karimov, and found both scenarios equally outlandish.

Thinking back to the conversation in the bar, he imagined holding a gun aimed at Coffin and couldn't say whether he would have shot him or not. Once again, Lapin heard the voice of his father as he told his mother about the gang, his face buried in his hands. He put his head under the cold water tap to wash away the troublesome memories that rang in his ears like bells.

Savage's daughter was born on the day Leo becomes Virgo so every morning she looked at the horoscope for both signs and selected the forecast she preferred. She kept a well-thumbed deck of cards hidden under her pillow and used it to seek advice. She couldn't bring herself to share this with her mother. Vasilisa knew only one way of telling fortunes. She was taught it by a wizened old lady in the south, who rented out a little house by the sea. Vasilisa laid the cards out endlessly until the aces turned to sixes and the queens to jokers, predicting what she wanted.

"I'm not lonely when I'm on my own but I am lonely when I'm not on my own," she admitted once to her mother whose unhappy female lot she wore like hand-me-down clothes. Her mother put it down to a phase.

Vasilisa skipped school with her friends, going through pockets for change to buy beer. Hiding in the entry-way, the girls sat on the steps, tucking their handbags under them. They passed the bottle round like a peace pipe, each girl swallowing the beer through a deep drag, like a man's, on her cigarette in a bid to get drunk more quickly. Vasilisa used to spend the evenings in the Three Lemons, leaving crimson traces of lipstick on cigarette butts left glowing in ashtrays, on glasses and on men's shirts. Now, however, the security guards wouldn't let her into the bar and the phone appeared to have gone dead. When she skipped school, she roamed the streets aimlessly, managing to go three times round the whole town in a day. Pictures of her father had been posted over the adverts on the lamp-posts and Vasilisa felt as if he were watching her every step.

"If he puts in an appearance, we'll take the money and

get out of this dump for good," snapped her mother, pulling a torn-off poster out of her bag.

Vasilisa turned her mother's comment over in her head, kicking a crumpled beer can down the street. When she was little, her father used to take her to a derelict playground. The wooden swings were broken, the rusty slide had collapsed and cracked bottles littered the sandbox, but she and her father liked it there. Her feet took her along the familiar path, but where the playground used to be the place was empty as a beggar's palm. Vasilisa suddenly felt orphaned, lonely and of no use to anyone.

"Shall we go?" A heavy hand came down on her shoulder.

The girl had no chance to come to her senses before she was grabbed by the neck and dragged off to a car parked by the side of the road and pushed onto the back seat, her head pressed to her knees.

"Don't move!"

Vasilisa was taken to the wooden house the gangsters met in, tied up and tossed onto a sofa in a large room. Two grubby boys stood guard, cracking sunflower seeds and spitting shells into their fists. Vasilisa sobbed, her head buried in a greasy pillow that smelt of sweat and tobacco. One of the boys awkwardly stroked her shoulder.

"Don't cry. We won't touch you."

The other boy brought a mug from the kitchen. He rolled Vasilisa over and gave her a drink, spilling icy water on her face and chest.

In the evening, the gangsters huddled round with their battered faces and malicious eyes that wandered under her clothes.

"So has Daddikins turned up? Has he called round? Or phoned? Sent anyone?"

The girl shook her head.

"Where's he hiding? Do you know?"

"I don't know. I don't know anything..."

The gangsters exchanged looks.

"Maybe she really doesn't know?"

"Never trust a chick. She'll tell you lies even when there's nothing in it for her."

"Please, please don't do anything to me," Vasilisa sobbed. "I haven't done anything wrong!"

"What do you mean? This is all because of you! Four dead, the best in town, and all because of one little slut!" spat one of the gang, rubbing the spittle into the floor with his foot.

Vasilisa's mother hung around outside the wooden hut, unsure whether to knock. Vasilisa hadn't come home and, after ringing round her friends, she had a feeling the gangsters who had been keeping watch in their courtyard of late, squinting up at the windows of her flat, had to have been involved.

"What d'you want?" a fair-haired lad who reminded her of someone asked, frowning.

"I need to talk to Saam," she cooed plaintively.

"He's busy!"

"My daughter's gone missing. I'm scared to go to the police. Maybe Saam knows where she is…"

"Don't go to the police," said the boy, pulling a face and unlocking the door. "Don't trouble trouble…"

"Just get Saam, please!" the woman shouted after him. "I don't know what to do!"

She walked round the house like a beaten dog, nervously tugging at her hair and drawing curious glances from passersby. Wherever she went, there were whispers behind her that she was Savage's wife and everywhere she saw posters of her husband looking at her with a contemptuous curl of his lip. "I hate you. God, I hate you!" she yelled inwardly, turning away.

In the afternoon, she took a random route across town to the forest and, turning to watch her go, the townspeople exchanged animated whispers.

"Where's she off to? She's going like crazy!"

"Maybe they've found Savage?"

The final houses parted before her and the forest

172

swallowed her up, its trees closing behind her. Sobbing aloud, the woman simply ran around calling with all her strength:

"Savely! Savage! They've taken our daughter! They're going to kill her!"

Only now did she realize how much her husband's surname, the one she used to make fun of, actually suited him!

"Savely! Damn you!"

Falling in the damp moss she howled like a factory siren, clawing at her face in her grief, and when she came to and looked round, she realized she was lost in the forest and didn't know which way to go. The trees crowded round, aiming their branches like guns, and she gazed around in fear. Damp rose from the swamps. She was frozen through and had begun to shake with the cold, standing there in just one shoe, unable to remember where she'd lost the other one. She was holding the keys to her flat, which seemed like useless bits of metal now, and her mud-spattered coat was in shreds. She was scared of having to spend days, weeks, months wandering around out here and rushed off blindly, calling for help. Suddenly, she imagined coming across Savage and each picture of their unlooked-for encounter was more terrifying than the last.

A dog barked in the trees and the hunters, returning from the taiga, appeared. They gave the hysterical woman a swig of alcohol from a flask then wrapped her feet in coarse cloth, bound with string, and took her into town, telling her they'd been searching for the notorious murderer Savely Savage who had vanished into thin air.

"He won't last long in the forest," said the hunters, shaking their heads. "It will be so cold at the end of August that he'll either drop dead or give himself up."

Taking their leave of the woman by the garages, they turned off to the dog runs, never knowing whose wife they'd rescued in the forest that day.

Savage's wife plodded home, trying to conceal her torn dress and passersby gaped at the sight of her scratched legs and the rags on her feet. Leaves and fir twigs were sticking out of her hair like feathers from a torn pillow and her face was like an overripe apple.

Not far from home, a gangster with a sloping forehead approached and led her without a word to a car parked on the pavement. Flopping down on the back seat, Savage's wife burst into tears: there in the car was Vasilisa. The girl was rubbing her wrists where the rope had eaten into them and her face was puffy from lack of sleep.

"No hysterics, okay?" said Saam, leaning towards them from the front seat. He ran a damp handkerchief over his forehead and screwed up his eyes in fatigue. "You didn't find him then?"

Savage's wife shook her head, snivelling into her fist. That same fair-headed boy she'd seen outside the gang's house was in the driver's seat and she was certain she'd met him before but couldn't remember where.

"Take yourself home. Sort yourself out," said Saam, leaning across the seat to open the door. "And don't bear a grudge," he said with a wink, taking her hand and kissing her on the wrist.

She clambered out of the car and Vasilisa looked around in alarm, clinging to her mother.

"That's a present for good behaviour," said the driver, putting a plump bag on the roof of the car.

The boy wore a malicious, mocking expression as he rolled a sweet around in his mouth and cracked his knuckles as he flexed his muscles.

"What's your name?" the woman asked, taking the bag.

"Lyonya," the driver said with a sneer.

But the name meant nothing to her. When she opened the bag, Savage's wife saw clothes, trinkets and two bundles of banknotes tied with a ribbon.

"Is Dad going to come back?" Vasilisa asked when the gangsters had vanished around the corner, honking their horns in farewell.

"I hope not."

"Will he go to prison?"

Her mother didn't answer and tried to think where she could have seen the fair-headed boy before.

Lapin was keeping a look out for them at the house entrance. He quickly looked Savage's wife up and down. She looked like a beggar with the rags wound round her feet but she was behaving as though nothing had happened, even as she put a hand over a breast that was showing through the holes in her dress. Lapin sniffed cautiously. Savage's wife burst out laughing.

"I don't drink in the middle of the day, son," she said, winking at Lapin, adjusting her hair flirtatiously and pouting playfully as she removed a dry twig.

Vasilisa hid behind her mother, hands behind her back, her dirty hair hanging over her face like icicles. She looked as though she hadn't been home for several days.

"I have to talk to you about that night," said Lapin, confused. "Are you prepared to repeat your statement?"

"I want to tell you what really happened," the girl blurted out, hiding her face.

They went into the flat and Lapin pictured Savely Savage going through that door year after year. Now he was wanted by the whole town and there wasn't a single flat that wasn't talking about a man whose neighbours couldn't even remember what he looked like.

Savage's wife disappeared into the bedroom with an apology while Vasilisa put cups on the table, embarrassed by the investigator's stare. She pulled down her sleeves to hide the rope burns on her arms and Lapin could smell her stale odour like that of the little kids who spent their nights in basements.

Savage's wife came out wearing a short red housecoat that matched her crimson cheeks. She'd hurriedly tidied herself up, washed her face and combed her hair, and Lapin, flustered, couldn't take his eyes off her scratched legs.

"Well, please, take a seat," she said with a strained smile.

The shaking of her hands conveyed itself to the cup which rattled so much in its saucer that she stopped talking and went to get the kettle from the kitchen where she opened a bottle of vodka and had a swig as a tranquilliser.

"I'll tell you everything that happened," she gabbled as if reading a script when she came back, carrying a tray. "Savely was on his way home that evening. As usual, he went through the square. That's the sort of person he is, always in the wrong place at the wrong time."

Lapin broke in and spoke to Vasilisa: "You said your father…"

"They frightened her!" said Savage's wife, not letting him finish and adjusting the housecoat. "They threatened the poor girl, promised to disfigure her, cripple her… And where can you find any protection from them? You know yourself, no-one will help!" Her voice sounded so false that Lapin winced. "She even kept it from me and I'm sure my husband…" She fell silent as if her tongue couldn't repeat the accusation against her husband. "Although actually, I think it's funny. You need to know Savely to understand that it's ridiculous." She burst into hysterical laughter by way of confirmation.

"But why are you saying this now? Why have you kept quiet for so long?" Lapin asked, knocking over his cup with a clumsy movement and soaking the tablecloth.

"We were intimidated," Savage's wife stubbornly maintained, her lips thin as a thread.

"And now you're brave all of a sudden?" said Lapin, teasing her as he wiped the wet table down with napkins. "What's happened to make all of you so brave all of a sudden? All of you." Lapin said again with a helpless gesture as if he were asking the walls for an answer.

Savage's wife opened a jar of gooseberry jam and licked her fingers.

"Who shot Coffin?" asked Lapin helplessly.

"Karimov," whispered Vasilisa.

"I'll tell you how it happened," said Savage's wife, sinking into her chair, her legs crossed.

Her wheedling tones bound him hand and foot and, as he

picked out the tea leaves with a spoon, Lapin listened to the new version of Coffin's murder word for word as he had heard it from other witnesses.

Lapin slammed a heavy file down on his boss's table.

"Shit!"

"They all said the same?" asked the prosecutor, raising an eyebrow in mock surprise.

"Every one of them. And it's so faultless. You can't pick holes in it. Security, gangsters, passersby, even Savage's daughter. They're all retracting their old statements. They sound like they're reading from a script. No-one contradicts anyone else. New witnesses have come forward."

"Send the case back."

"What about Savage?"

"Are you short of witnesses?"

Lapin was flummoxed.

"But they said ..."

"Don't you know how they manipulate witnesses?"

"What about Antonov? And Trebenko?"

"You don't really believe that was Savage..."

Lapin clammed up. The prosecutor rubbed his hands as if soaping them up over the sink and looked inquiringly at the investigator.

"But the blood on Antonov's body?" Lapin mumbled, perplexed. "Trebenko's gun that was used at the bathhouse?"

"The only thing we know is that we don't know anything. The blood and the gun could have been planted."

"By the police?!"

There was a weighty silence from the prosecutor who looked at Lapin over his glasses.

"And Krotov?"

"Who said Savage was even there? Karimov? The whores? We don't know what Krotov had been eating and drinking in the bathhouse. Maybe Karimov helped him along..."

"So why were the gangsters looking for Savage? Why did

they offer a reward? What does Karimov get out of all these killings?"

"That's for you to find out." And the prosecutor buried himself in his paperwork, indicating that the conversation was over.

Lapin backed out of the room, pushing the door open with his back.

The banging of hammers, along with swearwords as sharp as nails that littered the workmen's speech, could be heard in the area from early in the morning. They were knocking together a new fence from freshly-cut planks that smelt of the forest to surround the gangsters' den. The construction netting was torn and it trailed on the ground so that passersby tripped and got entangled in it. Small boys dragged it away from right under the workmen's noses and raced through the courtyards, turning it into knights' cloaks or sails for their wooden-bench boats.

"What are they saying in town? Are they going to send another mayor?" a gangster asked, cleaning his nails with the end of his knife.

Another shook his head and watched the boys hiding behind the trees and rolling the construction netting into a ball. Perched on a stone, a workman smoked, ignoring the little thieves.

"They changed their minds at the last minute. They're scared of a war. If they brought someone in from outside, he wouldn't know how we do things or our people. Just imagine the chaos!"

The gangster with the knife smirked showing his gap-toothed mouth.

"When you're weighing up pros and cons, it's always cons that win! So who's going to replace Krotov?"

"One of our own. Smart and biddable."

There was rarely any news from the little town hidden like a needle in a haystack out in the taiga near the frontier, and it was always bad. The regional authorities had decided to send in their own people to restore order but no-one would take the position, avoiding the job like the plague. In the end, in the superstitious belief that it was better to leave well alone, they simply gave up on the town, remembering when its residents had been left without light and the town had been as lawless as a prison camp. Trebenko's assistant became chief of police and Krotov's deputy took over as mayor.

A small town is like a communal apartment where people are crowded together, take no pains to hide what they're whispering about and can recognize their neighbours by their smell. These people don't like change, they expect nothing good from it and so, when they saw the new mayor, they sighed with relief. "At least he won't be any worse than Krotov," they said, gesturing towards the central square.

The new mayor was the spitting image of his predecessor, with an ample belly and a nose that was constantly sniffing, moving from side to side like the rod of a metronome and his face was as round as the template for a circle. Once he occupied Krotov's seat, he began to wear the same type of suits and the wide-striped ties Krotov had favoured. The thin hair he'd previously combed to the left now lay to the right so that he was virtually indistinguishable from his late boss.

Saam sat out on the veranda, rocking on his chair, while the gangster with the scar that split his face in two, cracked sunflower seeds and spat them into his paw.

"Isn't the hunter back yet?" Saam asked.

The gangster shook his head.

"The hunter's getting old," Saam frowned. "He's never taken so long to track someone down."

The new mayor left the local government building and, adjusting his shirt that had come untucked, got into a car that dipped on that side. Saam felt as if he'd seen a ghost, as if Krotov, lying naked on the lake shore, had flashed before his eyes.

"Does the new mayor support us?" asked the gangster, picking his teeth.

"He does," Saam ground out. "Like a noose and a hanged man. Trusting civil servants is like trusting the weather forecast. They promise sunshine and it rains anyway."

The Chief was wandering around the square, dragging his foot. He took passersby by the hand but they gently pushed him away and quickened their pace. He had a sausage protruding from his pocket and a dirty piece of string on his leg left over from a tin can the kids had tied on for a laugh. The Chief chased them, the can rattling until it came off when it caught on an iron bar sticking out of the ground.

"Name?" the Chief demanded leaning across the veranda fence to grab Saam by the arm.

"Get lost!" the gangster snarled, nervously pulling back his leather jacket. "And you, get him out of here!" he yelled at his assistant, indicating the crazy old man. "Sort it!"

The gangster with the scar pushed the Chief away with a nasty look.

"Come on, get out of it, Chief! You're stinking the place up!" He turned to Saam and added, "Who would have thought he'd outlive Trebenko?"

"Just put him away in a home, will you? I can't stand the sight of him."

The working day was coming to an end and miners were coming home from the factory, spreading out through the town like ants. Saam suddenly imagined Savage, chewing on a loaf of bread he'd bought on his way. He jumped up, gazing at a man with a stoop, carrying a worn briefcase, and the gangster with the scar froze as he tried to work out what Saam was looking at.

"I thought I saw…" said Saam, plonking himself down on the chair when he realized he'd got the wrong man. He took out a dirty handkerchief and wiped his sweaty neck.

The Saami took the fugitives in and provided them with a patched-up tourist tent they'd found in the forest. They fed them on cured reindeer meat and a soup of meat, flour and berries, and made Salmon a pine bark infusion. The Saami's faces were cracked like antique portraits and their half-moon smiles looked like they'd been stuck in place. The herders spoke good Russian but asked no questions. They tutted just looking at Salmon, with the skin stretched tight over her bones and her frightful face with its huge, protruding eyes.

The Saami had come from depopulated towns and settlements where drink was the only diversion. Russians took to drink quickly but for the Saami it took only one glass. Alcohol became an utter disaster that cut down their tribe like weeds. All that was left was to move into the taiga where they could breed reindeer and live the nomadic lives their forebears had led on the Kola Peninsula for centuries.

The herders brought Savage a sweater left by a previous guest. "Black face," the Saami said of him and Savage couldn't tell whether they meant he was actually black or from the Caucasus. He had almost drowned in the swamp that had ingested his bag. He had taken a wrong turn and lay on a cold stone, clutching it in his arms. The Saami rescued the runaway, plied him with herbal infusions and escorted him to the border. The herders believed guests were brought to them by spirits and so as not to anger them they took everybody in, fed them and warmed them up.

The Saami liked their new guests. They were sitting silently close to each other by the fire, listening to the mutterings of an elderly female shaman and swaying to their rhythm. In her ornate, guttural melodies they could hear the wind tickling the trees that gurgled with laughter and then the whole forest swayed and laughed confounding the hunters who were on their trail.

"Our settlement closed. My dad went south," mumbled Salmon, keeping them awake. "And Mum took to drink. There were carers, going around, picking up abandoned kids and, when they heard me crying, they dragged me out from under the bed, like a lost ball. They took me…"

181

"What about your mother?" asked Savage, propping himself up on one elbow.

"I don't know what happened to her. I can hardly remember what she looked like. When I think about her, she's mixed up with the nanny at the orphanage. I can't even say what colour eyes she had... At the orphanage, we were ten to a room and slept two to a bed. They fed us porridge and soup with about as much taste as water. The only joy was the aid. The Finns used to send us things and food and we stuffed ourselves with sweets so that the next day the whole home had stomach ache. We hung around in the streets, begging for change and cigarettes and no-one took any notice of us. The ordinary kids didn't play with us. They stayed clear of us. If some girl was seeing an ordinary boy, they used to hide in the entryways. He'd be embarrassed to be seen with her and she'd be scared the kids from the home would beat up someone from outside."

Savage remembered the grubby, shaven-headed kids who moved in crowds. You could recognize the orphans by their blistering frowns and imported hand-me-downs, rumpled and ill-fitting. Someone would have sleeves that hung down round their feet. Someone else wouldn't be able to fasten up their jacket.

"Coffin looked after us," said Salmon, clutching her legs to her chest and cringing at the memories. "He made a gang out of the cleverest and meanest ones and people were more frightened of the kid gangsters than they were of the grown-ups. Saam let the little boys call him Daddy and, for that, they were ready to tear apart anyone that was pointed out to them."

When his daughter was small, Savage used to take her to the playground. The rusty slide had fallen on its side, the swings were broken and the benches covered in adolescent declarations of love. The place was littered with bottles and garbage and the ground bristled with shards of glass. Savage liked going there, getting away from people. He always picked quiet, secluded spots. A small boy in a pair of girl's bright green dungarees started to appear in the playground. He would watch Savage's daughter from a distance as she messed about in the sandpit but he didn't go any closer. Savage offered him a toy and the boy took it and hid behind the slide. The next day Savage brought some chocolate. He began to take a bit out of his minuscule salary to buy the boy treats and they soon made friends. The child complained that the carers at the orphanage hit him and let him go hungry. To begin with Savage believed everything he said but the stories grew more and more outlandish and contradicted one another. Savage wasn't cross. The kid wanted people to feel sorry for him and he did.

Even so, Savage called in at the orphanage.

"You want to adopt Lyonya?" The manager waved her hands.

Stammering in embarrassment, Savage mumbled that he hadn't made up his mind. By then, he was already being taken down a long corridor painted a pale pink. Children seized his hands, gazing into his eyes and whispering: "Have you come to get me?" A small girl ran after him holding out her doll and Savely could feel the children looking after him, frozen to the spot.

Savely was told about the boy's parents who had got to know one another at school and made their baby after lessons. They both had families now so they never visited Lyonya, putting him out of their minds like an unwanted object and when they ran across the shaven-headed little boy in town, they didn't even know he was their son. Savely was shown the little boy's room, his school planner and drawings and he was already sorry he'd come.

The manager brought Lyonya in dressed in funny trousers that were too long for him. The boy kept pulling them up so as not to tread on them. Biting his nails, Lyonya looked at Savage with shining eyes and Savage's nose tickled. He turned away and secretly wiped his eyes, determined to adopt the boy.

"The ones who were going to be adopted were never forgiven," Salmon mumbled as if she could read his mind.

"They became outcasts. They were beaten up. Nobody talked to them and when they were collected we spat at them. Even I felt that all my misfortunes came from a little girl in my room, who'd been selected for adoption. I set fire to her curly hair one night and was locked in the basement for a few days."

That evening, Savage explained everything to his wife, banging his fist on the table, trying to persuade her and win her over. He even threatened divorce. She merely bit her pale lip, nervously twiddling the edge of the tablecloth. Pressed against the door, Vasilisa listened in on their argument and couldn't understand whether to be delighted that she was going to have a little brother or to cry. In the morning, Savage's wife set off for the orphanage, red lipstick on her bitten lips, thick mascara on her lashes which she fluttered as if they were giving a round of applause. Closeted away in the manager's office, she liberally cursed children and carers alike, coming out in blotches with shouting.

The little boy never showed up in the playground again. When the manager met Savage in a shop, she pretended not to know him. And when he plucked up his courage to go to the orphanage, she lowered her gaze and told him quietly: "You'd better get the hell out of here!"

Savage held Salmon more tightly and his face burned as if he'd been slapped.

"And the gangsters went out with the girlies. They married them. Saam was going to marry me. I was so beautiful. But then he drove me away..."

Savage reached for a bundle the old Saami woman had given him. He broke a sweating creamy cheese in half and offered a chunk to Salmon.

"I've got a different name now and I'm different too. The old woman said they change the name of a poorly baby to deceive the evil spirits. Maybe that's why I'm still alive, because my death got confused and can't find me."

"What were you called before?"

"Severina. I didn't know my real name. The nanny at

the orphanage wasn't all there, she used to give the children unusual names. We had a Serafima and an Isaura. Life was shit but at least you had a pretty name."

Savage ran a finger over a blue vein as hard as a rope beneath her skin.

"I was dealing, started to dabble a bit, then I got hooked," she said, hiding the track marks. "I got jaundice from all the withdrawals. I was like a skeleton... And I used to be so pretty... Coffin suggested getting rid of me. He said I wouldn't last long anyway. I was with him all the time. I knew all his business, heard all his conversations. I know who he killed and why, where they're buried ... Saam took me off into the forest. I knew why straightaway, but he was sorry for me."

The one-eyed hunter hid behind a fallen pine, its tangled roots sticking out. His dog curled up at his feet. The old man watched the Saami busy at the fire and a narrow-eyed small boy jumping around with a wooden toy while a wrinkled woman, her face yellow as a rotten apple, pounded poisonous spurge laurel into a concoction offering protection from their enemies.

But the old man wasn't the only one who had found Savage. The blue-tattooed runt arrived at the Saami camp just behind him, following him like a predator out of the ravine. "You have to shed someone else's blood to liven up your own," he used to say when he got involved in other people's fights. Now, scratching his nose with a crooked nail, he licked lips that were dry with excitement.

The dog whined and the hunter shushed it with a kick in the side. It fell silent, hiding its nose in its paws. The hunter was bent with age. The damp made his bones ache and blocked his chest and he wanted to get rid of Savage so that he could go home quickly. Suddenly he was aware of the steady gaze of someone behind him. The dog gave a hollow bark. The old man cocked the gun. It gave a dull click as though a branch had snapped under foot and the runt, who had been hiding in the ravine, drew himself up to his full height. Covered in tattoos his neck was blue like a corpse's and there were rings tattooed on his fingers. The hunter sneered when he saw his empty hands but the runt, his stance wide, was coming right at him, ignoring the gun. He had the eyes of a killer. He snapped his jaw like a crazed wolf and the one-eyed old man took fright and trembled. He stepped backwards, still holding the gun. The runt leapt at him and sank his teeth into his neck then watched, teeth still clenched, as the hunter's old dog, fled, tail between its legs. The gun fired, splintering the white trunk of a birch. Sap welled up and the Saami leapt out of their houses in a great commotion.

The runt appeared before them, wiping his bloodstained mouth, and took a picture of Savage out of his pocket. Without a word, he unfurled it in front of the old woman.

"Where is he?" the runt kept saying, poking the picture. "Where is he?"

"He, he," the Saami woman repeated, offering her guest a fragrant herbal elixir, in which black and red berries floated. The runt recoiled from the bitter smell but made himself drink it to get in the old woman's good books.

When Savage came out of the tent, smoothing his hair with his fingers, the runt was already writhing on the ground and the herders were watching how long it would take him to die. Biting her fist so as not to cry out, Salmon hid behind Savage who whistled when he unfurled his picture. He realized he couldn't go back into town where it was open season on him. He would have to keep roaming the forest in search of food and shelter.

The old Saami woman found the body of the hunter in the ravine and, rolling her eyes, called out in her own language. The Saami surrounded the body of the murdered old man, shaking their heads and looking at his torn throat. Savage was assailed by a wave of nausea and turned away, his hand over his mouth.

"Manhunter!" a Saami boy whispered in Savage's ear. "Many people tried to get away from him but he got them all!"

They threw the bodies onto a ragged wide skin and

Savage with two of the Saami dragged them away from the camp. Their faces, frozen in death, were so full of malice that the young Saami tried to avoid looking at them.

As he towed the skin along, Savage recalled dragging bodies to the morgue on the days the town had been without electricity and corpses were being thrown out of the back of the hospital. Savage imagined the cold he would endure in the taiga and decided that winter in the forest would be no worse than a town without electricity.

"Yavr!" said the young Saami, pointing to the lake.

"Yavr!" said Savage trying out the new word. "Yavr, yavr, yavr…"

The Saami laughed, imitating Savage.

"Yokk!" The boy pointed at the river.

The one-eyed hunter bared his teeth as he bounced over bumps and stones and the runt stared up morosely as if reproaching the Saami for killing him in such an underhand fashion.

"Yokk?" said a delighted Savage at the sight of a stream glistening on the other side of a hill.

The Saam shook his head.

"Yuay!"

It was Savage's turn to laugh.

"You only have four-letter words!"

The Saami didn't get the joke but they laughed anyway and their laughter rolled down the rocky slope like a loose stone.

Standing around the bodies, the Saami took one last look at them, and whispered something in their own language that rustled like leaves in the wind. Their final expressions frozen on their faces, the hunter and the runt appeared to be staring at one another in hatred. The Saami threw the bodies into a narrow gully, overgrown with bearberry and flowering water hemlock. They covered them with soil and damp moss then burnt the skin on the bonfire, dousing it with petrol which the herders kept in a small plastic bottle.

"If they found us, it means others will too," Savage told

Salmon fatalistically when he joined her at the camp. "We've got to get out of here!"

The girl shook her head.

"No, no-one else is going to come."

She recalled the cruel face that looked as if it were carved out of rock and thought that only the one-eyed hunter could go so far into the taiga. Salmon had visited him in his home that reeked of sour cabbage soup and the oil he used to grease his gun. When Saam was settling up with the hunter, the girl would hover in the corridor, and when the old man gave her sweets, she would blush and hide them in her pocket only to throw them away later. Saam laughed at her but to her the hunter's sweets were as bitter as the smirk fixed on his lips.

The old Saami woman, who resembled the goddess Beaivi, hid the one-eyed hunter's gun in her tent and forbade the Saami to go anywhere near it. She scattered grass over the place where the runt had bitten through the hunter's neck, spattering the mossy stones with blood, and said that all that had happened that day should be forgotten.

Gathered round the bonfire in the evening and serving up platefuls of meat stew, the Saami counted their herd on their fingers and, snorting like reindeer, talked about the autumn that was already hard on the heels of summer: before you knew it, it would be winter, white as doe's milk.

Salmon was snuggled in a mangy pelt that smelt of dogs. As she listened to the Saami, she wandered in memory, going back to the orphanage where the nanny with her cracked dry hands had sung her to sleep in her arms. Savage smoothed out the poster the runt had been carrying and tried to imagine what his daughter was doing right then.

"People are unhappy and that's why they're bad," Salmon said, taking the poster from him.

"People are bad and that's why they're unhappy," said Savage with a shake of his head.

"Are you going to kill Saam?" the girl suddenly asked. Savely hugged her and kissed her on the temple.

The old dog raced around the herders' encampment for a long time, catching its dragging lead on snags. Salmon slipped it food, saving up leftovers but the old Saami woman cursed him, throwing stones at him in the belief that its owner's wicked soul had taken up residence in the dog.

The pictures on the hotel walls showed the green hills that huddled around the town, the smoking factory chimneys, and reindeer teams bogged down in snow as thick as cream. Since Karimov could see all this from his car window every day, he first hung the pictures upside down, then turned them to the wall. He hated the long, dark winters, the damp marsh air and the polar sun that crept under the blankets at night. But like the chalked outline of a magic circle, the Arctic Circle wouldn't let him go.

The visitor from Moscow was in the next room. In the evenings, Karimov could hear the old man singing Italian arias in his unbearable, squeaky voice, the device at his throat. It made his stomach churn. In the times when many quarrel were settled with a bullet, Pipe always had the last word. People said he didn't trust his dangerous rivals to a hired killer but took up arms himself. He had become sentimental in his old age, however, and allowed his enemies to live a life worse than death. In the past he had been a man of few words whereas these days he loved to chat, aware that people trembled at the sound of his voice and longed to plug the hole in his throat.

Pipe kept to the shadows, hiding behind placemen he moved around like chessmen on a board. But Karimov dreamed of being rid of the foster father who tailed him so relentlessly, popping up behind him like a jack-in-the-box so that Karimov felt as though Pipe was living his life, biting out pieces as if it were an apple and making him voice other people's opinions and play someone else's role. Once Karimov even made up his mind to try and kill Pipe but when the car blew up, the old man was lingering outside a wine shop, perusing the dusty bottles. Pipe realized straightway where the fuse led but rather than wrapping it round the traitor's throat, he sent Karimov to the North and made him manager of the factory.

"You'll like it there," the old man squeaked, jabbing at a remote corner of the map. "It's said to be very pretty. The harsh climate is character-building."

"Then I'd be better off further south," Karimov quipped.

"One year is like two in the Arctic Circle. It's instead of the military service you didn't do. It'll make a man of you!" he said, patting Karimov on the head and sadly taking note of the traces of grey already showing among the dark curls.

There was a noise in the corridor and unfamiliar voices. Karimov heard his bodyguard engaged in a protracted argument with somebody and then there was a loud, insistent knock. Two lanky young men in uniform came in, automatically wiping their feet at the door.

One went unceremoniously around the room, opening cupboards, turning out the drawers and looking through paperwork left on the bed while the second muttered some phrases he'd learnt by heart that Karimov simply couldn't apply to himself.

"Witness saw you shoot someone."

Karimov shuddered and swallowed.

"Shoot someone?"

"That's right. We've got a dozen witnesses. And several killings where you're the main suspect. Get your stuff together. We're going to the station."

Karimov leapt away when they tried to handcuff him.

"Are you mad?" he yelled, raising a hand at the officer.

The officer quailed and clipped the cuffs to his belt. He gestured towards the door, asking Karimov to accompany them to the car.

"What am I being accused of? Murder?" Karimov asked as they went downstairs.

"Murders," the cop said, correcting him.

Grey smoke from the factory chimney mingled with the clouds and trailed across the sky in a dark band like a smear from a dirty rag. Out on the balcony, the visitor from Moscow watched the policemen escort Karimov to the car. There were crowds of onlookers and local reporters drawn like bees to honey. Cameras clicked and Karimov hid his face behind his hand. He was pushed into the car and before climbing into the back seat he turned to look at Pipe but he had already disappeared into his room where he would pack his suitcase.

Karimov felt abandoned as he had on the orphanage steps that night when he was gathered up by the stranger who adopted him.

Karimov was put in a dark, damp cell with a chipped bench and a rusty sink. Initially, the prison warders brought him hot meals and the morning papers. The television in the corner was on all the time and the bedding smelt of scented soap. Karimov cursed Pipe and calculated how much his release would cost. The old man never lost and this time too he had outplayed him.

Pacing the cell, Karimov had an attack of claustrophobia that brought him out in a cold sweat. A lump rose in his throat, preventing him breathing, and he was about to shout for help. At that very moment the lock rattled and a policeman strode into the cell, presenting a document which charged Karimov with three counts of murder.

"I won't even have the trousers I stand up in," said Karimov, screwing up his face with a laugh. He was convinced he would be blackmailed so that he repaid Pipe for the factory a hundred-fold.

"We'll give you prison trousers," said the policeman, holding his gaze. "An honest confession…" he said, mumbling the well-rehearsed phrases and holding out a sheet of paper.

"You've got to be joking," said Karimov, shaking his head, when he heard he was being charged with Coffin's murder. "Everyone saw Savely Savage kill him!"

"The witnesses are saying they were threatened, forced to malign Savage on pain of death."

"Malign him?!"

"Despite their false testimonies," said the officer, stressing the word "false", "no-one really believed that a decent citizen just brought down a gangster like a moose in a hunt. Even less that he'd started picking everyone off one by one like the hero in some stupid film."

Karimov wiped his forehead, struggling to get his act together.

"So, I'm the one who killed Coffin?"

"Is that a confession?"

"I'm asking you."

The officer didn't answer and just held out the sheet of paper.

"And Trebenko? That was me? And Antonov? And whoever used a gun to shoot at me, was that me as well?"

The policeman put the paper and a pen on the bed and left without a backward glance.

"So why did I kill them all?" yelled Karimov, hurling himself at the closing door. "What for?"

When he was little, his foster father used to threaten him when he was naughty: "I'll put you in the orphanage." Or he would hide behind a tree and watch the little boy running around the courtyard wailing and rubbing away the tears with his dirty little fists. Then he would emerge, holding out his arms, and Karimov would cling to him, choking with mortification. Even now, he expected the bolt to be drawn back and the door opened and Pipe to come in laughing and holding out his arms.

But he didn't come.

Lapin looked at Savage's photo and tried on Savage's life like a jacket, imagining being married to Savage's wife and the father of Savage's daughter. Warming to the part, he imagined coming home in the evening amid the throng of factory workers, buying a loaf of bread at the stall and munching it on the way, then passing the veranda of the Three Lemons and seeing Coffin, snoozing at the table, surrounded by bored bodyguards. He imagined talking to Coffin, gesticulating in front of the dumbfounded clientele who regarded him as a madman. The bouncers take him by the belt and see him out. He sits on the dusty kerb, rubbing his temples. He pictured the gangster offering him the gun and himself taking it in trembling hands sweating with terror, training it on Coffin and pressing the trigger.

As he got to know Savage better, he had discovered that they were very much alike. Savage had always been superfluous and alone wherever he went and Lapin had always been alone and superfluous wherever he went. He allowed loneliness to get under the blankets at night and in the mornings he spent so long looking at his reflection that he no longer knew who he was seeing in the mirror. Running a finger over the crumpled photo, he could sense Savage circling the town, afraid to return but not knowing where to run.

One evening, the prosecutor put his head round Lapin's door. The building was empty and quiet and when the prosecutor passed Lapin's office he could hear him leafing through the weighty pages of the Savely Savage case, muttering to himself.

"You're like someone colour blind. You don't distinguish half-tones," the prosecutor smirked. "But, after all, life isn't black and white."

"What is it then?" Lapin asked, looking up.

"Grey."

Lapin yelled inwardly, "It's grey for grey people and black and white for black and white people!" Aloud, he said nothing. But, as if he'd read his response, the prosecutor's face suddenly darkened and, spinning round on his heels, he left without saying goodbye.

They didn't meet again after that evening and when Lapin called at his boss's office, he ran up against the thick mascara of his secretary's eyelashes like bayonets at the ready.

He had now spent an hour sitting outside the prosecutor's office but no-one asked him in.

"Perhaps he's forgotten about me," he said, leaning towards the secretary as she typed. She was wearing a polka-dot dress and her full breasts swelled above the neckline like rising dough.

"He doesn't forget anything," the woman ground out in irritation. "He's busy."

Lapin attempted to count the dots on her dress and lost count every time. Noticing the investigator staring at her fixedly, the woman looked him up and down contemptuously. Lapin got up and walked the length of the shelves laden with files. He drew a finger over them to count them, reading all the titles on the spines, then sat down again. Suddenly, he leapt for the door to his boss's office and yanked the handle with all his strength.

Looking up, the secretary gazed at him in triumph.

"It's locked!"

Lapin flopped onto a chair.

"Is he there?" he asked without any particular hope.

The woman didn't answer. She continued to type, burying herself in the flashing screen. Squinting short-sightedly, she dictated something quietly to herself and, by reading her lips Lapin could make out an official letter couched in bureaucratic tongue-twisters.

The office door swung open, slamming into the wall, and his boss emerged.

"Ah, Lapin," he said, distracted, wiping his glasses on the edge of his jacket. "Don't sit there. I'm busy. Get back to work."

"But the Savage case..." the investigator tried to say.

"There is no Savage case!" the prosecutor broke in. "It's gone back to the police. There's a new suspect in the case and Missing Persons are handling Savage now."

Lapin was taken aback but the prosecutor donned the expression he reserved for feisty defence lawyers.

"It's got nothing to do with you anymore. And stop getting under my feet!"

Lapin ran into the senior investigator on the stairs. He was running up taking two steps at a time. Lapin grabbed the stair rail and decided he wouldn't get out of his way but since he didn't step aside either they bumped shoulders painfully.

Turning round, the senior investigator measured Lapin with a glance, looking him up and down, and said, with a sneer:

"You know, life is just like being in court. Some people get to be the judge, some get to be the prosecutor and some live their lives as if they are on the bench facing trumped up charges!"

Severina had disappeared as though she'd never existed. A new cleaner had appeared at the bathhouse, a young girl with short legs, bleached hair and a nose ring. She walked barefoot on the cold ground and spat in her hands before taking up her mop.

"So where's the girl who was here before you?" Lapin asked, catching her at the door.

"How should I know?" she said dismissively. "I never saw her."

"Do many people ask about her?"

"Saam goes on about it every day: has she turned up, is there any news, has anyone said anything…"

After the orphanage, Severina was assigned a room in a hostel with an ashtray-stinking corridor, where the light bulbs were always being stolen. There was a shared shower on every floor. The shower room was small and dark as a larder and the water drained away through a black hole in the floor. The shower itself was made from a thick hose, fixed to the tap. The doors had been staved in and the women would put up a shower curtain, while the men washed in full view, splashing water into the corridor so that puddles formed in the corners.

The plank floor buckled as if someone had been buried beneath it. It seemed about to kiss the low ceiling that was losing flakes of dirty plaster. Her own room was so small that Severina felt like she was putting a tee-shirt on when she went in and with two people it became tight as a coffin. "It might be like a gas chamber but it's mine!" she said, running her hand along the painted wall.

Severina was rarely in the hostel, making her way to her room late at night when no-one could see her. She would lock the door and tiptoe in an attempt to prevent the floorboards creaking. She wouldn't answer any knocks, pretending she wasn't there. She was afraid of the police coming after her but they had long since forgotten all about her and only Lapin collared her and tried to persuade her to tell him all she knew. Severina maintained a stubborn silence.

Lapin couldn't forget her begging change for cigarettes from passersby, then marking out hopscotch on the road and hopping, a smoking cigarette held tightly between her teeth. Sometimes she had seemed to be a little woman, at others a child who had grown up too soon. Now she had aged as if her life had gathered pace like someone running on the spot. She was visibly shrivelling and it was almost impossible to recognize the person who used to be Severina in the unsightly, pinched little old woman with the burnt face. The girls at the bathhouse nicknamed her Salmon for resembling a fish, and it stuck like a leech. She even used the nickname herself.

Lapin was often at the bathhouse, waiting for Severina behind a thick pine, sticky with resin, and she would sneak away from the prying attendant to go and see him. They would walk in the forest where no-one could see them together. Lapin would bring news from town in the hope that the girl would soon decide to make the confessions he was sure were on the very tip of her tongue, and Severina would ask about Coffin's murder as if she were hoping for new details from each retelling.

"The chair toppled over and Coffin fell to the floor. There was blood everywhere. Savage threw the gun away and ran out of the square," said Lapin for the umpteenth time.

"Didn't anyone stop him?" Severina asked, kicking a stone on the path with the toe of her shoe. "Didn't anyone go after him?"

"No! It was as if they'd all been struck by lightning!"

"So who killed Trebenko? Was that Savage too?" The colonel's smug face rose before them.

Lapin shrugged: "Hardly. One of his own people."

"What about Antonov?"

The investigator shook his head, kicking the cap off a worm-eaten mushroom with his boot.

"It was him," the girl said with certainty. "I know. He'll kill them all. Tell me how he shot Coffin again!" she asked and, laughing, Lapin told it all over again from the very beginning.

After Krotov's death Severina vanished without trace and Lapin had little hope of seeing her alive again.

On his way back from the bathhouse, he went through the forest, thinking back to the day he had given her the teddy bear she hid drugs in and thought that life always makes blind use of us. There was no Severina, no elderly watchman thrown on the bench outside the police station with his neck wrung, no Krotov promising support, there was just tiny little Lapin, all on his own, plodding through the rusty-yellow autumn forest where he was as much alone as he was in town. The trees exchanged whispers as if swapping the latest news. The wind like a drunken bully-boy buffeted his back. Dry leaves lay like handprints on the pale reindeer lichen and Lapin remembered Savage who was no doubt roaming the taiga now, imagining like him that the trees were gossiping and the wind jostling him, challenging him to a fight.

There, in the path, arms crossed, stood Saam. Lapin started and looked around. He slowed his pace and the gangster sneered, taking an unfiltered cigarette from behind his ear.

"Are you looking for Severina?" he asked, lighting up.

Lapin stopped in front of Saam, his shaking hands hidden in his pockets.

"Won't I find her?" he said, answering the question with one of his own. Saam stared at him as if trying to work out whether this was just bravado on Lapin's part.

"I don't know," he admitted all of a sudden, realizing

that the investigator didn't know where the girl had gone. "She disappeared the day Savage showed up. Have you heard anything about him?"

Lapin shook his head.

"Not a thing…"

Saam stepped aside, letting him through.

"Well, if you do hear anything about her, let me know."

Lapin went past, aware of Saam's eyes on his back.

"And you tell me if there's any sign of Savage," he said, looking back.

Saam didn't answer but nodded and they went their separate ways, going over the conversation and scouring their words, looks, and gestures for a hidden meaning that wasn't there.

The local paper wrote up Karimov's arrest and put his picture on the front page. Out-of-town TV crews arrived and moved into the room recently vacated by the visitor from Moscow. Even the general from the regional centre who had put in an appearance after the death of Trebenko was content at how things had turned out and full of praise for the new chief of police. True, he couldn't bring himself to visit the town, mindful of the angry snarls the forest had bestowed on him as a stranger.

Lapin clutched at the reporters' sleeves but they only listened if they were talking and talked when they were listening, sniffing out sensational items like pigs in search of acorns.

"The gang rules the entire town with terror. They are law and order," Lapin gabbled, trotting after a swarthy journalist. "The police have been bought off. The residents have been intimidated. Even crime bosses from Moscow are scared to show up here! The town's out of their control and they've written it off!"

"Did you know Karimov?" the journalist asked. He slowed his pace, headlines glittering in his eyes.

"Savage shot Coffin in front of dozens of witnesses. I

handled the investigation. Karimov's arrest is sheer lunacy!" the investigator pressed on.

But the journalist lost interest even before Lapin finished talking and dashed ahead, adjusting his camera bag.

The faded posters of Savage were still stuck on the lamp-posts and billboards but the conversation was all about Karimov, building up the story of the murder from police reports and overheard gossip. Blinking as the cameras flashed, the new chief of police recounted the story to journalists, their microphones like guns at the ready.

"Karimov was wilful and stubborn. He looked on the gangsters as scum and who likes that?" he said, leaning back in his chair. He could feel his certainty grow while he talked as if reading from a script. "Karimov himself was scarcely any different to Coffin, well, apart from his expensive suits and his handsome looks. On the inside, he was just another gangster..."

"So what happened that evening?" a narrow-shouldered reporter asked impatiently, licking his lips.

"Coffin was having a snooze on the veranda at the Three Lemons. He spent his evenings in the bar and everyone knew where to find him. Karimov drove up in his car and got out with his bodyguards – he never went anywhere without them," explained the chief of police.

"Had they had some kind of falling out?"

"Yes, over the protection money Coffin had demanded from the factory. He didn't miss a trick that one. He would have extorted money from God Himself and profiteered on the Devil. There was nothing he wouldn't do and nothing he was afraid of. There are people who live by the law of the land and people who live by the law of the underworld but Karimov lived by his own laws and had no intention of bowing down to a gangster. He gave Coffin an ultimatum. Coffin told him to stick it. They started arguing and when he was threatened Coffin clicked his fingers and asked for his gun."

"To give Karimov a fright?" asked a journalist, clicking his fingers as if copying Coffin.

The chief of police screwed up his face and shrugged:

"His sidekick Saam got a double-barrelled shotgun and Coffin gave it to Karimov. Go on, then, he said. Either you shoot me or I shoot you. He wanted to make him look stupid, for a laugh. Who would have actually fired? But Karimov, not missing a trick, shot him right there in front of everyone."

The next day the serial killer's story was in all the local papers and on everybody's lips. Examining it like bedding in the daylight, everyone found their own evidence, drawing out of their memory like grips out of hair something they had happened to see, something someone let slip or an encounter that confirmed what the journalists had written.

"Savage was destined to act as the scapegoat!" said a fat man surrounded by curious listeners, raising a finger.

"We're all scapegoats," said a blue-faced alcoholic with a broken nose. "Of our own destinies!"

The bar was packed and the waitress, flushed from lack of air, fanned herself with a folded newspaper. The customers went from table to table, interrupting one another and breaking into other people's conversations like burglars into a flat. It was noisy. Everyone was arguing, yelling and gesticulating like windmills. No-one was listening to anyone else but they could all hear what was being said because it was what people had been talking about all over town of late.

"They say his daughter's lovely."

"Not so much lovely as a slapper!"

"It's the same thing! She got mixed up with Antonov and her father went to the Three Lemons to sort things out. Karimov shot Coffin then got in his car and drove off as if nothing had happened. His bodyguards got rid of the finger prints and went to work on the witnesses..."

"Bollocks!" said the blue-nosed drunkard, nearly knocking his glass over as he waved his arm. "Utter bollocks!" He hesitated as he tried to find the right words but spat and just said again. "Bollocks! Can't have happened."

"Anything can happen here!" said the fat man, shushing

him. "Do you remember them turning off the lights? My neighbour gutted his mother like a chicken then said he'd wanted to do it his whole life but hadn't had the guts. He said she'd tormented him, lived his life for him so that she'd had two lives and he hadn't had even one. He went down for 20 years! And he was a nice chap, a geography teacher."

Lapin stood in a corner behind the counter, sipping his beer. He chased it down with conversations, turning first to one table then another.

"Savage had no choice but to go on the run," the fat man went on after a swig.

"What about Saam?" said two lanky men, bending over the table like shadufs. "How could he stand it?"

"Oh, he was pleased. Coffin was out of control. They were all fed up with him being so high-handed! On the other hand, the way they see things, it was a betrayal and so they started settling scores just like the bad old days."

"There's talk about several people having gone missing."

"And the shoot-outs? We could hear them shooting every night!" said a man at the next table turning round to join the conversation.

"You could smell the gunpowder in the air," the lanky pair agreed, nodding their heads in tandem.

"The papers are saying Trebenko was the first to have had enough and to decide to do something. Everyone could see how he stood with the gang. He wanted everything to be nice and peaceful more than anyone."

"What's Karimov got to do with it? Saam knocked off Trebenko!" the alcoholic with the broken nose said, interrupting. "Remember the Chief? Who beat him half to death?"

"And he got rid of Antonov because he was an important witness!" said the fat man in a louder voice after clearing his throat. "After all, he saw who shot Coffin and his evidence would outweigh the rest."

He was interrupted by the waitress who opened the crumpled paper she had been using as a fan.

"It says Karimov was a bit, you know," she said and twirled a finger by her temple "And he killed because he got a taste for it! The prison shrink asked him if he thought of himself as a serial killer," she continued, running a finger along the crumpled paper and reading the article out loud. "And Karimov had some sort of fit, laughing fit to burst until they took him back to his cell." She folded the paper up again and looked at the fat man in triumph.

"And he set up the shooting at the lake as a distraction," said a man hunched over behind the counter. "What I can't understand is whether Krotov died by accident or whether Karimov knew he had a bad heart and deliberately turned the heat up in the steam room."

"Yes but Savage. What about him?" someone yelled.

"Sod Savage!" the fat man said with a yawn watching the foam on his beer settle. "Maybe he starved to death or maybe Karimov got to him…"

Lapin slammed his empty glass down on the table and went out, blinking in the sun. It was dazzling after the darkness of the bar. He picked up a dirty, sticky newspaper that lay next to an overflowing dustbin and read the article about Karimov, whom the reporters had dubbed a serial killer. The drink clouded his brain and the letters jumped around like fleas so that he had to read every line twice to understand it. "When he looked around, Saam, the head of the group, saw that he was surrounded by dead men. Everyone he had been close to and on whom he could rely had been killed by Karimov. So Saam was afraid he would be next. It was then that he went to Investigator Lapin and told him what really happened on the fateful evening that turned the town upside down. The killer has not got away with it."

The car sped along the broken, bumpy road, bouncing over the potholes. Pipe only remembered what he wanted to remember and forgot everything he wanted to forget and so, when he passed the road sign with a broad line crossing out the name of the town, he crossed the town out of his memory too, forgetting even its name.

"The killer has not got away with it," Pipe read in conclusion before rolling up the paper and hiding it in his pocket. "People like fairy stories and believe in them more than they believe in themselves."

"Be ye as little children," said the driver with a smirk.

"It's a shame I'm not a writer," the old man sighed, looking at the red of the autumn forest, dark as dried blood, and contemplating the serial killer story he had just read.

The driver raised his eyebrows in surprise and turned the music down.

"I'd write a detective story, seasoned with murders like meat with pepper, and then," Pipe thought for a while, "and then I'd actually do everything I'd written about, following my own book like a recipe. Everything grows dull, my friend, everything needs novelty whether it's food, women, or killing…" His mechanical voice through the device placed at his throat was like a radio broadcast.

The driver kept his eyes firmly on the road, unable to bring himself to ask his boss about his foster son.

"When I die, he'll forget about me the very next day," said Pipe as if reading the driver's thoughts. "Now, though, he'll remember me for the rest of his life. He'll wake up in his bunk and his first thought will be about me. He'll look in the mirror and see me. Every single second he'll be thinking about me. To his dying day…"

When Karimov found out from the warders that his foster father had left, he became limp as a rag doll. He signed the confession and stretched out on the bench, staring at the ceiling. "Nobody needs anybody," Karimov muttered and he felt as though he lay wrapped in his mother's faded frock which he had never ever seen.

Summer in the north is short as a woman's best years. The air smelled of rotten leaves. The young trees had already lost their leaves and stood naked, shivering with cold. Berries scattered like broken strings of beads and Salmon gathered them up in her skirt while Savage cleaned skins with the Saami and dried meat, cutting it into thin strips and hanging them over the fire.

It seemed to Savage as though there were more hours in the day. While previously dawn peeped out of nightfall like an underskirt from under a dress and the days ended even before they began, now the days were as long as an echo in the taiga, coming back like a boomerang, only to take flight through the forest once again. Savage started smoking, making his own smelly roll-ups. He scraped off bark and planed off fine strips that he pulverized between two stones, then rolled into sheets to dry in the sun. And so he kept himself busy during the long, drawn-out days as thick as Saami soup.

Wrapped in reindeer skins, Savage smoked a roll-up, warming himself by the fire, and mentally reviewed his life. He felt as though he hadn't lived before. As if his skin had been peeled away and he were naked now, aware of the slightest breath of wind, the cautious steps of a wild animal keeping away from the Saami camp, and Salmon, shivering as she snuggled up to him.

"If I could have my time over again, I'd live life completely differently," her toothless mouth mumbled as she drifted through reminiscences of her own, in which she was a beautiful young girl with eyes blue as berries. "And why do we only live once? After all, you write things out in rough first, deleting things, crossing them out and redoing what you don't like. Then you write it all out nicely. But we only live once, without any rehearsal. We leave blots like birthmarks and it's only when we look back that we realize we lived in the wrong place, in the wrong way, with the wrong people... And we die without even being born!"

These were Savage's own thoughts chewed over in solitude for years like a cold supper and when he looked at Salmon, it struck him that life, like the Saamis' traditional songs, had no beginning, no end and no rhyme. It was pure feeling, drawing us along like a guide dog on a lead.

"There's no way you can change anything." He shook his head. "Our life is spelled out from the cradle. We don't choose our parents, the town we're born in, the colour of our eyes, our friends, our wives, our children or our ailments... You can't escape your fate like you can't leave your own body. The play can be stopped mid-word with a noose around your neck but who knows, perhaps that too is the only possible ending, the one that was predestined."

Salmon remembered the nanny who suffocated babies with pillows, chanting, "You poor, unfortunate things," and she recalled her, hair loose, stepping out of the window and into the night.

"We are poor, unfortunate things," the girl repeated, burying her face in Savage's shoulder.

The herders talked the way they sewed their Saami shirts, piercing the conversation with their tongues like needles through cloth. They decorated the shirts with beads and coloured ribbons and their conversations with songs and sayings that made their faces tickle as if stroked by a blade of grass. Savely joined the Saami in their circle and they talked to him, smiling, even though he didn't know their language, but he nodded in response or threw out his arms as if he understood what they were saying.

"Happen it did or happen it didn't, be it a fairy story or a tall tale, but heed it well, my dear, if you've nothing better to do," said the old woman in a sing-song voice, a smile in her slanting eyes. "I can't remember who told me this tale, Old Father Reindeer or a passerby or whether I made it up myself..."

Salmon was cleaning fish with a knife and the old Saami woman, spattered with flour, was rolling the fish in flatbread to bake over the fire.

"Once upon a time there were three sisters. They went into the forest and turned into bears and all summer long they stayed away from people. Then, when winter came, they settled into a lair."

Tucking up her legs, the old woman demonstrated how they had curled up in the lair and Salmon laughed so much she dropped the fish.

"But they were discovered by huntsmen who woke them up and killed them. As they were skinning the carcasses, the youngest sister sprang out of the lair. She threw herself onto the outstretched skin, all but one paw. She regained her human shape but one hand remained a bear's paw…"

Salmon thought for a while, wiping her fish-stained hands on her skirt.

"What's the point of the story? What does it mean?"

"What's the point of life?" blinked the old lady. "Or of the day gone by? Or the night? Unless we learn from our mistakes no story can teach us anything." the Saami woman laughed, daubing Salmon's nose with flour.

Rolling crushed bark in leaves, Savage watched young boys packing reindeer-antler buttons into packets. The Saami loaded them on to a sled, along with the tanned skins, and took them into town to be sold or exchanged for much needed items. The boys' father, a round-faced man with such fat cheeks he seemed to have his mouth full all the time, used to take the goods into town. Once he met some local freight handlers, jolly red-faced drunkards with whom he spent all his earnings on drink. Then, so as not to go back empty-handed, he sold the reindeer and the sled but drank the money away in a nearby bar. He couldn't remember how he got home. He walked for many miles with his pockets emptied out and his spirit as black as the forest after wildfire, until he collapsed in the snow and into a fever. The old Saami woman nursed him with an infusion of wormwood and heather, spiced with prayers and charms, and the children wept at his feet but he died all the same without regaining consciousness. From then on, his wife pulled the loaded sled, keeping her purse beneath her shirt and her lips sealed. All the crying over her husband had cost her the sight of one eye and, looking at her, Savage was reminded of his own wife, widowed while her husband was still alive.

The old Saami woman took a bottle of vodka from under her skirt and the men held out their mugs that had small stones or a coin at the bottom. The old woman poured out thick coffee-like brew made from pine bark, splashing in vodka measured out by sight like medicine. The men drank, smacking their lips to avoid swallowing the stones. Savage, draining his cup in one gulp, admitted that he wanted to stay.

"Everybody wants to," said the Saami shaking their heads, "but no-one ever does."

But Salmon did. She went into convulsions and her arms clutched at the women like the branches of a dry tree. Her chest heaved so fiercely it seemed that the beautiful girl she once was might leap out of it at any moment. Wailing like the wind in a churchyard, the old Saami woman battled to drive out the demons. She shook her head and beat her drum and the others took up her songs which rolled around in the mouth like pebbles in a river. Salmon just kept getting worse. Already she lay still, staring in terror at the Saami women who looked to her like evil spirits. And then, mouth wide open in horror, she died and her whole life, gone in a flash like a terrible dream, was reflected in her still gaze. The old woman lifted the edge of the tent like the hem of a skirt and the women shouted out loud to drive away Salmon's soul, which, they believed, could get lost and fail to find the world of the dead. As he came out of the tent, Savage saw an old Saami man fashioning a cross. He had a vision of a girl dancing in the coiling smoke over the fire, her ashen hair streaming in the wind like a flag. Savage lit a roll-up from the fire and, listening to the lament of the Saami women, he decided it was time to go home.

"A single log can't burn for long," said the Saami, huddling together like children afraid of the dark. Savage was sick and tired of his wanderings. There was no longer anyone to cling to and feel that he wasn't alone. He felt as he had on the burning rubbish tip when he had abandoned the red-haired

207

woman and all of a sudden Savage became indifferent to his fate that was as wild and free as the wind in a burning ruin. He understood that for many months he had lived like a wild beast, reliant on his instincts, taking no thought for where he was heading or why. Now, though, he had come to his senses, there in the middle of the Saami encampment, suddenly aware that he was running away from someone he couldn't escape – himself.

Reading his mind, an old Saami man took Savage by the arm and said, "Death is like life, rain, sun and snow. It's given us whether we ask for it or not."

"What's left?"

"To thank the heavens or curse them. Either way, they won't hear you!"

As required by ancient custom, an empty coffin, hastily cobbled together from planks of wood, was buried on the lake shore. Salmon herself they buried in the Saami cemetery, hidden on one of the islands in the vast lake. From the lakeside, the island with its rocky shores was the same as all the others and it was only on going closer that wooden crosses could be made out, peeping from behind boulders. The Saami believed water stopped the dead returning to the land of the living and so they buried them on islands or the other side of a river.

The Saami tied their boats to a tree and came out on the shore. They set about digging a grave while Salmon's coffin lay in the bay, rocked on the waves like a baby in a cradle. The old man placed the cross on the ground and began to draw Salmon's face on the cross with a piece of coal: first one oval then a slightly smaller one for her large toothless mouth, a stripe for a nose, wavy lines for her hair and black dots for eyes. The portrait reminded Savage of the children's drawings stuck up on the walls of the orphanage and it occurred to him that the whole world was an orphanage, for children forsaken by their Father.

The coffin was lowered into the ground, covered in earth and marked with stones. A cross was set at Salmon's feet and a moss-covered boulder at her head. Food, a headscarf and a knife were left on the grave and Savage, kissing the cross in farewell, secretly slipped a little pebble into his pocket.

The Saami bury their dead silently, without songs or lamentations, because they believe the best funeral song is silence.

Lapin roamed the town, pocketing snatches of conversations, newspaper headlines and inadvertent sighs as he tried to work out how the Savage case had suddenly dissolved and where the evidence against Karimov, seemingly written in invisible ink, had come from.

"I had him down as suspicious straightaway. Dark as a gypsy, a real predator and putting himself up in the hotel as if he were always ready to do a runner," Karimov's secretary told him when he waylaid her after work.

The woman's heels clicked rapidly like fingers on a keyboard and Lapin, struggling to keep up, tried to decipher her Morse code.

"People say he used to help the orphanage," he reminded her.

"That's right. He went there as if he were going to work," the woman said, curling her lip. "He hugged the kids and stared into space like a zombie. He could stand there for a whole hour, not moving a muscle. You can imagine what the carers had started to think but who could they complain to?"

What Lapin picked up from the click of her heels, however, was: "Talk about the things you don't know, keep quiet about the things you do know."

Lapin wandered the streets like a lost soul, joining old ladies on their benches, popping into the bar and starting up conversations with all comers. Lapin thought to himself, "A man without other people is like a letter without a word." He tried to understand why he had dropped out of the world around him like a word missed out of a poem. He remembered Savage, as superfluous as an exclamation mark in the middle of a sentence, and regretted he couldn't look him in the eye and ask, "What makes a man so lonely when he's surrounded by other people?"

"But do you remember how Karimov tried to find Savage? He wanted to blame everything on the dead man!"

"He probably polished him off as well! What sort of life is it when people are being killed for nothing?"

Hands behind their backs, two old men were strolling down the avenue, discussing the latest news. One limped on his right leg and the other on his left and Lapin slowed down to listen to their chatter as if he might learn something useful from them.

"Was Saam in it with him?"

"You can't understand these gangsters. They think one thing, say another and then do something else…"

Lapin thought back to the time when the town emptied of people when there was a price on Savage's head and its residents took up guns and garden rakes and galloped off on a manhunt. It reminded him of the days when the town had no light and turned into a massive gangsters' den and every flat produced murderers, thieves and profiteers who would trade a candle for gold. Robbers smashed down doors to break into flats and, brandishing kitchen knives that cut the darkness to pieces, they went off with everything of value.

There was no room in Lapin's office for the fat files that recorded the details of crimes perpetrated by decent citizens. Ultimately, an emergency meeting of the mayor, the prosecutor and chief of police, decided to destroy the evidence of those days, crossing it out of the town's history so that everyone who had been arrested, except the murderers who had settled scores with their relatives, were allowed to go home.

"And how are we any better than the gangsters?" Lapin exclaimed loudly. The old men looked round, startled.

"We haven't stolen anything or killed anyone!" they replied in annoyance, looking him up and down.

"When the lights were out and the doors were smashed

like bits of cardboard, I didn't bother locking my flat but I did sleep under the bed so that I didn't get killed for an old TV and a tape recorder," Lapin began and the old men prepared to listen. "I didn't even wake up when I had visitors at night. I only discovered there was something missing a couple of days later."

"So what?" an old man interrupted impatiently. "The day before yesterday the fence was stolen from my wife's grave!"

"But then I saw my tape recorder when I went to see some friends. They swore they'd bought it cheap on the black market. Maybe they did but who can find out now?"

The old men waved him away and carried on, limping and spitting out the bitter saliva of the old.

"And the second-hand shop which at one time could hardly make ends meet expanded so much they had to lease another building!" Lapin yelled after them, thinking that he was like an old man to whom no-one listened.

He had been suffering from headaches for several days, the tablets weren't helping and he was haunted by a recurring dream. In it, there was an open book in front of him that was written in Russian but when he leaned over it he realized he couldn't read a word as if all the letters had suddenly become strange and incomprehensible. Waking in a cold sweat, Lapin would grab the first newspaper that came to hand or a crumpled draft report and only calm down when he'd read it. The next night, however, he had the dream again.

"Name?" the Chief popped out of a garden like a jack-in-the-box and grabbed his arm.

"Lapin, Comrade Colonel," the investigator said, drawing himself up, and the Chief subsided, burying his face in his shoulder.

The crazy thought occurred to Lapin that if he shot the Chief, it would put an end to the hapless cripple's sufferings and be the best thing he'd done in his life. Watching the Chief blowing bubbles, he thought back to the angry man who had scoured the town, shaking his fist at the gangsters: "I'll put the

211

lot of you behind bars. I'll get you!" Fear had silenced the little boys when they saw the chief of police and he self-consciously raised an eyebrow as he went by as if trying to appear even more menacing.

"Comrade Colonel, why is it that you think you're digging up a treasure and it turns out you're digging your own grave?"

"Grave...Coffin..." said the Chief, and Lapin thought he saw a flash of awareness cross his mad countenance.

"Why is that, Comrade Colonel?" Lapin said again but the Chief didn't answer and they went on standing by the garden for some time, arm in arm, as if communicating wordlessly with one another.

The Saami assigned a young lad with short, quick legs to accompany Savage. The herders lined up in the clearing and came up one by one to shake Savage's hand or, hugging him, to give him three kisses, Russian-style, taking his cheeks in their cracked hands. The Saami woman stuffed a bundle of food into his bosom and whispered charms into his ear to ward off evil. "I was so beautiful once" were the words he heard in the old shaman's mumblings, and the lake that showed white through the trees was laughing like a toothless mouth.

Savage took the same road he had once fled along with Salmon when they were hiding from the hunters. He thought that life offered many roads but we choose only one and travel along it back and forth, never deviating. He could already think about the town without horror or revulsion and, as he mentally went back over his past life, he could feel his heart tingle with yearning. His escort said nothing, recognizing Savage's need to be alone and to probe his inmost self in order to find the Savely Savage who had fled into the taiga several months earlier.

The youngster ran through the forest as if he knew every corner of it, guided by unseen paths and signposts. As he made his way through the alder groves, the boy held the branches up carefully to let Savage pass as if afraid of hurting the trees and when he picked mushrooms he bowed to the earth in thanks for feeding him. Savage thought of the people who had hearts like shoe soles and minds eaten away by spiteful thoughts like a wormy apple, and again he wanted to stay with the Saami whose thoughts were simple and hearts kind.

Many years ago, Savage had gone to St Petersburg. Like a brightly decorated shop window, the TV lured him in with offers of another life that seemed more interesting and more intriguing than the sleazy everydays in the horrid little town he knew like the back of his hand. His wife and daughter were squabbling in the next room while Savage imagined travelling to the northern capital and plunging into its mysterious life. He imagined women with thin, mean lips, reading the poets of the Silver Age, a long cigarette holder clasped in their teeth, and men with manicured hands who thought that life was a confrontation with yourself in which some people forge their own path while others split in two like walnut halves and in living out one destiny, lose the other they might have had. Savage himself sensed that his own life, like the moon, had a dark side he would never see.

He brought the old suitcase he'd inherited from his father down from the attic, threw in his stuff and sat down all alone for a moment to compose himself for the journey. He slapped his knee: "Time to go!" His wife, lips pursed, scowled after him from the window.

The train arrived early in the morning. A full moon bobbed amid blackening clouds and sleepy passengers hurried along the platform, bumping into one another with their suitcases. There was a smell of diesel and the homeless. Eyes watered from the acrid smoke and Savage, wiping his eyes with a handkerchief, bumped into a grinning taxi driver.

"The metro station's closed for repairs," he told Savage. "Look, everyone's waiting." He gestured towards the people crowding round the entrance.

"Surely, it won't be long before it opens," said Savely missing the point.

213

The taxi driver shook his head.

"Not till late in the evening. If you don't want to wait, get in the car."

Plonking himself down on the back seat, Savage noticed that the doors into the station had opened and the crowd was swallowed up by the subway. Savely would have liked the driver to stop but he had already started the engine.

"Hotel?" the driver asked matter-of-factly and Savage nodded. Dropping Savage off at a hotel the driver charged him well over the top and, looking at his wooden face and his big, dirty hands, Savage realized he would have to pay up. The hotel room was dirty. The window looked out onto a wall and old newspapers gathered dust on the table. But the only thought in his head was to walk around the city although he didn't know what he expected of it. He wanted a shower but there was only cold water so after a quick wash and without stopping for breakfast he went out onto the streets.

The tram rattling along the street was crammed with passengers like a pumpkin with seeds. Savage took the first one available and got out at a stop with a tempting, cosy-looking cafe where the tables stood close together and the nonsense of lovers had been written with a finger in the dust on the dirty windows.

Savage sat down in a corner and ordered a black coffee, his gaze wandering over the crowded room. The café was stuffy and smoky and the blades of the fans turned lazily, grinding up snatches of conversation. A young couple chatted about mortgages, two solid chaps engaged in a heated discussion of the latest stock exchange news, a girl in a short dress shouted into her phone, gesticulating so wildly she nearly spilt her tea while the music wafting from the speakers stuck in the mouth like unripe berries. Savely spread out a magazine that had been left on the table and ran his eyes over the headlines but they only repeated the conversations that were going on around him as if the café's customers were reading the articles aloud to one another.

214

The cook could be heard singing in the kitchen. Fat as an opera singer, he sang arias as he made the soup and love songs as he prepared the meat then moved on to more modern melodies as he worked on the desserts. The waitress's heels kept time as she ran between the kitchen and the dining room. Having assessed Savage with a look in which Savely could read how low he was rated, she brought him the bill which he hadn't requested.

Savage paid and went on to a nearby café where the music was muffled and the conversations raced between the tables like beggars. Gossip, exchange rates, prices, brands and the names of celebrities hung like whores on every lip. Savage ordered a brandy, choosing the cheapest.

Rain scraped along the window and a woman, bored on her own and nervously lighting one cigarette from another, scrutinized the blurred shapes of passersby that flickered past the window. She appeared mysterious because she wasn't talking and Savage couldn't take his eyes off her. After a drink, he grew bolder and moved to her table to suggest, with a stammer, that they spend the evening together.

"You w-w-would th-th-think we had l-l-language so that we could communicate b-b-but it t-t-turns out to be quite the r-r-reverse. W-w-we t-t-talk to k-k-keep our thoughts hidden from the p-p-people w-w-we are t-t-talking to."

"Your coat cost 10 bucks," she drawled with a slight trill as she clicked her cigarette case shut. "You're one of the have-nots. What could you possibly offer me?"

Clapping a hand to his forehead as he might to an empty pocket, Savage backed out of the café.

A fine rain was falling. Pedestrians streamed past, slipping by like the wind-chased leaves. Savage walked through the streets, turning the word "have-nots" over on his tongue and ducking out of the way of the umbrellas that threatened to poke out an eye. The houses towered over him, the mouths of their stone arches yawning, and there was always rain in this city to be waited out under umbrellas and its conversations were the complete reverse of provincial gossip. He set off for the station that same evening and as he watched the platform recede he felt like an insect landing on fly paper only to leave its feet behind when it took off again.

And so Savage learnt that loneliness comes in many guises. In the countryside it's as quiet as a whisper behind you and in the big city it hits you over the head like a burglar with a bludgeon and roars in your ears with a thousand voices. To women it's as cold as an empty bed and to men it's as cold as a singleton's supper. Loneliness has ages just like people: in its youth it's as lachrymose as love poems inscribed on a wall and in old age it's cantankerous and decrepit so that everyone is lonely, each in their own way.

When he spotted the smoke from the factory chimneys drifting over the tree-tops, Savage felt a hot lump in his throat and nearly burst into tears, astonished at how much he'd missed a town in which he'd been so unhappy. His escort gave him a gentle prod in the back and, without looking round, ran back the way he had come, whistling to himself as he went.

Once on his own, it was all Savage could do not to hurl himself after the boy but the Saami had already vanished in the taiga and Savage knew very well that forest paths disappear as soon as they are walked on while others appear in their place to confuse you and make you lose the trail as they take you in a completely different direction.

Yellow leaves jumped under foot and a cold sun hung like a drawing of itself, offering no warmth at all. The Saami used to say that, at night, the sun would leave the sky on a reindeer doe and turn back into a man who had a wife and children as all men do. It had seemed to Savage in the forest that there were people all around him: the frozen expressions of the stones, the laughing rivers, the embracing trees, their branches entwined like lovers. He collapsed into the shaggy paws of fir trees held out like arms and sobbed aloud as though leaning on the shoulder of a friend.

The little town that he had previously found quiet and sleepy now seemed as clamorous as the metropolis. Klaxons and car horns, noises from the factory, laughter, tears, snatches of conversation – there was such a din, so much bellowing and ringing that it made Savage's head spin. A man stuck out of the gaping maw of a car and Savage imagined a monster had gobbled up the driver who was rootling around in the boot, while the grey houses crowding in on all sides seemed like craggy fjords. Stumbling backwards, Savely was close to diving back into the forest but onlookers had already gathered behind him. Armed with sticks and stones, the men stared at him, scratching the back of their necks. Savage saw the walls covered in his pictures, one of which the murdered runt had brought to the Saami encampment.

"Hey, toe rag, where did you come from?" yelled one of the men, taking a couple of steps towards him.

"Keep back. You can see he's a nut job!"

Savage touched his broken nose, tangled beard and long, matted hair littered with twigs and dry grass and realized that any resident of the town looked more like his picture than he did. Meanwhile, the men continued to argue, looking over the strange tramp who was more like a wood demon than a vagrant.

"He's really weird. Maybe we should call the cops?"

"He does look crazy…"

"I'm Savely Savage!" he shouted, gesturing towards the photos.

The rags on his feet trailed on the ground as Savage plodded on and the bewildered men followed, keeping their distance. "Savely Savage," they said to one another, trying to get a feel for the name and threatening him with their sticks whenever he turned round. Passersby stopped to look at them curiously, shrugging their shoulders or joining the procession without knowing why. "It's Savage!" came a loud shout and a frightened whisper went up on all sides: "It's Savage! It's Savage! Savage!"

The news raced through the town, stirring up the anthill. The inhabitants dropped what they were doing and rushed to look at the man they had first regarded as a murderer and then thought had been murdered himself. They didn't know what to think now but they did want to see him for themselves.

"No way is that Savage!" the crowd argued.

"It's him!"

The streets were noisy. Women, hands clasped to their chests, gasped and wailed, children cried and men hollered and poked the shaggy tramp. Seeing the crowd processing along the street, passersby hurried over to see what was going on so that the numbers kept on growing.

Curtains twitched with curiosity and those inside threw open the windows and hung out.

"What's happened?" they asked, cupping their hands over their mouths. "What sort of meeting is it? Where's everyone going?"

Savage rounded a corner onto the central square to go past the veranda his life had careered blindly towards like a crazed elk three months ago. He felt as if he would see Coffin there, smirking and holding out his gun, along with a tipsy Vasilisa and Antonov, the marks of the wire visible on his neck. Looking over his shoulder, Savage was startled to see how many people were following him. Dirty little boys kept running forward and peering into his face, asking: "Are you really Savage?" then scattered with a shriek if he tried to touch them.

A car with darkened windows crept slowly down the street. Saam looked at the hunched, dishevelled vagrant and couldn't believe it was the same Savage who had arrived at the veranda, stammering in confusion, his battered briefcase clutched to his chest.

"It's not him!" whispered Savage's wife, pressing a handkerchief to her lips. "It's not!"

"It is!" Saam cut in. "Out of the car!"

"What happens now?" the woman whined. "Now what? How are we going to manage?"

"Like you did before," the gangster replied, gesturing to the driver to stop. "Out!" he said again impatiently.

"I'm scared," the woman said, shaking her head and cuddling her daughter. "He's crazy! Mad! I'm scared!"

Saam took hold of her chin and his pupils narrowed to slits.

"Out!" he rapped out and Savage's wife crossed herself and got out of the car.

Dragging her daughter along like a doll, she went towards Savage, her shaking hands straightening a hair-do that had slipped to the side. Savage stopped, perplexed, and the crowd behind him slowed down. Savely felt tears welling up and his wife, eyes tightly closed, gave him a hug then stepped back overwhelmed by the stench.

"Hello, Savage," she whispered, trembling as she looked over this man who was so unlike her husband.

"Hello, Mrs Savage," said Savely, screwing up his face and attempting a smile. "Well, here I am," he muttered, holding out his arms, unable to come up with anything else to say.

His wife ran a hand over his hairy face, then jerked it back as if it were burnt. Savely thought that this woman had never been so distant from him as she was now. He looked into his daughter's eyes, empty and viscous like her mother's, and saw only anger and fear. Savage longed to embrace his daughter but Vasilisa shrank back and hid behind her mother. The crowd came to a halt. Only a couple of steps separated them from Savage. Shifting their feet, they watched him and waited to see what would happen.

Sirens blaring, patrol cars made their deafening way through the crowd. Police officers leapt out and Savage put his hands up to show he was unarmed. The officers didn't move, however, their jaws dropping as they gazed at Savage before they stood back to let him through. For a long time, Savely couldn't bring himself to lower his hands. They moved further back and, acknowledging them, Savage went cautiously by. He kept looking over his shoulder, afraid they would attack him from behind.

The square was packed as if it were a holiday. The veranda was crowded with the bar's customers, bouncers and waitresses, fearfully hugging their round trays to their chests. "Shoot me, or I shoot you" – Coffin's words rang in their ears. Savage stared at the table the gangster had sat at that evening and once again was assailed by a feeling that he had simply imagined it all.

Savage was pulled up short when he saw his reflection in a window. He was wearing short, ragged trousers, there was cellophane wrapped round his feet and his jumper hung in rags on a body as dry as a stick. His beard was a filthy mat of hair and his broken nose appeared to have fallen asleep on his cheek. Savage turned towards his daughter and saw her cover her face with a handkerchief, the stench from her father overwhelming. He couldn't resist and stroked his daughter's head. She jumped back in disgust and burst into tears.

Lapin pushed through the crowd to get to Savage. He had heard that Savage had turned up from a woman next door who had been spreading the news like a newspaper boy. He had raced down the stairs without even locking the door, buttoning his shirt as he ran. The investigator flew through the streets but passersby pointed him in different directions like broken compasses and sirens were wailing all over town so that in the end he was so confused he despaired of ever seeing Savage. Then, a passing police patrol told him he was in the central square and Lapin dashed off.

"You've got to tell the truth!" he said, grabbing Savage by the shoulder. Several shaven-headed characters pulled him off.

"Savage! Savage, do you hear me?" he yelled. "You've got to tell the truth!"

The shaven-headed gangsters wouldn't let him take another step. Every time the investigator tried to get closer to Savage they grabbed his arms or stood shoulder to shoulder to block his path, pushing Lapin back towards the crowd.

Gazing around, Savage saw that people surrounded him

on all sides like impenetrable fir trees. They were staring at him greedily.

"Savage, did you see Coffin get killed?" they shouted at him.

"Were you hiding in the forest?"

"Are you scared?"

Savage's wife tried to push back the press of people to shield her husband from their questions.

"Stop! Can't you see he's not well?"

Savage had spots before his eyes. The curious glances pierced him like needles and the faces merged into a shapeless mass. He felt as though the yelling mouths wanted to bite him and he veered out of their way. He stepped forward and the crowd parted with a gasp.

Police officers ran up and took him by the arms and Savage went limp as if his backbone had been removed. His legs wouldn't obey him. His head fell forward onto his chest as if his neck were broken and in the noise of the crowd Savage could hear the singing of the Saami women as it hopped from one rhyme to the next like birds on the branches of trees.

"Stand back! Let us through!" bellowed a chubby sergeant running ahead of Savage. "Stand back!"

They took pictures of Savage, thrusting their mobiles in his face and reaching out to try and touch him but the pungent stench of his unwashed body made them turn away in disgust, holding their noses. There was no end to the flood of people and when Savage arrived at the police station it seemed as though the entire town had followed him.

Savage was taken down long corridors where dim light bulbs blinked like conspirators and shadows like sneak-thieves crept along behind him. He abandoned himself to his fate and didn't think about anything, regret anything or fear anything as he followed his escorts as obediently as a dog on a lead.

The leather-upholstered office smelled of brandy, money and torn-up police records. On the walls there were pictures of the Chief and Trebenko, his oppressive gaze fixed on Savage.

Taking a bottle out of a locker, the chief of police poured a cloudy liquid into their glasses just as Trebenko had done when Savage appeared at his garage door, and he shuddered. They drank without clinking glasses, looking askance at the pictures. Then, before Savage had a chance to open his mouth, the police chief unfolded a newspaper and read out the story of Karimov, the serial killer, which had caused a sensation far beyond the borders of the little town. Savage's head ached. It was as if the town, its people and this office were just a dream and the news about Karimov was a trick of his sick imagination.

"We know you were intimidated and had to leave town," the chief said, putting his newspaper aside quite matter-of-factly, "but murder will out, as they say… Anyway, the killer has been apprehended and, please, don't worry, we'll give you all the help you need. See a doctor, get well…"

He threw open the windows to air the office that reeked of Savage.

"Has the killer confessed?" Savely asked cautiously, running his hand through his hair.

"Of course!" said the chief of police. "He's confessed to everything and repented!"

Savage looked up at Trebenko and thought he saw the colonel narrow his pupils.

"He was a fine man!" the chief said, intercepting his gaze. "Honest, incorruptible! Let's drink to him!"

Pouring out another glass, he drank it down in one gulp, wiping his mouth on his sleeve. Hunger and the brandy made Savage feel sick and he took out the bundle of food the Saami woman had given him and stuffed a piece of fish greedily into his mouth. Breaking off a piece of flatbread, Savage offered it to the policeman who waved it away with a forced smile.

"No, thanks. I've just eaten."

Savage was taken to a tiny, cramped and smoky room, where a sleepy officer gave him some papers to sign. Savage didn't even look at them before writing his name.

"We've written this in your name to make things easy for

you. These are just formalities. Just in case though, go through it at home, before the trial…" the officer handed Savage copies of the signed witness statements.

Once outside the office, Savage fiddled with the rolled up papers and couldn't work out where to go. His legs wouldn't obey him and a wave of terror suddenly grasped him by the throat like a murderer and stopped him breathing. Sinking into a chair against the wall, he collapsed and fell into drunken oblivion until the cleaner woke him up by slapping him across the face with a wet rag.

"Get out of here!" she told Savage, wiping down the chair he'd sat in. "Go on, get out!" she cried, waving the wet cloth. Savage fled.

Wandering along the various floors, he squatted down in a corner, his head in his hands, but the drink scattered his thoughts and they crept away like blind kittens. Savage took out his bundle of food and fell on the fragrant bread that the old Saami woman had made with rain water. He sobbed at the thought of the herders' kind faces.

"Where's that stink coming from?!" said a girl carrying a batch of documents as she put her head round the corner, holding her nose. "What are you doing there?" she yelled at Savage, folding her arms.

Savely offered her the papers he'd been given by the police officer but couldn't get his cotton-wool tongue to work and just mumbled something helplessly by way of a reply.

The woman knocked at one of the offices for help.

"Look who you've got sitting here!" she said, nodding to the two fat men who peeped out.

"Come on, you, out," said one, giving Savage a kick. "Up you get. There's the exit!"

"Bloody tramp! It'll stink for the rest of the week," said the woman, unappeased. She fanned herself with her clutch of papers.

The second fat man pulled a face and took Savage by the collar:

223

"Get lost or we'll lock you up for a month!"

"That's just what he wants. To be fed and tucked up in bed!" said the furious woman. "I wouldn't let them anywhere near the place. They can live in the forest if they can't cope around other people!"

Savage staggered back towards the stairs and the fat man gave him such a kick that he lost his balance and fell down the stairs.

Savage's ears were ringing and he couldn't see straight. He didn't know where he was going. He hung onto the wall to avoid falling down and, missing the door, he tumbled right into an office.

Cigarette smoke almost concealed the table and the officers who were sitting at it, engaged in a lively squabble over a bottle of wine.

"Look at this!" said a lanky young man, arms open wide, when he saw Savage. "Over here, darling, come on!" he said, looking kindly at Savage and closing the door behind him to general laughter.

The duty officer who had once driven Savage out of the station and persuaded him to leave town didn't recognize him in the filthy vagrant smelling of spirits. He shoved him into a cell where a trio of drunken tramps greeted their fellow with catcalls and laughter.

Shoving the papers into his shirt, Savage stretched out on the floor and suddenly recognized them as down-and-outs who'd lived at the tip.

Collaring one of them, Savage pulled him closer:

"The red-haired woman? What about her?"

The tramp pushed Savage away and crashed down beside him. The other two rushed over to help.

"The woman with red hair?" Savely asked, grabbing the tramps' legs.

They lost their balance and fell down on top of him so that when the duty officer looked through the hatch he saw a heap of bodies on the floor.

"Break it up!" he said, entering the cell and giving each of them a kick. "Break it up, I said!" Once he'd got them all in different corners, he slammed the door shut.

"The red-head?" yelled Savage but the tramps mumbled and turned away from him as ruffled as sparrows.

Blood trickled from his split lip. Savage spat out a rotten tooth, curled himself into a ball and fell asleep. A crowd of memories assailed him in his deep, drunken sleep, slapped his cheeks, spat in his face and pulled him in different directions, tearing his clothes. "Shoot me or I'll shoot you!" said Coffin over and over again, staring at him with eyes as prickly as burrs. "Run where? You don't need to run anywhere," said Trebenko, pouring out the drinks and hiding his battered head under his cap while Salmon, her shroud pulled up to her chin like a blanket, sobbed like a child.

Savage was woken by shouts from the corridor. The face of the chief of police appeared at the barred window. It was a tight fit.

"Idiots!" he yelled at his subordinates. "He's here!"

The lock grated and policemen burst into the cell, taking Savage by the arms and legs and dragging him along like a sack.

"I was starting to think he'd run off again," sighed the chief, wiping the sweat from his brow, while the duty office tutted and stared wide-eyed at Savage, unable to see in him the frightened and bewildered man who had come to the station to hand himself in three months ago.

"I'm Savely Savage who shot Coffin!" The words rang in the duty officer's ears but, stealthily crossing himself, he drove away these bad thoughts and put them down to a vivid imagination.

The hospital reception area was cold and the doctor, wrapped in a soft shawl, was warming her hands on a mug of tea. The radio wheezed and spluttered as if it had a cold and the music was drowned out by the static. A jaundiced attendant made the sign of the cross over his mouth as he yawned and put his ear to the speaker.

"Can't hear a damn thing!" he said, tapping the radio and pulling the flex out of its socket.

Savage sat on a couch, dangling his feet and listening to the silence. A clock ticked sonorously. The patients thronging the corridor groaned and the doctor tapped her feet in time to a tune only she could hear. They removed the bundle hidden under Savage's shirt, took his temperature, gave him an injection that made his chest burn and dumped him on a stretcher.

"Get him out of here!" the doctor ordered and the attendants carried him out feet first.

"He is still alive, you know!" said an indignant police officer. "At least, carry him properly!"

Banging Savage against the doorframe, they turned the stretcher round and took him out head first.

"Where are you taking him? We haven't got any beds!" shouted a nurse, blocking their path. She stood in the door to the ward her hands on her hips. "I'm sick of these wretched tramps! Take him to the morgue!"

The police officer who was hurrying to keep up with the stretcher took out a warrant and opened it under her nose.

"Hey, you, out of the way!" He threw open the doors and stepped aside, letting the attendants go through. "Bring him in!"

The white-tiled bathroom looked like a mortuary. The sink leaked. There was a smell of medicines and bleach. Putting the stretcher on the floor, the attendants stripped off Savage's clothes, wincing at the stench.

"Christ! What on earth have you brought in?" said a plump female attendant, throwing up her arms at the sight of Savely. Embarrassed, he hastened to cover himself with his hands.

"Don't worry, Lyuska! He'll scrub up nicely when you wash him and warm him up!" said the attendant with a familiar laugh as he pinched her breast.

He set about shaving off Savage's beard and his matted

hair. The woman took a pair of clippers from her pocket and went to work on his curved, yellow nails that were like bird's claws.

"Are you the one the whole town's been looking for?" she asked Savage. "You poor thing, you," she said shaking her head. Then, turning to the attendants, she exclaimed, "Why have they been chasing him? You can tell he wouldn't hurt a fly!"

Lifting Savage by the armpits, the attendants put him in the bath and directed the shower hose at him. The woman rolled up her sleeves and scrubbed him with a rough cloth, delivering harsh little comments that made his nose sting.

They put Savage in pyjamas, the issue number marked in blue ink, sat him in a wheelchair and set off, pushing aside the curious patients who had gathered in the corridor to get a look at Savely Savage. He was put in a separate ward where the neatly made beds were empty and the door locked from the outside. Doctors and nurses fussed over him all night. Drips were replaced by tablets and nurses by policemen who crept up on tiptoe to study him with interest.

Savage had a fever. He went from hot to cold and, like busy nurses, ghosts huddled over him, holding hands and swaying like sleepwalkers. Antonov's lacerated throat was bleeding. The red-headed woman was spattered with soot and Savage felt himself dissolving on the bed like putty melting in the heat. He tried to sit up in bed to call for help but at that very moment he woke up and the nurses hushed him, settled him back down and tucked him in.

Unbeknownst to Savage, a nurse filled a syringe with a tranquilliser and gave him an injection like a wasp sting. Savage abandoned himself to a leaden sleep in which events and people were all mixed up, the past was no longer the past and blood turned into paint and only the voice of Coffin rang in his ears all night: "a little man in a little town…"

Everything in the ward was white: white walls, white curtains, white sheets, the milk-white skin of the nurses in their white uniforms, white wraiths peering out from behind them. Savely jabbed a finger at them and the hallucinations vanished and the nurses rolled up his pyjama sleeves to give him another dose of tranquilliser. They waited until he was asleep to produce a greasy deck of cards and set up their game right on the bed. The tranquilliser made his dreams bitter and his waking hours as cloudy as misted glass and Savage couldn't tell one from the other as if the days and nights had been reshuffled like a deck of cards.

"You haven't overdone it with the meds, have you?" came a voice that sounded like it came from a funnel.

Savage tried but failed to unglue his eyelids and, pursing his lips into a straw, he tried to catch every word.

"He's not himself," lisped the doctor. He swallowed his vowels like pills and talked in consonants. Savage knew who he was from this obscure way of talking. "Our j-b is to m-ke him b-tt-r!"

"Your job is to get him back to normal so that he's walking, talking and eating, not just lying in bed like a block of wood! Are you giving him psychotropics?"

"We are," the doctor said innocently. "He's d-l-r-ous, hall-c-n-ting."

"Sort it out!" The answer was barked back.

A few days later Savage was already out of bed and wandering around the ward. An auxiliary nurse treated him to a cigarette and he smoked it at an open window in secret from the doctors. Savely asked the girl to bring him local newspapers but she shook her head with a frown:

"That's not allowed!"

The corridor was packed with beds. It smelled of boiled cabbage, medicines and the ball of soiled sheets a nurse was dragging along the floor. Savage walked holding on to the wall and the patients whispered to one another as they looked him over. The toilet was full of smoke. A crowd of men in the passageway chatted about nothing in particular, blowing tiny smoke rings for want of something to do.

"Have you heard about the actor?" asked one patient, his head in bandages.

"The one who hanged himself?" asked another, nodding and adjusting his catheter. "What did he want for? Money, fame, women…"

"They say he played a suicide in his last film but they just couldn't get the scene right where he put the noose around his neck. The director was even threatening to tear up the contract and bring someone else in. He was so scared of someone else getting his part that he started rehearsing at home. He read up on the Internet how to make a noose, hooked it round the ceiling light, stood in front of a huge mirror and acted out the suicide. But he slipped on the chair and accidently hanged himself…"

"Good God! What about the film?"

"They had to do it with a different actor."

They both fell silent, letting Savage through. Their eyes bored into his back as he stood at the urinal.

"Life's a disease," drawled the man in bandages.

"No," said the other, screwing up his face. "Death's the disease and the incubation period lasts a lifetime!"

Again they fell silent, drawing thoughtfully on their cigarettes.

"That one's not long for this world," said the man in bandages, exhaling smoke through his nostrils and jabbing at a urine sample pot.

"And this one's like dew. Look at it! Whose is that?" the other nodded, peering short-sightedly. "Go on, can you read the name? Lucky bastard!"

"Kuznetsov," read the man in bandages. "You're not Kuznetsov, are you?" he asked Savage.

Savely shook his head.

"So who are you?"

"I'm Savely Savage," Savage mumbled keeping his voice low.

"The one who was found in the forest?"

The men lost interest in him and turned back to the samples.

"I wonder what ward that Kuznetsov's in? How old is he? What do you reckon? The same as us?"

In the evening, the whole ward gathered around the TV. Those with broken legs tossed their crutches aside. Ulcer patients sat in one corner, hands folded on their stomachs. Plump heart cases were in another. A nurse pushed them aside and brought over a wrinkled old man in a wheelchair who never spoke but merely rolled his eyes from side to side.

"He can't understand anything anyway," the patients shouted, pushing the old man into a corner where he spent the whole evening, staring at the paint peeling from the wall.

Savage, perched on the edge of a sofa, looked at the television and it seemed as if everything that had happened to him was just a film he had seen on the screen. He kept turning round as if something were breathing down his neck. He felt as if there were a crowd behind him, tossing a single phrase to one another like a hot potato: "It's Savely Savage!" But there was no-one there. The patients had soon lost interest in him and Savage himself couldn't tell what was real and what wasn't. He drove away the thoughts that pursued him like hungry hounds and wept for joy at being back from the forest when he looked at the windows of the nearby blocks of flats, their residents peeping at the hospital windows from behind their curtains. His bedside table contained the documents he'd been given at the police station. He would cast superstitious glances at them but couldn't bring himself to read them.

A tall, solid woman in a torn shirt wandered around the department, looking in at the wards. She was barefoot and dishevelled and a blissful smile played unbidden on her features like a cat.

"Rina, Rina, come and join us!" the men called, tearing themselves away from the television. "Come on, gorgeous!"

Every year, Rina Oktyabrina would be brought over from the psychiatric hospital where she had become pregnant, God knows by whom. She would wrap a pillow in a sheet, cradle it like a baby and sing it a lullaby. Her ward had doors without handles, windows with bars and fat half-drunken nurses. The only man was the old, gout-ridden doctor so they didn't know who to blame. Oktyabrina would be tied to her bed, locked in the back room and kept under constant observation on her walks and yet once a year her stomach stubbornly swelled. "It's the Holy Ghost's!" the nurses would say blasphemously, crossing themselves and dispatching her to the hospital where she would be scraped out like a pot of burnt porridge and then wander the floors of the hospital, empty and insane.

The women's department didn't have enough nurses who could perform both deliveries and abortions and they were always losing Oktyabrina, like a needle in a haystack. She would pop up here or there and, arms outstretched like a scarecrow's, she would snatch bags of fruit from visiting relatives. A stranger to shame, she would sit on men's laps or shrug off her top to reveal her drooping breasts. The men lured her into their wards where she hid under the beds from the nurses and during the night staff from the women's wards would search every floor in the hospital for their missing patient.

"Now, now, back you go!" said a nurse blocking her path. She dialled a number and yelled into the receiver: "Come and collect your star patient. She's wandering half-naked round the surgical ward!"

"Honestly, she should have been sterilized long ago!" said another nurse, shaking her head as she peered out of the treatment room and wrung out a wet cloth over a bucket. "Every year, she comes here. Without fail!"

Oktyabrina pushed the nurse out of the way and ran over to the television, tugging down her short top. Her curvaceous hips covering the screen, she cast a triumphant look at her audience and stamped a bare foot.

"Rina, lift your shirt!" whispered a man with his leg in plaster, hand over his mouth. "Come on, Rina!"

As everyone laughed, the woman lifted her shirt, revealing

the curly hair low down on her belly. Savage jumped up as if he'd been scalded. He turned away from the madwoman and the men nodded at him.

"Look what a gentleman! Turning up his nose!" shouted the leg patient, scratching the skin under his plaster. "She might be an old bag to you but she suits me fine!" he guffawed.

"You've no shame!" said a nurse with a waggish shake of fist. "No shame at all!"

Savage stretched out on his bed, which rocked on its springs. His future seemed less and less clear to him and suddenly it occurred to him that he might escape – into the forest, back to the Saami, to the down-and-outs at the tip, anywhere as long as it was far away from this town.

He took the paperwork out of his bedside table and ran a finger along the leaping lines that detailed the murder of Coffin, of which he had now become an inadvertent witness.

He was met outside the hospital by his wife and by police officers who supported him by the arms as they led him to a car. He was suddenly stricken by a dreadful feeling of weakness as if the months of wandering were hanging on him like drunken girls. He couldn't take a single step unaided.

His wife had managed to plaster a smile on her face as if she'd used some special lipstick, but over the years the smile had become increasingly false and now, watching her curl her lips into a sneer, Savage lowered his gaze. His old life was coming back like a flood tide, washing over a bereft shore and Savage felt he was just the same as he had been three months earlier, the unloved husband of a domineering wife.

Pulling the door to, Savage's wife stayed out on the landing for a long time whispering to the policemen, while Savely, like an uninvited guest, hovered in the hallway, too timid to cross the threshold. He gazed around as if seeing the walls he'd spent his life in for the first time. Taking in the smell of the flat, he recognized the tartness of lemon peel hidden in the wardrobe, the pungency of lipstick and the smell of the cigarettes his daughter disguised with cheap scent. There was the odour of old wood and leather boots, of dust on books and family meals, of a pillow wet with tears and the withered violets Vasilisa had forgotten, as always, to water, and the many other aromas that made up the smell of his home and were evident only on returning from a long journey.

He found his slippers under the chest of drawers. He popped into the kitchen and opened the fridge out of habit to find his shelf was bare. Gnawing on a piece of cheese, he went into his room that he had recalled so wistfully at the town tip. He fell onto his bed, which was magically soft, and fell asleep, fully dressed, still holding the cheese. When his wife looked in on him, it was a long time before she could take her eyes off this stranger who had appeared in the flat.

"Vasilisa's staying over at a friend's," she whispered into the telephone. "I'm scared to go out and staying in… Yes, yes, you're right," she nodded at her friend's advice. "I'll put a knife under my pillow."

Savage stood in front of the mirror inspecting his dried-up, yellow body, covered in cuts and bruises. Gnarled blue veins had appeared on his legs. His ribs jutted out over a hollow belly and his chin was as sharp as an old man's.

"I look terrible," he said, pulling a face and running a hand through his hair when he met his wife in the hall.

Fidgeting with the belt of her housecoat, his wife, embarrassed, said nothing.

"E-e-everything's so mixed up, s-s-so w-w-weird…" Savage tried to say, stammering as he had before. "I feel like I've gone mad."

"So what's new?" snapped his wife, unable to resist and immediately biting her lip in a rage.

Savage simply thought that there are no truces in domestic battles.

"I'm glad you're back," she lied, embarrassing them both with the falsehood. "Have you read the statements?"

"Wh-wh-where it s-s-says K-K-Karimov shot Coffin?"

233

Savage gave his wife a long, challenging look but she didn't bat an eyelid. "What d-d-does Vasilisa have to say? A-a-after all she w-w-was there."

"How could it possibly be any different to what you said?"

Pulling her housecoat more tightly around her, his wife vanished into the bathroom, locking it noisily behind her.

Vasilisa came back in the evening and looked at her father with mean and frightened eyes. His daughter avoided him, hiding away in her room, and when he did come across her in the kitchen, she jumped away in fright, a hand raised in self-defence.

"Vas-s-silisa, shall we have a chat?" Savage asked, standing in her way.

The girl was sullen and silent, her gaze turned away.

"L-l-let's t-t-talk about that n-n-night," said Savage lowering himself onto a stool and taking his daughter's hand.

"H-h-have you r-r-read w-w-what's in the papers?"

Vasilisa licked her lips and nodded.

"A-a-and what do you think about it?"

She twirled her hair round a finger and didn't reply.

"What d-d-do you think ab-b-bout K-k-karimov?"

"He's a terrible man, that Karimov. It's a good thing they caught him," she said, choosing her words as if she were feeling her way across a mossy swamp, checking where she could put her foot down safely.

"And that n-n-night?"

"I was really scared when he fired," she sighed, lowering her gaze. "I only saw Coffin fall and then everyone started yelling and running around and I didn't understand any of it and then people said you were the one who shot him..." Vasilisa breathed in deeply and fired out, "I even believed it myself for a while."

You could have cut the silence with a knife. Savage looked at his daughter's bitten lips and recalled the crimson lipstick she'd worn that night and how he'd wanted to rub it off with his sleeve. Unable to bear his silence, Vasilisa jumped up, knocking the stool over.

"I've got to go," she said and, without looking at her father, she rushed out of the kitchen, leaving him alone and at a loss.

Savage's wife often thought about a divorce but a school friend with as many divorces as marriages to her name dissuaded her, shaking her head:

"Every new one's worse than the last!"

Her friend couldn't bear officialdom and to avoid having to change her identity papers she kept the name of her first husband even after their divorce. She wore it like a wig. Her ex-husbands all seemed the same to her and when she met them in the street she got their names mixed up and they had to remind her which number husband they were.

"Love takes the years off, marriage piles them on," Savage's wife agreed, wiping away a trickle of mascara.

She changed her lovers the way she changed her clothes and thought of her husband as a well-worn housecoat. Her initial terror wore off and once again she reigned supreme in their relationship like a wrestler standing over a prostrate opponent.

"Your colleagues want to know when you'll be back at work," she said, dropping it into the conversation in such unctuous tones that Savage broke out in a clammy sweat.

He thought back to his desk, piled with drawings, the pot-bellied computer he just couldn't get used to so that he continued drawing by hand out of habit, and the limping coat stand that tipped sideways whenever he passed which made his colleagues sigh meaningfully, their gaze going through him like thread through the eye of a needle. After college, Savage had dreamed of soaring like a bird but instead had plodded off to work like a cur, tail between its legs and teeth chattering.

"Have they really not given me the sack?" he marvelled. "For all the time I've had off?"

"They've given you unpaid leave," his wife answered, her eyes glittering. "But you mustn't take advantage."

Savage's wife attempted to revive family meals. She spent all day at the stove, spread the table with a freshly ironed cloth and put out the best china.

Conversation at the table failed to flow and the silence swelled like clouds full of rain, threatening to break into thunder and lightning. Savage simply couldn't get used to a fork, put the crumbs off the table into his mouth and virtually licked his plate clean, but his wife's eyes glittered, trapping him in his chair like a moth on a pin. Vasilisa was taut as a string. She didn't touch her food while her mother rolled little balls of bread and struggled to start the conversation.

"The f-f-fate of man is the s-s-sum of circumst-t-tance," muttered an embarrassed Savage addressing his daughter. "We are p-p-powerless over it..."

"Come again?" frowned Vasilisa.

"Well, t-t-take C-c-christ," said Savage, nodding at the Orthodox calendar on the wall. "If th-th-things had b-b-been different, he c-c-could have been Judas..."

"How?" His daughter couldn't follow him.

"Well, if s-s-something h-h-ad h-h-happened..."

"Like what?" asked Vasilisa. So Savage gave up, biting his tongue.

"Was it tough, being in the forest?" his wife asked to change the subject.

Inwardly Savage cried: "Better than at home." Aloud he muttered: "It was."

With a clatter of her fork, Vasilisa left the table without a word and Savely crumpled like a deflated ball. Savage's wife hastily poured out the tea and cleared the plates away. Watching the wreaths of steam above their cups, Savely thought back to the bonfire the Saami had lit in the clearing. Dusk was falling but they left the lights off so that it soon went dark in the kitchen but Savage and his wife sat on in the darkness for another hour without saying a word.

A pink-cheeked police officer turned up on the doorstep unannounced. Staring at his scarred face Savage took him for a gangster in disguise and went white with terror. One of the scars split his top lip in half so that when the policeman wasn't speaking, it looked as if he had a harelip.

"Scars look good on a man," he said when he spotted Savage's look.

Savely glanced doubtfully at the cuts on his own hands which until recently had been as smooth and white as a lady's.

"Soon be good as new!" the policeman chuckled. Savage found this deeply irritating.

Sprawled in a chair, the visitor took out some papers and licked his finger to flick through them. Savage drew back the curtain and took a quick look at the patrol car that had been keeping watch outside for days.

"I just need to clarify something," the officer said, chewing his pencil. "About the night Coffin needed a coffin of his own..." He giggled at the pun.

Savage winced and nodded.

"Where were you standing when Karimov fired?"

"I was next to Antonov's car, talking to my daughter..." He paused after every word as if seeing how it felt. "A car pulled up and Karimov got out."

There was a shriek of brakes from outside and Savage stopped talking, nervously loosening the neck of his jumper. The policeman looked up, frowning in surprise. Savely swallowed and continued repeating his statement word for word, as if reading it from a piece of paper. His visitor crossed his legs and turned a page in his notebook and Savage could see that there wasn't a word in it. The whole page was covered in noughts and crosses. A chill ran through him and, shivering with the sudden cold, he threw a blanket round his shoulders.

"Thanks for your time," said the policeman and left, putting the notebook away in his pocket.

Savage saw him out then tried to work out why he'd

come. Closing the door behind him, he looked through the spy hole to make sure he'd gone. The visitor went down a couple of stairs then came back, creeping up on tiptoe and listening with his ear to the door. To Savage it seemed as if his ear were a stethoscope that could hear his heart beating wildly and he held his breath, afraid to release it and give himself away. Adjusting his cap, the police officer whistled and dashed off down the stairs.

Back in his room, Savage checked that nothing was missing. Then he took a broom and swept away the mud from his boots and the stupid jokes scattered by the suspect policeman.

Savage closed his eyes and went over the evening Coffin was shot, reliving it minute by minute as he remembered it before turning it inside out and rearranging it back to front. He only became more confused. He kept getting stuck right at the second the shot was heard and the weapon jerked as if in its death throes and fell from his hands. It seemed as though he'd never pulled the trigger or, if he had, that he'd pointed the gun upwards and that then there was a second shot and a third or perhaps he hadn't fired at all or the gun fired a blank and fell from his grasp without killing a soul. And where was Karimov at that moment? Was he even there? Savage felt as if his doubts were starting to eat away at him, like rust corroding his recollections and confusing them with imaginings and overheard conversations.

Going through his old clothes which were now several sizes too big and hung on him like sacks, Savage thought back to the cold nights in the taiga when brushwood had kept him warm and he'd rigged up a hut from dry branches and rotten, mouldering trees. He felt cold all the time as if he'd been so frozen out in the forest that he still couldn't thaw out and, pulling on several sweaters, he sat under a camel-wool blanket, listening to his teeth chatter.

His daughter stayed out at night and his wife came home late, concealing kiss marks under her blouse. Just as before, she took no more notice of her husband than of the furniture. She seemed to have put the last few months of her life out of her mind like the torn-off pages of a calendar being flicked into the bin.

All that was left for Savage was to talk to himself and wander through the mazes of his imagination, which presented events in a new pattern each time like a kaleidoscope. Looking in the mirror, he could no longer tell what happened the night Coffin was shot.

Howling with loneliness, he dialled telephone numbers at random then said nothing when he heard a voice at the other end until the receiver was replaced. Once, however, he did bring himself to reply.

"Yes, hello?" a woman's impatient voice repeated.

"H-h-hello," Savage drawled, nerves making him stammer more than usual. "I just h-h-happened to d-d-dial your number. I j-j-just w-w-wanted to hear a h-h-human…"

"Are you lonely?" came the sudden response. "Are you having a tough time?"

"I really am," Savage admitted, dropping the phone in his agitation. "Hello, c-c-can you hear me?"

"Yes, yes. I can hear you…"

"I am very, very l-l-lonely. All m-m-my life, I have b-b-been as lonely as if I were in a lifeless desert but now it's like b-b-being in outer space and infinity is all around… Do you understand?"

"Of course, I do. We should meet!"

"R-r-really?" Savage said in surprise. "Are you s-s-serious?" Then, hesitating, he added, "M-m-my n-n-name is Savely Savage…"

"Great! You need specialist help. Come to our psychology centre. We can help everyone," the woman replied in a soothing tone. A cactus sprang up in Savage's throat. "Jot down the address."

Savage shuffled into the kitchen, opened the bottle of vodka with his teeth and took a gulp. He threw away the crumpled bit of paper on which he'd written the address and leaned on his fist against the cold glass. The patrol car was still keeping watch over the entrance to the flats. An officer got out and flexed his stiff joints. He looked up at Savage's window and Savely hid behind the curtain, cursing himself for being so childish.

In a little town, people get set in their sedate lives like flies in amber. People there like the old jokes that stick in your teeth like last year's jam. They wear their clothes until they wear them out and they read the same books, year in year out, delighted that the story doesn't change and they know the ending. Newspapers, unlike women, don't age in the provinces. Nothing goes out of fashion here because no-one follows the trends anyway and every tomorrow is a carbon copy of yesterday. Savage used to believe that a person should die where he was born and live quiet as a mouse. Now that he had put his former life on like a hat back to front he believed that before he died he needed the chance to be born, to hatch like a baby bird from the eggshell of his own fate. He felt as if he'd been used as a tool of revenge but he didn't know who by. He was terrified when he looked at himself in the mirror. He told his reflection, "You think God's leading you by the hand. But it turns out the Devil's leading you a merry dance!"

"It's just a formality. We won't keep you long." The officer spoke hoarsely into the receiver as he invited Savage into the station. "We need to go over your statements…"

Savely was bored being stuck inside his own four walls and was pleased to be going out. He quickly got ready and put the crumpled witness statements in his pocket. He'd read them so many times he dreamed about Karimov arguing with Coffin by the veranda and firing a gun at him.

"Now, don't hesitate to ask if you need anything," said the rotund policeman at the wheel, turning to face Savage. "The car's always outside. We'll take you where you need to go."

"I d-d-don't know w-w-where I need to go," said Savage with a shrug. The fat man smirked understandingly.

At the police station, they read the witness statements out again and pointed at the papers to show him where to sign. The letters jumped about in front of him like fleas and Savage glanced superstitiously at the records, in which the words kept changing places and altering the meaning. He felt as if everyone but him could read the new meaning.

"Why are we bothering with him?" the officer shrugged. "It's high time we wrapped this case up."

His small black eyes were like two fat flies in his face and it seemed they would fly away at any moment.

"We've been told to give him time to get back on his feet. They said he's not himself since being in the forest and he might still say something he shouldn't. But what could that be when everything's known already?"

Savage ran into the chief of police in the corridor.

"How're things?" The chief held out a hand. "Are you feeling better? Glad to be back?"

Trebenko's features could be seen in his fleshy face and Savage stammered, unable to spit out the words that stuck to his tongue. The chief of police shifted from foot to foot, already sorry he'd stopped. Looking at Savage's trembling lips, he grimaced in disgust. Then he took his leave, citing his work.

"I am," Savage sighed after him.

Savage found himself as lost in the police station as a babe in the woods. He hammered on all the doors. Every one was locked and every floor was empty. He had raised a fist to knock when he heard voices, the door swung open right in front of him and out came an officer with Karimov in tow. His hands were handcuffed behind him and the dark thoughts that kept him awake at night could be seen in the furrows on his brow. Recognizing Savage, he turned to look at him, ignoring the threats of the sergeant, pushing him from behind.

Subsiding onto the back seat of the car, Savely asked the driver to take him out of town.

"That's not allowed," he said, hesitating. "But as long as you don't get out of the car…"

The officer switched on the flashing light and raced past the garages, through the rabbit-warren of single-storey houses and the open spaces of squares littered with the rusting carcasses of cars like skeletons that had been picked clean, on past the cemetery dense with monuments and crosses and the last signpost with the name of the town crossed out. Savage opened the window and stuck his head out, gulping down the air as greedily as drinking water from the kettle for a morning hangover.

"Do you think you could stop, please?" Savage asked. "I need some fresh air."

The fat man turned the wheel and braked at the side of the road.

Savely stretched out on the dusty grass and lit up greedily. The forest that overlooked the road was like a theatre curtain and Savage felt as though Salmon, Trebenko, Antonov, Coffin and the red-headed woman were hiding behind it like actors before the start of a show.

"Better?" the officer asked, bending over him. Savage nodded and gave him a strained smile. "In that case, I won't be a second." With a whistle, he went off into a gully by the side of the road.

Savage made a break for it, going the opposite way, plunging into the faded autumn forest that closed behind him like the gates of a city. When the fat cop came back onto the road, there wasn't a trace of Savage to be seen and no matter how much he ran this way and that, calling him, the only answer was the rustle of falling leaves like idle gossips whispering in amusement at the hapless policeman.

Lapin had already been pacing the corridors of local government for several days in the hope of waylaying the new mayor. Finally, his secretary, grey locks peeping out from under her black wig, called him in and, drawing her eyebrows into a single line, she pointed to the door. Lapin popped a sedative into his mouth. It was the only way to stop his lips twitching and his hands trembling. Then he strode into the office as if stepping off a cliff.

He nearly crossed himself when he saw the late Krotov sitting at the desk.

"It frightens everyone," the mayor told Lapin soothingly. He didn't offer him a chair so the investigator stood, adjusting his jacket in embarrassment and smoothing his hair.

The mayor had been Krotov's deputy for so many years that he knew everything Krotov had known. What's more, he knew what had gone on behind Krotov's back. So, when Lapin opened his mouth he interrupted with a wry face:

"I know all about it but there's nothing I can do. The local authorities are concerned with economic matters, with a peaceful life, so to speak, but crime's not our business."

"What if the police are corrupt and the prosecutors are in league with the gangsters?" cried Lapin, catching his breath.

The mayor ran a hand over his right cheek which was burning as though it had been slapped. Saying nothing, he turned the other cheek.

"And what if it's the criminals who lay down the law and if that's to everyone's liking?" Tears leapt from Lapin's eyes.

The mayor flexed his stiff joints and Lapin could read in his face the sentence that had already been handed down at work.

Towering over his desk, his boss had handed him a piece of paper.

"We're putting you up for promotion. Our little town cramps your style. You're going to the regional centre."

"But I don't want to go," said Lapin, shaking his head. "I won't go. I won't!" he repeated raising his voice.

His boss put the paper on the edge of the table, wedging it under an ashtray.

"There's no need to answer right away," the prosecutor said, turning round at the door. "You've got a week to think about it…" He paused then went on, "Incidentally, there's been a complaint about you. It seems we'll have to launch an inquiry. An in-house one to start with and then we'll see. If you do decide, however, we're not going to spoil things for you. But for now, you're suspended."

Lapin was gutted. He felt as superfluous as the teddy bear he'd given Severina when it had been tossed into a rubbish bin like an abandoned baby. He put his head down on the table and stayed like that until the evening when twilight crept into the office, gathering under the table and chairs, solidifying in the corners and settling in dark circles under his eyes. He picked up the paper about his transfer, scribbled his resignation on the back, rolled it into a tube and stuck it on the door handle of the prosecutor's office.

The clouds were clustered together like frightened sheep and the sun sought refuge behind them. The cold had settled in Savage's joints and he was doubled up with the pain of stomach cramps. He chewed the leaves and berries that used to deaden his hunger but now they merely tantalized. Savely was trying to find the tip, lurching at random like a drunk here, there and everywhere. He couldn't get Karimov out of his head. No matter where Savage looked, he could see Karimov's eyes black as crowberries, boring into his throat.

Pushing through the thorn bushes as if they were a crowd, Savage tripped and fell on the damp, squelchy moss. He felt lethal despair descend on him, keeping him down.

"So, Little Savage, did you imagine you could administer justice? Think you were running the show? Turns out the director of the play is someone else entirely!"

Savage gazed around to see where the voice was coming from until he realized he was talking to himself.

"He gave it his own meaning. After all, it's not only works of art that can have different interpretations!"

"How can life have an interpretation? Or events? Things either happen or they don't," said Savage, interrupting himself.

"You can live life in any order, in any sequence! You can turn what's happened into something that hasn't happened by

244

sewing a figment of your imagination on to the fabric of the past like a clever seamstress's patchwork."

"But who's doing the sewing?" Savage yelled. "Who if not me?"

"You're just the patch!" said his inner voice, guffawing. "Wherever you're sewn on, that's where you'll be!"

So he realized that the other Savely Savage who had been like a separated Siamese twin hadn't disappeared but had stayed behind in the forest. Then Savage ran towards the town, guided by the television tower rising above the forest like a signpost, while the other Savage laughed as he watched him go.

The houses brooded like giants with a hundred glittering eyes. Empty-hearted people passed him by. Savage scraped together what change he had to buy a bun at the bread stall, choking as he chewed it eagerly. People looked round at his hunched figure in surprise.

The bread filled his aching stomach but the town had nestled into his breast, deadening the flood of emotion. Savage cursed himself for running away. He could tell that he was carrying madness inside himself like a baby that could kick out to remind him of its presence at any moment. The insanity that had split him in two when he was in the forest boomed in his head and terror was hot on his heels. He hurried home in the belief that crossing the threshold into his flat would act like an injection. He'd feel better and his memories would scatter like frightened rats.

They were waiting for him in the entry way. Hunched on the rough bench was a young man in a creased grey jacket of the kind usually worn by office workers or investigators who flick out their ID like a knife. He stood up to meet Savage. The man seemed familiar and it occurred to Savely that in a small town all the residents remember one another's faces so that everyone seems to be an open book. Turn them inside out though like a reversible coat to show the inside and you'd go crazy, realizing you didn't even know the people closest to you, the ones you'd spent your life with.

Savage stopped impatiently but Lapin said nothing. He'd had his questions prepared but they seemed ridiculous now. He felt he'd been lost in a maze for a long time, then hit a blank wall just when he'd found the way out. All of a sudden he wanted to reach out and ask whether it had been lonely in the forest, whether Savage had heard the whispering of the trees and how to go on living when you don't know what for. Savely shuffled from foot to foot, Lapin licked his chapped lips and their gazes searched one another like blind men's hands.

"Are you here for me?" Savage asked after a minute.

"That's right," Lapin nodded.

They were both silent again, looking at their shadows which had merged with those of the trees that were thrashing in the wind. Lapin remembered the unkempt tramp he'd seen in the square, so unlike the nondescript character who now stood before him. He pictured him with a gun but couldn't imagine him as a killer. An eternity seemed to pass but the men didn't say a word. Lapin drew in the dust with the toe of his boot, wondering why not saying anything didn't make him feel uncomfortable.

A neighbour coming home with her shopping glanced at Savage and walked between them, breaking their interlocked stares and Savely shook off his stupor. He stepped back, still facing Lapin, and tried to key in the code for the lock without looking. The investigator strode towards him. Yanking the door open, Savage dashed into the entrance but Lapin raced after him and they climbed the stairs in step, eyes fixed on one another like boxers in the ring. Savely kept walking backwards and Lapin trod carefully after him. Savage quickened his pace and Lapin walked faster to keep up. Savely shot up the stairs and Lapin ran after him and when Savage pressed the bell, Lapin held on to the wall to get his breath back.

A police officer appeared on the threshold, looking from

one to the other in astonishment. He stepped back to let Savage into the flat, slammed the door and turned back to Lapin.

"Haven't you been warned about getting under our feet?" the cop asked, nudging him with his shoulder. "What are you doing here?"

Lapin ran downstairs and the officer slowly followed him down. His Adam's apple moved nervously and the lines on his forehead were as taut as strings.

"Well, do I call for back-up?" the policeman asked.

"You've no right! You don't have the authority!" Lapin blustered, going down another flight.

But the policeman squared his shoulders, becoming even taller and towering over Lapin like a mountain, he shoved him off the stairs, giving him no option but to leave.

The house was as crowded as the police station. The fat sergeant was clicking the remote in the living room. Two plainclothes officers were smoking in the kitchen and men's voices could be heard from his daughter's room. A cop took off Savage's mud-spattered coat and supported him while he took off his shoes.

"What's all this then, Savely? Trying to pull a fast one?" The cop frowned, helping him into bed. "We've put a wanted call out."

"S-s-sorry," Savage mumbled as he pulled the blanket up to his chin. "I'm sorry."

"We're going to keep you under guard until the trial. Just until you adapt, get back to your old life…"

"How long will that take?"

"Not long," the officer assured him. "In the meantime, get some rest. Your wife will give you sedative injections. Your nerves are shot. Well, it's understandable," he said, not letting Savage speak. "Now get some rest."

Skulking in the doorway, Savage's wife listened in, biting her lip. She dialled Saam's number and whispered, her hand over the receiver:

"He's back."

The sergeant had stretched out in the big room and his presence was like something in your eye. Mrs Savage wrung out a wet rag and cleaned the well-walked floor. Then she ran a bath and sat in it into the night, crying without knowing why.

As he counted the days like beads, Savage couldn't find the one when he'd turned into a killer. His three months of wandering around the taiga were fading from his memory, their only reminder his scratched hands and a nervous tick that made the right half of his face twitch and tighten like cloth caught in a zipper. When the ghosts whispered like mice in the mornings or the stench of the burning tip filled his nose, Savage would repeat the witness statements he had learnt off by heart, as if praying for salvation.

Once, he gave in and asked to go to church. The sergeant shrugged his shoulders and called the patrol car. It took Savage to the tiny, grey-brick church, its domes painted the blue used in entrance halls.

A service was under way. A young-looking priest was leading the prayers and the congregation's discordant voices chorused the responses. The candles in their hands melted and appeared to bow low before the icons. Savage stood off to one side, head bowed. When the policeman came in he slammed the door so that everyone turned round and shushed him. Unsure what to do with his hands, he stood to attention as he would for his senior officers and looked apologetically upwards where God was usually sought.

The service was soon over and a queue formed for the priest to hear confessions. Awkwardly shifting his feet, Savage stood at the back of the queue breathing down the shaved nape of a broad-shouldered lad in a leather jacket. Some made their confessions in whispers. Others declared their sins aloud as if listing their achievements while a pale girl in a grey headscarf faltered at the last minute and backed away from the altar.

It was the shaven-headed lad's turn. He had been constantly looking around and the priest, seeing the slashes on his face, smiled to himself as he noticed that the scars made a cross like a crucifix.

"The sixth commandment of Our Lord is 'Thou shalt not kill'," Savage heard and he moved forward.

"That's the job, Father," the gangster said by way of explanation. "You either kill or get…"

The priest quickly crossed himself and rolled his eyes.

"The Lord gave us life. He alone may take it away."

"So what? You can't nick purses either?" The gangster smirked but immediately lowered his head guiltily. "Everyone's trying to grab a piece of the pie for himself."

"Do you really repent? Are you tormented? Do you pray for those you kill?"

"I am in torment, Father, I am, honestly! I pray. I repent. I give money to the church so that God will forgive me for everything."

The priest held out the cross and the Gospel and, bending down awkwardly, the gangster kissed them apologetically the way he used to kiss his mother when he came back from prison.

"Bless me, Father, to fight my sins," he rapped out words he knew by heart.

When the priest turned to Savage, he was already heading for the door, turning away from the faces of the saints, dark in their gilded covers.

"Evil is hidden behind good like darkness behind an icon," he thought as he went down the church steps. "You set out towards God but it's the Devil you encounter…"

Recalling the heavy smell of the incense, the priest's ruddy face and the shaven folds of the gangster's scalp, Savage tossed and turned all night, unable to sleep. "Confession's just the same as sterilizing a needle before a lethal injection," he whispered when the grey and twisted face of dawn hung outside his window like a suicide.

When he heard that Savage had shown up, Karimov paced his cell like a caged wolf. He called for the lawyer he'd previously refused and began to retract his earlier statements. As he prepared for their confrontation, he trimmed his nails, changed his shirt and noticed in the mirror that his curls had got thinner.

Savage was clean-shaven but out of habit he fiddled with his beardless chin that stood out in his sun-burnt face. His clothes hung on him as if they were someone else's and his sleepless nights showed black beneath his eyes. He sat hunched on his chair legs crossed, and shuddered when Karimov sat down on the other side of the table.

Clapping Savage on the shoulder, the investigator put an ashtray between them and Savely, unable to stop his hands shaking, took a cigarette from the packet with his teeth.

"See, I've taken up smoking," he grinned sheepishly. "Do you mind?"

Karimov pulled a face and took a crumpled cigarette from behind his ear. He leant over the table towards Savage and lit up from his match. It quivered like a baby bird in its nest of fingers.

"Can you tell us what happened on the veranda the evening Coffin was killed?" the investigator suggested.

"I wasn't in the square that evening," snapped Karimov, breathing smoke from his nostrils.

Lighting one cigarette from another, Savage repeated the confession he had by heart, staring at Karimov's right ear as if the text only he could see was written on it. He appeared calm and scarcely stammered. Only his trembling fingers, nervously squashing the cigarette filter gave away his agitation.

"I d-d-didn't see him fire. I just saw Coffin go down with a shot to the head and the gun he threw on the floor." Unable to bring himself to use Karimov's name, Savage stumbled over "he" and lowered his gaze.

Karimov couldn't help it. He snorted loudly but the investigator slammed his fist on the table.

"Shut it! You've had your say!"

Savage related how Karimov's bodyguards had threatened him to make him take the blame and how he hid in the forest too scared to seek police protection. Karimov took his head in his hands. His shoulders shook noiselessly and it was impossible to tell whether he was laughing or crying.

Turning round in the doorway, he pierced Savage with a glance and Savely couldn't hold his gaze.

"The court will rise."

The court rose with a scrape of chairs. There was scarcely enough room in the little court building for everyone who wanted to attend. There were chairs in the aisles and security men kept tripping over the spider's web of wires that reporters had laid around the courtroom. Separated by bars, Karimov was rocking on his chair and muttering to himself: "Nobody needs anybody..." The court officials picked up the refrain like a rash and used it in conversation where appropriate and where not appropriate. They also picked up his melancholy, which had turned the corners of his mouth down and his temples grey.

During the month of the trial, bouncers from the bar, accidental witnesses, the bathhouse attendant, wiping his brow with shaking hands, and Savage's daughter avoiding looking in his direction, all passed before Karimov. He listened to what they had to say indifferently. Like the lines on his palm, the wrinkles that had appeared on his face revealed his fate while the outcome of the trial, which he knew in advance, lay in the creases by his mouth.

"He checked whether the gun was loaded, smirked and fired!" said a waiter from the Three Lemons, straightening his glasses.

This was echoed by a bouncer who said, "He turned the barrel towards Coffin and – bang!"

"He got drunk at the bathhouse and boasted about killing Coffin," confirmed the attendant, so agitated he trembled.

Saam was called several times. He talked about the murder of Coffin, acting it out, and the judge listened open-mouthed. Seeing Lapin in court, Saam gave him a friendly wink so that the prosecutor and the lawyers looked round to see who the wink was meant for. Seeing his former subordinate, haggard and crushed, the prosecutor grimaced and whispered something to his secretary.

When Savely Savage took the witness stand Karimov leaned eagerly against the bars and Lapin, half-rising, stared at him so intently that when Savage intercepted his gaze, he felt as if the investigator were shaking him by the collar.

The court was so quiet it was possible to hear the prosecutor's rasping breath and Karimov's whispering which reminded Savage of the old Saami woman's fortune-telling but he couldn't make out what he was saying.

"Who killed Coffin?" came a shout from the public and the judge banged her gavel and called for order.

Savage cleared his throat, loosened his shirt-collar and looked at Karimov. There was whispering in court and it seemed to Savage that the wind was rubbing the forest up the wrong way and the aspens were jingling leaves as round as coins, their tops leaning towards one another. Savage's cheek twitched as if an invisible hand had patted his face and he looked fitfully around the room, afraid that he would see one Savely Savage looking at Savely Savage and tugging on his matted beard. "Just don't split in two like a tree hit by lightning," Savage thought in a fright, stroking his shaven chin.

"Why did you run away into the forest?" The judge's voice was like a dash of cold water.

"I was a-a-afraid for m-m-my daughter," Savage replied, rubbing his temples. "They threatened to get rid of her. I was prepared to do anything for my daughter's sake even to take the blame…"

The now quiet courtroom tried to catch his every word. When Savage was asked about the details of his wanderings, muffled gasps were heard from the seats.

"What did you eat?" inquired the lawyer. "How did you survive for so long?"

"Mushrooms, berries, roots, leftovers from the tip…" said Savage, ticking them off on his fingers.

Saam exchanged looks with his sidekicks and pursed his lips:

"I said to check the tip!"

"We did. We couldn't find him," one apologized.

Savage covered his twitching cheek with his hand, embarrassed by the appearance of the nervous tic that twisted his face into hideous grimaces.

"Did you come into town?"

Savage shook his head. He was squeezing the cold pebble from Salmon's grave and, as he looked at Saam, sitting astride a chair in the back row, he recalled her protruding cheekbones and face like a skull.

"I look at myself in the mirror and I wonder, 'Severina, Severina, where are you now? Where have you gone?'" the girl whispered, head bowed as she admired a bead and feather bracelet the old Saami woman had given her. "Where are you now?" Savage asked himself, thinking that it was Salmon they had buried on the island beneath a rough-hewn cross and Severina, whom he'd never seen, in the empty coffin on the river bank.

Savage rolled the stone in his hand and thought about where that Savely Savage had gone who had tightened a wire round Antonov's neck and listened to his last gasps. Would he come back? Or was he now inside him and contemplating, as he looked at Saam sitting in the courtroom, something the other Savely Savage could never bring himself to do?

"Did you shoot Krotov?" the lawyer asked again, bringing him back to the courtroom.

"Who?" Savage asked in turn.

"The mayor, Krotov," he repeated. "Were you the one who shot him at the bathhouse?"

"I don't know how to fire a gun," said Savage with a shrug and the courtroom burst out laughing.

As he left the witness stand, some journalists ran up to him but he was still squeezing his stone and held out a fist so the puzzled reporters shook that.

Lapin was waiting for him in the corridor. He was

nervously playing with his jacket collar and Savage would have liked to go back into the courtroom but the door was already locked.

"I just need to know," Lapin whispered to him heatedly, taking him by the elbow. "It won't change anything now but I need to know! Or I'll go crazy. Just give me a wink…"

"Sorry, sorry," said Savage. He detached his hand carefully.

"Just give me a wink. I'll understand. It's all such a mess. You said one thing then another. I'm losing my mind. I beg you. Just tip me a wink… I won't tell anyone! I just need to know!"

Savage turned away so that the investigator couldn't take the nervous twitch of his eye for an answer.

"They've forced me out of my job, you know!" Lapin called after him. "Forced me out! Can you imagine? So that I don't get in their way…"

Savage hastened down the stairs but Lapin leaned over the railing and carried on shouting:

"Just give me a wink? What would it cost you?"

The final day of the trial was held in camera. Everyone was heartily sick of the murders and only a small crowd of onlookers and reporters had gathered outside the court. With nothing else to do, they talked about the weather that was as changeable as the mood of a capricious woman.

A court official recounted that when Karimov heard the verdict he burst out laughing and shook his head as if he'd lost his mind. Stretching his arms out through the bars, he yelled at the judge: "It was you in the snow drift! I recognized you straightaway! Do you remember me? Do you?" But the judge ignored his cries, continued reading out the sentence, straightened her skirt and left the court. Karimov carried on laughing as he remembered how he couldn't bring himself to kill the drunken woman lying in the snow.

Back in his cell he mused, "If everything in life is

254

predetermined, if everything is mapped out by the Almighty who knows the manner of our deaths even before we are born, the Almighty is an evil joker like my foster father."

"You had it all," said a prison warder, shaking his head as he put his face up to the viewing window. "Money, power, a flat in Moscow... Everything. What more did you want?"

Karimov grinned, stroking his cheek as if checking whether he'd remembered to shave.

"I've got what you can't buy for any amount of money – freedom!" He gestured at the cell.

The warder laughed:

"Freedom? In jail? You haven't got it. You've lost it!"

Karimov rolled on to his stomach with a yawn and buried his face in his pillow. The warder waited to hear what he would say but deciding he wasn't going to get an answer, was about to close the window, still laughing at Karimov. All of a sudden, Karimov leapt up and looked out through the bars. The guard could feel his fevered breath on his face.

"Freedom means freedom from everything and above all from freedom itself!" Karimov said poking the warder in the face. He jumped back and slammed the window shut.

"You had it all: money, power ... what more did you want?" he continued to mutter to himself as he went off along the corridor.

Karimov received a letter from his foster father before he was sent off to prison camp. He went around his cell, caressing the walls as if he wanted to remember every bump and scratch of the peeling paint but he didn't open the envelope. He held it up to the light, palpated it and sniffed it as if he could tell what it said from the smell of its postal odyssey and the printer's ink. He thought that a person is a letter by an unknown writer, sent out to a random address. The lucky ones are opened and read but most come to rest in rusting post boxes full of papers and adverts and never discover their intended recipient.

Karimov went over his life, trying to understand why his soul had been behind bars before his body and imagining himself as a prisoner in an Arctic Circle that would grip his throat like a dog collar, preventing any escape.

The warder was sorry Karimov was being taken away. He enjoyed listening to his tales about life in the capital and women who smelt of spicy scent, about expensive resorts and financial speculations. Karimov told stories of lives spent as small change and his tales filled the warder up like a money box. More than anything else, the warder loved it when Karimov talked about the murders and recounted the deaths of Trebenko and Coffin, who the warder feared and hated even though they were dead.

He lectured Karimov, saying, "You should have been cannier. Do you know how many people get killed here? This many," and he drew his hand along his neck. "And no-one gets sent down. It's a little town. Everyone knows who did it but they can't prove it."

Karimov smirked and carried on packing his bag.

"And now you'll be locked up for the rest of your life," insisted the warder. "To your dying day!"

"Prison is whatever's all around us," said Karimov, gesturing at his cell. "We are all imprisoned by circumstances, habits, weaknesses, by our heritage and our biography, ultimately by our body which dictates how we live our lives. As for the flat where the years go by, its locks are stronger than the bolts on my cell and its walls are thicker." Karimov looked again at the grey sky and said: "And isn't this town a straitjacket in the end? You live as if you're behind barbed wire here and the whole country is as unattainable for you as freedom is for prisoners, as if you were all serving sentences…"

Shaking his finger, the warder cracked a broad smile that showed the gaps in his teeth:

"No," he drawled. "You're the one banged up and I'm the one who's free. I go where I like and live how I like."

And slamming the window closed with all his strength, he limped off down the corridor, chuckling.

The cheerless sky hung over the hills like a deflated circus tent. There was a grimy locomotive at the platform, a solitary carriage hitched to it, no different in appearance to a goods wagon. The prisoners were driven into cells, separated from the corridor by bars. Karimov stretched out on the bottom bunk, staring at a blank wall. His cellmate dangled off the top bunk to look at him, drumming a military march with his fingers. He grimaced evilly, his face spongy as a lump of dough.

"Hello, sir," he smirked. "I recognized you right away…"

Looking at him, Karimov tried to remember where he could have seen him.

"You don't remember," the man said, licking his lips. "People like me are like stones under your feet. If we get in your way, you chuck us out. If we don't, you won't even notice we're there."

Half-standing Karimov turned towards the guard but he was coolly going through the list of prisoners, ignoring what they were saying.

"I was a custodian at the factory. The stuff I carried off wasn't much really. You had a driver. I walked every day. And now here we are in the same carriage. But I've only got two years and from what I hear you're there for life…"

For the whole journey, he hung off his bunk, gazing at Karimov and cracking his knuckles.

"For life!" the man said again with an evil laugh.

Karimov took out his father's unopened letter and tore it open. Smoothing out the sheet of paper which had been folded in half, he read a single sentence written in Pipe's uneven hand:

"Life is a trial in which just one case is heard: the case of fate against the individual."

The doorman was frightened of every visitor, he wrapped himself in his tattered sheepskin coat, his pockets clinked with medicine bottles and he was hard of hearing so that he never heard what was going on in the hostel. Savage went up the stairs, reading the graffiti on the walls. He jumped back at the scrunch of a syringe under foot as if he'd stepped on a scorpion.

"Even in the hostel, I got room No. 13," Severina had lamented, cursing the absurdities of her life. The town had three hostels. At the first, Savage was shown in by a tipsy young woman who was breastfeeding a wizened baby. Savely had a lump in his throat. He staggered back and took the stairs like a slide.

A domestic squabble could be heard from room No. 13 at the workers' hostel. It reminded Savage so much of his arguments with his wife it seemed he need only push open the door to see himself and his wife, covered in the red blotches from her yelling.

The third hostel was in wasteland that had once had a football pitch but was now a rubbish dump for packing cases, broken furniture and plastic bags stuffed with garbage from God knows where. Empty windows gaped in an upper storey, left grimy by a fire. Tramps gathered there in winter and the watchmen kept away from them, afraid of being knifed. One night, one of the tramps fell out of a window. No-one tried to find him and he lay under a snow drift until the snow started to melt and someone spotted a hand sticking out of the drift.

The corridor smelled of burnt frying pans and cheap eau-de-cologne. Numbers had been daubed on the doors in floor paint. Inside, the TV burbled away like a demented old man. The floorboards creaked like aching joints and Savage took every step gingerly as if afraid of falling through the floor.

There was a mess of crumpled receipts and cigarette butts outside Salmon's door.

"She hasn't been around for a long time," said an old woman with a long, hooked nose, who put her head out of the next room and looked Savage up and down. "She could be dead." She closed the door without waiting for an answer.

Savage picked the flimsy lock with a knife and slipped inside like a thief. The room was furnished with a narrow bed, a humming fridge and a couple of chairs with clothes hung over their backs. Savage found a lump of mouldy cheese and a swollen carton of kefir in the fridge. A partially completed crossword lay on the bed. He took a framed photo off the wall, lay on the bed and looked for a long time at the girl who was so pretty she looked lovely even in a distorting mirror.

A lieutenant-colonel went to Savage's work. He walked so heavily it seemed as though he found every step difficult. Looking over Savage's papers, he peered at his drawings and recounted Karimov's trial while Savely's colleagues clustered round wondering how he was able to say one thing while reading another.

Coming to a halt, the lieutenant-colonel said:

"Give the guy some support. He was wandering around the forest for three months. He's been through a lot. God forbid anyone…"

"They told us he'd shot a gangster," whispered a secretary standing in the doorway.

"Have you worked with him for long?"

"We've sat next to him for about 15 years," one colleague answered, adjusting his glasses with a nervous gesture.

"And what do you say? Could he have shot anyone?"

Adjusting his glasses again, the man laughed.

The next day Savage himself appeared. As he walked down the long corridor, he was accompanied by stares that prodded him from behind. He felt as though he had walked down that corridor the previous day, the day before that and a month before that, and in the evenings had struggled to put his arms in the sleeves of his coat as he ran down the stairs, his steps counting out the final seconds of the working day. During that time, it had been someone else, not him, who had lived in the forest, sheltering from rain as light as mist in a hut made of twigs.

All talk ceased as he entered the office. Embarrassed, Savage hardly opened his mouth to say hello and his colleagues couldn't hear him. He squeezed through to his desk and caught himself thinking that his movements were so familiar it was as if the three crazy months that had been extracted from his life like rotten teeth had never happened. Hidden behind the tub with its dried-out palm, Savely hung his coat on a nail, switched on his computer, took his pencils out of their case and began to sort out the papers that were scattered untidily over his desk.

His colleagues, with whom, as before, he had no common language even when not talking, watched him apprehensively over their computer screens, but by lunchtime they had forgotten about Savage and were buried in the daily grind. A sleepy fly bumped against the window and their chatter merged with its buzzing.

At the lunchtime break, Savage went down to the canteen that smelled of food and gossip and a sturdy waitress, fat thighs brushing against the tables, swept the crumbs onto the floor.

"You're an unlucky chap," she said, looking at Savely and shaking her head. "With you, nothing's like it is with other people…"

Embarrassed, Savage concentrated on counting out his change. Behind the counter, a skinny woman with an elongated face that had scarcely enough room for her wide, plump mouth, didn't wait to be asked to serve him the bowls of soup and pasta that, true to habit, he had bought every day in his many years of going to the canteen at exactly the same time. Savage would have liked to ask for mashed potato but took what he was given, tipping the money out for the woman at the counter.

"What did you eat out there?" asked the waitress. She sank down at his table, propping her chin on her fist as she prepared to listen. "Tell me, go on."

"Leave the bloke alone!" laughed the woman at the counter but, waving her away with a cloth, the waitress leaned towards Savage. "Go on, tell me."

Savage ate in a hurry, his face fixed on his plate and his spoon banging against his teeth but the waitress still stared brazenly at him.

"So, why don't you say something?" she said, trying to draw him out, as he embarked hurriedly on his pasta.

Stacking the bowls, Savage jumped up, nearly knocking over the table, and worming his way between the curious glances, he dashed out of the canteen. The waitress shrugged her shoulders and collected the used napkins. As she looked through the glass at the huddle of plates of food, she tried to imagine what she would have done if she'd been lost in the forest.

It seemed to Savage that his straggly beard was full of pine needles, his torn shirt hung like a sack and when he went down the corridor all the offices could hear the rustle of the plastic wrapped round his feet. He was constantly running a hand over his face, wiping his mouth, and sniffing the heavy odour that rose from his unwashed body. When he passed a mirror, however, he could see that he was clean shaven and wearing a pressed suit and tie rather than rags.

His colleagues soon got used to his odd ways and, as before, paid him no more attention than the dried-up palm in its tub, which hadn't been watered in his absence. Hidden away behind the cupboard, he thought that some people live like a needle in a haystack and others are like a beam in the eye while Savely Savage was superfluous everywhere, an outsider to everyone.

News of visitors to the town travelled faster than the wind. The townspeople had grey faces covered with dust from the mines and glancing smiles like the northern lights so that new arrivals stood out in a crowd like stars in the sky. After a few days, however, they grew dull and their hearts became overgrown by despondency, turning into moss-covered stones and they drowned their northern melancholy in drink and couldn't wait to leave.

The ore quarry, a serpentine road cut into many kilometres, was so vast that the small town huddled on its edge seemed as though it was bound to fall into its gaping maw at any moment.

"How can you live in such a hole?" muttered a bald man with sharp ears. "This isn't a town, it's a common grave!"

"Like life, death takes some getting used to," grinned a grey-haired man, scribbling in his notebook. "Mind you, dying here wouldn't be too bad!"

When they looked at the eviscerated innards of the ore deposit with bulldozers working at the bottom, which could hardly be seen from the viewing platform, the Moscow visitors felt tiny and insignificant. In order to shake off this unpleasant sensation, they popped into the Three Lemons and stayed there till the morning.

"Southerners are tight-fisted," the barman said, distracting them with conversation as he poured out their drinks. "People from the temperate zone are mean and envious but northerners are wise and hospitable!"

The visitors laughed and emptied their glasses.

"That's because," the barman went on, "there are no indigenous people here, apart from the Saami. People were sent into exile here or assigned here for work. Some came looking for easy money. The best people came along, intermixed and adopted each other's customs and traditions. It's a melting pot, like America. Here in the North, we're all visitors.

The grey-haired man looked around the room then at his watch.

"Any girls in that pot?"

"Of course. They come along in the evening."

The bald man threw a bundle of money onto the table.

"Close the bar. Only let girls in. All the drinks are on us."

His companion raised his eyebrows but the bald man showed him the prices in the menu.

"And the snacks!"

The bouncers stood legs apart and blocked the entrance, admitting only girls who flocked in like bees to honey. In the dim light the women seemed more beautiful, the men more intelligent and the adulterated brandy potent.

"You can certainly drink here in the North!" the bald man said, leaning towards the barman.

A kaleidoscope of girls flitted by, dancing and downing

their drinks, with heavy sighs and a shake of their heads. Well and truly plastered, the Muscovites turned out their wallets and scattered their money around, flinging it onto the counter, throwing it on the floor and stuffing rolled up banknotes into cleavages. To them, the women's faces merged into one and in their drunken haze the bar seemed chock-a-block with twins, their cheeks flushed from the brandy, their eyes cold and their mouths wide open like the quarry as they laughed and yelled in an ear-tingling clamour.

"Do you feel like an oligarch?" the grey-haired man shouted, cuddling three girls at once.

"We are oligarchs!" said the bald man, doing a little dance, his sharp ears sticking out like wings.

The bouncers made way and Saam came into the bar with a retinue of gangsters. He looked at the dancing Muscovites then, with a nod at the barman, crossed over to his table, which was immediately vacated by the girls.

"Be quiet!" he bellowed and the music broke off. Conversations, laughter, the clinking of glasses and the scraping of chairs could be heard.

"Get them out of here!" the Muscovites yelled at the bouncers "Put the music on!"

"There's no point, guys. Be quiet. Don't cause trouble," said the barman beckoning them over to appease them but the bald man, staggering, made for Saam's table.

"There'd be a shooting if Coffin were still alive!" a waiter said to the barman who nodded and reached for the pistol he kept under the counter.

"This is a private party!" the bald man shouted to Saam, knocking an ashtray off the table. It echoed as it rolled around the floor. "Come back tomorrow. Tonight's just for us!" He turned to the barman and clicked his fingers: "Music!"

Saam looked him up and down and then stood and headed for the exit.

"Put the music on. Let them enjoy themselves. So that they don't go away and say our town's mean and inhospitable!"

he called to the barman and the speakers screamed back into action.

In the morning, shivering in the cold wind, the Muscovites stuck three puffy-faced girls into a car and off they went through the sleeping streets, the horn blaring as loudly as possible. The rest of the girls, dragging their feet, left the bar and melted into backstreets and alley-ways where their heels rang out in the quietness.

The disappearance of the visitors from Moscow, who failed to return to their hotel, was discovered in the afternoon when they didn't show up at the factory either. They didn't answer their mobiles and their hired car had last been seen at the Three Lemons. With a shrug the bouncers said their guests had left in the morning, taking three girls with them, and the barman produced a lengthy bill with four zeros together with the broken crockery. The alarm was sounded in the evening and the police alerted. Patrol cars wailed, rooftop lights flashing, as they hurtled along the forest roads.

"We're all visitors in the North!" a bittern boomed in the bushes as they brought the smashed car, full of broken bodies, up from an overgrown gully.

It was quiet and empty in the bar. The cleaner swept away the drunken laughter that had crept into the cracks between the floor boards, the trampled cigarette butts and the sweet wrappers. A fan chased away the stale air that had gathered below the ceiling. The chairs were put on the tables, legs up, and the women's dust-grey yearning hung in tatters from the cobwebs.

"Southerners are greedy," said the barman, resuming his usual line with a little yawn as he wiped the glasses. "People in the temperate zone are evil…"

Saam picked at his eggs distractedly agreeing with his chatter.

"And we're hospital here in the North!"

"What about Muscovites?" Saam looked up at the barman, his pupils narrowed like a snake's ready to pounce.

"Muscovites are rich," the barman replied without batting an eyelid. "But they don't know when to stop."

Savage woke early in the morning before the alarm clock went off. He was woken by the sound of car horns and shouting coming from the street. Bare branches traced the sky and banged on the window and Savage had a vision of Antonov hammering on the glass, his hands reaching for his throat.

A leaky tap took him back to the taiga reminding him of the wash-stand the Saami had rigged up from a plastic bottle suspended from a tree. In the mornings, Salmon, sputtering like a cat, washed her face in the icy water and her cheeks turned so red they looked frost-bitten. Savage drove away these recollections that tore at his heart. In the corridor, he bumped into his daughter coming back from a party. Vasilisa smelled of brandy and acrid male sweat. The kisses on her lips gave her away.

"Let's get away from here," Savage suggested, taking her chin in his hand. "There are so many towns. Pick any one!"

"You go," Vasilisa muttered drunkenly. "No-one'll miss you."

Swaying she went to her room where she collapsed, fully dressed, onto the bed.

Here and there the lamp-posts still displayed the yellowed pictures of Savage although he had long since become a victim rather than a criminal. People had discussed his ordeals, spicing up what they'd heard with inventions of their own, until their tongues were swollen with gossip. And the plump woman, who was hanging her washing out on the balcony, already believed that she had actually seen Karimov aiming a gun at Coffin.

"Mum, did he kill them all or not?" asked Vasilisa, rubbing her puffy eyes. "Sometimes I don't think he actually fired."

Her mother tore herself away from her love story and looked her daughter up and down.

"If he'd been capable of killing someone..." she began. She pursed her lips and slammed the book closed. "If he'd been capable of anything at all, I would have lived like Antonov's wife – half the year on holiday, the other half at the beautician's."

Vasilisa lay down beside her, her head on her mother's shoulder, and thought back to the night in Antonov's car, when he stroked her legs as he talked to her father through the open window.

"I sometimes think that what never happened did happen and what actually happened was made up..." she whispered, gnawing at a hangnail.

Her mother hugged her. She recalled how a blushing Savely had been too shy to speak to her and had bought her a bunch of roses that he left on a window sill in the lobby, unable to bring himself to give it to her. She read once in a women's magazine that "a domineering man makes a good lover but a hen-pecked man makes a good husband". Frosted lipstick in place, she had pressed his bell. Savage hovered self-consciously at the door and she went in without being asked. The next morning, she kissed him on the forehead and proposed. Now, as she looked back over their life together she felt that her past was full of gossip, advice, film serials, empty chatter and other people's husbands like a scarecrow stuffed with straw, like an old glossy magazine that becomes unbearably dull when you've seen its tawdry headlines a thousand times.

Knocking gently, she pushed open the door of her husband's room and, sinking into a chair in front of him, she stared at the bridge of his nose. Savage switched the TV off with the remote and silence hung in the room like an axe.

Savely looked at his wife as she sat in the chair but what he saw was her, stretched out on the ground, pulling off her boot with its broken heel, and running through the forest barefoot, swearing, as she tried to keep up with Saam. "He won't last long in the forest. Where else is he going to go? He hasn't got any friends or relatives" – her words rang in his ears and Savage thought that women have many faces and none of them is real.

"Savely," his wife began, crossing her legs. It occurred to them both that this was the first time she had used her husband's name. "Savely, tell me, did you kill them all?"

Biting her lip, she straightened her housecoat with a nervous gesture. Savage said nothing, looking at his wife in consternation, twisting the control he was holding and choosing his words carefully

The previous day she had been with the lover she saw whenever his wife went to visit her sick mother. Toppling her onto the marital bed, he tickled her neck with a moustache as stiff as a brush.

"For three months he lived in the woods, frightened of being sent to jail for something he didn't do," the man laughed as he unbuttoned her blouse. "You can't find losers like that for love or money."

Savage's wife pushed him away in a fury.

"He'll come and kill you for sleeping with his wife. We'll see how much you laugh when you get shot in the head." She tried to fasten her blouse but got the buttons mixed up.

She broke her long nails trying to fasten it and the saying went round in her head that "once you've missed the first button hole, you'll never finish the job".

The man paled and put an arm around her shoulders in an attempt to make amends.

"Did you hear what he did to Antonov?" She ground out vengefully. She pulled down her skirt and the man's eyes bulged.

When she was putting on her coat and straightening her hair at the mirror, he suddenly burst out laughing.

"Oh, come on. He apologizes when you tread on his foot. They're calling him Sissy at work. Can you imagine?" He continued to laugh, pulled off her coat and laid her down on the floor.

267

Savage's wife continued to fiddle with the edge of her housecoat, looking curiously at her husband.

"Savely," she said again and her voice trembled. "Please tell me you killed them!"

She moved to sit next to him on the bed and covered his hand with her own hot one that to him felt as cold as a corpse's.

"I-I-I," Savage stammered and nodded. "I–I-I did…"

His wife looked at him sceptically.

"So you lied?"

"Yes," Savage nodded. All he wanted was for her to go away as quickly as possible.

She leapt up as though scalded and rushed out.

"I hate you so much!" she yelled at the door and Savage thought it was time he went back to the forest.

The bus bounced over the bumps like a bucking bronco. The forest flashed by the window, once again wild and alien, as if the months he'd spent wandering the dank swamps of the taiga had never happened. The last stop was the abandoned mine. It was only a few miles from there to the tip. Bottles tinkled in his bag and the scissors he had in his pocket for a weapon jabbed into his side. He recalled how the tramps buried him alive under a pile of rubbish.

Fallen leaves lay on the ground like crude brushstrokes on canvas. Savage went through his memories of his days of wandering as if telling beads and it seemed it was just his sick imagination or a film he had seen before he went back to a real life as dull and grey as the rubbish tip.

Savage found the tramps by the smoke from their fire. It was cold and the tramps were clustered around it, scorching themselves as they held out their red, frost-bitten hands. Savage wanted to sit down next to them as he had in the past but they grew wary when they spotted him. Two men stood up and went towards him.

"It's me!" said Savage, shifting uncomfortably from foot to foot. "I'm back."

The tramps looked at him maliciously, shaggy eyebrows drawn, and their compressed lips augured nothing good.

"I've brought something…" Savely held out his bag, rattling the bottles. "Help yourselves!"

The tramps didn't so much as twitch. He took out his gifts and placed them on the ground. A dirty, soot-smeared little boy grabbed the food and carried it closer to the fire. The tramps crowded round and began to share it out. Savage, the scissors hidden in his sleeve, squatted by the fire.

"The woman with the red hair," he said, leaning towards one of the women. "Red hair, wearing a hat…"

The woman deftly patted his pockets then jumped away to hide behind the men. One of them produced a knotty stick and drawing himself up to his full height Savage showed them the scissors. They stepped back, chewing the sandwiches he'd provided.

"I'm a friend," said Savage, putting up his hands. "I'm one of you. Do you remember I was with you? I've just brought some food…"

"And money?" A vagrant's mouth stretched into a smile that showed the gaps in his teeth. "Have you brought any money?"

Savage nodded and pulled some rolled up notes out from his shirt.

"I'm looking for a woman with red hair," he reiterated. "She was with you. I would see her here a lot."

"These are all our women," the tramp said with a gesture. "Pick any of them."

Savage ran his glance over the homeless women but the one he was looking for wasn't among them.

"I'm looking for a woman with red hair," he stressed. "She vanished after the fire…"

The tramps shrugged and an old man with bushy hair went over to Savage and snatched up the money. An open bottle was passed around. Smacking their lips, the tramps took a slug then passed it on but when it was Savage's turn, the old man drank for two and tossed him the empty bottle.

"Get out while you're still alive," he rasped, showing him a crooked finger.

Savage backed away, keeping hold of the scissors. He tripped over bits of iron and wood sticking out of a pile of rubbish. The tramps watched him go, leaning shoulder to shoulder, then went back to the fire and got started on another bottle.

"What did he want?" one asked, wiping his mouth with his sleeve.

"A woman!"

"Hasn't he got enough of his own?"

"You try and understand them…"

Savage looked round one last time at the tramps. Suddenly he envied them as he imagined himself going home to his lonely little room where he could talk to the television or to his reflection in the mirror but couldn't lean on anyone's shoulder. He thought of moving in with the vagrants, loving their women, drinking vodka, bedding down in the rubbish to sleep and feeling life sticking into his back like a broken bottle. Savage calculated how much money it would take to provide food and drink for the whole tribe of tramps and decided to put money aside from his very first pay check. So that he'd have nowhere to go back to, he would slap a divorce on his wife together with the keys to the flat, and throw away his passport to be a real homeless person – no home, no family, no name.

When he got home, however, he put his dirty clothes in the washing machine and spent a whole hour in the shower, washing off the smell of the tip, the vicious looks of the tramps and his foolish dreams of a vagrant life.

Lapin lay in wait for him by the entrance, loitering beneath the windows. Savage would look round the corner and wait for him to leave. If he saw him in town, he would dive into an alleyway or the nearest shop. Lapin wandered around unkempt, in a dirty crumpled coat, his nervous shadow getting under people's feet. Sometimes he would jump out from behind a passerby and shake Savage by the shoulder, watching every movement of his lips:

"Just wink at me if it's you. I won't tell anyone!"

"L-l-leave me al-l-lone. I'm tired," Savage said. He hurried away but Lapin was right behind him.

"Just wink at me. I need to know or I'll go out of my mind!"

People turned to look at them and, pretending they were friends, Savely would put an arm round Lapin's shoulders, muttering some nonsense into his ear. The investigator would try to find a secret sign in his gibberish and to work out as he roamed the streets just what might be hidden behind the "ba-ba-ba" or "la-la-la" Savage used to imitate conversation.

Savage hung around outside the police station but couldn't bring himself to go in. The door was forever bumping against him like a cocky little boy and the snub-nosed sergeant, smoking on the bench, looked at him apprehensively.

Savage sat on the steps and looking at his shadow, curled up at his feet like a cat, he thought that a man is attached to the town he lives in like a button to a jacket and it is no more possible to escape fate than your own shadow.

The sergeant, stamping out his cigarette butt, crossed his arms.

"Who are you waiting for?" he called to Savage.

"I'm just waiting," Savely replied, pulling down his old-fashioned hat with its upturned brim.

The duty officer had long since spotted Savage from the window and, hiding behind a forlorn fig-tree in a tub, had watched his hunched figure and wondered why he was there. He mixed some mint and valerian into a glass, pulled a face and drank it down in one gulp like vodka. Then he cautiously opened the window.

"What do you want?" asked the duty officer cautiously. He had long since persuaded himself that he had imagined Savage that evening.

Savage didn't answer, looking at his watch as if he were waiting for someone. Embarrassed, the officer shut the window.

"Who are you waiting for?" the sergeant asked again, tearing himself off his bench. Savage shook his head and hurried away.

"Name?" shouted the Chief, popping up from around a corner.

"Ivanov!" Savage lied on impulse.

He remembered Trebenko, lying in a pool of blood on the garage floor and the sharp black smoke that rose above the trees as he fled into the forest, clutching his gun and the rubber boots, wrapped in a reindeer skin. "Judas!" Savage spat out.

Two beggars were digging in a dustbin, standing on tiptoe and raking through the rubbish with a gnarled stick. The taste of mouldy bread filled Savage's mouth. His nose tickled as if the tousled hair of the red-headed woman had tickled his face and, bent down by the weight of his memories, he went on by. "What makes us any different to tramps? Having somewhere to spend the night?" he thought, recalling the burrow in the congealed rubbish he'd slept in at the tip.

With every step, the road seemed longer and life shorter and he couldn't understand why he was looking for justice where no hope or love existed and people's hearts were as dark and empty as their stomachs.

No sooner had the people started forgetting about Karimov's trial than news of a fresh attack came. There was an attempt to cover it up but it was blurted out by a warrant officer at the military unit after more than his usual amount to drink and the next day the town was buzzing like a hive.

The phone rang in the office of the new chief of police whom people sometimes called Trebenko out of habit.

"Now what's going on over there?" the general ground out with ill disguised irritation. Dismissal hung in the air.

"It's the military," the chief offered by way of an

excuse, wiping his sweating forehead. "They've got their own investigation. It's got nothing to do with us."

"It never does have anything to do with you." The general swore and slammed down the phone.

Gossip spread through the town like rats and, sensing a story, the visiting journalists turned back, microphones at the ready that were more scary than guns.

Whether he had been attacked or not, no-one could say, but the unit commander wasn't seen in public for several days. When he did put in an appearance, everyone noticed that he was finding it hard to walk and every step hurt.

Whispers in town rehashed what the warrant officer had said in his cups: that, after drinking a whole bottle, some other officer had lain in wait for the commander and thrown a heavy box of tinned meat down on him from a window. As he threw it he shouted, "Die, bastard!" The commander had a narrow escape when the box hit him in the small of the back. He was confined to bed for several days unable to move, leaving the doctors to marvel at his heroic health.

The mayor summoned the chief of police and the prosecutor who bent over their drinks scratching their stubborn necks. After Karimov's arrest, the phone calls from Moscow had stopped and the turbulent little town had been left to its own devices. And now once again, their seats threatened to be pulled from under them and, as they poured out the bitter liquor, they racked their brains as to how to hush up the scandal. When Saam turned up at the door, the chief of police had the feeling that his chair had turned into a stake.

"Four heads are better than three," grinned the gangster, examining the label on the bottle.

Saam was less violent than the cruel Coffin. He knew how to negotiate and haggle and, if necessary, to lie low. If people didn't talk, he would loosen their tongues like ties. If they talked too much, he'd tear them right out. If Coffin had clenched the town in his fist, Saam had it under his thumb.

"Life is a theatre!" he declared, blowing his nose onto

the floor and perching on the edge of the table. The men shuddered. "Ten actors can play the same part and the audience will believe water is tears and paint is blood."

"No blood, please!" said the mayor in fright.

"We'll put a marked card in the deck and when the time comes we'll take it out," said Saam, trying another angle.

"What have cards got to do with it?" The prosecutor frowned.

Saam spat and straddled his chair.

"In short," he said, abandoning metaphors. "We'll replace the officer who's lost the plot with one of our own and there you go!"

The others turned his suggestion down outright.

"What's done can't be undone," said the mayor, knocking his glass over. "And the army's not your theatre."

"Everything's got to be legal and above board!" said the chief of police with a shake of his head using one of Trebenko's favourite phrases.

"Laws are there to be broken," objected Saam with feigned indifference. "And courts are there to be bought off."

The men heard the hidden threat in his voice and, with a dismissive gesture, decided things couldn't get worse.

"Do what you think best," said the mayor, giving in. "Just don't drag us into it."

At that point, Saam noticed with surprise that the fat mayor had a tiny, darting shadow like a mouse.

"For the first time in my life I felt like a man," smiled the officer when the door to his cell opened like the gates of heaven. "It's like I haven't lived."

"Then you haven't died either," retorted the gangster, taking the already lifeless body by the feet.

They put the body in the boot. Saam, who had a weakness for rituals, demanded that the ill-fated box of tinned meat that he'd thrown at the commander should go in with him.

When the journalists showed up at the army unit along with

an inspection team, it appeared there had been a false alarm and the attack had been a fiction. The unit commander talked about lumbago as he clutched his aching back swathed in a woollen shawl. The officers he lined up in front of the barracks were smooth-shaven and well turned out. The inspectors questioned everyone, leafing through their records, and by evening they were enjoying the steam at the lakeside bathhouse.

The hapless officer had no family and the neighbour on the same floor who had been worried about his drinking companion was told he'd left the force. Removal men with coarse faces and broad shoulders took the furniture out of his flat and loaded it into an ancient container. For several days the neighbour drowned his sorrows in drink, telling the wall: "We drank together for so many years and he never even bothered to say goodbye."

"And no theatricals," warned Pipe before he left. He took his speaking device out of his pocket the way he used to pull a gun. "No accidents, heart attacks or suicides. Look after him like the apple of your eye. Otherwise, I'll send in my boys and they'll kill you, your kids and your friends, and raze the town to the ground."

His mechanical voice turned Saam inside out: when he thought about the old man, he winced and ground his teeth. The gangsters carried out Pipe's instructions and didn't lay a finger on Savage. When they came across him in the street, they stepped aside, their evil looks at his back like penknives stuck in wood.

Once, they called him over, pointing him to a car parked at the side of the road. Clasping his briefcase to his chest, Savage looked around to call for help but the gangsters pinned his arms to his sides and pushed him onto the back seat. The fair-haired driver switched off the ignition and slammed the door, leaving him with Saam who leered as he picked his teeth with a matchstick.

"Well, hello, Savely Savage!"

Savage felt terror return, standing out on his forehead in beads of sweat. Saam thought back to the evening when Coffin died and was astonished that it was Karimov he saw aiming the gun.

"We spent a long time looking for you," Saam said, shaking his head. "Some of us never came back. They died out there in the forest…"

Savage remembered the old hunter, his neck torn and bloody like a rag, and nausea rose in his gullet.

"You know, it's a piece of piss to turn a popgun into a firearm," Saam said, scratching the back of his neck. "But people are pretty quick getting rid of a gun with a history attached…"

Savage felt a stabbing pain in his chest but he hid his fear under his coat and licked his dry lips.

"Lawbreakers leave a trail of broken necks."

"It can't be easy playing with fate," the bandit grinned, letting the words go over his head. "Let alone playing Russian roulette."

"It's not easy to play against people who never lose," replied Savage, amazed there was no trace of his stammer.

They fell silent and exchanged glances via the windscreen mirror. Each waited to see what the other would say. Savage was aware that his back was soaked while Saam was fighting the desire to turn round to get a better look at him.

Remembering how Salmon had feared the shadows on the wall when she lay dying, Savage heard the death rattle that tore at her chest in Saam's heavy breathing. "I was so beautiful once," her voice whispered. Staring at the gangster's rough hands that he had laid upon her, Savage felt his terror giving way to devastating hatred.

Saam shuddered as if he had read what Savage was thinking in the colourless eyes that had turned cold and angry. Like an animal ready to pounce, he slowly reached towards his pocket that held a knife, but Savage spotted the movement and shrank back in his seat, his hands raised.

Facing in opposite directions, they leaned against the windows, watching the passersby. The dark windows made it look as though it were dusk outside and Savely chanced a glance at his watch.

"Put it all behind you," said Saam without looking round. "Go back to how you used to live as if none of it ever happened."

"Put it all down to my imagination? Think of it all as a dream?"

"If nobody remembers something that happened, it means it was a dream."

Savage held out his scratched hands like dry, broken twigs.

"Scars heal," said Saam dismissively. "And those to the heart heal more quickly. But do you know what corpses smell of?"

"What?" asked Savage encountering his mocking look.

"Human filth. The worse someone was, the more he stinks after death..."

Savage remembered Salmon's shrunken corpse that smelled of reindeer milk, mouldy pelts and the orphanage. "What's that supposed to mean?" Savage asked, struggling to remain polite.

"That people die the way they lived."

Savage wanted to talk about Salmon but hesitated.

"And how should you live?"

"With no regrets for the past and no thought for tomorrow. The main thing is to remember that life has no meaning and that that is its main meaning."

His maxims made Savage's head hurt.

"You have a daughter," said Saam with a conspiratorial wink, concealing a threat in his smile like the knife in his coat. "Think about her, nothing else..."

Savage's mouth felt full of prickles: Vasilisa had drunk her youth away by the glassful. Her glazed eyes had pierced her father like needles and he had felt his daughter drifting away like a chunk of ice-floe borne away by the current.

"I think he's a bit, you know," said the driver, twirling his finger at his temple as he watched Savage go.

He remembered running from the orphanage to the abandoned playground. Savage's little girl had been digging in the sandpit and he, a sweet hidden in his cheek, had nestled into Savage's shoulder wishing the moment to last as long as possible. He had boasted to the children in the home that his father had shown up and had put up with their beatings as he waited for him to collect him.

Lyonya flushed and the old hurts hung like leeches on his heart.

"Perhaps we better get rid of him before it's too late?" he asked, pupils narrowed.

"I don't want the old man for an enemy," Saam said, pulling a face as he thought about Pipe. "Let's wait till he dies and then..." He made a gun with his fingers and aimed it at Savage's back.

Savely's memories clung to one another and became confused. He suddenly saw the red-headed woman getting into Antonov's car, Salmon choking on the smoke at the burning tip, and the Saami lowering his daughter into a rough pine coffin, her shrivelled body laced as if in cobwebs by prominent blue veins.

"If life's an empty dream, death is a dirty trick!" said a passerby and Savage plodded after him like a stray dog.

He was all ears as he walked, waiting for the man to throw him his well-chewed thoughts like crumbs to a dog.

"Death is madness because life is stupidity. Each person has their cross to bear and that cross is himself."

All of a sudden Savage realized that he was following his own shadow and talking to himself.

He wandered home, waving his arms and muttering to himself and passersby shied away from him, frightened by his mad, contorted face. Rain trickled down inside his collar. His boots mashed the slush and Savage dissolved in his recollections like sugar in water. He felt as if he were being pursued by ghosts that grabbed onto his coat.

At home Savage carried on talking to himself and, looking into his eyes, his wife read in them something that turned her lips down in a half moon and made her heart shrivel up like a baked apple.

In the morning, a psychiatrist arrived with a nervous giggle as he straightened his shirt cuffs.

"The p-p-past is all m-m-mixed up with my imagination and I can't tell what really happened and what I only imagined and I think I'm going mad."

The doctor listened to Savage and made out a prescription which he left on the bedside table.

"B-b-but what's m-m-most terrifying," said Savage grabbing his hand, "is when the d-d-darkness p-p-passes and I r-r-remember what really did happen."

"There's no cure for memories. All we can do is give you medication to get rid of the thoughts..." He rose to go.

"Will it be easier if I do forget it all?"

"It could be even worse," the doctor said, shrugging his shoulders. Savage's wife tugged at his sleeve.

"Is he ill?" she asked in the corridor.

"Definitely," the doctor nodded.

"What ails him?"

"Himself."

Savage kept the tablets close to his heart like a baby and felt the hallucinations subsiding and giving way to an unbearable, oppressive indifference that bent him to the ground as if he'd become a hunchback. Previously Salmon had come to him at night as he alternated between dreams and memories. Sometimes she was young as she was in the photo. Sometimes she was disfigured by disease. She whispered as she shivered in her fever: "I was so beautiful once..." and her trembling transferred itself to Savage who also shivered beneath his blanket. Every night they ran through the impenetrable taiga and took refuge in the Saami encampment and the kind herders warmed their frozen souls like the heat of the fire. Every night the shaman woman lowered an empty coffin into the ground and in it, according to their beliefs, they buried her soul. To Savage it seemed as though he'd left his soul in the coffin as well and that without it he was like a stone covered in moss. He dreamed of holding Salmon close and kissing her withered cheeks and in the morning he would stare at the ceiling trying to remember whether it had really happened. Since he'd started taking the tablets, however, the girl had stopped coming. Savage missed her and took her photo out from under his pillow.

Savely was losing his mind, scared by the shadows overhead threatening to attack him. He stared at the madman twirling his finger by his temple until he realized he was looking in the mirror. It felt as though he weren't in control of his own body, that someone else was, and that he smiled and moved his limbs at someone else's behest. The minute that person stopped being in charge, however, Savage would collapse on the floor, unable to take a single step.

"No regrets for the past and no thought for tomorrow," he said, repeating Saam's words. "No regrets and no thought. No regrets..." The walls of his room held him in a vice. The ceiling bore down like a tombstone. Savage poured out his tablets, weighed them in his hand and put the handful into his mouth, washing them down with water. He stretched out on the bed and lay for a long time, listening to himself. His heart was pounding crazily and the blood raced through his veins like a new resident examining his home. A weight was pressing on his chest like Antonov's body when they fought on the stairs. His blanket was soaked with sweat and the trembling of his body transmitted itself to the walls which started to jump before his eyes. They sought to collapse, as if he were lying in the old box the tramps had slept in at the tip. Savage waited to lose consciousness and sink into the blackness, oblivion and silence of the everlasting Polar night.

He only fell asleep as morning came, worn out by his distress. When his office rang to find out why he hadn't come in, his wife couldn't wake him. She shook him and slapped his face, but he was sleeping the sleep of the dead, pale and cold as a corpse. When she saw the bottle of tablets on the floor, She put her hand over her mouth and tiptoed out of the room.

Several times she was tempted to call an ambulance but put the receiver down each time. Pacing the room, she fought the temptation to feel his pulse. But when he rose from the bed in the evening, she cried out as though she'd seen a ghost.

Savage didn't leave his room. Watching him through the keyhole, his wife saw a trembling bundle on the bed. He woke in a sweat so cold it iced up the windows and he felt frozen under his blanket as if it were a snow drift. "No regrets, no regrets…" he whispered, trying to work out why the way to himself was longer than a lifetime. Turning his life inside out like a jacket, he realized that he was living it back to front and that in order not to go out of his mind he had to become part of the general madness.

Several days later the fever passed and feeling better Savage went into the kitchen. The kettle was boiling, its lid tapping gently, and the window had steamed up. Savage felt as though he had been released from an obsession. Only then did he realize that he hadn't eaten in all that time. He made some coffee and chewing a sandwich on the go, he saw Trebenko smirking in a corner. His head like a deflated ball, the colonel reached out to him with burnt hands. Savely covered his face and the cup fell from his hands.

Savely made a dash for his medication to get rid of his oppressive memories. He searched his room, turning out the drawers of his desk, looking under his pillow, emptying out his pockets but found only an empty bottle that had rolled under the desk. He trod on it and it snapped like a branch in the forest or a broken bone. Savage felt better as if he had been dusty and stuffy inside and had opened a window to let in the cold, fresh air.

"I was so beautiful once," he heard and, taking his head in his hands, he burst into tears.

Savage put his arms into the sleeves of his coat and plunged into the twilight. He had put on his old life too, like his coat, but it fitted him as if it didn't belong to him. "You can't stick life back together once it's broken, you just can't," he said, shaking his head as he roamed the dark sidestreets.

The evening was thick as coffee and a nibbled moon hung over the town like an apple core. "Demons are eating it," the old Saami woman had said, poking her finger at the moon, and Savage grew wistful at the thought that he would never go back to the Saami encampment where the slant-eyed herders kneaded their songs like dough and Salmon, legs stretched out by the fire, wandered through the days of her youth, which had broken off like a conversation in mid-word.

Bent into a question mark, Lapin came towards him. Flinching from the cold wind that blew in his face, he was muttering something to himself and waving his arms, and Savage realized he wasn't the only one seeing ghosts. When he noticed Savage, the investigator slowed down and when Savely stopped, he too froze expectantly.

"Just a wink. What would it cost you?" Savage read in his tormented face. Lapin had grown a moustache that bristled over his upper lip. His sunken cheeks were blue with stubble and the end of his nose twitched nervously. The biting wind got under his collar and Savage felt he was drowning in Lapin's eyes that were as restless as the waves. Reining in his shadow, he went on by.

The awnings on the veranda at the Three Lemons had been folded up and the plastic furniture stacked away but Coffin's chair stood off to one side like a naughty child. Its seat sagged and a leg had broken. Savage thought that things last longer than their owners.

A security guard, shrouded in sheepskin, stamped his feet in the doorway and the first frost nipped at them like mischievous puppies. Savage peeped through a faint twinkle of multicoloured sparks in the bar window. His breath clouded the glass and he wiped it with the palm of his hand until he spotted

Saam. His face looked like wax in the dim light and the dark circles under his eyes like empty sockets packed with earth. The bar was wreathed in cigarette smoke and the gangsters' heads bobbed in the smoke, as if cut off from their bodies.

Savage imagined going into the bar down the worn wooden steps, rapping out the rhythm of the Saami rites on the railing. The security guard, hand over his holster, would follow him in and with a practised gesture the cloakroom attendant would reach out for his coat, his other hand proffering the tag. Savage would take his coat off slowly, watching the guard's frightened eyes monitor his every move in the dusty mirror. He would smooth his thinning hair, exchange a meaningful look with his reflection and hurry into the bar-room. The tables would be occupied while couples out on the dance floor shuffled their feet. Savage would sit in a free chair at a table in the corner where the night was thickest and tobacco smoke coiled as soft as cotton-wool.

To keep his emotions under control, he would take out a cigarette, strike a match behind his hand as if to keep the flame from the wind and light up. He would blow the smoke noisily through his nostrils and call the barman.

The latter would start up his usual refrain: "In the North people huddle together to get warm..." Hearing it out, Savage would order a drink.

The dancers would look askance at him and his daughter, sitting on the lap of some beefy guy with a squashed nose, would throw back her head and laugh loudly and deliberately. One of the gang would come and sit next to him, right up close and search him with his deft fingers, his sour breath hitting him in the nose. Then, with a sign to the others the gangster would down the drink the barman brought Savage and go back to his table.

With a click of his fingers, Savage would ask the barman for another and, stubbing his cigarette out in the ashtray, he would head for the toilets.

Savage would have already been in the bar earlier in the

day when it had just opened, shaking off its drowsy torpor, and, unfazed, the sleepy security guard would have let him into the empty room. In the gents, behind a rusty pipe leaking water that pooled on the floor, Savage would have hidden the kitchen knife his wife used for cutting onions, wiping away her tears with the edge of her apron.

Savage would take it out, tucking it into his sleeve blade first. Rehearsing in front of the mirror, he would take out the knife and smile at his reflection. The door would bang open and, leaning over the tap, Savely would turn it on and pretend to be washing his hands.

"Great evening, eh?" a drunken hulk would grin, unfastening his flies at the sink and Savage would nod in reply. "Just a habit," he would add with a laugh and Savely, looking at the urinals, would hurry out.

Crossing the bar-room, he would head towards Saam who would be hunched over the table, cleaning his nails with a matchstick. A neglected cigarette would be smoking on his lower lip and a fat fly would land on the back of his head. Waving it away, Saam's hand would brush against him and the gangster would stare at him expectantly, his teary eyes covered in red thread veins. Savage would stand there in front of him, hands at his sides, one clutching the handle of the hidden knife, the other turning over and over the tiny stone from the grave of Salmon-Severina who had died, mouth open wide as though she didn't understand why she had ever lived.

Savage would lean over Saam and rasp out: "But she was so beautiful once, you know!" Saam would look at him blankly and Savage would calmly wait until he could read in his eyes, like a response to his own words, "You poor, unfortunate things. What have you got to live for?" Then, like a cardsharp with the ace of spades, he would draw the knife from his sleeve and run it across Saam's thick throat.

Seeing Savage lean against the bar window, Lapin came closer, treading gingerly over the crisp crust of ice that covered the pavement. He tripped over Coffin's chair and it fell sideways like the gangster who'd been shot, and Savage turned round at the sound. He saw Lapin, hands hidden in his pockets, looking at him like a beggar expecting a handout, his eyes expressing the bitterness of his father's tears, and his dreams like stale crusts. Turning up his collar, Savage hurried away, melting into the blue-grey twilight.

Lapin raced to the window, trying to make out who he had been looking at in the dense half-light. Someone's glance tickled the back of Saam's neck and he turned to see the investigator, his nose flattened against the glass. Lapin thought he could see a jagged wound gaping on the gangster's throat and put his hands over his mouth, afraid to cry out, while his heart thrashed like a fish caught in a net.

The light swayed in the wind and the shadows staggered from side to side like drunkards as Lapin stood, an unmoving exclamation mark, and from a distance people took him for a post. "Fate has so many twists and turns no-one's immune," he thought, staring into the void, unable to tell whether Savely Savage had indeed given him a wink or whether he'd merely imagined it.

COMPLETE GLAS BACKLIST

Peter Aleshkovsky, *Skunk: A Life*. (Bildungsroman set in today's Northern Russian countryside.)

Vasil Bykov and Boris Yampolsky, *The Scared Generation*. (Two novels by modern classics.)

Alan Cherchesov, *Requiem for the Living*, a novel. (Extraordinary adventures of an Ossetian boy against the background of traditional culture of the Caucasus.)

Vlas Doroshevich, *What the Emperor Cannot Do*, *Tales and Legends of the Orient.* (Highly relevant parables about the eternal conflict between the authorities and the people.)

Asar Eppel, *The Grassy Street*. (Striking stories set in a Moscow suburb in the 1940s.)

Nina Gabrielyan, *Master of the Grass*. (Long and short stories by a leading feminist.)

Maria Galina, *Iramification*s, a novel. (Adventures of today's Russian traders in medieval East.)

Nikolai Klimontovich, *The Road to Rome.* (Naughty reminiscences about the later Soviet years.)

Sigizmund Krzhizhanovsky, *Seven Stories*. (A rediscovered writer of genius from the 1920s.)

Leonid Latynin, *The Lair*, a novel-parable, stories and poems

Mikhail Levitin, *A Jewish God in Paris*. (Three novellas by a world-famous stage director.)

Anatoly Mariengof, *A Novel Without Lies*. (The turbulent life of a great poet in 1920s Bohemian Moscow.)

Larissa Miller, *Dim and Distant Days*. (Childhood in postwar Moscow.)

Irina Muravyova, *The Nomadic Soul*. (A family saga about a modern-day Anna Karenina.)

Alexander Pokrovsky and **Alexander Terekhov,** *Sea Stories. Army Stories*. (Realities of army life today.)

Portable Platonov, a reader. (For the centenary of Russia's greatest 20th century writer.)

Valery Ronshin, *Living a Life. Totally Absurd Tales*

Lev Rubinstein, *Here I Am*. (Humorous-philosophical performance poems and essays.)

Alexander Selin, *The New Romantic*. Satirical short stories.

Roman Senchin, *Minus*, a novel. (An old Siberian town surviving the perestroika dislocation.)

Andrei Sergeev, *Stamp Album*. *A Collection of People, Things, Relationships and Words.*

Andrei Sinyavsky, *Ivan the Fool*. *Russian Folk Belief.* A cultural history.

Boris Slutsky: *Things That Happened*, by Gerald Smith. (Biography and poetry of a major 20th century poet.)

Andrei Volos, *Hurramabad*. A novel in facets. (Post-Soviet national strife in Tajikstan.)

ANTHOLOGIES

Beyond the Looking-Glas. (Russian grotesque revisited.)

Booker Winners & Others. (Mostly provincial writers.)

Booker Winners & Others-II. (Samplings from the Booker winners of the early 1990s.)

Bulgakov & Mandelstam. (Earlier autobiographical stories.)

Captives. (Victors turn out to be captives on conquered territory.)

Childhood. (The child is father to the man.)

Jews & Strangers. (What it means to be a Jew in Russia.)

Love and Fear. (The strongest emotions dominating Russian life.)

Love Russian Style. (Russia tries decadence.)

NINE of Russia's Foremost Women Writers. (Collective portrait of women's writing today.)

Revolution. (The 1920s versus the 1980s.)

Soviet Grotesque. (Young people's rebellion against the establishment.)

Strange Soviet Practices. (Stories and documentaries illustrating inimitably Soviet phenomena.)

War & Peace. (Army stories versus women's stories: a compelling portrait of post-post-perestroika Russia.)

A Will & a Way. (Women's writing of the 1990s.)

Women's View. (Russian woman bloodied but unbowed.)

NON-FICTION

Michele A. Berdy, *The Russian Word's Worth*. A humorous and informative guide to the Russian language, culture and translation.

Contemporary Russian Fiction: A Short List. (Eleven major Russian authors interviewed by Kristina Rotkirch.)

Nina Lugovskaya, *The Diary of a Soviet Schoolgirl: 1932-1937*. (The diary of a Russian Anne Frank.)

Alexander Genis, *Red Bread*, essays. (Russian and American civilizations compared by one of Russia's foremost essayists.)

A.J. Perry, *Twelve Stories of Russia: A Novel, I guess*

THE DEBUT SUBSERIES FOR YOUNG AUTHORS

Anna Babiashkina, *Before I Croak*. (A novel about five women who come to an old age home to experience their "second youth.")

Arslan Khasavov, *Sense*. (A novel about today's political struggles.)

Anna Lavrinenko, *Yaroslavl Stories.*

Mendeleev Rock. (Two short novels about modern-day urban life.)

Off the Beaten Track. Stories by Russian Hitchhikers.

Russian Drama, Four Young Female Voices.

Igor Savelyev, *Mission to Mars*. (Disillusioned young Russians, the product of the wild capitalism of the 1990s.)

Alexander Snegirev, *Petroleum Venus*. (Psychological tragicomic novel about a lone father of a Down-syndrome boy.)

Still Waters Run Deep. Young women's writing from Russia.

Squaring the Circle. Selected stories by Debut Prize winners.

Dmitry Vachedin, *Snow Germans*. (A novel about repatriated Germans and their cultural and psychological problems.)